a **WALTZ** *in* **TENNESSEE**

a WALTZ *in* TENNESSEE

FRANCINE THOMAS HOWARD

Andrew Benzie Books
Orinda, California

Published by Andrew Benzie Books
www.andrewbenziebooks.com

Copyright © 2015 Francine Thomas Howard
All rights reserved.

The characters and events in this book are fictitious.
Any similarity to real persons, living or dead, is coincidental
and not intended by the father.

No part of this publication may be reproduced,
distributed or transmitted in any form or by any means,
or stored in a database or retrieval system without prior
written permission of the author.

Printed in the United States of America

First Edition: June 2015

10 9 8 7 6 5 4 3 2 1

ISBN 978-1-941713-04-4

Cover and book design by Andrew Benzie

I THOUGHT I TOLD MY GRANDMOTHER'S STORY
FULLY WHEN I WROTE *PAGE from a TENNESSEE JOURNAL*,
BUT SEVERAL TRIPS BACK TO ILLINOIS CONVIINCED ME
THE TALE OF GRANDMA'S LIFE WAS NOT YET COMPLETE.

Mama, this one's for you.

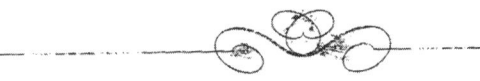

CHAPTER ONE

Crack! The sound sent a jolt through Annalaura's shoulders. She shook her head at her foolishness as she tested the slipperiness of the concrete steps leading off the porch of her house. How long was it going to take not to startle at the sound of icicles cracking off her very own roof? A person would think by now—after all, it'd been sixteen years since she and John settled in Brugestown—she'd be used to all this Illinois ice and snow. She squeezed her elbows to her sides as her fast-chilling feet sent up spires of cold to her chest. She hadn't bothered to put on her galoshes—no need for a quick step to the mailbox. Now she wasn't so sure. She picked her way down the walkway glistening in the pale afternoon sun.

This was the middle of April, and the storm had sneaked up on them three days ago. Took all six streets of Brugestown by surprise. Even her Polish, Italian, and Belgian neighbors—that is, those who didn't mind speaking to colored—grumbled that April snow was a bad thing. Annalaura shrugged against the chill as she spotted the up-flag on her mailbox. The cold stung her lips and rushed into her throat. She shivered again. April snow in Illinois a bad thing? Not easy, for sure. Yes, it might mean a little delay in putting in the pole beans, green onions, and lettuce, but a hard ground in the middle of spring didn't really matter all that much in

Brugestown unless you were a farmer. The closest big-sized cornfields were a good five miles away. But back in Tennessee, a late freeze like this one could spoil... There it was again. Tennessee.

Annalaura fixed her eyes on the mailbox, now almost within reach. She clamped her lips over her teeth. A gust of wind made her eyes sting. She didn't like to think about Tennessee, but sometimes, and she was never sure when a smell, a sound, or even the way Dolly tilted her chin, would bring on a full-blown memory and snatch the breath right out of her mouth. She reached out a hand to lower the mailbox flag. The cold metal grabbed the skin of her fingers. Annalaura gritted her teeth, unpeeled her hand, and pulled down the sleeve of her coat to fumble open the mailbox lid. She laid a hand inside the box and lifted out the afternoon's delivery.

She turned toward her house and glanced at the thin stack in her hand. A bill from the coal company caught her eye. She slid the envelope to the bottom of the pile as she began the trek back up her stairs. A folded-up flyer from the Sears Roebuck showing the newest in 1930 wringer washing machines stared back at her. Why, it looked like the thing might even have a cord attached. An electric washing machine? Not that she'd ever bother with such a contraption. Fire coming out of a wire. Who'd ever thought of such a thing? She'd stick to the coal oil lamps and the good old washboard, thank you.

Annalaura stepped onto her porch and shuffled the flyer to the bottom. Now an ad from the grocery store. A big loaf of bread at the A&P cost five cents. Five cents? Lord, have mercy. Why, back in Tennessee, she'd made do with just a scant cup of flour and a pinch of baking powder to make her bread—and that'd been for the five of them. Why... There it was again. Tennessee. Sometimes, the scent of her buttermilk biscuits conjured up the gassy smell of cows offering their teats for the milking and pitched her head-first into Tennessee-and that barn. Lord, the memories were batting her mind good this day. She shook her head so hard her short braids waggled as she opened her door and stepped into the living room. Warm again. She rushed to the big furnace standing in the center of the space, dropped the mail bundle on the daybed pushed against the front window, whirled around and held out her hands for the warming. She glanced down at the almost full coal bucket.

After three weeks of regular April weather, John had shut down the furnace. But when the storm hit on Tuesday, he went to the shed out back and brought in a fresh bucket. Her husband hadn't even missed a beat. He'd promised her that—all those years ago—she would never want for anything. Not ever. And ever since that day on the train leaving Clarksville forever, he'd delivered.

The heat from the red-hot furnace worked its way up her arms and into her shoulders. She shook off her coat and hung it on the hook by the front door. She headed to her kitchen, the smell of neck bones coming off her bottom oven signaled less than five minutes 'til the meat was fork-ready. She reached up and cracked open her top oven. Six more minutes of browning and out would come her cornbread.

She shut the oven door and gave it a little pat just when she heard the familiar footfalls.

"Mrs. Anna," Gina began like always, "okay I take-a one peach preserve?" Her next-door neighbor rattled open Annalaura's kitchen door.

"What's that?" Annalaura pointed to the tin can Gina clutched in her hand as she stepped through the always unlocked door.

"Olives, Mrs." Gina, her gray-going-to-silver hair bound tight at the back of her neck, tugged down her heavy sweater. "That's the what, and they come-a in the mail this day straight from the Napoli."

"Olives? How many times I got to tell you, my family don't eat no olives." Annalaura turned to her stove to hide her smile. "You can have one of my last jars of peach preserves, but I don't want no olives." She eased herself around to face the woman she guessed she'd call her best friend if the woman hadn't been white. Of course, Gina Maggiora didn't look all that white to Annalaura. Not by Tennessee standards. Skin too brushed with sun, just a shade lighter than Dolly. And Gina's wavy hair-why Dolly's was way straighter and... No, not Tennessee again.

"Mrs. Welles-" Gina could play the game as well as Annalaura, "-you know the truth like I know the truth. You tell me the last jar of the peaches? Did I no stand beside you all the last Fall with those damn peaches?" She made the sign of the cross against her chest. "I peel. You peel. I boil. You boil. I smash. You smash. I put in the jar. You put in the jar. And...I do the count."

Gina won. Annalaura laughed first. Gina, with her not-so-great English, had lightened her day again. Annalaura played exasperation on her face as she looked over at the big-bosomed woman, who had gone a little too far to the stout side. Annalaura felt her head wobble in a questioning shake. When was Gina ever going to figure out the North's way of doing things? Poor white folks and coloreds might live next door to one another, but they sure weren't supposed to be the best of friends.

The three-thirty whistle blared through Annalaura's shut kitchen window. Another day at the coal mines without the cave-in alarm making that God-awful sound. Annalaura grunted. She always did when she heard that whistle. She'd only heard that other—the cave-in sound—twice since John moved her into the little gray house on Lattier street, thank the Good Lord. She was positive-sure that when that chill-to-the-marrow noise blasted, even the Devil would wet his drawers. Annalaura peered over at Gina. The woman's shoulders hunched up in that little jerk of relief Annalaura knew so well. No matter how many years went by, everybody in Brugestown always said their quiet hallelujahs—even the Catholics—when the three-thirty sounded. Another day and their menfolk still lived.

Gina's man was in the mines—had been ever since the

two of them came to Brugestown, three or four years before Annalaura's time. Gina said they'd come from some place in Italy called Napoli. Said Annalaura had to know about the place. Some singer fella—what was the name? Oh, yes-Caruso. He'd come from there, too. Annalaura just pretended she'd heard of the man. For all she knew, this Enrico Caruso might have been one of those Chicago speakeasy jazz singers spewing the Devil's music, or worse, one of those Al Capone bootleggers.

"These olives you give the try." Gina's voice sounded a little huskier than a minute ago. "I bet you, you Dolly no turn up her nose at what is good."

"That girl will eat anything just to be different." Annalaura turned to her neighbor, aiming her stirring spoon at the woman. "Don't you go tempting my girl." Annalaura dropped her eyes. "She's got too many big ideas already." For a colored girl way too good-looking for her own best interest.

"Ideas are good, no?" Gina walked over to Annalaura's food safe, opened the glass door like it was her own, and pulled out the jar of peach preserves. "Ideas and a girl learning to do the cooking. No stopping you Dolly, eh?"

Annalaura gave her pole beans a stir. She jabbed a fork into the flavoring fatback. Just about ready. "She won't make sixteen until next month. She's got the hang of cooking. I want her to study her lessons, but I don't want my girl gettin' ahead of herself."

"Ahead of herself?" Gina sat the olives on the kitchen table. "You Dolly the first one in your family to finish the high school. Like my Guido. Is good, no?"

Annalaura sucked in her lips as she opened her lower oven, grabbed her tea-towel and lifted out the pan of neck bones. The brown juices mingling with her preserved tomatoes told her dinner was just about ready for the serving. Dolly was not Guido. A dream of college for an I-talian white boy was just fine. But a colored girl like Dolly... Girls were always a worry. Yes, her Lottie's man had turned out all right, but what colored man living in Brugestown could do right by her smart-as-a-buggy-whip and good-looking youngest? A bead of sweat dripped from Annalaura's forehead.

"My Lorenzo had the idea to come to the America." Gina squinted as she inspected the jar of peaches.

"Mmm." Annalaura managed as she forced her mind off her youngest child. "Saw a piece in the paper about Illinois needin' coal miners." She recited the oft-told story.

"I say to him, we no know nobody in this America. You know nothing about the coal, why for we go to this place?" Her full lips pulled back over her yellowing teeth. "He say to me, Gina, *mi adore*, in America, we be the millionaire." She laughed and ran a finger around the seal of the Mason jar. "You betcha. I tell him, we make it big with my good cooking!"

Annalaura lifted out her cornbread. "Don't know no millionaire, but coal minin' puts the food on the table, I reckon." She headed toward the safe and her plates.

Gina stepped aside. "And making the zinc like you John and you boys. Put-a the food on the table. We no make the millions with the mines, not with the zinc, not even with my cooking"-she sucked in lips almost as plump as Annalaura's- "but we—me and you—we gotta our house, the food, a little money for our children, and for our old age." She took two plates from Annalaura. "It's a good-a life, and it's a good-a thing for you Dolly to go to the school." She stood straight.

Annalaura pulled out her sharp look—the one she used to warn Gina she was moving too close to the line.

"How many you gotta for dinner tonight?" Gina received the message.

Annalaura breathed out a sigh. "Cleveland's comin'. Doug usually wolfs down a plate or two befo' he heads out to see some gal or t'other. Now Henry's out sparkin', too. So I reckon I'm layin' on for six."

"I think you gotta two good-looking boys." Gina narrowed her eyes as she looked up. "Anna, you keep straight that Doug and you Henry so they don't fall-a in the trap like Cleveland." She set down the two plates and headed back to the safe.

Annalaura wagged her head from side to side The good Lord and Gina both knew how much she fretted over her Cleveland. "I tried to tell that boy to stay away from loose women. You knows as well as me that wife of his got to be thirty-two, maybe thirty-three—a good five years older than my boy."

Gina nodded like she'd just heard Annalaura's lament for the first time. "You Cleveland, he the hardworking man. A woman like that see a man with the good-pay job, and she rolls the hip at him." Gina bent her knees and moved her own hips in a circle.

Annalaura felt caught between laughing and getting mad all over again. "You know that hussy puts rouge on her face—even on her knees!" She stared at Gina, remembering very well she'd told her neighbor the same story at least a hundred times. She didn't care.

"It's the flapper, she is." Gina lifted her own calf-length dress over her knees and moved her legs in and out.

Annalaura laughed out loud. Gina had a way of keeping Annalaura's worries in their place.

Her neighbor marched to her side in a flash. She laid a firm hand on her shoulder. "You do all the right thing for you boy. You teach him the rights from the wrongs." She wrapped both arms around Annalaura's shoulders. "But he the man now. And when that flapper woman bounces her big bosoms at him...well." She took a hand and lifted up her own breasts.

"Oh Lord, woman. You'd better get on home. Your Lorenzo be walkin' up the road any minute." Annalaura stifled a fresh laugh.

"Not before you own men come from the zinc plant." She turned to the door, gave her backside one more wiggle, "They gotta the brand-new car to ride in. Not Lorenzo. He walk." She closed the door behind with her usual double thump.

Annalaura laughed. That woman. She could tell her anything, no matter how awful. Gina always had a way of making her feel better. Lord knows, she'd never had that with John. Not even with Aunt Becky, God rest her soul, or anybody else, for that matter, except…" She moved to the stove and cut the fire off under the eye. Her pole beans were ready. She poured the neck bones onto her serving platter and set it on the oilcloth covered table. She walked to her safe, cornbread plate in hand, and got out the butter she'd churned yesterday. She looked over her kitchen table. Everything was at the ready. She wiped her hands on her apron and headed to the living room to chunk another piece of coal into the fireplace. She wanted the place toasty when Dolly got home. Where was that girl? That child knew to be home in time for dinner. She'd told her girl she could spend one after-school hour studying with her French friend, Claire. But that was it. Those two, together, were the smartest students at Brugestown high. A France-born girl and a colored. Back in Tennessee, never would Annalaura have thought it so. Yes, this Illinois was a paradise standing next to Lawnover. But for her girl…Lord, Dolly was going to worry her to pieces. She jabbed the poker into the furnace, stirred the coal chips, and closed the fire door. Her eyes dropped to the daybed as she turned to lay the poker in its resting place. Have mercy, Jesus, she'd forgotten all about the mail.

She brushed aside the grocery store ad and picked up the pile. An envelope slipped out. She frowned. A letter? From some hussy after her Doug? Don't let it be for Henry. He was barely twenty and way too young for marrying. But no. She stared at the writing. Annalaura Welles. It was for her. Who would write her? Sometimes letter writers put their own names in the corner of the envelope, but not this time. Her fingers peeled open the envelope. She unfolded the letter. Leotha? Why in the world was John's cousin's wife writing her?

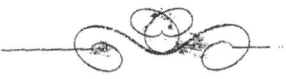

CHAPTER TWO

"Lord, Lottie. Get that baby off of that chair befo' he falls and breaks his neck--and my good china!" Annalaura dipped the plate into the rinse water before she handed it to her eldest daughter.

"Nooo!" Two-year-old Sammy wailed as Lottie swung him to the floor with one hand. "Gammaw, I wanna wash dishes."

Annalaura threw the dish towel over one shoulder as she walked to the doorway leading to the outside porch. "Dolly, ain't you through pumpin' that well water yet?" She turned to Lottie. That girl's been drivin' me crazy ever since that letter from Leotha came." She frowned as she faced Lottie. "Why didn't you talk some sense into yo' brother?"

"Like this is my fault, Mama?" Lottie made a lunge at Sammy as the toddler readied his stubby legs for a climb onto a second chair. "It was Doug. Said wouldn't a trip back to Tennessee be nice for Dolly's graduation? Since she was co-valedictorian and all."

"Uh-huh." How much did her children remember? "It never would of come into Leotha's head to invite y'awl down to Lawnover if Doug hadn't put the bug in Cousin Richard's ear when he came up here summer last." Annalaura fumbled with the button on her Sears & Roebuck dress, but it wasn't the button that was worrying her. It was her racing heart. She had to keep Dolly out of Tennessee.

"Okay, Mama. Here's two buckets." Dolly slammed the containers down on the sideboard like she was carrying the weight of the world.

"Won't do no good to sulk." Annalaura mopped up the spilled drops with her tea-towel. "I said no Tennessee, and I mean that."

"But, Mama…"

"Don't you but Mama me. We'll take us a nice trip to Danville to celebrate your graduation and that 'dictorian thing. Maybe even have us a dinner at the five and dime."

"Woolworth's? Danville?" Dolly looked like she's been threatened with a whipping. "That's only five miles away. What kind of a trip is that?"

"Lottie, you better tell yo' sister to watch her mouth."

"Unca Doug! Unca Doug!" Sammy squealed as the screen on the front door opened and Annalaura's second boy walked into the kitchen.

Doug had been ten when they all left Tennessee. Surely, he must remember something about that hurried train ride in the dark of night that got them all out of Tennessee and into the safety of Illinois. At least "safety" had been the word John told all his children—including Dolly—about their deliverance north. Cleveland knew the truth—all of it. But her eldest was closed mouth, and ever since Annalaura made her dislike of Cleveland's wife, Lucille, known, he didn't talk much to his mother.

"Thanks for dinner, Ma. Got to go up to Hoopeston." Doug tossed Sammy in the air, raising his arms to catch the boy at the very last second.

"Oooh." The toddler squealed his delight.

"As long as its Hoopeston you're goin' to and nowheres else, it's a fine thing with me."

"Ma, not that again." Doug tossed the boy in the air a second time. "Won't be gone long. No more'n two weeks. Got to work, you know. Me, Henry, Lottie—if she can get away—and..."

"Don't none of y'awl need to go to no Tennessee. You want to sleep in a barn again?" There, she'd said it. To bring up the barn and that 1913 year when John left them all alone to forge for themselves only to be rescued by Ale... Yes, it was a tricky memory to stir, but with the bad might come the good. "Sides, Lottie can't go nowhere. Husband won't allow it. Tell him, Lottie."

"Lottie?" Dolly swiped down the last of the plates. "What about me? I don't remember Tennessee. You say I was born there, but I don't remember a thing about the place. I want to see for myself where I came from."

Thank the Good Lord for Dolly's ignorance. Until this "dictorian" thing, Dolly had spoken almost nothing about Tennessee. She understood from her parents—especially John—that Lawnover had been a segregated hell. And Dolly always believed every word her Papa said. Annalaura shrugged. Her daughter might hate her forever, but at least the girl would be safe and away from... "Lottie, speak up your mind."

Lottie retrieved Sammy from her brother. "Mama's right. Can't leave Sammy with Rusty, and I'm sure not taking my son down South." She looked over her shoulder at Annalaura. "Mama, you know my husband can't tell me what to do. I am your daughter, after all."

"Ma, didn't Cousin Leotha promise they'd look close after Dolly?" Doug ignored his sister as he walked over to the water buckets, dropped a corner of a rag into one, pulled it out and scrubbed at his teeth. "She'd only be around Welles kin. Wouldn't even take her into town. Into Lawnover. None of yours left down there anymore. Aunt Becky was the last of the old ones."

"What kind of graduation trip is that?" Dolly scowled.

Lottie shifted Sammy onto one hip. "Just to church and prayer meeting, Mama. Nothing else."

"No! I'm not in the arguin' business with you three. I said no, and that's that." Annalaura ripped off her apron, tossed it at the sideboard, missed, and stalked out of the kitchen and into her dayroom.

John liked to stretch out after dinner. Doze off. Said his almost fifty-year-old bones needed a rest after eating Annalaura's fine cooking. Annalaura glanced at her husband's daybed snugged between the side window and John's locked cabinet, where he kept his liquor and the stuff he didn't want her to see. Never mind. She had her own bookcase right next to the kitchen. She passed it now as she crossed in front of the big furnace toward her own daybed.

"Uhh." It was John's grunt that alerted her. Husband John was only faking sleep.

She turned toward him as she lowered herself to her bed. His eyes were wide open, forming a question right through the bottom of their dark brownness.

Annalaura shook her no just as Dolly bounced into the room, that, butter-would-swirl-itself-to-nothing-in-her-mouth look on her face. She headed straight for her father. While Dolly plopped herself on the floor beside John's feet, Annalaura repeated her mouthed, "no".

"Papa, you and Dickie are first cousins, aren't you?" Dolly put on her smile. She begged Annalaura to allow her to wear lipstick when she turned sixteen last week, but Annalaura knew that paint on those already pouty lips would make her girl all the more dangerous.

"Richard-family calls him Cousin Richard-only white folks calls him by Dickie." John doted on the girl that looked not one thing like him. Always had since that night on the train when he promised Annalaura he would treat the newborn as his very own.

"How's he our kin, Papa?" Dolly tilted her head and let the sun catch her eyes to make them look stretched between blue and green. "I know he's your cousin and all, but how?"

About two years ago, Dolly worried Annalaura with about a million and a half questions why she looked like none of her brown-skinned, brown-eyed relatives. Annalaura told her to hush up. Didn't Dolly understand she was a throwback to their Cherokee great-grandmother and Charity's blue-eyed mulatto husband, Ned? It happened some time, Annalaura told her girl with as straight a face as she could muster, that light-colored straight hair and eyes like a just-washed spring sky might skip three or four generations and then pop up in an offspring-a child who looked almost white despite having two brown-skinned parents. Annalaura never gave the lie the slightest bit of concern. She wasn't a big churchgoer anyway, and the real Jesus would understand and praise her goodness for protecting an innocent girl.

"My kin." John's deep voice still brought a thrill to Annalaura. "Richard's daddy and my daddy were brothers. Uncle Sherman, Richard's daddy, raised me when my own folks died. Richard's more like a brother to me than a cousin."

"You must miss him a lot." Dolly stroked John's feet.

"Humph." Annalaura muffled what she really wanted to say to her child for all the girl's obvious shenanigans.

"Mmm." John grunted his pleasure.

Of course, he loved to have his feet rubbed. Who wouldn't after standing all day smelting zinc? It was a pleasure she would never deliver to her husband. Not after he raised his hands to her in that barn.

"Papa," oh-oh, Dolly pulled out that 'here-it-comes' tone. "Don't you miss not going back to Lawnover to see your Cousin Richard? I bet he misses you." Dolly, who always sounded just like a three-generation born-and-bred northerner, soothed. Not a Tennessee twang, anywhere.

"Miss him?" John sounded as though he were snapping back to himself. "Richard comes up this way at least once a year. How could I miss him?"

"Not him so much, but Tennessee. You know, the homeplace."

"I told you, girl, I didn't leave nothin' in Tennessee to make me want to go back." John pulled his feet away as he sat up on the daybed.

Dolly dropped her hands. She sucked in her cheeks lower

lip. She batted those eyes, looking all the world as though her entire family had been wiped out by the Spanish Flu. "I tried so hard to make you proud of me, Papa. I studied awfully hard in school. I got good grades, but I still can't go to college. Claire already got her acceptance." A real tear threatened to trickle down the girl's face. She swallowed and turned to the floor.

John swung his feet off the bed and laid a hand on his daughter's shoulder. "Girl, you know I'm awful proud of you. Would give you any present you wanted. I wish to the Lord God that I had 'nough money to send you to that University of Illinois place you been wantin' to go. But with all this Depression talk, I just can't see my way clear."

Dolly shifted, her hands grasping John's arm. "I know that, Papa. You can't send me to college. I understand, but I was hoping"-she captured John's eye-"I just want one little thing special…if I could just, pretty please, go to Tennessee for a little while. Everybody remembers something about the place except me. Doug and Henry would both look after me. They promised they would. Cousin Leotha swears she'd take real good care of me. And I would go to church with her every Sunday, and to Bible Study, and to Sunday school and to Wednesday night prayer meetings and to…" Dolly sucked in a breath. "In fact, why don't you and Mama come back to Tennessee, too? You could look after me yourselves."

John stared over Dolly's head at Annalaura. He understood his daughter. The child was so desperate to take away the sorrow of losing college, she would even settle for a trip with the old folks. Annalaura read the permission in John's eyes before the words came anywhere near forming on his lips. Was her husband really ready to take that risk? Dolly's risk? His own risk? They'd been safe for sixteen years. But that would all end if Dolly showed her face in Lawnover. Why would John chance it? She stared at her husband. The muscles in his jaw hardened, and the regret in his eyes faded. Oh, my Lord! That was it! He had to know. John Welles had to finally have his answer about her-Annalaura.

Most likely, their daughter would face no physical harm in Tennessee. He loved that girl way too much to risk her safety. But that other—the real question—the one that must have wadded itself around his heart all these years, finally demanded an answer. This trip was all about her-Annalaura. Not Dolly. Given her druthers and without the pressure of Tennessee, who would Annalaura choose—him or Alexander McNaughton? The dinner turnips that should be settling in her stomach right now, instead tied themselves into knots.

No matter how well her husband treated her since the family settled in Brugestown, Annalaura's sin still gnawed at John. She looked into those eyes that mixed seeing with not seeing, as they stared back at her own. She understood John's truth before he did. Someplace deep within her husband's soul—a place his awake mind hadn't dug all the way out of his sleeping one—John Welles couldn't live another day without his answer. The turnips threatened a return to her throat. Her own truth weighed over her shoulders like six filled-to-the brim buckets of coal. She had no say. Dolly was being sent to Lawnover to test the heart of Annalaura Welles. God, Jesus, and Aunt Becky, blow enough strength into her to save those she loved.

CHAPTER THREE

"Ben Roy, get yo' ass out here and take a look at these niggers!" Wiley George, his hair and mustache more messed up than usual, banged through the open front door of Bobby Lee's, the only general store this close to the Tennessee/Kentucky border.

Ben Roy shot a quick glance over to the cotton-goods section, where Fedora and their daughter, Tilly, were looking over the latest in summer-dress yardage under the guidance of Mrs. Bobby Lee. Looking couldn't hurt none, though Ben Roy wasn't as all sure he should spring for all the fine goods Fedora fancied—not with all this Depression talk. But thanks to Jesus, none of the women lifted their heads this Saturday morning towards Tilly's good-for-nothing husband, Wiley George.

"Would you hush it up!" Ben Roy sneered at the son-in-law he'd been condemned to tolerate these last eighteen years. The fool was ignorant as all get-out. Wasn't worth a rat's ass at farming the Thornton acres—not even that itty-itty patch he'd been given to supervise as his own. Couldn't hold his liquor worth a damn. Low-class to boot. How many times did Ben Roy have to tell the clown not to use the nigger word in front of Thornton women? Thank God Eula Mae had not been at the mercantile. His sister would have had a head stroke, for sure. That word was too harsh for the ears of refined women like the Thorntons, the biggest tobacco farmers from Lawnover clean into Clarksville. He and Eula's mama had always preached that the Thorntons were a couple of cuts above all the rest of the folks in Lawnover—even old Dr. Starter and Judge Bigelow had to take a back seat to the Thorntons. Not that his Fedora had been all that refined when the two married. But Big Mama Thornton had drilled right from wrong and the Thornton Way into his wife's head before that powerful mother-of-the-family passed on to Glory.

"But, Ben Roy," Wiley George belched as he staggered through the door, "you gotta see these nig...coloreds. They drivin' a brand-new car!" Wiley George moved next to Ben Roy, last night's homemade hooch stinking up his breath. "Nineteen-thirty Illinoise plates!"

"What you say?" Ben Roy stared at his son-in-law.

"That's what I say. Illinoise plates. 1930." Wiley George looked over at the yardage counter.

Ben Roy kept his eyes on his daughter's husband. Fedora had heard every word. Ben Roy was positive-certain by the way his wife raised her voice to mask the men's' conversation. Keep high-strung Tilly out of this talk as long as possible. He loved his daughter, the Good Lord knew, but if the truth be told, Tilly wasn't the brightest of his girl children, even if she was the only white one. "How do you know they wasn't drivin' some white fella's car down from Chicago?"

"Because of that gal."

"What gal?" Ben Roy shook his head. Making sense had never been one of Wiley George's strong suits.

"That gal they had in the back seat." Wiley George leaned into Ben Roy, almost brushing his ear. "Good lookin' wench. Prettiest I ever seen. Hair colored like straw. Skin brighter than yo' own outside nig—colored gals."

Ben Roy clapped both hands hard into his son-in-law's work-shy, flabby upper arms and backed him through the door. He slammed him into the brick fronting the outside of

Bobby Lee's mercantile. "Listen to me, you moron. Don't you never, ever, mention no such a thing in front of Fedora or Tilly ever again!"

Wiley George's head bobbed as Ben Roy shook him. "I know. I know! You kind of sensitive since Hettie took off north two years back with yo' three kids."

Ben Roy drew back one fisted hand. "By God, Wiley George, I'm about to do what I shoulda done all them years ago when you got my Tilly pregnant. Killed you right then and there."

"I ain't meanin' nothin', Ben Roy. I won't never say no more Hettie's takin' off like that...after twenty years livin' on yo' back forty." He tried to squirm away from Ben Roy's grasp.

Ben Roy popped the flat of his hand hard against the side of Wiley George's cheek.

"No, no, Ben Roy." I won't say another word,... Not even Eula's husband, Alex, and that Welles woman. Annalaura, wasn't that her name?"

"Ben Roy," Fedora stepped through the mercantile door, her voice as cool as sitting Wake before a funeral. Only the flush covering her cheeks and racing down her neck told those who knew her best, something was terribly wrong. "Me and Tilly goin' over to the Five-and-Dime and have us some sweet tea. Why don't you and Wiley George go on over to the barber shop? Pick us up later."

Ben Roy nodded and cracked his lips into what he hoped would pass for a smile. He slipped his arm tight around Wiley George's shoulder and headed him toward his own five-year-old car. Now what was his son-in-law babbling on about Chicago coloreds and a brand-new automobile? Why, colored never even owned their own horses. Except for working white folk's acres, coloreds didn't even ride on a horse since... By God Almighty, why had he thought of John Welles?

"Sit here, Wiley George, until I come back." Ben Roy pushed his son-in-law into the barber chair. He turned to old

Charley Ray, "If he opens his mouth about seein' up-north colored, pay him no mind. I'm takin' care of it myself. Be back to get the fool in an hour."

The filling station was just two blocks west and three more toward the highway running down from Chicago straight to Memphis. Ben Roy parked the Model T at the pump. Didn't really need gas. He'd just filled up right before he and the family headed to Bobby Lee's.

"You got troubles, Ben Roy?" Eddie Lee, Bobby's pretty-far-gone-into-senility uncle, took off his cap and scratched his head, sweat drippin' off his brow.

Ben Roy stepped out of the Ford, grateful that no other cars had pulled into the station. "Wiley George said he saw some up-north colored troublemakers headin' this way. You seen 'em?"

"Why? What's Wiley George tryin' to say me?" Eddie took a step backwards.

"He ain't got the sense to say nothin'. Was they just passin' through Lawnover? Ain't no trouble in that."

Eddie rubbed the stubble on his chin. "No, I don't reckon they was passin' through." He jerked his head toward Ben Roy. "I ain't sayin' they did or didn't stop here, mind you."

"Eddie Lee, I don't give a damn if you served colored or not. A man's got to make a livin'." Ben Roy cocked his head. "As long as you didn't let 'em use the rest room or nothin'."

Eddie's shoulders released, and he slapped his cap back on his head. "Do I look crazy to you, Ben Roy? Them boys stopped in here just to get some gasoline. Tole 'em to fill it up themselves. I don't wait on no colored." He stroked his neck as he leveled his eyes at Ben Roy. "'Course, I was curious."

"Yeah?"

"Yep. Tole 'em best to keep on drivin' to wherever they was off to befo' dark." He pulled out his handkerchief and wiped at his forehead. "That's when them uppity coloreds in that new car asked me."

"Asked you what?" Lord, Eddie was almost as addlepated

as Wiley George was dumb.

"The way to the Welles place." Eddie Lee let the words hang in the air. "Dickie Welles. Said they was cousins."

God damn it to hell! "Dickie and Leotha Welles?" Ben Roy tried to hold his voice steady. "How old was these coloreds?"

"Young. But it was the gal I was lookin' at most."

"Gal?" Ben Roy's mind went into a flurry. A Welles gal? It couldn't be so. How long had it been? Nineteen-thirteen, nineteen-fourteen? "What sort of lookin' gal was she?"

The grin pasted itself on Eddie Lee's face, old as he was. It was that I'm-gonna-get-me-some-blackberry-juice-tonight look. "Young, sure 'nough." He raised a hand. "But she was ripe. Fifteen or sixteen at the most. High yella. Had to take me a second look to make sure them boys didn't have some Mexican gal or t'other in the car. Couldn't be no Mexican cause that gal had awful light hair. And them eyes...why, Ben Roy, I'm here to tell you they was blue with a little tinge of green here and there. Reckon I'll..."

"Reckon you'll stay put 'til I check on these coloreds. Did you hear any names called?"

"Sure did." He wadded up the handkerchief.

"Well?" The sun was way too hot this Saturday afternoon for all this back-and-forth with a man this far gone into losing his mind.

"'Stay in the car'...that's what the shorter one said to the gal—he looked to be the boss of the outfit. 'Stay in the car—Dolly.'"

Good Lord Almighty! Dolly. As many times as that day played in his head these sixteen years, he'd know that name. Dolly. Ben Roy forced his eyes back on Eddie Lee who looked at him like he was the one ready for the Old Folks Home for the fog-headed.

"Ben Roy? You hear me? Said that good-lookin' gal's name was D..."

"My hearin' ain't gone bad yet, Eddie Lee. You just keep that name and them boys to yourself. Though I don't put no truck in it myself, some folks just might mind you servin' gas to coloreds. Offerin' them the facilities." Ben Roy spewed out any old words while his mind whirled after the real problem. If this Dolly really was Alex's outside chil... Good God in the land of milk and honey, he'd have to get to Alex before his brother-in-law acted the fool again. Like he did all those years ago when Annalaura Welles... And then there was Eula. "Eddie Lee, I'm off to take care of these Welles coloreds. You just set quiet on this one."

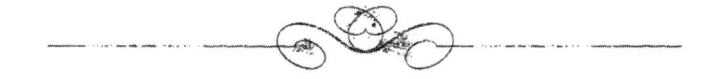

CHAPTER FOUR

Ben Roy didn't feel all that comfortable driving into the colored outskirts of Clarksville, the place where the uppity colored lived—school teachers, undertakers, preachers, and such. Dickie Welles had managed to get his own plot of land here—no more than twenty acres, but the family was making do. Didn't own their own horses, but they rented enough mules to plow the ground when the time was right, and they could hire on their own help at tobacco harvest time. Most of all, they owned their own house. Ben Roy could spot it now as he trundled his 1925 Model-T off the main road betwixt Lawnover and Clarksville and onto the gravel path leading up to the fading white, two-story house with the porticoed front porch. Hell, those colored better be careful. That house looked like it was almost good enough to belong to some low-class white folks. Like Wiley George.

The afternoon sun caught Ben Roy in the eye as he dodged a squirrel running across the gravel. Squirrels and houses be damned. He had to see what Dickie Welles was up to. He didn't have long to wait. There it was, sure enough. Ben Roy couldn't see the license plate because the shiny brown 1930 Model-A was turned sideways and half hidden behind the Welles' house. But he could hear the laughter, all right.

"Boy, you growed so tall even since last year, I don't reckon I'da knowed you." Dickie Welles's voice boomed out through the open front door.

"Ahh, Cousin Richard. It's just me. Doug. I'm only six-one."

"How old is you now, boy?" Leotha Welles

"He may be taller, but my brother's still a squirt to me, even if he is nineteen years old."

Whose was that fourth voice? Wiley George had said there were two colored men in the car. But where was the girl?

"Hey, Dickie, you in there?" Ben Roy called out. "It's me, Ben Roy Thornton."

The dark green door swung open and clattered against the lighter boards of the house.

"Mr. Ben Roy?" Dickie Welles, in his Saturday overalls and checkered shirt, stepped out of the inside gloom. His head was bare. No need to remove his hat. "What can I do fo' you, suh?" The man looked wary.

Ben Roy walked up to the wood stairs leading to the front porch and door. He spread his legs and crossed his arms. Dickie Welles took no time clattering down the steps. That colored knew he had no business standing on a platform that would raise him above a white man.

"Yes, suh?" He lifted his eyes to Ben Roy's.

Colored had certainly gotten a lot bolder in these last fifteen or so years. Sometimes they even looked a white man in the eye. When some of Fedora's folks came up from Alabama they would always say Tennesseans were too soft on their colored. For such a misdeed, coloreds in Alabama would get a good ass-whupping.

"You need somethin' the tobacco?" Dickie's voice cut through.

Ben Roy shook his head as he pointed to the car half concealed behind the house. "You got yo'self a new car, Dickie boy?"

Was that a little stiffening in Dickie's shoulders Ben Roy spotted before the colored man shook his head a slow no.

"Naw, suh. Ain't none of mine."

Ben Roy looked over Dickie's shoulder and up toward the porch. Leotha stood framed in the doorway, but neither of the other voices made their presence known.

"Look to be brand-new." Ben Roy let his eyes take in a slow sweep of the vehicle, Dickie, and Leotha. "Thought I heard me some talkin' when I pulled up. You got visitors, boy?"

There it was again, that little shudder of the shoulders that disappeared almost as fast as it came. Dickie Welles pulled out a smile, "Mr. Ben Roy, you care to have some of my Leotha's sweet tea? She's makin' some fresh for my kin. They's here fo' just a short visit. Passin' through, you might say."

For a fact, colored could cook good. Why, his own Hettie used to... "Auntie, bring me out a glass of your good sweet tea. If you got a chunk of ice, thow that in there, too." Ben Roy called out. "How many kin you got visitin', Dickie? Wiley George says he spotted three of 'em." He looked for Leotha, who had scurried back inside. "Auntie, I hear tell you got a gal visitin' you folks, too." No need to pull punches. If Wiley George's story was god-awful true, Ben Roy had to get back to Lawnover before Eula got wind of anything from his wish-that-gal-was-a-little-bit-brighter daughter, Tilly.

"Girl?" Dickie stood there looking for all the world like he wished Gabriel would blow his horn here and now and whisk Ben Roy straight to his Reward. "Mr. Wiley George seen a girl?"

"Here you is, Mr. Ben Roy. Pleased to serve you. Have some of my fresh pound cake, if you please, suh." Leotha had raced down the steps so fast, he wondered why the woman—she had to be sixty—hadn't fallen and snapped a leg bone.

"Now, Auntie, weren't no need for you to run like that." Ben Roy took the glass from Leotha's hand, and took in a swallow. He reached for the plate holding the cake. Oh my Lordy, good. How did colored make sweet tea and pound cake so much better than his Fedora? "Why didn't you let that gal—what's her name, Auntie?—bring the tea?"

"Kate." Leotha piped up.

"Not that one. Not your own girl." Ben Roy shook his head. That woman was hiding something. "The new one. One of your visitin' kin."

Leotha turned to Dickie. The man's eyes swept his wife's face before they looked up toward his porch and turned to fear.

"Cousin Leotha, here's a glass of tea for you and Cousin Richard, too." The voice was smooth, cultured, and northern.

Ben Roy turned to see the slim girl-child in her Sunday-go-to-meetin' dress make her way down the wooden front steps. Her straw-colored hair, cut in one of those new-style bobs, swinging with each step she took. Damn it to hell! The girl looked straight at him as she handed the two Mason jars to Dickie and Leotha. She smiled.

"Pleased to meet you." She held out her hand to Ben Roy.

Maybe it was those blue eyes, spotted here and there with green, but Ben Roy didn't think so. No, it was more the oval shape of her face and the way her light-colored brows angled across her forehead that told him the truth. Good God, Almighty! This gal sure as hell was Dolly, daughter to Annalaura Welles and... He took her hand before he could stop himself.

"Dolly, get on in here and help me with this ice!" The voice was commanding, and it belonged to Kate, Leotha's oldest daughter. Kate bounded down the stairs, grabbed the visitor by the shoulders, yanked her from Ben Roy's light grasp, and marched her into the house before Ben Roy could get his head to working straight again.

"I...I...." Dickie stuttered as he shot frightened glances toward Leotha, who looked like she was searching for a groundhog hole.

"She's...she's...," now it was Leotha's turn to stutter, "Mr. Ben Roy, suh, she won't be here no more'n two weeks. We'll most keep her in the house." Leotha mumbled to the ground. "She...she don't know. She from...from up north."

Leotha lifted her eyes. "We'll get her straightened out lickety-split." Leotha managed a little curtsy and backed her way up the steps. Ben Roy gave a quick look at Dickie Welles. He knew he should have lectured the fellow about his ill-bred kin but Ben Roy had more important business back in Lawnover—his brother-in-law, Alexander McNaughton.

CHAPTER FIVE

"What? Why are you looking at me like that?" Dolly stared at her cousin—at least that's what Mama had instructed her to call all the Welles family. Cousin this and Cousin that. Seems it was a Southern sign of respect. But Cousin Kate didn't look like she'd earned Dolly's respect at all. Her face was stuck somewhere between scared-to-death and the funniest-thing-I've-ever seen.

"Don't you up-north girls know nothin'?" A grin broke out on Kate's brown-toned face—looking every inch like Papa's side of the family. "That was a white man!" Kate, stood in the kitchen, chunking ice off the big block sitting in a small washtub. She berated Dolly as though Dolly was supposed to know what the girl was talking about. Kate acted as though that extra year—she'd just turned seventeen a month before Dolly's own sixteenth birthday—gave her the knowledge of the ancients.

"Yes, that was a white man." What else did Cousin Kate expect her to say other than the obvious? Dolly turned toward Kate's little sister, Dodie, who emerged out of a shady corner of the kitchen like some kind of tan-skinned ghost.

The eleven-year-old carried the most gosh-awful smirk on her face.

"The man had a lemonade." Dolly frowned. Why in the

world shouldn't Cousin Richard and Cousin Leotha have the same? They were all standing together out there in the hot sun. Hotter than the fires from *Dante's Inferno.*

"You talk funny. Dodie's eyes made a slow trace across Dolly's face. "Look funny, too. Colored don't have eyes like that."

Dolly sucked in her wrath. Mama had laid about two volumes of do's and don'ts into Dolly's head about how to behave in the South. Mama said she was sorry she and Papa couldn't get away, but if they gave their okay for a trip to Tennessee, Dolly had to mind her caretakers and her manners at all costs. She'd promised Mama she'd be a docile as Cleveland's dog, old Rags. Dolly clamped her lips shut. Cousin Dodie needed a good comeuppance—like some of the phrases Dolly and Claire perfected when they answered back those classmates who condemned the two as "brains," and thus unworthy of social interaction. But Dolly had promised Mama.

"I talk funny?" Dolly forced restraint on herself.

"All proper like." Dodie tilted her head. "Why's yo' hair so straight? Don't look like you use no pressin' comb."

"Shut up, Dodie. And you, Cousin Dolly," Kate tugged the ice tin onto the back porch and hefted it into the icebox, "Colored don't go around shaking hands with white folks," she called out.

Dolly blinked her why-nots as Kate walked back into the kitchen, wiping down her wet hands on her dress.

"Lord, girl." Henry laughed as he emerged from the front room, followed by Cousin Richard and Cousin Leotha. Doug brought up the rear. "I think you just about broke every rule Ma gave you."

"Henry!" Cousin Richard yelled. "I promised your pa I'd take good care of every last one of y'awl." He turned to Dolly. "Now, looky here, girl. You ain't sup…

"Richard, you take Doug and Henry on over to the Carruthers. I'll have me a talk with Dolly." Leotha smiled, but the effort seemed to crack her lips.

"Yes." Dolly twitched her mouth into as agreeable a grin as she could manage.

"Yes, m'am." Doug put on his big-brother face. "Dolly, don't forget your ma'am's and sirs." He turned to Cousin Richard. "Who are the Carruthers?"

"Grandpappy Welles' daughter's kin. They gonna put you and Henry up for the stay. Got more'n enough room there."

"What about Dolly?" Henry sounded alarmed.

"After what I seed today, she best stay here where Leotha can eagle-eye her." Cousin Richard beckoned the boys through the back door. "'Sides, I wants me a ride in that new-fangled car y'awl brought down from Danville." His chuckle thawed the air.

"But..." Dolly turned from Henry and Doug to Kate, and back again. "You're leaving me here with...with her?"

Leotha waved the men through the door, and pointed to one of her kitchen chairs. "Set yo'self down, Dolly. Dodie, you go on yo' business. Kate, you get after yo' sister." After the girls frowned their way out of the kitchen, Leotha sat and grabbed both of Dolly's hands in hers. "Girl, nothin' more in this world I wants than to sees you have a good time. It does my heart good to set eyes on you after ever so long." She squeezed Dolly's hands. "I'm gonna take you around to see all yo' Welles kin. They just rarin' to set eyes on John's girl." Her smile seemed real this time. She stroked Dolly's wrist. "Everythin' gonna be fine if you just keep it in yo' head that you is in the South."

"I will...I do, Cousin Leotha." Dolly felt herself returning Leotha's warmth.

Leotha shook her head. "Yo' mama wrote me that you was a very good girl. Right smart in school, but she's yo' mama, and she worries." Leotha loosened her grip and dropped her eyes. "Just a few things I wants to get into yo' head befo' we heads out tomorrow."

Dolly shook her yes. If she played her cards right, maybe she wouldn't be a prisoner for the entire two weeks of her visit.

"First, don't go shakin' no white folks' hand lessen they offer it to you first. And that ain't never gonna happen." She grabbed Dolly wrist again. "You understan' that?"

"Yes...uh, yes m'am." She didn't really understand, but if following that rule got her paroled from the house, she'd do it.

"Next 'un." Leotha's sounds almost made words Dolly could decipher as English—about half the time. "Don't never, ever, look no white man in the eye. He might take it the wrong way." She paused. "Get my drift?"

Dolly's face muscles twitched. What was Leotha talking about? Drift? "Yes, m'am, Cousin Leotha, I won't look any white person...man in the eye. No matter what." What a silly rule. Hadn't she grown up tomboying with Guido Maggiora?

Leotha withdrew her hands. "Cain't say when I'm takin' you to town, but it'll be Clarksville, never Lawnover." She stood from the table. "Fo' now, I want you in some of Kate's old clothes. Them you got on look too store-bought." She shook her head. "I'da thought Annalaura woulda knowed better."

Dolly stared back at her new cousin. Wear hand-me-downs? She'd never put on even one of Lottie's old dresses in her life. Annalaura's rules pounded in her ear. "Yes, m'am, Cousin Leotha, but why can't I wear my own clothes? Mama bought some from the Sears Roebuck catalogue and the others from a store in Danville. And I really would like to get to town—Clarksville. Maybe to the movies?"

"Movies?" Cousin Leotha looked at Dolly as though her mind had skipped more than one cog. "Girl, girl, girl." She shook her head as she took a step closer to the table. "You gonna wear some of Kate's clothes—they's new enough. I won't have you tellin' Annalaura I put you in rags. And you most certainly will wear a head scarf. Now get on upstairs with Kate while I ponder this one out."

Face Kate and that odious little sister of hers? Wear old clothes and tie her hair up in something that looked like Aunt

Jemima on the pancake box? Oh, no. Dolly had a plan. Throw herself on the mercy of her brothers. Doug and Henry would get her out of this jail Cousin Leotha determined to make for her.

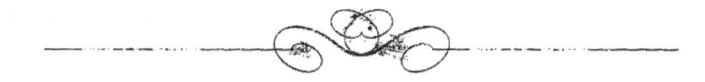

CHAPTER SIX

Eula Mae hadn't gone to town this morning when Ben Roy brought in Fedora and Tilly. Ben Roy prayed his sister was still in her farm house while Alex was out somewhere checking on his stock. This was mid-June, and most Lawnover farmers liked to take their ease from the fields on Saturdays and Sundays—the tobacco was already in the ground and harvest was almost three months away. Ben Roy decided to park the Model-T a little ways back from the path leading up to Eula's house. That way, maybe he could slip into the barn and catch Alex without Eula finding out.

He mopped his forehead as he headed the long way around the farmhouse to the work shed. He huffed his way to the back corner—it'd been a good ten-minute walk with the sun getting hotter with every step. "Alex, you in there?" Ben Roy tried to peer between two wide slats.

"Huh?" The sound of metal slammed down against something wooden.

"Alex, that you?" Ben Roy raised his voice. "It's me. Ben Roy."

"What the hell you doin' at the back of my shed?" The voice got closer.

"Where's Eula?"

"On the back porch churnin' butter. Go on up there,

you'll catch her." The voice walked away.
"No!" Ben Roy shouted. "Come on back here. I got somethin' to tell you."
Ben Roy heard grumbling and more tools slamming against something hard. He heard the shed door slam open. Alex turned the corner, his face more sun-red than usual. He ran a hand through his gray hair, still thick, which was far more than Ben Roy could say about his own almost gone strands.
"Ben Roy, what're you doin' playin' possum out here? Get on up to the house and get yourself some lemonade. I'll join you as soon as I get these harnesses rigged right." He stopped about half way to Ben Roy and the back of the shed.
"Don't stand there!" Ben Roy mouthed his words. "Eula might see you."
Alex tilted his head as though his brother-in-law had lost each and every one of his marbles.
"I mean it, God damn it. I got somethin' to tell you about...well, some up-north nig...colored just drove into town."
Alex lifted and eyebrow then dropped it down. He started to turn back toward the front of the barn.
"Illinoise license plates." Ben Roy slowed his words.
Alex shook his head, first like his hearing had gone bad, and then he eased himself around. His forehead scowled down to his hooded eyes. "Ill..." he walked next to Ben Roy. "What you mean, Illinoise license plates?"
As soon as Alex stepped close, Ben Roy grabbed his shirt sleeve and pulled him behind the shed. "Ain't no need upsettin' Eula Mae."
"Eula Ma...? Illinoise...whereabouts in Illinoise?" Alex's breathing picked up.
"I don't know all that, but I do know I just come from the Welles place, and I..."
"The Welles place?" Now Alex's breaths sounded caught in his chest.
Ben Roy looked around for shade to shelter his brother-

in-law. Eula would blame her brother if her husband had a heat stroke.

"What Welles place?"

"Dickie Welles. You know 'em. He's the one lives up near Clarksville."

"Of course I know him." Alex's shout rocked Ben Roy back.

Ben Roy raised his finger to his lips and shook his no. "Eula Mae can't hear tell none of this 'til I get you ready."

Alex bumped Ben Roy with his chest. "What the hell you talkin' bout? Dickie Welles is kin to…to…another Welles I used to know. I been to his place a time or two askin'…askin'."

"Well, you don't have to ask no more."

"What are you sayin'? John Welles? Is he back? And Anna…"

"Hell, no. That's what I come to tell you, Alex. You got to get hold of yourself. You can't be takin' on like this. John Welles nor that wife of his—you hear me, the man's wife—ain't neither one of 'em in town, but three of their get is."

Alex blinked at Ben Roy though the sun was at the man's back. Peculiar how the shape and color of those eyes looked so much like that gal holed up at Dickie and Leotha's. Alex's lips opened, closed, and then opened again. His cheeks puffed in and out like he was trying his God's mightiest to get out some words.

"Now I got it on Dickie Welles' word that he's gonna keep them three nig…colored out of Lawnover. Them boys is old…why, Alex, I'm here to tell you them coloreds is drivin' a brand new car! A 1930 Model-A."

"Car?" Alex's voice sounded like it came from the bottom of a rain barrel, but his eyes widened like they were trying to fight their way back to the here and now. "Ben Roy, whose car? Whose boys? Annalaura's?"

Ben Roy jerked Alex further behind the barn. "Would you hush it up? Eula Mae might step out here any minute. She don't need to hear nothin' more about this mess. She…"

Alex grabbed Ben Roy's shirt front before Ben Roy could get out his next word. "Mess? I'd say your Hettie was a mess—especially when she took off with your own get in tow, leavin' Fedora the pity stock of all Lawnover!" He shook Ben Roy once before he pushed him away. "Now I want you to tell me good and clear who the hell is stayin' up at Dickie Welles place?"

"Alex…" Ben Roy pointed a finger, "this here is just what I feared. Fedora might a been a mite shamed when all that old business came up, but my wife can take the hits much better than Eula Mae. Fedora understands that sometimes a man's got to go cattin' around. But Eula, she ain't good at it."

"Ben Roy—" Alex's voice took on that quiet tone signaling a threat—"I told you more than once, I ain't never aimed to hurt Eula Mae." He swallowed. "But what business I had—it's been over for sixteen years. I just want to know who is…"

"Sixteen years? Are you tellin' me you didn't take yourself up to Chicago more than once to look for her…that Annal…"

Alex took a step closer, his face clouding over like a spring tornado. "Ben Roy—" he drew out the name—"I don't need to hear her name comin' out of your mouth. Now you tell me straight, who's stayin' up at Dickie Welles' place?"

"Doug and Henry Welles…that's the names I heard called. I believe they're both John Welles' boys."

Alex stared at the ground like he was looking for mole holes before he looked back up at Ben Roy. "Anybody else?"

Ben Roy's mind raced. By the looks of him, Alex was going to act the fool again—the way he did that last morning sixteen years ago. That morning he and Alex tussled pretty good on the back porch. The same morning Eula finally faced the truth. Since that day, his sister had kept her counsel to herself, unless she spoke her business in private to Fedora. But Eula had never really been the same. Alex had done what wasn't right before a God-fearing Tennessean. Yelled out his love for the Welles woman—shouted it out right there where

Eula and most of Lawnover could hear. In his way Ben Roy had his feelings for Hettie, all right, but he'd never called them out loud, not even to Hettie. If the Good Lord gave him the strength, Ben Roy would do all he could to keep Alex away from the Welles' place.

Alex kept his hands at his side but Ben Roy could see the man's fingers release and tighten into fists over and over again.

"I said, anybody else up there with Dickie Welles?"

"I need your word." Ben Roy gave his head a slow shake. "If you go a runnin' off in all directions, won't nothin' but harm come of it. You understand me?"

"Is she here?" Alex's words took almost the full move of the second hand on a good table clock to turn one minute.

"I'm tellin' you, Alex, if you get to actin' up, not only Eula will suffer, but the colored's will be on the warpath themselves. "A white man ain't supposed to put on no big show over his outside family."

"Show?" Alex looked for all the world like he was going to pay no mind to Ben Roy. "You tellin' me my girl's here for show?"

"Tell you what." Ben Roy had to talk, beat, or scare Alex into reason. "I can give you what you want."

For the first time, Alex stared hard into Ben Roy's eyes.

"I ain't sayin' she is or she ain't at the Welles place, but if you can get a hold of yourself, I'll figure a way for you to get yourself a look at that gal without tippin' off nobody. Especially her. Don't look like to me she knows a thing you. I'll get you to Clarksville."

The few lines between Alex's eyes deepened. "She don't...you tellin' me she don't know nothing about me?" He took in a big breath like the thought had never entered his head that his colored-lover woman would keep her daughter's papa a secret from the girl herself. "You'll let me see my girl if I keep quiet about it?"

"Ain't no other way." Ben Roy's neck felt like it'd been stretched tight as he nodded his own slow answer. "Yeah, your Dolly is here."

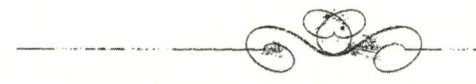

CHAPTER SEVEN

It hadn't worked out. At least not yet. Three days and two nights, and the only places she'd visited in Tennessee were six or seven Welles' family farms. And farms they were, too. While Dolly often lamented the small townness of Brugesville with its fewer than five hundred population, at least the neighbors were only a driveway distant and not a half mile or more of unrelenting tobacco fields. Worse, Dolly knew none of these Tennessee Welles. Yet she had to sit there with Cousin Leotha drinking tea sweet enough to gag even the most ardent possessor of a sweet tooth. Doug and Henry had been little help. They were in their own dungeon, confined to rides only in the back of Cousin Richard's hay wagon. The car all the Illinois Welles men pooled their zinc-factory earnings to procure had been pushed into the back of Cousin Richard's barn. Its shiny new brown paint now covered with bales of scratchy straw.

"I'm gonna tell." Dodie, sitting on the cot positioned against the high side of the sloped roof upstairs bedroom where Leotha had insisted Dolly be given the best bed, cocked her head at her sister. "What you gonna give me if I keep my mouth shut?"

"Your life!" Kate barked as she pulled on the satin slip she'd stitched up herself. "You say a word to Ma or Pa...one word, and I'll drop you out this window." She reached for a powder puff and dabbed the floury stuff across her nose. "I'll tell Ma you slipped and fell befo' I could grab yo' ankles and pull you back in." Kate slid on lipstick so red, she looked like she could paint a barn door with her mouth.

Lipstick and powder? Even if the stuff was way too light for Kate's medium-brown skin, why was she slathering powder on at seventeen? Mama would lock Dolly in the house for six months straight if she even thought her daughter used powder and paint. Tools of the Devil, according to Annalaura, and used by only the most brazen of hussies and her daughter-in-law, Lucille.

"You won't do no such a thing." Dodie put on her smirky face again.

Before Dolly could blink, Kate stormed across the wood-plank floor, grabbed Dodie around the neck, marched her to Dolly's newly assigned bed in the alcove, and forced the child's head through the half-open window.

"Say another word and I'll drop this pane smack dab across yo' neck. I'll cry real tears fo' Papa, too. Tell him how sorry I am you is dead. What's it gonna be, you little brat?"

"Nn..." Dodie tried to speak.

"Uh, Kate." What to do with crazy cousins? Dolly, on her knees on the cot, readied herself to pull Kate off Dodie if it came to that. "I think you'd better let her back in. She's scared."

"She damn well better be scared." Kate yanked Dodie back into the room and slammed her to the foot of the bed.

The child rubbed her neck. Dolly frowned at Kate. Had Kate said "damn," an honest-to- goodness cuss word? Annalaura would tan Dolly's hide if she even thought of using a swear word.

"Now what's worryin' you?" Kate jabbed a hand into Dodie's shoulder as she shoved Dolly to the head of the bed. Kate settled herself between the two. "You never heard anybody say 'damn' befo'?"

"I...uh..."

Kate shrugged. "Don't tell me you up-north girls is prissy, too?" You wanna get out of this house fo' a spell?"

Dolly startled. "Get out of the house? I...uh...thought it would be nice to see a little more of Tennessee than just..." She'd said too much.

"Well, Miss Priss, I heard you beggin' yo' brothers to take you out on the town."

"No. I mean only for a little trip into Clarksville for a movie, maybe."

"I knew it. You don't have the sense you was born with. Colored can only go to the picture show on Thursday nights, and then we have to sit up in the balcony. 'Sides, those brothers of yours better not be seen drivin' that new car around these parts."

Now what was Kate talking about? Movies only on Thursday nights? "Cousin Kate, I think I'd rather spend the rest of the time with the Carruthers, with my brothers. I think I'll speak to Cousin Leotha about moving out."

"You'll keep yo' mouth shut." Kate growled.

Dolly and Claire had taken a lot of taunts at Brugestown High and they learned to give back more than they got. Cousin or no cousin, Kate moved too far too fast. "I'll keep my mouth shut when I see fit, and orders from you do not make me see fit." Dolly rose to her feet, careful to heed Annalaura's warning not to toss her hair for fear of setting Kate off all the more. "Now I'm going downstairs and tell Cousin Richard and Cousin Leotha that I've had about enough of Tennessee. If I'm to be a prisoner here, I'll just go on back to Illinois." She headed for the door. "I'll not say a word about Dodie." She looked at the little girl who stared back at her. "That's up to her."

"Hold on, Dolly." Kate called out. "You're such a Miss Priss. Nobody can warm up to you."

Dolly turned her most withering glare on this annoying cousin before she reached for the doorknob.

"I said hold on." Kate leapt from the cot and reached the door before Dolly could twist the knob. "Okay, I got a deal for you. Keep yo' mouth shut, and you can come with me tonight."

"Come with you? Tonight?" Dolly stared at Kate who hovered just an inch over Dolly's own five-foot-two frame. "If you promise to keep yo' northern ways down and put something on yo' head to cover that hair, I'll take you with me." Kate shot one more 'I'd-sooner-see-you-dead-than-alive glares at Dodie.

"Take me with you?" Dolly shook her head. "I'm not into one more ice cream social."

"Are you really this stupid, or is you just playin' dumb because you think all Southerners is ignorant?" Kate waited for no reply. "Hell, no, I ain't goin' to no ice cream social." She reached for a dress that looked short enough to show her knees. "I'm goin' to a juke joint. You gonna join me or not?"

Dolly could still hear that snapping sound. "A juke joint?" She'd saved her chore money—hours of ironing shirts and pants for her unmarried brothers and bought herself a record by Bessie Smith—"Mississippi Delta Blues." As soon as she'd put it on the Victrola Papa bought for Mama, Annalaura stormed into the living room, snatched up the recording in one grand move, and snapped poor Bessie into four jagged parts. "No Devil music in this house!" Annalaura tossed her head as she stormed back to her kitchen, though her hair wasn't the kind that moved. Nothing in this world was ever going to change Annalaura's mind. Dolly blinked her way back to Kate. "Where?"

"Never you mind where. It's fun you want, it's fun you'll have if you listen careful to me."

"Will there be boys there?" Dolly had never had a proper boyfriend. None of the colored boys in Brugestown—the few who weren't relatives—had any ambition other than working in the zinc plant, to them, a considerable step up from the coal mines. They were not for Dolly. The handful of colored girls in town were slated to be housemaids. Not Dolly. She didn't know just how, but she'd find her way to a better life in Chicago, even if a college education had been denied her. As for boys worth something…well."

"Of course, there'll be boys there. Most of 'em with they girlfriends. They won't be happy to see the likes of you but I reckon I got to take that chance. What you say? Keep yo' mouth shut, and I'll take you out fo' a little fun."

"Jazz music? Boys and music—that's okay with Aunt Leotha?" Dolly tilted her head. Out of the corner of her eye she spotted Dodie, who seemed to make a rapid recovery back into spy-mode.

"Oh good God, Almighty." Kate stamped a foot. "How dense can you up-north girls be? Of course it ain't all right with Ma and Pa. We don't tell them, you ninny."

"She sneaks out the window." Dodie sounded fully back in control. "She pays me, of course, and I keeps what I knows to myself. What you gonna give me, Cousin Dolly? I likes me that pair of patent leather shoes you bought."

"My shoes? Dodie, we don't wear the same size." Dolly glanced down at her young cousin's sizeable feet. "Besides, my black patents are high heels, and you're only eleven years old."

"Oh, I'll grow into them. What do you say?"

She should say no to these crazy cousins, but another full day with Cousin Leotha dragging her off to another tobacco farm to sit around some farmhouse kitchen sipping lemonade with a pipe-smoking, hundred-year-old-plus great-great aunt was way more than Dolly could tolerate. "I can be ready in fifteen minutes."

Kate shook her head. "The old folks go to sleep right after their after-dinner chores. Wait twenty minutes mo', and we're out of here." She tossed a black snood at Dolly. "Cover yo' hair. Colored don't have hair that looks like dryin' tobacco."

"Don't forget my shoes." Dodie chortled.

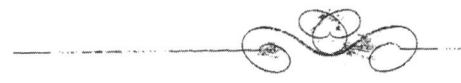

CHAPTER EIGHT

Ben Roy stuffed the handkerchief into his back pocket. The air was breath-drowning wet tonight. He'd taken his Saturday night bath in that back room Fedora asked him to convert into some kind of a bathroom with an inside toilet. Fedora insisted all quality folks had indoor plumbing nowadays. Didn't seem quite sanitary to Ben Roy, but Fedora begged him hard. She promised him one night a month—for the rest of her life—to do all the bed things Hettie used to do for him. Even that business with the... After she proved she meant her words for truth, two weeks straight, he'd grabbed his hammer and saw. Yet tonight, despite his douse in that claw-footed bathing tub, he still felt wringing wet. The stars were out, but even they seemed to be pouring water off their points. He could tell by the rising moon that it was most nine o'clock, and Bobby Lee's poker game was about to commence.

"Hey, Ben Roy." Wiley George grinned like he'd forgotten all about this morning's ruckus.

"Hey, Wiley George." Was he never to be free of Tilly's husband?

"Hey, Grandpa." Little Ben jumped out from behind a building just as Ben Roy reached the door of Bobby Lee's back room.

"Little Ben, what you doin' here?"

"Pa said it was time for me to start actin' like a man." The boy puffed out his puny chest. "I'm seventeen now, Gramps. I been practicin' my poker playin'."

Lord help us. Little Ben was looking and acting more and more like Wiley George with each passing day.

"I reckon I know how old you are, Little Ben, since you is my oldest grandbaby. What I want to know from yo' daddy is why in tarnation are you comin' to a poker game? Your grandma won't have no truck with that. As for Tilly, you tellin' me your mama okayed your playin' poker in the house?"

"I told him he could come. Be a man right soon enough." Wiley George pulled open the back door.

"A man? Why he ain't even a good sized boy quite yet." Ben Roy judged his grandson stood not much taller than his ma, Tilly. And Tilly never had reached over five-foot-five.

"Hey, Ben Roy." Bobbie Lee stepped through the curtain separating the front mercantile from the back storeroom he turned into a gambling den every Saturday night these past twenty-five years. He set down a tray loaded with ten whiskey glasses. "Yo' usual seat's waitin' for you, Ben Roy."

"Hmm," Ben Roy managed, as Wiley George rushed past him and grabbed the first glass of moonshine. "Bobbie Lee, bring me a glass of the good stuff after a bit." That down-country farmer's moonshine never did set well with Ben Roy. The stuff tasted like turpentine, and only those too poor to pay for the real Chicago hooch or too stupid to know the difference, like Wiley George, would ever put a glass of that moonshine swill to their lips.

"Pa, you think I could have me a taste, too?" Little Ben's whisper to his father caught Ben Roy's ear.

"Bobbie Lee," Ben Roy called out to Bobbie Lee's back as the proprietor aimed his way toward the dividing curtain, "Little Ben here ain't but seventeen. Why don't you bring him a Dr. Pepper?"

Bobbie Lee turned and scowled at Wiley George. "You

know I ain't partial to nobody under twenty-one comin' into my place. Never know when the revenuers might turn up. All I need is to have 'em find a kid in here along with the booze." Wiley George lifted both hands as he kicked out one of the chairs next to Ben Roy's playing table. "I brung him here to talk business. A little taste of yo' beer won't hurt him none. Give him courage for what I got to say." He sneaked a look at Ben Roy. "His ma don't know for sure, but I suspects she knows her boy's 'bout to become a man. She wouldn't object to jest a little taste."

Ben Roy grunted as he settled himself, his back to Wiley George and all his maneuverings. Ben Roy didn't fancy drinking until the game got going good. Let the others get drunk first, then he'd clean them out. He'd do his own celebrating later. He frowned as Little Ben settled in beside his father. "Business?" Ben Roy looked over his shoulder at his son-in-law. "What business Little Ben got at a poker game?"

"I was gonna hold back sayin' 'til the others got here." Wiley George downed his first drink of the night, not that Ben Roy doubted for one minute that four or five other libations had come earlier in the day.

"What you talkin' 'bout, Wiley George?" Ben Roy nodded to the three other players at his table—all old friends and damn good poker players.

Wiley George leaned in closer. Ben Roy was right. That liquor coming off his son-in-law's breath had stewed there all afternoon.

"My boy wants first dibs." Wiley George's lopsided grin with drool easing out of the left side of his mouth was enough to turn Ben Roy's stomach.

Ben Roy wrinkled his nose as he turned to the deck of playing cards on the table. "Who's holdin' the pot tonight?" He glanced over at Wiley George. "That why you brought Little Ben?"

"Hell, no, Ben Roy. This ain't about no card playin'. I seed her first, and I calls first dibs."

"What the...?" Good Lord, Jesus. Ben Roy swiveled so hard in his chair, his lumbago called out to him. Was Wiley George talking about Dolly? "Won't be no callin' dibs, tonight. We playin' five-card stud. Now send Little Ben over here. He can hold the pot."
Wiley George shook his head. "Ain't doin' it. That gal's fo' my boy. Just 'bout the right age. Looks fresh, too."
Drink usually made Tilly's husband more defiant and definitely more stupid than usual. Ben Roy clamped down hard on his teeth as he shoved the deck of cards toward Thaddeus Davis—the second best poker player in the place and a damn good tobacco broker. "You take first deal."
"Ben Roy," Thaddeus Davis tilted his head into a question, "what the hell is your boy talkin' 'bout ? What fresh gal?"
"Ask him." Wiley George swept up the drink set in front of one of his poker-playing partners. "I spotted them three up-north niggers this morning, and I told Ben Roy. He said he'd check 'em out." Wiley George downed the second drink while the farmer next to him scowled. "You shoulda seen that gal. Pretty as they come. High yella with hair jest about to match."
"Pa." Little Ben squirmed in his seat, his head staring at the spit-stained floor. "Maybe we oughta head home."
Ben Roy clutched the first card Thaddeus Davis dealt. "That gal ain't none of your business, Wiley George."
Thaddeus tilted his head. "Up north, you say. Maybe these coloreds was just passin' through. On their way to Memphis."
"Had theyselves a brand-new car. 1930. Illinoise plates." Wiley George belched as he shook his head.
"Wiley George," Thaddeus Davis had far more patience with Tilly's ever-so-dumb husband, maybe because as a businessman, he had to deal with all sorts of boneheads as he graded, bought, and sold tobacco, "what makes you think these folks wasn't just passin through town?"
Wiley George leaned so far forward in his chair, he almost slipped to the ground. Only Little Ben's quick lurch to grab

his father around the chest, saved Wiley George from an unceremonious splat on the dirty floor. "Cause them niggers told me they was puttin' up with Dickie Welles up near Clarksville." With Little Ben's help, the man righted himself.

"Dickie Welles, you say?" Now Jeff-Davis Pinkerton joined in the party. A decent poker player but one who lost five out of six times to Ben Roy. "Don't I recollect Dickie Welles havin' kin up north?" He turned to Ben Roy. "Chicago, weren't it?"

"There you go, then." More drool made its way down Wiley George's chin. "If that gal's local, then she's fair game."

"Tobacco's in the ground, sure enough," Thaddeus Davis—Jeff's second cousin on his papa's side—didn't look so sure, at all. "Still, don't need no trouble with the coloreds."

He shot a look so fast at Ben Roy that most of the other players likely missed it. Not Ben Roy. It all played out right there in that one quick glance—all of it in the eyes of Thaddeus Davis. That day—so long ago—with Johnnie McKnight. About that fine horse that Ben Roy's father gave to his colored outside child. That day—now thirty years gone—when jealousy made Ben Roy so all-fired blind-mad, he could think of nothing except gathering his friends around him, suiting them up in their white hoods, and paying a nighttime visit to his half-brother. Ben Roy had meant nothing by the costuming except to scare Johnny and that ma of his—Rebecca. How the rest of it happened he could never fully explain even to himself. Not to mention the Davis cousins, who had ridden with him that night.

"I'm thinkin' on it." Somebody's voice—the fourth man at the table—shook Ben Roy's head back to Bobbie Lee's back room.

Ben Roy struggled to bring himself back to the here and now, away from that rope and that tree and Johnny…Oh, God's Help in Ages Past.

"Won't be no trouble." Wiley George searched the table for a third drink.

"These are delicate issues." Thaddeus Davis was the

smartest business man in town. "Gals, especially up-north gals, can't just be there for the takin'. All kinds of trouble can come from it. What say you, Ben Roy?"

"Huh?" In Ben Roy's ear, Thaddeus' voice felt like a hammer pounding on an anvil. "Takin'?"

Thaddeus-Davis laid the cards on the table. "I seem to recollect some Welles leavin' Lawnover 'bout fifteen, sixteen years back. Didn't the fella sharecrop one of your places?"

Ben Roy pushed the very dead, the very lynched body of Johnnie McKnight to the back of his mind, where he prayed to the Good Lord his half-brother would stay without another of his frequent hauntings. "Eula. Was on Eula's place." His mouth felt stuffed with tobacco leaves wrapped in cotton.

"Seem like to me," Jeff-Davis opened his mouth, "if there's a colored gal that good-lookin', and from these parts, and fresh—" he worked his mouth like he was chewing tobacco— "then some 'commodations can be made for her." He frowned at Wiley George. "'Commodations for that kind of gal don't come cheap."

"And somebody's got to talk to her folks." Thaddeus looked straight at Ben Roy. "Could be lots of interest in the right kind of gal, if her folks…her daddy…gives his okay."

Lawnover was a small town—never more than three hundred in all the surrounding tobacco fields—even counting the slaves back in the day. Thank the good Lord, quality folks always knew how to play by the rules. The Davis cousins knew almost as much as Ben Roy about the events of sixteen years ago, and they had just laid down their requests. Get the white father to give his okay, and his outside girl could have a decent life with a house in her very own name, and a good education for their almost-white children. Wasn't that colored Fisk college still over there somewhere in Nashville?

"What y'awl talkin' 'bout?" Wiley George wobbled to his feet and snatched his fourth glass of moonshine from a fellow sitting three chairs away. "My boy here will give that gal all the 'commodation she needs. Little Ben has his way, then we sends her on her way back north. Won't nobody be bothered by none of it." Wiley George looked at the men at Ben Roy's table. "If my boy gets to her first." Wiley George swayed into the player to his left. "Tell 'em what you heard, Little Ben."

"Wasn't nothin', Pa." Little Ben looked about twelve years old as his face reddened.

"What you mean, wasn't nothin'?" Wiley George slurred. "These fellas is tryin' to say you ain't good enough fo' a fresh nigger gal." He swayed backwards. "Well if that gal goes to that juke joint party the niggers is throwin tonight, she won't be no kind of ways fresh tomorra mornin'."

The Davis cousins frowned all the more.

"Little Ben!" Wiley George shouted. "Tell it."

"Pa..." the boy looked like he was about to wet his pants. "I just overheard A.C. tell his mama he was goin' to the juke joint tonight. Kate Welles would be there." He squirmed. "Ain't nobody said nothin' 'bout the girl bein' there." Little Ben voice ended on a hopeful note. "'Sides, A.C.'s mama said he couldn't go."

"Y'awl hear that?" Wiley George finished off the moonshine. "The coloreds is having a party at that juke joint up in the woods near Clarksville. Sure-as-shootin' that up-north gal will be there. Then you can fo'get about fresh. I want my boy in there first before the coloreds take their ways with her. If it's just my boy, then ain't nothin' to it. One or two pokes ain't gonna mean nothin' to a nigger gal." Wiley George tried to find his chair with his foot, missed and fell flat on his behind.

"Ben Roy," Bobbie Lee, standing at the curtain partition holding his liquor tray, shook his head, "beggin' yo' pardon, but can you get that buffoon off a my floor and outta here? I'll hold yo' drinks 'til you get back."

"You boys get to playin'." Ben Roy pointed to Little Ben, "Somebody help the boy get his pa on his feet." Ben Roy looked around. "I'll see to it that he gets on home." He nodded to the Davis cousins. "Bobbie Lee, you can give my drinks to the others. Fact of the business, give drinks all around. On me. I'm out the notion of card playin' tonight."

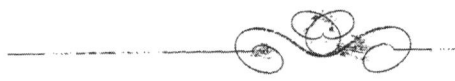

CHAPTER NINE

What in thunderation was all that noise? Good thing Eula was a sound sleeper. Here it was almost ten o'clock, and outside, Ben Roy ground his Model-T to a window-shaking halt. What could be the problem? Lord, don't let it be Dolly. Alex was trying with all the might God gave him to stay away from the Welles place until Ben Roy could arrange the secret meeting so he could see his girl.

Bam! Damn. Ben Roy had just slammed the car door loud enough to wake half the Christian world and Eula. Alex jumped from his seat at the kitchen table and walked over to the door leading from his kitchen to his front room. He cocked one ear to hear any movement from his wife. Nothing stirred. He shut the door. Eula usually went to bed around eight in the summers. Alex liked to have her fall asleep before he came to bed. He rarely disturbed her since she just laid there like the dead, anyway. Now that he was almost sixty, he didn't much need Eula in that way. Once a month was more than enough for him.

"Alex, thank God you still up." Ben Roy sounded like most of the air had been punched out of him. "Eula asleep?"

Alex rushed through the kitchen to the back door leading to the enclosed back porch. "If she is, it ain't because of you. What you makin' all that racket for?" He stared at his brother-in-law, the words he wanted to say, the question he really wanted to ask, refused to form on his lips.

"Alex, we got to talk." Ben Roy lowered his voice as he pulled Alex onto the back porch and shut the door. "You sure Eula's asleep?"

"Went to bed just about sunset, like always." Alex felt his heart pound almost through his checkered shirt. "What we got to talk about, Ben Roy?"

Ben Roy scratched at his neck, lifted his eyes to meet Alex's, then looked at the floor. "You got to make arrangements."

Alex felt his cheeks twitch, "Arrangements? Ben Roy, what you talkin' about?"

Ben Roy straightened himself like a probing rod had been laid down his back. "Her. That gal…Dolly."

"What the hell's happened?" Alex heard his voice rise. Somewhere in his mind he knew that wasn't a good thing for Eula, but the rest of him didn't care. "I swear to God, Ben Roy, if somethin's happened to my girl, I'll…"

Ben Roy grabbed Alex around the shoulders. "Would you keep it down. Your girl's all right—" He dropped his hands—"for now."

Alex shook his head. "What you mean, 'for now'?"

"Had no business comin' down here to Lawnover. Them damn brothers of hers. What was her ma thinkin' anyway?" Ben Roy shot an accusing look at Alex, "You ain't had nothin' to do with that, did you?"

"God damn it, Ben Roy, for the past sixteen years I haven't had me the slightest idea where Laura…Dolly…where my girl went."

"You sure 'bout that? I know you went up to Chicago a time or two. Did you find 'em there?"

Chicago. Alex stared at Ben Roy. Lawnover was a little town, and he reckoned some folk did put two and two together and figured out that his three absences, when he said he was going to Nashville on business, were really trips up north. In 1914, Chicago held over a million people. Even when he walked the scary streets of the colored part of town just south of Lake Michigan and asked folks if they knew anything about a Welles family, he'd been told no. In 1920 he'd gone back and checked all the black churches. No Welles there. On his last trip—Dolly would have been about nine—he searched the schools in the colored neighborhood. No Doug Welles. No Henry Welles. No Dolly Welles. Alex shook his head at Ben Roy. "They wasn't in Chicago. Wasn't nowhere I could find 'em."

"Well, your Dolly sure as hell is here now." Ben Roy glared at Alex as though it—the entire affair with her, with Anna—had been Alex's fault.

Alex tried to blink the memories away. They hurt way too much. John Welles disappearing, leaving his wife in a fix—no money and four children to feed. Alex was just a man. What was he to do? His eyes pained with the images. Was the vision of her ever going to leave his mind? Laura—her skin the color of burnished copper, the feel of her like silk, the smell of her like the most precious perfume. Alex stared at Ben Roy, watched his mouth move, not caring one whit that none of the man's sounds reached his ears. "I want to see her. My daughter—my Dolly."

"That's what I come to tell you. Most of Lawnover knows your girl's in town. Everybody, 'cept Eula Mae. I pray to the Good Lord." Ben Roy scanned the walls, the floor, and the ceiling of Alex's back porch. "There's been offers."

Alex stared at Ben Roy's mouth. His lips moved and sounds reached Alex's ears, yet they made no sense. "Offers?"

"She's a good-lookin' gal. I seen her myself. Mighty fine lookin'."

Alex tried to make sense out of the sounds spewing from Ben Roy's mouth.

"You know what that means." Ben Roy stared at the door hinge like he thought that object would know what he meant.

Thoughts rumbled and tumbled in Alex's head. Offers? Offers. He couldn't get the words out. He couldn't take his eyes off his brother-in-law.

"You hear me, Alex?" Ben Roy slowly moved his eyes from the door. "The Davis cousins...seems like they might have some interest."

"Interest? Davis?" Alex heard his own babbling.

A hard look crossed Ben Roy's face. Hinges had disappeared. "Looky here, Alex, we ain't got much time. That girl of yours has been noticed in town. Wiley George is jumpin' up and down 'bout his boy bein' the first..."

Alex's fist made contact with Ben Roy's chin before his mind gave him the okay to swing. Ben Roy staggered backwards a step or two but did not fall.

"Ain't no call for all that, Alex. Me and you got to figure this out to protect our women. Fedora and Eula Mae." He rubbed at his chin. "Now ain't no way Little Ben's gonna get nowhere near your girl, but something's got to be done. She can't stay here. Not here in Lawnover. Not even Clarksville without a proper provider. And if what I hear 'bout that juke joint party tonight is the God's truth, then we got to act fast."

Alex rubbed his bruised knuckle. "Juke joint? Little Ben? What the hell you talkin' 'bout now, Ben Roy?"

"I'm tellin' you straight, Alex. Little Ben overheard my washer woman's boy say he was goin' to a party at that juke joint down in the woods near Clarksville. Said he heard Kate Welles was bringin' her up-north kin. You know what that means."

"No. I sure as hell don't know what that means." Alex raised his voice again.

"Yeah, you do. If that gal of yours gets messed up by some colored boy, she won't be worth nothin'. Right now, you got the chance to make a good deal for her. The Davis cousins—either one of 'em—is willin' to set her up in style. She won't want for nothin', and you can see her any time you want."

Alex shook his head, buying time for his heart to stop that loud thumping and his chest to release enough air so he could speak. "Where..." he got out the first sounds, "juke joint. Where is it?"

"Hold on now, Alex." Ben Roy looked scared. "I can't have no boys ridin' with you tonight. This ridin' thing's serious business. I've got to talk 'em into it."

"I don't need no nightriders." Alex lowered his voice. "I don't need you, Ben Roy, 'cept to tell me where this juke joint place is. I can take care of my own business."

Ben Roy shook his head. "Hold on, Alex, we can't have no trouble here in Lawnover. Just say which of the Davis cousins you want for your girl, and...." Ben Roy looked confused.

"And you'll what? You just told me you ain't got time to round up the boys tonight. Could be too late after tonight, you just told me. Got to act fast, you say." All those rambling thoughts in Alex head pushed themselves into order. "I'll take care of this myself, and I promise there won't be no ruckus." Alex walked to the hanging hook where he kept his holster gun. He pulled it down and strapped it around his waist. "I'll be back before morning. Even before Eula wakes up and tends the cows."

Ben Roy took a step toward him. Alex held up a hand.

"Won't be no trouble, I promise you that." He looked Ben Roy in the eye. "But Hettie's children—wouldn't you do what you could for them if they was to turn up again in Lawnover?"

"Uh..." Ben Roy looked like he wanted to nod his yes as Alex brushed him aside and headed off the back porch.

CHAPTER TEN

Eula Mae shifted the thin cotton of her summer night dress off her knees. The wrinkled cotton covering her left leg was making a dent right over her kneecap. She'd knelt there by the upstairs bannister still as a cat, since she heard the back porch door slam shut twice. The first she reckoned was Alex going out, the second, her brother, Ben Roy. No, she hadn't heard everything they said, but she'd heard a name—Dolly. And then there was Fedora this afternoon acting all strange. That must be it. They were back. Eula Mae held on to the bannister to ease herself to her feet. Getting this close to sixty was no fun. She was getting used to the pain in her knees—old age, young Doc Starter had called it. But that other, that pain she'd fought so hard to bury these sixteen years, it was making wiggles like it wanted to return.

But how could that be? Her heart had been crumbled into tiny pebbles so long ago, how could it possibly revive itself now? Yet something was stirring inside her. When Alex's voice carried through two closed doors and up a flight of stairs yelling that name, she knew she had to crawl out of bed. She'd been awake way before then, of course. Ever since Ben Roy pulled into her driveway and she heard all that car-door slamming. The two men didn't want her to hear their talk. That was clear. But hear what? The most secret thing

Lawnover men believed they kept to themselves was their colored mistresses. As far as Eula and the rest of Montgomery County knew, Alex only had that one, but he had carried her in his silent heart all these years. Til now. Dolly—that was the child's name. Alex's child. Alex and Ann—There it was again—that pain that wiggled like a tapeworm inside her gut, growing stronger with each movement. A-n-n-n-a-l-a-u-r-a. There. She'd gotten it all out before her breath swept away. The name Alex had screamed at the top of his lungs on that day in May. He loved her—Annalaura—he said it right out loud in front of everybody under God's heaven who had ears. But how could that be? Alex had never said such a thing to Eula—not straight out—and she was his legally wed wife. But that other—Annalaura Welles—was she actually back in Lawnover?

Eula let her thin cotton nighty slip over her body as she stood. She tugged it a bit over her hips. She'd put on no more than thirty pounds in her thirty-seven-year marriage to Alex. Not that being skinny or fat meant a thing to her husband. Whenever he looked in her direction after that dreadful day, his eyes reflected back nothing of her. But she saw what dwelled deep within his own eyes—pain beyond belief. And now that woman, at least her daughter, was in town. Eula doubled over, her hand rubbing at the cramping in her stomach. She made her way down the stairs and through the quiet of her kitchen.

She stood there, her hand on the knob. The room at the back of her kitchen had once been Eula's pantry. For years after that day, Eula felt sick every time she reached for a can of peach preserves or a jar of green beans. The cradle—that cradle. Eula pulled open the door to the room that was pantry no more. Alex had finally converted the space into an indoor bathroom. And when he did, somewhere deep inside of what remained of her soul, Eula's heart fluttered a tiny bit of living. Maybe, just maybe, her husband's longings were fading away.

Eula stepped inside. The white bath tub, its claw feet plain, not painted red like Fedora's, greeted her. She knelt down to run the water for her bath. She'd already taken her weekly dousing last night, but now she felt grime and dirt cover her body. Like always, when she stepped over the edge of the tub, she kept her eyes away from the back corner of the room, and that covered cradle—now some thirty-seven years old. Alex had made the wooden baby bed himself for their only child—his and Eula's stillborn daughter. That cradle had been Eula and Alex's memorial to their dead infant, and on the spring day in May 1914, Alex had polished and shined the cradle to brand-new perfection. For that other—Alex's newborn, Dolly.

Eula crammed into the almost too small tub, her knees bent. She let the water caress her belly and the lower part of her sagging breasts. She shut her eyes. On that day sixteen years ago, Fedora told her she had to let it go—all the pain, the betrayal, and the anguish. Such feelings were selfish, Fedora declared. Eula had to buck up like all the other white wives in Lawnover. It was their duty, and now Eula's, not only to tolerate their husbands' dalliances but to fawn over their men all the more.

Eula opened her eyes, and tears splashed down her cheeks. She flicked them away with a hand, disgusted with such foolishness. Her sister-in-law had been right all those years ago. Eula had bucked up. She'd done her duty and followed all the rules of a good Southern wife. In all these years, neither she nor Alex ever mentioned that woman or the child the two of them produced. After that first shock when pain turned her into a woman raging mad enough to kill, she reformed herself into a being who breathed, walked, talked, but did not live.

About five years ago, during the time Alex converted the pantry, she set about her milking chores. One bright morning, a ray of light filtered through a small crack in one of the barn's wood sidings. It seemed to carry a message straight from the heavens. Yes, each day of Eula's dawned and set as dead as the last. She was the walking dead. But the sunbeam told her that was a good thing. The dead can't feel pain. She'd clung to that truth every waking day and each dreamless night. Until now.

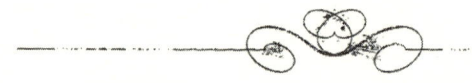

CHAPTER ELEVEN

Dolly had no trouble keeping up with Kate as they trod through the dirt and brambles in the near dark. That was not the problem. But having dust cover her new high-heeled white shoes was asking too much. Maybe she should have borrowed a pair of Kate's after all.

"Cousin Kate, are you sure there isn't a sidewalk or at least a regular road nearby? My shoes are getting ruined walking through all these fields."

Kate, a pace ahead of Dolly and only because she knew the way to the juke-joint, didn't bother to look back at her cousin. "I tole you to take them things off and walk barefoot like every other sensible woman in these parts." She shot a quick glance over her shoulder at Dolly. "Everybody with good sense knows you carry yo' shoes in yo' hand 'til you get to the front door." She waved her red leather shoes with their rhinestone buckles over one shoulder. "And don't no respectable woman here own a pair of silk stockings."

Dolly looked down at the shoes Papa had gone into his savings coffee can to purchase. Her parents weren't frivolous, and Dolly had to beg Annalaura for anything her mother considered nonessential—like shoes and clothing not meant for school or church. Any sort of jewelry and hair doodads were especially forbidden. When Annalaura put her foot down with a definite "no", Dolly knew to turn to her father. Papa most often came through. He said the white shoes with their crisscross leather strappings across the front were his graduation gift to her. She kissed him on the cheek, though Papa wasn't a man to show his affections out loud much. Now her shoes were covered with about an inch of tobacco field dust. She'd scrub them with every known cleaning substance before she'd ever let Papa see them again.

"Quit yo' complainin'." Kate stopped and pointed to a wooden building in the distance that looked built off-kilter. "Listen. Can you hear the music?"

The sounds of a guitar blasted through the wooden slats of the building still some fifty yards distant. From where Dolly stood, the windows, fronted by weeds almost to the bottom sill, looked boarded up. Light eked out only around the edges of the windows and doors. She followed Kate as the two walked closer.

"Kate, I mean, Cousin Kate, listen." Dolly stopped. All the growing animosity she'd been harboring toward this awful Tennessee cousin faded. "That's a Ma Rainey's song! 'See See Rider.' Dolly clapped her hands as she sung out in her near monotone voice. 'Lord, Lord, Lord. Made me love you. Now your gal has come.' She'd heard the recording at least three dozen times, but that was only when she could sneak over to Cleveland's house. Sister-in-law Lucille, had all kinds of jazz and blues records that were banned as Devil's music at the Welles home. Dolly adored music, except for those dragging church hymns. "Who's playing the guitar?"

"Oh, that's A.C., Savannah's boy. His mama does the wash for Miz Fedora Thornton." Kate bent over and slipped on her shoes, She took the hem of her dress and dusted them off. She looked at Dolly. "Well, get yo'self fixed up. I can't disgrace myself by bringin' somebody to a party that looks like somethin' the cat drug in."

"But..." Dolly looked down at her shoes, hopelessly swallowed in dirt.

"Here." Cousin Kate grabbed Dolly's knee. She lifted the

girl's foot and slipped off the shoe. She used the underside of Dolly's blue dress—this one a present from Cleveland—to swipe it clean. "Now you get the other one—" she dropped Dolly's foot—"and put that thing on yo' head." She pointed to Dolly's beaded pocketbook.

Shock of shocks, Mama had gotten her that one for graduation—with five whole dollars inside. Dolly pulled out the black netting and stared at it.

"Give me the thing!" Kate sounded as though Dolly had tried the patience of all the angels. "You put the thing on like this." Kate slapped the heavy black net over the top half of Dolly's head, gathering up the strands of her bob and stuffing them inside the net. She tightened the strap at the back of Dolly's head.

Dolly's new purse held a mirror, but she couldn't bring herself to look at her image. What must she look like? Her light hair sticking out of the black holes in all directions, just like straw poking through the torn seams of a scarecrow. Kate marched toward the front of the building. The musical strains of Ma Rainey's blues now accompanied by a female voice doing a pretty good imitation of the singer—*I'm going away. Won't be back til Fall, Lawd, Lawd, Lawd*—rang out through the walls of the juke joint.

"Ooh." Dolly's silk-stockinged foot, no doubt now covered in runs, scraped against something hard. She hopped onto her right leg.

Cousin Kate gave her a quick look before she tapped some sort of a signal knock on the front door. Just like in the gangster movies. "Oh yeah, that's a well. Be careful."

The door eased open, and a tall, muscular young man dressed in what Dolly guessed must have been his Saturday-best creaked open the door. He poked out his head. "Kate, girl, that you? Get on in here. I hear tells you was bringin'..." His eyes lit on Dolly.

Dolly put on her friendly smile and extended a hand for an Annalaura-instructed polite handshake. The young man pushed Kate against the door frame in his haste to grab

Dolly's arm.

"Girl, who is you?" He squeezed.

"Alvin Jay, get yo'self offen my cousin. She's not fo' you." The side of Kate's hand slammed down hard on the forearm of the man she'd called Alvin. She elbowed Dolly through the door.

"I'm gonna buy me a pistol just as long as I is tall. Lawd, Lawd, Lawd," the singer intoned as Dolly stood in the doorway.

This was heaven. Already, Dolly moved her body to the music. The place was smoky and her eyes teared, but she fought through the haze to stare at all the occupants. Almost every square foot of the place was crammed with party-goers. The little house—she spotted two inside doors she guessed led to other rooms—gyrated with the sweat and pounding feet of at least two dozen couples thumping, bumping, and slithering their bodies against one another. The Ma Rainey-like singer stood on a stage made of three wooden crates marked "sorghum molasses," a guitar player to her left, and an upright piano on the floor at her right. The musician punched home the beat with his nimble fingers flying over the black and white keys.

"Hey, Kate. Who's this you brung with you?" A brown-skinned man, more round than tall sidled up to Dolly.

"She's my up-north cousin." Kate leaned into the young man who looked close to twenty. "Don't know much 'bout nothing."

"Let me loosen her up a bit." The fellow grinned a gap-toothed smile.

"I'll do the loosening up." Alvin Jay shouldered the shorter man aside. He turned to Dolly, a glass of something brown in his hand. "Gal, you know how to do the hoochie-coochie?"

Kate grabbed the glass from Alvin Jay. She downed it in one gulp. "She's a church-goin' Miss Priss. She don't know no hoochie-coochie"—she turned to Dolly—"now do you, girl?"

Dolly was right. Cousin Kate was as awful as she suspected. Mama had always told her that sass was good, but you had to be careful when and where you played it. Kate had way over-played her hand. And now it was Dolly's turn. "The hoochie-coochie is older than my mama." Dolly lifted her chin like this news was so old, even people in Tennessee should know it. "Back in the last century at some World's Fair or other." Truth be told, she'd only heard of the unspeakable evils of the hoochie-coochie. Even Lucille, with all her wild ways, had never performed that scandalous dance in front of Dolly. "Don't you know how to swing?" She let her eyes settle first on the short, round kid, then Alvin Jay, and finally bore into Kate.

"Uhh." The short, round one looked impressed as he struggled to answer.

Alvin Jay poked out his lower lip like he was thinking about it.

"Some up-north dance, I bet." Kate frowned. "Come on, Alvin Jay, let's show her how the hoochie-coochie should really be done." Cousin Kate shoved the empty glass into Dolly's hand and elbowed her way onto the crowded dance floor. Alvin Jay followed.

Oh, my Lord. Dolly stood next to the short, round one, who stared at her. She could hear his breathing getting heavier with each breath. Was he that anxious to dance with her? Even without Annalaura haunting her, Dolly never wanted to put on an exhibition like that! She blinked away the smoke and haze clouding her eyes. What was Cousin Kate doing? All the girls wore dresses above the knee, the homemade fringe at the hems swinging around their rouged knees. But it wasn't the girls' bent legs moving in and out to the beat—the girl's hands tapping the opposite knee cap as she moved—that got Dolly. Lucille did that when Cleveland was at work. She'd even taught Dolly a step or two of the Charleston. No, it was what Cousin Kate did after she turned her backside to Alvin Jay and stuck out her rear end. Kate bumped square into the front of Alvin Jay's best pants and rubbed her behind against the man! Dolly realized her mouth must be open when she spotted the short, round one out of the corner of her eye. He grinned the most stupid smile at her.

"Wanna try it?" That had to be drool gathering on the fool's face.

"I'm waiting for a swing tune." She lied. Lucille hadn't taught her those steps, and the only time she'd seen the swing in person was when brother Doug took her for a brief visit to a dance party. But the two had been found out, and in front of the entire congregation of Brugestown's Nazareth Baptist church, they'd been forced to confess the major sin of dancing.

"*I'm goin' away, baby. I won't be back till Fall, Lawd, Lawd, Lawd. If I find me a good man, won't be back at all.*" The singer moved her hips in a slow circle until she faced the audience, then she thrust herself forward with great force.

Dolly felt a hand on her hip. She pushed away from the short, round one.

"Come on, gal. Jest a little dance." He sounded drunk. "I wants to see you hoochie-coo…"

Oh, goodness. What had she gotten herself into? Where was brother Doug? Even Henry would do. Short and Round grabbed her backside and hung on in a hurting pinch. She whirled around and smacked the boy across the face.

"Hey, g" Short and Round looked stunned.

"Hey! Hey! Y'awl." The male voice was loud and panicked. "It's Jessie Jim outside. He done fell in the well!"

The singer staggered through a few more notes, but the guitar player stopped.

"You funnin' me?" The piano player glared out into the crowd.

"God's truth. Y'awl, come help! Who got a rope?" The man stormed back out the door.

"Somebody say Jessie Jim?" Alvin Jay called out from the dance floor, where Kate stood sweating and bare-footed.

"Yeah, it's Jessie Jim." Short and Round answered back.

"Fell in the well."

"Hot damn!" Alvin Jay pushed his way through the crowd. "All y'awl, help get my cousin out." He rushed passed Dolly and out the front door.

Kate pushed through the crowd to Dolly. She stood next to Short and Round. "Oh Lord, anythin' bad happen here, and Mama gonna have my behind!" She grabbed Dolly by one hand as she shoved Short and Round in the chest. "Why don't you get yo' behind away from my cousin and go out there to help Jessie Jim?" She headed for the door, her hand tight on Dolly's wrist.

"Jessie Jim, you all right?" Alvin Jay in his Saturday-night-best clothes dropped to his knees at well's edge.

"Somebody, get me outta this damn thing!" The voice swelled up from under the ground. I don't feel me no water down here, but it's damn sure dark, and tight fittin'. Y'awl got to get me outta here."

"Who got the rope?" Alvin Jay.

"They's one in the backroom." The guitar player shouted as he headed back into the juke joint.

"Cousin Dolly—" Kate's voice almost sounded like a prayer—"Let's ease our way on outta here."

"What about Jessie what's-his-name?" Dolly tried to break free of her cousin's grip. No luck.

"They'll get him out. He's just drunk, is all. Me and you gotta get outta here befo' Mama and Papa find out there's been trouble." She yanked Dolly through the crowd. "Lawd help us all if my folks find out I been here. Never mind that I brung you. They already told me if I keep messing up, they gonna send me to my Mama's great aunt. Lord, Lord, she older than dirt, set in her ways, and lives at the church. I'll be at prayer meeting, bible study, altar guild, and who knows what all, seven days out of the week! Come on girl, I gotta get you home safe."

The two cleared most of the crowd surrounding the well when Kate stopped short. Dolly held back as much as she could. It just wasn't right to leave somebody in distress, even if he was drunk when he tumbled into a dry well. When Dolly stopped walking completely, Cousin Kate pulled her arm all the harder, then in one quick move, dropped her hand. Dolly turned to her cousin. Just yards in front of Kate and nowhere near a proper road, Dolly spotted the headlights of a car. And it wasn't a 1930 Model-T with Illinois license plates.

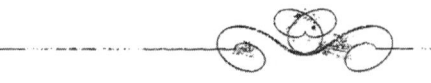

CHAPTER TWELVE

What the hell was all this commotion? Alex looked over the steering wheel of his truck. He could see the shack that passed as a juke joint for the colored. Ben Roy had been stingy in recounting the directions to the place. Alex had driven over every bump and lump off the main road to find this juke joint. Now he watched at a collection of party-going young colored people all gathered in a group staring down at something on the ground. He'd slowed his car to an idle because a few of the young folk fleeing the scene scattered awfully close to his truck. He looked to his left and spotted two girls. One he recognized as Kate Welles, Dickie's girl. But the other he had never before seen. Wait. That second girl, almost hidden behind Kate, didn't look right. He could see only half of her hair and face. A black thing covered most of her hair but light strands poked through here and there. And her face, even in the glare of his headlights, looked bright like Ben Roy's half-colored children by Hettie.

"Kate Welles, that you?" He rolled down the window as he glared at the girl, who looked stupefied. If she had led his girl here, and anything had happened, he'd…

Kate stared up at the truck, her face flooding over with her wrongdoing.

"What you doin' way out here at this time of night? Your

pa's gonna tan you go..." The words swallowed in Alex's throat as the other one—the girl with Kate—stepped almost full into the glare of his headlights.

There she stood, a hand shading her eyes. What color were those eyes? Too hard to see. But the shape of her—that body. Good God, Almighty. It was Laura. Alex blinked. His hands gripped the steering wheel of his truck. If he didn't hold on with all his might, he might fall back into his seat. The girl's face stared around the glare of the light beam. The wide open space between eyebrows and hairline, that way her cheekbones slendered down to her chin, her nose—oh, Lord Jesus, it was his face!

"Uh..." The sound coming out of Kate Welles' mouth sounded as though an unseen hand choked her. "Uh..." She tried again, louder this time. "Mr. Mc...Naughton, suh? I...we..." If she were a deer, she would have died of fright then and there.

"Who's that girl with you?" It all rushed at him like a blaze straight out of hell. That was his girl. Alex knew it. He opened the car door and jumped out. He stood by his truck. "What's her name?" He pointed to Kate's companion.

Kate looked behind her. Alex spotted a few of the party-goers looking in his direction. Kate nodded toward the truck. Alex took a step toward her.

"Gal, I said who's that with you?"

"My name is Dolly Welles, and this is my cousin. I'm sorry, are we on your land?"

Alex stared full at the girl. Blue. Her eyes. Tinged with green, sure enough, but they were blue, just like he remembered on the day he pulled her out of Laura in Rebecca's cabin.

"Mr. McNaughton, suh. We could use yo' help, please, suh." A male voice.

Was it A.C., Savannah's boy—the woman who did Fedora's wash? Alex hadn't noticed how many young people moved his way until A.C. spoke up. He kept his eyes on her. On Dolly.

"What?"

"Jessie Jim done fell in the well, suh," A.C. whispered. "It's dry, suh—the well—so's he ain't 'bout to drown or nothin', but we needs a rope and a truck to pull him out."

Alex forced his eyes off Dolly and onto A.C. "Well? Somebody fell in a well?" He heard his own voice rising. "Y'awl been drinking?" He turned back to Kate. "Did you give my...did...Dolly take a drink? If you did, Kate Welles, I'll tan your hide myself."

"No. No. Mr. McNaughton, suh. Ain't no call for any of that." Alvin Jay, his pants soiled at the knee, shook his head. "Miss Dolly here, she don't do no drinkin'. No dancin' neither. We got a rope, and Jessie Jim done tied it 'round his waist, but if we had a truck to pull..."

"I don't give a da..." He turned to Dolly, who stared her confusion at him. "Anybody...any of these boys...did they...mess with...."

A.C. spoke up. "No, suh. Weren't that kinda party. Jest some dancin' and singin' and..."

"Get in the car." Alex heard all the words, but he was certain of just one thing. He had to get her—his Dolly away from this place. "You," he pointed to her, "get in the car."

"Oh my God, no!" Kate Welles' scream could have wakened the dead. "Please, Mr. Alex, suh. Not my cousin!"

"No suh, no suh," Alvin Jay. "Mr. McNaughton, suh, we knows you is a good man. We'll see to it that Miss Dolly gets home all safe and everythin'."

"He wants me to get in the car?" Dolly frowned her disbelief as she looked at Kate before she turned to Alex. "You're Mr. McNaughton?" She stuck out her hand. "Pleased to meet you. Can you give Kate and Alvin Jay a ride home, too?" Too late. She remembered Cousin Leotha's instructions.

The screams and yells from the crowd almost drowned out his Dolly's last words. A pudgy boy advanced upon him. Alex moved his hand slow like. He tapped at the handle of the pistol on his hip. The tubby kid's eyes went wide. The lad's body shook. Alex squeezed his fingers around the gun handle. No tellin' what this many coloreds together had in mind for his girl.

"Please, Mr. McNaughton, suh, we don't need none of that." A.C.'s hands patted the air. "I swears to God, we'll take Alvin Jay's wagon and take Miss Dolly straight back to Miz Leotha's this very moment."

Alex looked over the crowd of twenty to thirty young people now gathering around him, almost encircling his truck, the engine still running. What were they talking about? Kate Welles rushed up to him and dropped to her knees.

"I'll go with you, Mr. Alex. I will, and I won't say a word 'bout nothin' to nobody." She looked around at the crowd. "Won't nobody say nothin'. Take me, not her. Dolly...she from up north, she don't know nothin' 'bout..." Her lips quivered as she lowered her voice, "I'll do anythin' you wants."

Want? Up north? Illinois. Alex felt his heart threatening to shred right through his plaid shirt. Where up north? "Kate Welles," Alex growled, "it's a good thing you're on your knees. You better be beggin' your Jesus for mercy. You ain't had no business bringin' a girl like her..." he pointed to Dolly, "to this here den of iniquity. Now I'm takin' her home. Straight home, and I don't want no foolishness out of you." He turned to Alvin Jay. "You tie that rope to the end of that wagon yonder. Pull out your worthless cousin, and then you take Kate Welles straight to her house." He turned back to Kate. "Get off your knees, gal. You look a fool. Do what I say, and your daddy just might not kill you tonight. I know I would." He took a step toward Dolly. "I told you to get in the car."

The girl shook her head. "I'm not supposed to get into a car with people I don't know. My mama would kill me if she found..."

Alex swallowed as he sifted through the northern sounds of this girl—his daughter. "Yeah. I don't reckon Lau...Annalaura would be too pleased to find out you been spending your time in a juke joint. Now if you don't want her to find out the truth, get yourself into this car. I'm taking you straight to Dickie and Leotha. You probably need a good hide-tannin' yourself." He reached for her arm. Dolly stepped around him and headed for the passenger door.

"You can take me home, but only after you pull Jessie Jim out of the well."

The smile crept on his face. It didn't belong there. He knew he had to act and look stern, but tarnation, this girl had all the spunk of her mother—Laura.

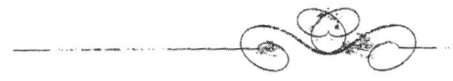

CHAPTER THIRTEEN

Dolly sat with her shoulder pressed against the passenger side door, her hand on the latch. The man—Alex McNaughton—wasn't driving that fast. And they still hadn't reached the road. If he made a move toward her, she would open the door, jump out, and run like crazy. Kate certainly was scared when Dolly climbed into the car with a man Kate seemed to know. Never mind that her cousin sat next to Alvin Jay in his wagon, prepared to follow the McNaughton car. If Kate looked terrified, Alvin Jay's whole body trembled for all to see as he sat on the buckboard seat, his hands tight on the reins tethered to the mule. As if those two weren't enough, Dolly heard more than one "Lord, Jesus, save us all," from the crowd of now-frazzled party-goers as McNaughton's car eased away. Each and every one of them looked scared to death of this man. But not Dolly.

There was something about Mr. McNaughton that was different from all the men Mama had warned her to run from, far and fast. He was old, for one thing. Had to be almost sixty. His hair was white with just a few streaks of yellow here and there. His eyes were blue, but not the fiery blue of a man on a rampage. Then there was something about his face that hinted familiarity. Perhaps the shape, the still-yellow eyebrows. Something she couldn't quite place. And she saw none of the warning signs Annalaura told her about. McNaughton didn't drool around her like Short and Round. Better still, he didn't have that stupid, eyes-wide-open-like-he-wanted-to-devour-you look on his face. But there was something else about his manner. What was that look as he stared straight at the road in front of him? Anger? No. He sure tried to act angry back at the well when his truck finally freed Jessie Jim. Want, like Mama said men sometimes plaster on their faces for women who aren't their wives? No, he was much too old for that sort of stuff, anyway. He didn't want her as a temporary fill-in wife, Dolly was confident. In fact, the man hadn't said a word in these five minutes since they'd driven from the juke joint and that dry well. But something definitely rode across the planes of his face. Concern? Worry? Why, and for whom?

"How do you know my mother?"

The car swerved so hard to the right, Dolly banged her shoulder against the window.

"Your mother?" Mr. McNaughton corrected the car.

"Yes. You called her Annalaura. That's her name. How do you know that?"

"It was a long time ago." The man's eyes fixed back on the fast approaching main highway.

"Yes, I know. My folks left here—Tennessee—when I was a baby. They don't talk much about this…here. Tennessee."

Did she hear the man try to gravel out a sound as he turned the truck onto the paved road heading back toward Cousin Richard and Leotha's house? "Did you know them when they lived here in Tennessee? "Lawnover." The word barely traveled the short distance between them.

"That's it! Did my parents work for you? I think they grew tobacco somewhere around here, but I'm not sure. They never talk about it, but my middle brother remembers a few things. He…"

"Doug?"

Dolly moved from the safety of her window seat toward this Alex McNaughton. "How do you know my brother's name?"

He finally glanced in her direction. "You're right. Your folks. They worked my acres a long time ago."

"Yes, I know it was a long time ago. I'm sixteen, now."

He nodded his head. "I know." He turned back to her for a brief instant. "You graduate from eighth grade?"

Dolly stared at this man who had once been her father's employer. She pulled up one of Annalaura's lectures about acting subservient in front of Tennessee white people. It seemed a strange way of existing to Dolly, but Mama had insisted. Yet this man was asking her all kinds of improbable questions. She nodded her head. "I just graduated…from high school. I was co-valedictorian." She started to smile but remembered another of Annalaura's thousand and one rules—modesty is a virtue.

He turned to her, ignoring the road for several long seconds. Thank God no other traffic was moving in either direction. "Valedic…what?"

"My grades. They were the best—well, I was tied with my best friend, Claire—for the top grades in the whole senior class. We were both valedictorians. We got to give the graduation speeches, and we each received plaques and everything." She remembered her day of triumph, then her disappointment. "Of course, Claire's going to college."

"And you?" The man turned to examine her once more.

Dolly sucked in her lips. Her mama was right as usual. Annalaura wanted Dolly to get a college education for sure, but that wasn't to be. It was best in times like these, Mama said, to carry on like you could win with whatever life dealt you. And life had not dealt a teaching degree in French for Dolly Welles. "My folks don't have the money." She looked down at her scuffed white shoes.

"You'da gone to that colored college in Nashville? Fisk." He turned his eyes to the road, but only for a few seconds before he scanned her face again.

"Fisk?" Dolly looked at Mr. McNaughton while she shook her head. "No. I wanted to go to the University of Illinois at Champaign-Urbana." She frowned as she sorted through this southerner's words. "We don't have 'colored' schools in Illinois."

"Um." He turned back to the road. His hands gripped the steering wheel. He hunched his shoulders. He said nothing as the truck rattled over the darkened pavement avoiding the occasional jack rabbit. "You're not but sixteen." He broke his own silence. "Just turned. In May. Too young for college."

"Yes, I turned sixteen two weeks ago." She stared at him. "How do you know that? This trip, it's my graduation present." Dolly recognized a farm house not two miles from Cousin Richard. Her stomach flip-flopped. "Oh, Mr. McNaughton, please, please, don't tell my mama about the party. She's so old fashioned. She'll never understand."

Was that a smile she caught on the man's face as he trained his eyes on the road. "That depends on you." He kept driving. "Promise me no more juke joints. No drinking. No smoking. And, positively, no boys."

Dolly sighed as she leaned back into her seat. "You sound just like my father. Of course, I pro..." Did the car lurch forward again?

Up ahead, the road to the Welles farm approached. The man looked straight ahead. "I know your folks, Dolly. They left here a while back. Went up to Illinoise. Not Chicago, I know." He turned to her for a quick glance. "I can't quite recollect the name of the town they headed to."

"Oh, you mean Brugestown, if you want to call that dinky little place a town. Nothing ever happens there. Dull as dishwater."

"Bruges..."

"Yep. Brugestown, Illinois." She brightened. "But Danville's only five miles away. That's a pretty big place, but of course, my folks rarely allow me to go there." She looked down at her hands, devoid of the nail polish Annalaura always forbid on the fingertips of a refined young lady. "One day, I'm going to live in Paris like my friend Claire's mother." Dolly looked over at Mr. McNaughton. "Well, she didn't exactly live in Paris. But somewhere near." She brightened. "Ury, I think it's called."

Mr. McNaughton pulled the car to a stop. "Paris, is it? Let's see if you can make it through Lawnover first." He reached for the truck door handle.

"Wait!" Dolly called out. "I'm sorry..." Annalaura's instructions pounded in her head. "Sir. I mean, sir, I thought we were going to wait until Kate—Cousin Kate—got here. She's the one to tell Cousin Richard and Aunt Leotha what happened."

"That's what you're thinkin', is it?" The man opened the car door and stepped out. "I don't need your cousin tellin' whoppin' lies about how you two run off to a juke joint. I suspect you two snuck out of the house without tellin' nobody. Now if you want me to keep this thing civil, then you get outta this car, right now."

Dolly looked at the man's stern face. Goodness, he sounded just like Papa when he caught her doing something forbidden. Her heart thumped. She was going to have to come up with something bold to protect both herself and Kate from adult wrath, even if that cousin was dreadful. She opened the door and slid to the ground. Mr. McNaughton motioned her toward the steps leading to the front porch. She followed him, her head down. A sound from the upstairs window brought her eyes upward. Annalaura had forbidden swear words out of the mouths of her daughters—ladies never swore—another Annalaura rule—but just this one time, Dolly determined it was justified. Shit. There, grinning down at her through a partially opened curtain, sat Dodie.

"Dickie Welles!" Mr. McNaughton shouted as he strode across the front porch and banged on the door. "Alex McNaughton, here. I need to talk to you."

Dolly, standing on the second from the bottom stair, heard the startled voices of her cousins and the stumbling of feet seconds before the front door creaked open. Cousin

Leotha peered through the crack.

"Mr. McNaughton, suh?" The half-moon shining through the foliage of the one tree in the front yard, only partially lit her face. "How's it I can help you, suh?"

"Where's your man? I need to talk to him right now!" Dolly slipped further behind Mr. McNaughton's shadow. Where, oh where was Kate? How slow could a mule move? Cousin Richard pushed the door wide open as he stepped in front of Leotha.

"Pleased to serve you, suh. What is it I can do fo' you?"

Mr. McNaughton whirled around, looked for Dolly, spotted her cowering against the stair bannister, covered the three steps down, grabbed her arm and yanked her to the front porch.

"This," McNaughton growled as he dug his work-worn hand into Dolly's arm, "is what you can do for me. You know where I found this girl?"

"Uhh." Cousin Richard's eyes grew wide, wider still when Mr. McNaughton pushed both him and Cousin Leotha aside and stormed into the front room.

Dolly stifled the cry she wanted to make as the man's fingers dug into her upper arm. He planted himself in the middle of Cousin Leotha's for-company-only front room, right next to her blue davenport. He dropped her arm and folded his own.

"Ben Roy tells me this girl's from Illinoise—up north. Visitin' her kin folks. That tells me her mama put her trust in you." He glared at Cousin Richard a second time. "You two know anythin' 'bout where I found her?"

Cousin Richard's mouth opened and closed as he shook his head. Cousin Leotha got the words out first.

"Suh...she...suh...I reckon..." Leotha turned toward the stairs leading to the upstairs attic bedroom. "Kate Welles, get yo' behind on down here!"

Mr. McNaughton shook his head. "Leotha, you tryin' to tell me you don't know your own girl was gone, too?"

Leotha faced her visitor, her head doing a slow shake like

she was trying to interpret an unfamiliar French sentence. "Kate," Leotha pointed upstairs, "she...all the girls is upstairs. They..."

McNaughton turned back to Dolly. "And if this ain't Dolly Welles—the one who's supposed to be fast asleep in your upper room—then who is she?" His mouth set in a grim line.

Dolly glanced at the pistol still on Mr. McNaughton's hip. She had kept almost none of Mama's admonitions about Negro behavior in the South, but one angry man carrying a gun versus a confused old couple who bore no weapons couldn't be good. "Sorry, Cousin Leotha."

"Sorry?" Leotha looked close to fainting. "What... why..." Her breath came in spurts. "Wasn't you upstairs 'til a minute ago?"

"I'll get you some water." Dolly took a step toward the kitchen. "You don't look well, Cousin Leotha."

McNaughton grabbed Dolly's shoulder. "You're going nowhere 'til I find out how you got to that juke joint."

"Juke joint!" Cousin Richard and Cousin Leotha screamed the words in unison, their tone sounding like they just heard Dolly pronounced to Hell by St. Peter.

"What juke joint?" Leotha gathered herself.

"Not the one up the road just outside of Clarksville?" Cousin Richard.

Three sets of eyes turned to Dolly, waiting.

"They climbed out the winda." Dodie, in her night dress, crouched on the bottom stair step, peeped through the bannister rails.

"What winda?" Leotha demanded. "I sent all you girls up to bed right after supper. Y'awls supposed to be 'sleep hours ago."

Dolly shook her head as she took in a big breath. Confession time. "Cousin Leotha, I did it. I climbed out the win..."

The braying of the mule and Alvin Jay's voice commanding the animal to a halt, brought all eyes toward the still open front door.

"Alvin Jay? What you doin' here?" Cousin Richard still looked rocked by confusion.

"Oh, he ain't by himself." Mr. McNaughton walked to the door. "Get on in here, Kate. You, Alvin Jay, you head on home. This ain't none of your business."

"Kate?" Leotha's eyes looked as though they were struggling to put together a very complicated puzzle. "My Kate and Alvin Jay?" She walked to the door just as Kate walked up the stairs.

"What in the name of God's Graces is you wearin'? You know I don't 'llow no dresses that short. And, what is that mess on yo' knees? Why ain't you in bed? And look at that goop on yo' face. Why…?."

Mr. McNaughton nodded Kate into the living room. "There's a whole lot of why's I want to know. I suspect Dolly," he nodded toward her, "didn't know nothin' about a juke joint 'til you took her there." He turned to Dodie. "You the one say you saw 'em both go out the window?"

Now even Dodie looked frightened. She looked first at her mother, then her father, and finally at Kate. Her head shook, but was it a yes or a no?

Mr. McNaughton advanced on the child. Leotha clutched both hands to her throat.

"Dodie, you better tell all you knows," Leotha squeaked, "befo' I beats the tar outta you."

The tears came quick and loud. "Kate, I didn't mean nothin' by it." The child sniffled as she backed up one stair.

"You ain't goin' nowhere, girl, 'til you tell your ma and me what you seed." Cousin Richard.

"Nothin', Papa. I mean," Dodie sent a pleading look to Kate. "I mean they said they was goin' out. I thought maybe it was a special Saturday night prayer meetin' is all."

"Girl, I gonna beat you 'til the end of time." Leotha rushed to the stairway.

Mr. McNaughton held up a hand. "You beat your girl all you want. " He turned to Kate. "'Specially that one. Right now, I want all these children out of here." He pointed to Kate and Dolly as he turned to Cousin Richard. "We've got to have ourselves a serious talk."

"Talk, suh?" Cousin Richard.

"I said I want these girls outta here." He nodded toward Dolly. "Now get upstairs. All of you. I gotta to talk to your folks."

Dodie scampered upstairs. Kate slithered past her mother and bounded out of sight, her red shoes in her hand.

"I'm sorry. I know this is all my fault. I should have said no." Dolly turned from her cousins to Mr. McNaughton. "Please don't be angry at Kate and Dodie. I knew better. I..."

"I think I told you to get upstairs. I don't like repeatin' myself. Now get!" He raised his voice.

Never argue with a Southern elder, Mama had said, no matter what the color. Dolly was used to making her point to her parents. She usually lost, of course, but at least they pretended to listen. None of these southerners seemed inclined to hear reason, especially Mr. McNaughton. Dolly nodded her yes and walked up the stairs as slowly as she could manage. She would never scamper and run like Kate and Dodie. Funny. Dolly never thought anything could frighten Cousin Kate. She had been wrong.

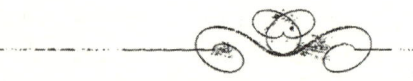

CHAPTER FOURTEEN

"Kate! Gal, you better close that door tight!" Alex barked up the stairs before he turned to face the Welles. "You can see as well as me this ain't gonna work."

Dickie looked at his wife. She shook her head while her face muscles twitched. Three girls under their roof, and these two had no control over any of them. He couldn't allow this, not with Ben Roy talking nonsense about the Davis cousins and Wiley George. Oh, Lord. Not Wiley George.

"I reckon we gonna have to make other arrangements." Alex scowled at Dickie Welles. "I hold you responsible for this mess. If I hadn't gotten there when I did," he turned to Leotha, "anything could have happened to those two. Boys and young girls mixin' together. No chaperone. It ain't right."

Leotha clamped her hand over her mouth. "Oh, Lord, glory. Mr. Alex, suh, I ain't had me no idea. I thought…"

"That's 'zactly what I'm sayin', Leotha. You ain't had no idea. How many times has your Kate climbed out the window and gone who knows where?"

"Some childrens is just high strung, Mr. Alex." Was Dickie Welles trying to defend his wife? "Kate's but seventeen. Feeling her oats. She…"

"Uh-huh," Alex grunted. "Well, I don't want her feelin' her oats around Dolly. She ain't that kind of girl."

Leotha put up her hands. Was that a little bit of mother sternness on her face? "Suh, I admits I been too soft on that girl. Oh, I whips her all right, but she's a good girl. Told her she had to come with me to prayer meetin' every Wednesday night, and Bible study on Thursdays 'stead of goin' to the picture show. And we at two services on Sunday. Been a month of discipline now, and she's done followed the rules."

"Spare the rod and spoil the child, I says." Dickie Welles' lower lip protruded as he shook his head. "I'm gonna tan her hide good. Dodie's, too." He held up a hand. "And I'm nailin' that winda shut. I don't care if they just 'bout smother up there."

Alex shook his head. "Take care of your own as best you see fit. But I'll take care of Dolly."

"Suh?" Dickie and Leotha talked at the same time.

They had to act surprised, Alex understood. Of course they knew all about Dolly and himself. All of Lawnover did. Didn't they? He felt his forehead crinkle into a frown. But then these Welles were kin to John... Alex laid a hand across his chest. There was that pain again. The thought of John Welles lying beside Laura always brought up the gall. His mind whirred. Would John Welles announce to his Tennessee kin that his wife's youngest child was not his own? Would...? Something gripped at Alex's heart—an answer he had to have.

"Dickie, I hear tell you're cousin to Dolly's...pa. Any more after her?"

Leotha stared the longest and hardest. Did she know the truth? But it was Dickie Welles who shook his head.

"Any mo children? No mo', Mr. Alex. John and Annalaura? Just the five—three boys and the two girls. Dolly's the last."

A boulder that burdened Alex these sixteen years lifted away. It hurt too much to imagine Laura lying under John Welles. When those god-awful pictures popped into his head, he bashed them back into the foggy place in his brain. But now he knew one thing. Dolly was Laura's youngest. Could that mean she refused her husband? He'd never heard of a wife telling her man, no, but Laura was like no other woman he'd ever known. Alex spotted the curious look on the faces of Dickie and Leotha. They were watching his mouth that now curved into a smile.

"Suh," Dickie Welles, "don't you fret 'bout a thing. We gonna take good care of our Dolly."

"Your Dolly?" The words popped out before Alex could give them any sort of measure. "She can't stay here." He caught himself.

Both Welles' stared at him as though his mind had flown off with a night bird.

"But…" Leotha looked as though Gabriel had blown his horn for the reckoning day and she was first in line. "What you say, suh? We the closest kin Dolly have 'round here. Just us—the Welles. Her mama's folks, Annalaura…they…"

Dickie didn't look that far behind Leotha in the waiting. "My Leotha, she meant to say…that is…I say…" his tongue waggled but no more words came forth.

"Leotha, get upstairs and get her ready." Alex's mind raced.

"Ready, suh?" Leotha was nowhere near recovery from her shock.

Alex nodded. "I'm takin' her outta here. Tonight."

"Lord, Jesus, no!" Leotha shouted at him.

Alex, stared at this colored woman. She had forgotten her place. His right hand stroked the gun handle still at his hip. He didn't expect any trouble out of these two, and he certainly didn't want to start a ruckus—Ben Roy's words banged around his head—but Dolly could not remain in this sort of danger.

"Leotha," maybe if he spoke to her better than she deserved, he might make some headway, "I think I know what's best for Dolly. Don't none of us—you, me, Dickie, here—want anythin' bad to happen to her. Now I know you done your best to keep an eye on her, but your Kate ain't exactly a good influence."

"No. No, suh, we sure don't wants nothin' to happen to our...to Dolly." Dickie. "But if she leave here, where will she go?"

Alex blinked. He'd suggested it once before and it hadn't gone too well, but that was sixteen years ago. "I'm takin' her to my place."

"Yo' place?" Leotha screamed.

Alex jerked his head toward the stairs. With Leotha carrying on like a banshee, the girls in their bedroom would surely hear all the commotion.

"Yo' place?" Leotha repeated, several sound levels lower. "Suh, how can that be?" She looked at him with eyes wider than any owl he'd ever seen.

Dickie shook his head without saying a word.

"Yes. My place."

'But...but....' Leotha wasn't going to listen to reason. "Yo'...uh...yo' missus, suh. Ms. McNaughton, she 'spectin' to see Dolly ride up to her house tonight? Round midnight?"

Alex felt a punch in the gut. Leotha was right. Eula Mae might need some preparing. She acted up that last time, but she'd been nothing but a caring wife all these years. He guessed she'd been caring. He hadn't given Eula or her ways much thought. She looked after him, the house, tended the gardens, the animals, the accounts and...come to think of it, when was the last time he'd seen her write in that account journal?

"You get the girl ready to leave at first light." Alex turned to Dickie, "I want you to stand guard over this house all night. You got yourself a squirrel gun, right?"

"Yes, suh, yes, suh, I do."

"If any colored man comes ridin' up here before mornin', you shoot 'em dead. You got that straight?"

Dickie Welles stared at him.

"If it's Wiley George, you hold him here with your gun while you—" he turned to Leotha. "Get your tail to my place lickety-split. Whatever you do, don't turn Dolly over to nobody. You got that? Especially Wiley George."

Leotha turned to her husband, who glanced back at his wife before two sets of eyes rested on Alex. They nodded their heads as though it was best to agree to anything a crazy man said—at least until he stepped out of sight. But there was no other way. Alex just had to pray that Ben Roy would keep a tight rein on Wiley George. The Davis cousins were gentlemen. They'd never touch Dolly until a proper deal had been struck, and the Good Lord knew that was never going to happen. Now off to wake Eula Mae.

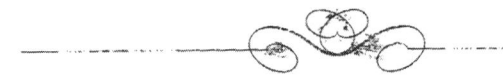

CHAPTER FIFTEEN

"Eula Mae. You awake?"

The sound of her husband's voice cut through her sleep. She lay on her right side, her knees half-curled under her on her side of the bed. Eula had never been a hard sleeper. Never thrashed around much—at least not since her marriage. In those early days when Alex had his needs, she only allowed herself to sink into a half-slumber so she could respond quickly to the feel of her husband's hand working its way around her bottom, across her thigh, and down to there. But after their girl died aborning, that hand didn't come so often. Twenty years into her marriage she still kept to her half-slumber. But back then, though she suspected it had to be some kind of a sin that even Reverend Hawkins couldn't pray away, she wished Alex would show he wanted her body a tad more often. And on that one magnificent Good-God-to-Glory night when her soul soared to the skies, he had. But that very next morning, Eula found out the why of her thrilling night.

"Eula Mae?" His tone was a shade louder.

Her eyelids fluttered, but in the dimness of the bedroom—Alex hadn't turned on the new electric lights—she still pretended sleep. What could her husband want of her this late at night? Alex only touched her every six or seven weeks these past sixteen years, and then the whole thing fled by so fast she wondered why he bothered. Not that she cared one way or the other on most nights. But every now and again one little spark in her dead heart threatened a flare-up. There were those times, they didn't come often, when she remembered that feeling. Maybe, if just one more time, she could feel that open-up-the-heavens-and-let-the-angels-sing moment— these years as a member of the walking-dead club might be worth it after all.

Alex gave her shoulder a little shake.

She eased herself to her back and opened her eyes. "Something you need me to fix for you, Alex?"

Her husband stood looking down at her from his side of the bed. He pulled off his boots, unbuttoned his britches, and let them drop to just below his drawers. He sat. "Eula Mae, you work too hard."

Good God, Almighty! Where had it come from? That slender dagger that pierced her dead heart. She'd heard those words before. Lord, why did they still hurt? Sixteen years back, right before... "We've had a hired girl these past ten years, Alex. And a washerwoman once a week. Don't need no more help." She scooted up, her back against the wooden headboard with its twin carved deer heads. Her heart pounded so hard her ears barely unscrambled Alex's words. Work too hard?

"I'm just sayin' you need more help around here—the cleanin' and all." He looked at her. "Not forever, mind you. Just 'til I can get things sorted out."

What things? "With all this Depression talk, you think we ought to spend the money?" Eula held her breath. In all these years she had done her duty by her husband. Despite the struggles of their early years, she never ever suggested that Alex might not have been the best provider for the eldest daughter of the richest tobacco clan in all of Lawnover. Thanks to her mother, Eula had been well trained to show gratitude toward any man who offered her overly tall, big-boned self marriage. And in one way, she knew she had been fortunate. What Alex lacked in economic sense, he more than made up with those looks that made even married women give him second and third glances. But he had always been faithful to her—until...

Eula grunted. She hated memories. "Might be best not to spend extra money." There. She'd spoken her own mind and broken her promise to herself. It felt good. If her husband flinched at her boldness, Eula didn't see it.

"Eula Mae" Alex put on his serious look.

She stared at him. What was that unusual expression on his face? Could it be that he considered her something almost as important as his favorite hunting rifle?

"I might as well just get to it." He looked passed her to her peony-printed wallpaper. "I need to take on a hired girl for a week or so. Just 'til I figure some things out. She won't be stayin'."

Hadn't he said almost those same words sixteen years back when he wanted to bring his...that woman... into her house? That woman and her child—Dolly. Eula had been past forty back then, but she had been as green as her slow-in-thinking niece, Tilly. And twice as blind. She had believed in her husband. Even if he paid her scant mind, Alex had always been true to her, and she as plain as a mud duck. Now she knew she understood it had been a lie—even if only one time. "I don't reckon I need much household help, Alex." She couldn't meet his eyes, but somehow her chest expanded.

She kept her eyes on his shirt collar as Alex looked down at the summer coverlet at the foot of the bed. "She's a girl—a child." He stooped a little to catch Eula's eyes. "Just sixteen."

The sound rushed down Eula's throat rather than out into in the air. "Sixteen?"

He nodded. Sixteen. Alex's colored bastard would be sixteen.

"And..." the words should have caught in her throat, but somehow they paraded out of her mouth in a most orderly fashion, "it's her... you want to bring here? To this house—to my house?" Her own raised voice sounded strange in her ears. "You expectin' me to take her—your daughter—into my house?" Her hands—one over the other—gripped tight. "I'm not Fedora."

The most peculiar look covered her husband's face. Not like he was about to have a stroke. More like his ears had gone bad and he needed a hearing trumpet. He shook his head and pulled up his britches.

"I don't want you to be like Fedora, Eula Mae. You're just fine the way you are." He finished buttoning as he walked toward the door. "I don't want this to be no kind of a trial for you." He stood in the doorway. "But I've got to do what I ought. It won't be but for a few days. I'll fix up the little room at the top of the stairs for her. Do it myself."

Do it himself? Did Alex know where Eula kept the extra sheets and pillows? Did he even know they owned extra linen?

He stepped through the doorway, stopped and turned. "She's a northern girl with northern ways. Don't pay her no mind. I'll take care of her." He closed the door behind him.

Eula felt the pain first in her jaw. That was it, was it? Her husband intended to bring his colored bastard into Eula's house no matter what her say-so. But she understood her man. In his way, he'd offered her an apology for his decision. Why wasn't that enough? Few other women in Lawnover ever got their husbands' I'm sorrys about their other families. Fedora had endured Ben Roy's second family for more than twenty years—living right there on her very own acres. His Hettie washing Fedora's clothes. Ben Roy's bastard girls canning Fedora's beans. Dusting Fedora's settee. Eula grimaced. The pain worsened and moved from her jaw to her shoulder. She should be grateful she knew. She'd talked back to her husband, and he hadn't given her a proper beating for it. Alexander had never been a beating man. In return, she'd pleased Alexander McNaughton in every way for the thirty-seven years of their marriage. With his bastard child living under her roof—even for an hour—would she have the strength to please him for the thirty-eighth?

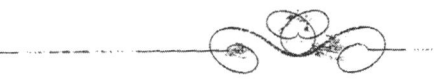

CHAPTER SIXTEEN

"I didn't know what to say," Dodie whimpered, curled up in the corner of the bed farthest from the window. "That white man...he...had a gun. I..."

Kate's hand flashed out in a blur and struck the eleven-year-old on the side of the head. "You shoulda kept your damn mouth shut, that's what you shoulda did!"

Dolly, standing no more than three feet away, reached Kate in one step. She clamped on to her cousin's arm. "Why are you blaming her? You and I are the ones who climbed out of that window. You keep hitting her, and she'll make so much noise, everyone will rush upstairs."

"You didn't tell on me." Kate's words strung half way between a question and a thank you. "Why not? You and me ain't exactly been getting' along great since you got here."

Dolly ignored the troublesome child. "Kate, we've got bigger problems than the two of us squabbling. I don't want this getting back to my parents in Illinois." Dolly brushed a strand of hair from her face. "My folks are almost as strict as yours. If they find out..."

"They gonna kill us all!" Dodie wailed.

"They outta kill you fo' damn sure." Kate glared at her sister.

"Would you two stop it!" Dolly looked between the two

sisters before she sat at the foot of the bed next to Kate. She leaned into her cousin and lowered her voice. "How bad can it be? I know we'll probably have to confess in front of the entire church." She hunched her shoulders. "I've already done that one."

"You?" Kate looked incredulous. "What bad thing you ever do?"

"Dancing."

Dodie, her knees scrunched to her chest, pushed her back against the head of the bed. "Cousin Dolly, did you dance the hoochie-coochie?" The child had a smile on her face.

"Of course, I didn't dance the hoo…that's not the point." She turned back to Kate, "What will they do to us? Your folks. All that talk about whippings, they were just kidding weren't they?"

"Kiddin'?" Kate hooted. "Mama just about tears up my behind every time she thinks I've misbehaved. Now Papa, he ain't that bad." She looked into Dolly's eyes. "Mind you, I'm not sayin' that takin' a lickin' from Pa is fun. It's just that he lays a lighter hand on us 'cause we is girls."

Dolly shuddered. "But, Kate, you're seventeen. You're too old for a spanking."

"Did I say anythin' 'bout a spankin'?" Kate snapped. "No, they both gives honest-to- goodness whippin's. Ma uses her stout belt. Papa don't use nothin' but his hand."

Dolly stared at Cousin Kate. Had she heard right? "A strap? We used to get spankings when we were kids—Lottie and me. Lottie's my older sister. Mama used a belt on my brothers—Doug and Henry, but never on us girls. And I haven't had a spanking since I was seven years old."

Both Dodie and Kate looked at Dolly as though her mind had snapped. Dodie spoke first, "Cousin Dolly, you tellin' us that you ain't had no whippin's since you was seven?" Dodie shook her I-don't-believe-a-word-of-it head.

"Well, you better get yo' behind ready fo' a shock 'cause…"

Dolly heard them first. Footsteps walking up the stairs.

Two pairs. But which two pair? She laid a finger across her lips to silence her cousins. The door flung open without a knock.

"I'm prayin' to the Lord Jesus," Cousin Leotha, her face looking like she'd just faced the devil and meant every word literally, stepped into the room first, followed by Cousin Richard.

Dolly looked at her two cousins. Kate and Dodie seemed to think the absence of Mr. McNaughton a good thing. But with all this talk of beatings and whippings, Dolly wasn't so sure. Cousin Richard looked like a man who'd been condemned to death in that new-fangled electric chair they had in Joliet. Did they have one in Tennessee, too?

Leotha turned first to Kate. "Girl, I know you ain't been one to pay me much mind in the past, but you got to follow what I tells you like I was Jesus hisself."

"I promised your daddy I'd take care of you." Cousin Richard looked ready to cry. "I wants us all to get down on our knees and pray that this thing come out all right."

Richard grabbed Dodie first and pulled her off the bed. Leotha reached for Kate. Dolly slipped to her knees before either cousin could lay hands on her. All five of them crowded together at the side of the bed, hands clasped in prayer. Four sets of eyes closed at Cousin Richard's command. Dolly squinted through half-shut lids.

"Lord Jesus, we ain't asked fo' this trouble. They is just high-spirited children. Ain't meant no harm. Let this be all right fo' these innocent girls, oh Lord. Amen."

Leotha motioned them to their feet, the girls lined up on the bed, she and Cousin Richard towering over them.

"This is how this is gonna go." Leotha began as Cousin Richard left the room. "Cousin Dolly, you got to pay me close mind. I knows this is unusual fo' you but it's got to be."

"Cousin Leotha, I'm so very, very sorry, and I'll take whatever punishment you give me, but I want you to know that I don't think going to church is a punishment. I'll go with you anytime you want. I'll..."

Leotha shook her head. "Ain't 'bout no church." Her chest heaved. "You goin' away for a bit."

"Going away?" Hallelujah! Her cousins had decided to allow her to join her brothers with the Carruthers family. She struggled to suppress her smile.

But Cousin Leotha wasn't smiling. "First light, I hear tell." She put a hand on Dolly's shoulder, "I don't reckon the work will be hard." She stared. "Girl, do you know how to do anythin' 'round the house? Can you cook a lick? You ever scrubbed clothes? You know how to turn a feather bed?"

Dolly shook her head. What was Cousin Leotha talking about? "Yes, I can...Yes, m'am, I can cook a little. I know how to sweep and dust. I iron my brothers' clothes—of course, they pay me."

Leotha grunted. "Humph," came out of her mouth first. "Don't reckon there'll be pay in this deal."

"What deal, Mama?" Cousin Kate's voice actually shook. "What's gonna happen to Cousin Dolly."

"Oh, she ain't the onliest one in this pickle of a mess." Cousin Richard came back into the room. He carried Dolly's new suitcase and a cardboard box. He set them both on Dolly's assigned bed. "You tell 'em yet, Leotha?"

"I'm jest gettin' to it." She shook her head once again, and took in a sigh loud enough to be heard by their distant neighbors. "Both of y'awl bein' picked up at first light."

"Both of who, Mama?" Dodie raised her voice. "Not me?"

Leotha shook her head. "Oh, missy, you ain't gettin' away scott free. You gonna get a tannin' like you ain't never seed befo', but no, you ain't the two that's going."

Dolly frowned as she looked at Kate. As wonderful as it would be to finish her vacation with her brothers at her beck and call, she did not relish the idea of having to drag along Cousin Kate. "Do the Carruthers have enough room for Kate, too?"

"The Carruthers?" Richard joined Cousin Leotha in confusion. "Y'awl ain't goin' to no Carruthers. Mr. Alexander

McNaughton comin' here at cock's crow to take y'awl to his house." He brought out his own loud sigh. "Leastways, that's the way it's got to go." He dropped his head. "Not while I has breath in this body will I lets that girl go alone."

Dolly looked from Richard to Leotha. What were they talking about? "I don't...Mr. McNaughton? Why is he coming here so early in the morning? And what does he want with me and Kate?"

"He's takin' you to his house." Leotha's face jumped between relief that she'd gotten out the words, and fear so great she looked pale beneath the brown tones of her skin.

"Taking who to his house?" Where in Annalaura's rules of Southern behavior was this particular oddity?

"You, girl," Leotha spoke. "He's taking you to his house to act as his maid."

"Maid?" Dolly jumped from her assigned seat at the foot of the bed. "I'm nobody's maid. I'll not go!" Oh, oh, she'd raised her voice to an elder—another in the long list of infractions Leotha was sure to write Mama about her graceless and insolent youngest daughter.

Leotha advanced upon Dolly, put her hands on her shoulders and pulled the girl to her in a quick embrace. "Ain't no way to stop it, girl, but Richard and me, we done thought it over careful." She pushed Dolly back and searched her face as though she were looking for a glimmer of understanding. "I knows Annalaura ain't trained you to be no maid. They's a better life fo' you up north, I know, but baby girl, you gots to find it in yo'self somewhere, somehow, to act the part fo' a little while."

Dolly didn't try to break Leotha's grip on her.

Cousin Richard walked beside the pair. He pulled Kate to her feet. "Dolly, you ain't goin' into this thing alone." He swallowed hard. "No matter what, I ain't allowin' that." He shook Kate's shoulder, "She's goin' with you. I'm 'fraid it's my girl got you into this mess. You both gonna be maids."

"Papa!" Kate screamed. "Mama, don't let him do this to me. You said I don't have to work as nobody's maid 'til I'm twenty-one years old, and then only if I don't find me a husband. Well, I've almost got me a husband. Alvin Jay. I know I can convin…"

"This ain't 'bout no Alvin Jay, rascal tho' he is." Cousin Leotha shook her head, her face suddenly clouding with anger. "This is 'bout you, girl. You brung this on yo'self. Mr. McNaughton, he don't think we doin' a good 'nough job of protectin' Dolly from wild boys—like yo' Alvin Jay. I reckon it was you who led him into that way of thinkin'."

"But, Mama, you know Alvin Jay's not wild. At least, not buck wild. Just high-spirited. You know, 'bitious."

"We ain't talkin' 'bout this no mo'." Cousin Richard raised a hand. "Dolly, get yo' valise packed. Kate, you take that there box. Mr. McNaughton be here 'fo you know it." He motioned Leotha out of the room and closed the door behind him.

"Is it gonna be like slavery times?" Dodie sounded more earnest than sarcastic this time. "A white man decides he needs him a maid, and he just comes and picks one up?" Now the child sounded frightened.

Dolly looked between Kate and Dodie. "Is this a southern thing? People can actually command you to go to work for them even if you don't want to?" Maybe that was why her parents rarely spoke of their lives in Tennessee. It must have been like slavery.

Kate shook her head. "Oh, it ain't pretty down here, that's for sure, but can't nobody make you work fo' them if you don't want to." She scowled as she scanned Dolly's face. "Unless…" the girl's eyes widened. Kate clamped both hands over her mouth.

"Unless what?" Dolly pulled Kate's hands away.

"You sure Mr. McNaughton ain't never set eyes on you befo'?" Kate trembled.

"Of course, I've never seen the man before in my life. How would I?"

"It's just that…just that…"

Dodie looked wide-eyed with curiosity. "What you know

'bout this?" She tapped Kate on the shoulder.

Kate shook her sister's arm away. She looked down at the floor as she slowly shook her head. "Dolly, I ain't gonna let it happen." She looked straight at Dolly. "What you know 'bout men?"

"Men? What do men have to do with us becoming maids?" How could she get word to her brothers? She leaned in to Kate. "Can your father get to the Carruthers place and tell them what's happening?" For the first time in an hour, Dolly felt a spark of hope.

That look of terror on Kate's face soon splashed water all over that spark.

"No. No. We can't get yo' brothers involved in this." She grabbed Dolly's arm. "Remember, you and me got to stick together. Never be separated. You never be by yo'self with him. Me neither."

Was Kate hinting at what Dolly thought? Ridiculous. "Kate, you're being silly. I don't know why that man wants us at his house, but it's not that. I rode in the car with him. Remember? He never laid a hand on me."

The door creaked open, and Cousin Leotha popped in her head. She scanned their faces. "I don't know what foolishness Kate been scarin' you with, but pay her no mind. Y'awl two jest do as you're told, and this will all work out jest fine." She turned to go. "Get on yo' knees and say yo' prayers. The Lord will make this turn out all right." She closed the door.

* * *

"It's 'bout that time, y'awl. He's here." Dolly opened her eyes to the sound of Cousin Leotha's voice.

Had she slept? When she lay down on her assigned bed, she knew she'd never get a wink of sleep. Dodie and Kate, too, said they'd be up all night worrying. Yet here was Cousin Leotha shaking Kate awake. "Bring yo' valises and get on downstairs. Dolly, he's willin' to let you set for breakfast."

Dolly was first to thump her suitcase down the staircase. By the time she reached the fourth stair riser, Mr. McNaughton walked up to meet her. He looked into her face before he picked up and carried her case downstairs. Dolly followed him while Kate had to wrestle the cardboard box to the bottom step.

"I've got eggs and grits and poke sausage and bacon and biscuits and gravy. Please to set yo'self down Mr. McNaughton, suh." Leotha stood at her kitchen table now ladened with platters, bowls, and pitchers of sweet milk.

"Don't mind if I do." Mr. McNaughton settled himself at the head of the table, the chair usually reserved for Cousin Richard.

This morning Richard stood. Leotha moved next to her wood-burning stove. Kate looked stranded in the doorway. Dolly pulled up a chair across from Mr. McNaughton. It was the gasp streaming from three mouths that first brought her attention to the Tennessee cousins. All three faces looked frozen in a Frankenstein horror movie. Dolly shook her head. Now what had she done wrong?

"You better eat hardy." Mr. McNaughton bit into a part of fat sausage. "Can't say much for dinner." His face brightened as he looked up. "Leotha, can you fix dinner and bring it to my house?" He pointed to Dolly. "She don't look like much of a cook."

Cousin Leotha turned to Cousin Richard. Each looked as though they were daring the other to speak first. Cousin Leotha lost.

"That's jest it, suh. Dolly, here…well, Anna…I mean Dolly was meant to do her studies. Never had proper trainin' in the housework stuff." She nodded her head toward the doorway. "Now my Kate, she's a right fine cook. That's why I thought…" Leotha's words hung in midair.

McNaughton shook his head as he piled a biscuit and scrambled eggs onto Dolly's plate.

"Suh, that's why we thought it a good idea if Dolly got some learnin' from our own girl, Kate." Cousin Richard joined in. "She'd be mighty pleased to go with Dolly to yo' house fo' a spell of trainin' in the cookin' and cleanin' business." Cousin Richard raised his eyes to the ceiling as though he were calling on the Deity to send him strength.

"Kate? You want yo' Kate at my house?" McNaughton shook his head. "Ain't no need for that." He looked at the milk pitchers sitting on the table. "Leotha, you got some coffee?"

Leotha startled as she moved to the speckled enamel coffee pot. She nodded, but her head movements looked more like the palsy to Dolly. "Yes, suh. I'll get yo' coffee. My Kate makes a mighty fine cup." Leotha stopped her trembling and turned to Mr. McNaughton. "Please suh, let her go with Dolly. She'll be big help to yo' whole family." She paused. "Make things a bit easier on..."

Mr. McNaughton stared at Leotha as though she were speaking a foreign tongue. He tilted his head, his eyes suggesting he'd finally translated. "Hmmm. I reckon Dolly should learn to cook. Why her mama was the best co..." Why did the man's face turn so pale?

He cleared his throat. Had he almost choked on that bit of egg? McNaughton pushed back from the table. "See to it that both girls eat hardy." He kept his back to the four as he headed out the front door. "I'll take my coffee outside. Dickie, put their valises in the back of my truck."

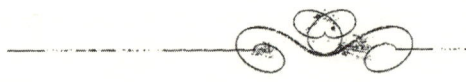

CHAPTER SEVENTEEN

Eula latched the gate to the chicken coop and made her way to the back pantry door, carrying nine just-laid eggs. She looked up at the sky, now twenty minutes past peeking over the eastern horizon. Alex had been gone close to an hour. She'd lay there, on her side of the bed 'til he got himself up, dressed, and out of the house. Eula checked the round-faced clock sitting on her bedroom bureau. Five o'clock. Unlike her, he'd snored through the night like he didn't have a care in the world. As soon as she heard the truck start up and smelled the gasoline fumes, Eula flung back the bedcovers, put on her wrapper and hurried down the hall to the little room at the top of the stairs. She pushed open the closed door.

"If I was a swearin' woman, I'd say I'll be damned." Eula wasn't in the habit of speaking out loud to herself, but the shock of seeing the spare bed spread with sheets, a pillow, and a summer coverlet jolted her Mama Thornton-instilled manners. Granted, the bed was a disrespectful mess, but her husband had done the job himself. She closed the door, trying to push the coming thought to the back of her head. No good.

Alex had never made a bed, washed a dish, or boiled a kettle of water for her. Not even when the pains came so bad for their baby. Eula had gotten herself downstairs and fixed her husband's breakfast that morning. Some nights, even all these years later, she wondered if all that effort had caused her baby girl to die before she could take her first good breath. And now, here was Alex, knocking himself silly to do for his colored get. Eula shook her head. Reverend Hawkins preached Christian charity, but where was the charity for her?

"Lord, forgive..." She couldn't finish her prayer. Reverend Hawkins said those with un-Christian thoughts would burn in hell. Eula clasped her hands. But even the good Lord couldn't expect her to put on her welcome face for her husband's dark-skinned child.

Wham. Eula jumped when she heard the truck door slam. Her eyes fixed on the closed porch door. Alex and...that...would be walking into her kitchen any minute. Eula stood flat-footed. She wanted to scurry from this place. Her legs refused to obey.

"Well, here we are. You girls come on up to the house. Dolly, I'll get your valise."

She was here! Good God, Almighty! Alex had actually done it. Brought his bastard daughter and...girls? Another child? Fedora never even hinted at more than the one for Alex, and her sister-in-law kept accurate count of every white man's "other family" in the whole of Montgomery County. The pain started in Eula's jaw and jerked to her feet. But at least now she could leave her kitchen table. She scurried to the top of the stairs, her knees crackling with each step. Should she go to her bedroom—shut the door, shut away Alex and his get? The kitchen door opened, and Eula heard the sound of footsteps entering. How many sets? She shook her head. Why should she hide in her own home? She knelt down by the top of the stairs, her knees offering up their usual protest. She couldn't see into her kitchen from her perch, but she could hear every word.

"Now where in thunderation to put you?" Alex's voice.

"I'm to stay with Cousin Dolly." A young girl.

Cousin? Eula let out a deep breath. Kate Welles.

"Dolly's goin' upstairs. We'll fix somethin' up for you out here on the back porch."

"Mr. McNaughton, I don't mind if Cousin Kate shares a bed with me."

Now Eula's ears joined her jaw, knees, and feet in paining. That girl—her up-north voice gave her away—actually stood in Eula's very own kitchen. The cry was soft, and praise the Lord, low enough to escape the ears of those downstairs, but it came up so sudden, Eula had no control over it. She slumped to her bottom, both hands clinging to the banister rails. "Lord, I want Your forgiveness for my sinful thoughts, but I can't believe I'm the only one who needs it." The words whispered out between lips frozen with pain. "I know I'm not to judge, but it's him, my husband, who needs You the most. Lord, please help the man 'cause I'm near 'bout to hating him!" She clamped one hand over her mouth as she bolstered herself to her feet. Church. Here it was Sunday morning, and she'd just blasphemed the Lord. Could she pray her way out of this one? If she was to believe Reverend Hawkins, she already had one foot in hell.

The Lawnover Baptist Church had stood in that same spot next to the two elm trees since back in Mama Thornton's mother's time. Reverend Hawkins had served the congregation as its one and only pastor since before Eula's wedding to Alex. Reverend Hawkins. He was God's messenger, wasn't he? Eula made her way toward her bedroom, careful not to step on that squeaky floorboard. Sixteen years back she'd brought up the courage to meet the Reverend in his office at the little parsonage. Back then, she'd let her respect for herself slip. She'd sobbed out her grief over Alex' treachery with his sharecropper's wife. Eula asked her pastor for the Lord's guidance. Surely it couldn't be a sin to divorce a husband who laid with another woman. Wasn't that adultery? The good Reverend Hawkins took Eula's hand, patted it as though she were a mite simple in the head, and told her to wear her knees out praying harder. If she was truly sincere in her repentance, the Lord would show her the way to the wifely skills she so sorely lacked to keep a husband happy. She must ask not only the Lord, but her husband, for forgiveness. Her sin: Vanity.

Eula stumbled out the proper words to thank Reverend, balled up her tear-soaked handkerchief, stuffed it into her pocketbook and walked out of the parsonage. Oh, she still attended church, all right—every decent person in Lawnover did—even poor white trash. But it wasn't Reverend Hawkins who brought her there all these years. Eula sat in her pew every Sunday morning, waiting for the Lord to come up through the floorboards, ooze his spirit through the clapboard walls of the drafty old building, and fill her body with the strength she needed to cope one more week with the likes of the men of Lawnover—Ben Roy and Reverend Hawkins included. And especially Alexander McNaughton.

"Wring its neck? Me?" Alex's girl, her excited voice carried up to the second floor.

Eula, almost at her bedroom, stopped.

"Ain't you never wrung a chicken's neck befo'?" The other young voice. "Don't you folks eat chicken up north?"

"Of course, we eat chicken. I've watched Mama wri...ugh...that awful squawking—but never me."

"We—that's you and me—got to get this man's dinner on. That means chicken. Now you come on out here to the chicken coop, and I'll show you what to do."

"No. I can't..."

Eula heard the sounds of a slight scuffle and then the opening of the back porch door. She stepped into the bedroom and looked at her Sunday clothes pulled out last night from the chiffarobe, now laid across a chair. This morning she stood in the center of her room. Something didn't look right. What had she forgotten? Oh yes, Alex's Sunday outfit. She always laid them out for her husband. Alex couldn't match his own socks. Not last night. She walked toward the bureau and pulled out her Sunday girdle. She sat on the side of the bed and slid the thing over her feet and up to her knees when she heard Alex enter the room.

"Eula Mae, I've brought you two girls for help. They'll be cookin' dinner today so you don't have to worry none 'bout that." Alex talked to her back.

Eula stood and tugged the girdle into place, her back to her husband.

"They'll be a bit of a help to you, Eula. I know it's gonna take a bit of adjustin' but…"

Adjusting? Eula tightened the belt at her wrapper as her jaws set firm. She turned, walked past Alex as though she were a ghost, and lifted her Sunday-best dress from the chair, its dark blue ruffle fluttering into the gray/blue splotches of the patterned bodice. She wasn't the one who needed adjusting.

"Ain't you gettin' ready for church a mite early?" His voice sounded confusion.

"I reckon I'd walk to church this morning." The words hurt her ears. "You bein' busy and all." She held the dress against her chest.

"Walk to church? Eula Mae, church is five miles down the road." You ain't never walked to church before." He moved to her side.

"Didn't know if you was goin' or not." Now why had she said that?

"Not goin' to church? Eula, you feeling all right? I knew it would be a good thing to get you some more help. '"Course I didn't know I'd get two of 'em. And it won't be but a few days. Then…"

Eula clamped her lips together, turned and faced her husband. She looked him in the eye. "You can drive me to church as usual, Alex, but Fedora and Ben Roy gonna take me back to their house. I'll be there a few days."

"Fedora?" Alex looked at her as though her mind had slipped. "You and Fedora already done your spring cannin'." He shook his head like he was trying to get all the wheels spinning in the same direction. "Too early for fall. I'll pick you up before supper tonight."

"No." Eula felt both the heat of summer and the

bubbling up inside her rush to her face. Had she refused her husband? Never in these thirty-seven years had she ever said no to Alexander McNaughton.

He stood there, staring, no doubt deciding if he should call Sheriff Andrews to haul her off to the Tennessee State Home for the Insane.

"Not canning. There's a quilt Fedora needs help with." Mama always said Eula was a quick thinker—not a good thing for a woman. "A special quilt." She stared into those blue eyes of Alex McNaughton. Did she even care if they believed her or not? "She's puttin' in pieces 'bout the Thornton family history. You know. Daddy's, pa's, pa. Way back befo' the War of Secession. Fedora needs me to help." Never mind the lie. It had come way easier than she ever thought an untruth would leave her lips.

"Can't Ben Roy help with that?"

Eula shook her head as she pointed to the chiffarobe, now caught in the glare of the morning sun. "Your church clothes are waitin' for you. Why don't you change in the spare bedroom?"

Alex's mouth opened, closed, and opened again. "Chiffarobe. Clothes? Spare...?" He gave his head a slow nod as he stared at her. "I reckon you're more tuckered than I figured." He took a step toward the bureau, stopped, and stared at her from head to foot. He turned and shuffled his way to the dresser.

She watched as her husband rummaged through the unfamiliar drawers. How long had she had that piece of knotty-pine furniture in this house? Thirty-seven years, a wedding gift from Mama, handed down from Grandma Thornton. Thirty-seven years and Alex didn't know the what of the bottom drawer to the which of the top.

CHAPTER EIGHTEEN

"Mrs." Two, three knocks on the door—more like pounding. "Annalaura, you come quick. You have-a the call on the telephone. From you Tennessee." Gina sounded frantic.

Annalaura pulled her hands out of the hot soapy water where she washed up the breakfast dishes. She dried her hands on her apron and rushed to the door. "Get on in here, Gina. You know my do' ain't never closed. What's this 'bout Tennessee? Dolly? My boys?" The kitchen was already warm from the cornbread baking in her coal-fired oven. She didn't need the extra heat that came from running across her floor this early Sunday afternoon.

"The cousin of you, she telephone on the party line because you no gotta the telephone. She asked Edith for the number of the neighbor. She—"

Annalaura grabbed Gina Maggiora's shoulders. "Gina! Never mind 'bout the telephone operator. Tell me! Dolly! My boys! Is they all right?"

Had she made a mistake? She'd worried ever since John gave the okay for this trip to Tennessee. Her Dolly, the boys...back in Lawnover. Couldn't John see danger written all over his okay? But John...he had to be sure of her. Of her. Why had Annalaura really chosen Brugestown? This whole trip—John's yes to Dolly—had been a test of herself. Was it a test she should have deliberately failed? Told John no to Tennessee. Refused Henry and disappointed Dolly? Had she sacrificed her children to make up for her own weakness, her refusal to decide?

"Come on, Mrs." Gina grabbed Annalaura's wrist and shook her mind free. The woman marched Annalaura across the porch, down the one concrete step, beyond the dividing driveway between their houses, through Gina's own kitchen smelling of steaming tomatoes, and onto her front room with its wall telephone. "Here, Mrs., you talk." Gina lifted the smaller piece and shoved it into Annalaura's hand.

Annalaura stared at the two-piece instrument. Both were connected by a cord. But which was the talking end and which was the listening? She turned to Gina. Her neighbor pointed.

"Is this you, Edith Dubois?" Annalaura put the ear piece to her head. Her voice trembled as she leaned into the mouthpiece.

"Mrs. Welles, you've got a call from Tennessee on the line. You want to take it?" Even Edith sounded excited.

"Of course, I'm takin' the call. Who is it, Edith?"

"One moment, please." Edith's voice sounded like something coming out of the long end of a molasses barrel.

Annalaura jammed the earpiece into the side of her head so hard it hurt. Gina pulled her close. She patted Annalaura's shoulder.

"Miz Welles, your party from Tennessee is on the telephone, and I've cleared off all the other parties." Edith sounded pleased with herself.

"Thank…Miz…Edith."

"Here is your party now."

"Annalaura, that you? This here is Leotha. Richard, he here too. He thought it best if I be the one to tell you."

"Leotha?" When things really got bad, Annalaura had always been able to think her best. This morning was no different. "How are things goin' down there?" She paced her voice so that every word came unrushed.

"I told Richard best to tell it right off." Her words crackled over the line. "Well, here t'is, but I don't want you to get to frettin' too much 'cause Richard, he…"

"Tell it to me, Leotha!" Yes, Annalaura raised her voice but only to help Leotha get the words out of her mouth.

"Dolly and Kate, well, truth to tell, it was Kate that done started it all and, Annalaura, I'm truly sorry 'bout…"

"Leotha." Truth? That truth had already settled into Annalaura's brain with Leotha's babbling. He—the man she'd left in Tennessee—had her daughter. Now what to do about it? "Where's my girl?" She waited for Leotha to tell Annalaura what she already knew.

"Oh, Lord, Annalaura. She's with… Mr. McNaughton, he done come and taken her to his house."

The ear piece slipped from her fingers. Gina caught the instrument before it dangled fully from its cord. She stared her own worries into Annalaura's face as she handed back the ear piece. Annalaura wanted to nod her thanks, but her mind took her to him—Alexander McNaughton. He had part of what he wanted those sixteen years ago—his daughter. Had he told his Dolly the truth about her actual father?

"Leotha, I want you to listen careful to me." Annalaura counted to ten. Enough time for Leotha to stop her crying.

"Annalaura?" Richard Welles. "I know this ain't the best of news, but I believes it's gonna be all right. Now, right off, I made him take Kate along, too. He said he won't keep 'em but a few days and then…"

"Have you told my boys?" Annalaura's heart thumped. She blinked her eyes to clear away the fear. It was hard to catch her breath, but the only who could know any of that was Gina Maggiora.

"No, no, Annalaura. I ain't told them nothin'. Good God, Almighty, all hell…'scuse me…would break loose down here if Doug and Henry found out."

"Good, Richard. Now I'm not sayin' a word to John just yet. Not 'til you do two things for me,"

"Anything you says, Annalaura." Richard's breathing puffed over the party line. "You ain't tellin' John right off?"

"Not if you do what I say."

"Annalaura, I appreciates. Cousin John, he counted on me to care fo' his chil'ren whilst they was down here in Lawnover. Is you sure I shouldn't tell him myself?"

"Richard, this is what I wants you to do. You tell Leotha to get a message to...to him." In all these sixteen years she'd never given sound to Alex's name.

"Mr. Alex? You wants my wife to give Mr. McNaughton a message from...you?" Richard sounded confused. "What is it you wants Leotha to say?"

"Ask him," Annalaura clamped her eyes closed for a second, "ask him what he wants. Now I don't wants him to give her the answer direct." She took in a deep breath. "Leotha, she's to tell him to use that telephone thing and ring up my neighbor." Annalaura kept her eyes on the wall phone, but, out of the side of her eye, she caught the surprised look on Gina's face. "Richard, is you there?"

Annalaura heard Richard's muffled voice, his hand apparently covering the mouthpiece as he talked his confusion over with Leotha. Annalaura closed her eyes. She could think under any circumstances, but right now it would be best to deal with the problem of Gina later. Dolly, Doug, and Henry needed all of her right now. Sixteen, seventeen years faded away. Her Dolly was in no danger from Alex. Neither were Doug and Henry. She'd kept herself well hidden from Alexander McNaughton all this time, but she knew the man maybe even better than she knew her husband. But then there was Ben Roy and the other night riders of Lawnover. How much colored and white, out-loud mixing could any of them allow, especially if Alexander paraded Dolly around all of Lawnover as his very own body child?

"Annalaura?" Richard's voice called out. "Leotha says he—Mr. Alex—don't know nothin' 'bout callin' y'awl up north. Leotha say..."

"Annalaura? This Leotha." She must have taken the

telephone from her husband. "Y'awl don't have no phone. I took me a chance on reachin' you by askin' the operator if any of yo' neighbors had telephones. We callin' you from up here in Clarksville, so's nobody in Lawnover will know what done happened."

"Do that again, Leotha. Whatever you did befo', do it again. Use the Clarksville operator to get to me. Tell Al...him...to telephone a Mrs. Gina Maggiora in Brugestown." She spelled out the names.

"You sure you wanna do that?" Leotha.

Annalaura swallowed. She had three children to save. Whatever Alex wanted, she would tell him yes just as she had those sixteen years ago when his addled mind told him to move her and Dolly into his house alongside his wife. Telling him yes was an easy thing to do, doing it was something altogether different.

"Leotha, I wants you to get to that house right away. Tell Richard, he's to watch his words 'round my boys 'til he hears from me." She'd gotten most it out on one breath. "Tell my boys they is to sit tight. Their father has a plan."

"Cousin Annalaura." Richard must have overheard and grabbed the ear piece, "That ain't the truth. Cousin John, he don't have no idea of what done happen."

Annalaura nodded. Richard couldn't see her, but the smile she felt forming on her face told her the man had fallen into her trap. "Don't you worry none 'bout you bein' the one who ain't kept a proper eye on any of his children. I'll tell him what done happened—and how—myself."

"Uhh," Richard's voice came out garbled over the telephone. "Now it don't have to be like that, Annalaura. Still, them is his boys. I believes it's best if I tell him the story."

"Richard Welles, quit yo' foolishness. You know as well as me what's gonna happen if my boys think they got to save their sister. Ain't nothin' John can do from up here in Illinois 'cept go on down to Lawnover and get all three of 'em killed. And maybe you, too. Once night-riders' hangin' fingers get to itchin', they don't know when to stop. Now you tell me if that's what you want?"

More grunt than answer came over the telephone wire. There was no more time to waste. "Richard, put Leotha back on the line."

Annalaura heard the line snap and crackle. "Now, Leotha, get yo'self over to...over to his place right now! Richard, you leave Leotha up the road a piece, back from his house. She can walk the distance to his back do'. Richard, he ain't to see you, just Leotha. You got that clear?"

"Yes'm, Cousin Annalaura. I'll wait fo' Leotha back a piece." Richard's politeness told Annalaura he wasn't at all clear.

"Leotha, you knows what you got to say?"

"Mr. Alex is to call yo' neighbor, but then what's supposed to happen?"

Annalaura stifled her grunt. She couldn't afford a mistake. "Leotha, you deliver that message just like I say—what do he want. Don't fret none 'bout the rest. Just make sure Mr....he call the name I give you. Richard, you make good my boys don't do nothin' 'til I give the say-so. Y'awl just sit there doin' nothin' 'til I calls you back. Won't be long." Annalaura slipped the earpiece back onto its hook, careful not to tangle the cord. She turned to Gina. "Sorry."

Gina, her arms folded over her ample bosom, pointed to her overstuffed brown chair. "You-a better sit yourself down, Mrs. We have the lot of talk to do."

Like a disobedient child, Annalaura settled into the cushions, her eyes on Gina's green-flowered carpet, now dappled in sunlight filtering through Gina's J.C. Penney lace curtains.

"Who is this man you gonna ask what he wants?" Gina's command of English got better every day, and she was not a woman to waste even one of her precious newly learned words.

Annalaura shook her head as she examined the way the leaves on Gina's floral carpet swirled to the right. Annalaura's secret had stayed locked up tight in her heart all these years.

"Annalaura. You tell me!" Gina had never been shy about using her no-nonsense voice.

That's why Annalaura liked her so much. The two were a match for one another. Annalaura lifted her eyes. "This is an America thing. I don't reckon you can understand."

"I understand the men and the women." Gina settled herself on her settee, opposite the overstuffed chair in the tidy front room of her house. "And I got the eyes."

Aunt Becky knew Annalaura's troubles—had known them from the beginning. But Rebecca McKnight was five years in her grave. Even when she lived, she never spoke about that last year in Tennessee. John neither. After Annalaura's finger landed on Danville on that train schedule—and John believed she had chosen him—her husband had never said a word about Tennessee. In his way, he had done everything to say his sorrys to her. He'd gotten his job right away, worked hard, and brought her every newfangled contraption that came out in the Sears Roebuck catalogue. He'd wanted to get her that telephone business, but the thing scared her. Not that John was a saint. She knew every year or so when Cousin Richard came up to visit, the two went out gambling and, she suspected, whoring. That he never brought Leotha or the girls never did set well with Annalaura. She suspected both Richard and Leotha knew the truth of Dolly, but they'd never said. And now here was Gina Maggiora—a woman not even from America—ordering Annalaura to give up her deepest secret.

"You've got eyes? What you believe you sees, Gina?" Annalaura stiffened despite the softness of Gina's chair.

"Don't you-a play with me, Mrs. My eyes see that you John and you Dolly, they no match." Gina stood from the settee. "You think over what you say to me while I get you the coffee." She headed toward her kitchen, the smell of simmering tomato sauce even stronger. "You think it over good because I know the truth when I hear it."

The truth. Could Gina understand how ugly the truth really was? Her friend stepped back into the front room—the best room in the frame house—and handed Annalaura a mug. The coffee swirled with fresh cream from the milkman and a good dose of sugar just the way Annalaura liked it. Gina sat back on the settee, holding her own cup of black coffee. She took a sip and waited.

"It ain't a pretty story, Gina."

"I think it's a hard story for you to tell, Annalaura." Gina took another sip. "You Dolly too pretty a girl to make her story ugly. I tell you my story first."

"Your story?" Annalaura clutched her still-full cup. "You ain't got no story, Gina. Leastways, not a true one. It's just been you and yo' Lorenzo."

Gina nodded. "Yes, I go to the church with Lorenzo and say the 'I marrieds.' No man before or after him." She swallowed a second sip. "But that don't mean I don't look. Now, Alfredo, oh that man, he coulda..."

Annalaura laughed. "Gina, you tellin' me a fib just to make me feel better?" She sank into the cushions. Oh Lord, her stiff back thanked her for the relief.

Gina played with the rim of her coffee cup.

"John run off on me." Annalaura took her first swallow to deaden the pain of those hard words. "Left me with just 'bout two dollars fo' food or rent or..." Where did that wetness filling her eyes come from? Annalaura had never shed a tear in Illinois—not even when Aunt Becky passed away.

"And the four children. Cleveland, Doug, Lottie, and Henry." Gina counted them off on her fingers. "How long you John gone?"

The hunger, the cold of the coming winter, the fear of having no more than two dollars to her name, all flooded back to Annalaura. "A year."

"*Dio Mio!*" Gina made the Catholic sign across her chest.

Annalaura sucked in her lips. "I figured me a way to care fo' my children."

"And what woman wouldn't?" Gina lowered her head as she looked at Annalaura. "This man you gonna ask what he wants, he the *patrone* of the farm?"

"*Patrone?*" The feel of the foreign word crossing her tongue felt unfamiliar, but not the meaning.

Gina leaned forward. "Annalaura, I know I not born here—in America, but I understand the *patrones*—the man who owns the land, he have the power over the woman who works for him. Especially the woman who have no man of her own." She finished her coffee and stared Annalaura in the eye. "But, my friend, there is more to you story, no?"

Annalaura opened her mouth. She wanted to answer. How could Gina know so much? She nodded.

Gina held up a hand. "This America have the laws that say no colored woman can marry a white man, no?"

Annalaura blinked.

"I no know, and you don't need to tell Gina, but if the America no have such a law, maybe the story of you would be different, yes?" She settled back into her settee. "What you plan to do, I know it is the right thing for you, Annalaura. This time, you make the story end the way you want."

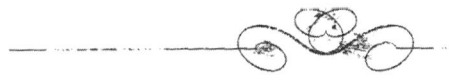

CHAPTER NINETEEN

"Eula, I know it ain't easy, but you got to put up with it." Fedora, sitting calm at the big walnut Mama-Thornton dining room table, let the words slip out of her mouth like a woman sentenced to hanging, and there was nothing to do but get on with it,

"Fedora, I know what you been through." Eula pecked at the lace covering the table. "Sorry to say it was with my own brother, but, Fedora, I'm not you." Eula Mae pushed the glass of sweet tea aside. No amount of Fedora's fried chicken, hush puppies, or stewed okra Sunday dinner was going to make Eula forgive her rascal of a husband. She didn't care if every other white wife in Lawnover had looked the other way for two hundred years.

"I know you ain't me. That's just the problem. You ain't yo' mama, either."

Eula and Fedora has never been particularly close, and this afternoon with the temperature about to break ninety, the distance felt even greater. They were sisters-in-law and civil to one another, but Fedora had never achieved that Thornton polish that Mama brushed on both Eula and her Kentucky-married sister. Eula cocked an eye at Fedora. "I'm not sure that story you told about Mama is so, anyway."

Fedora, sitting across from Eula at the now cleared dinner

table, slapped her palm on top of the lace cloth put there just for Sunday dinners. "All right, Eula Mae, I'm gonna tell it to you again. Your Pa, Old Ben, took Rebecca's mama to his bed. The two of them had Rebecca. Then Old Ben, he done took Becky to his bed, too—his own daughter. Then the two of them had Jo—."

"You can stop it right there, Fedora." Eula glared at her sister-in-law. "You can tell me every gosh-darn tale you want about every husband under the Lawnover sun strayin' from his wife, and how she got down on her knees and begged his forgiveness for the bother." Eula shook her head. "That's not me." She flapped one hand in the air to stir up a breeze.

"Eula Mae, what year we livin' in?"

"What in tarnation are you talkin' about?"

"You heard me. What year we livin' in? I'll tell you. This here is nineteen-thirty. You listen to me, and you listen to me good. In eighteen-thirty, husbands was takin' their colored women to their beds just like today." Fedora nodded her certainty. "And I'm here to tell you that in two-thousand-thirty, they gonna be doin' the same."

"I believe you're right, Fedora." Eula leaned across the table, now empty of the dirty dishes after Ben Roy, Wiley George, and Little Ben had their fill and left the house to take Tilly for a Sunday drive. "And I'll wager you every white wife from eighteen-thirty on up to two-thousand thirty gonna look the other way." She leaned back in the dining room chair. "Don't none of that mean I'm gonna forget and forgive."

"Eula Mae, you don't want me to call Ben Roy in here." Fedora scowled.

"I wish you would. Call in Ben Roy. Call Wiley George. Call Bobbie Lee, the Davis cousins, Alex. Call any damn man you want!"

Fedora's face blanched white under the suntan of her skin. "Eula, ain't no count for you to take up swearin' like a man."

Eula took a swallow of her sweet tea. "Fedora, I'm gonna be takin' on a lot of things I haven't took on before."

"No, you ain't. Let me put it to you this way. If you leave

Alex, where is it you think you gonna stay?"

"Stay?" Where was she going to live? Eula hadn't gotten quite that far. "At the farm, that's where. Let Alex be the one to leave."

"Judge ain't gonna see it that way. Not in Tennessee." Fedora examined the nails on her left hand.

"I'll come home, then. Here."

"No, you won't." Now Fedora scanned her right hand. "Ben Roy ain't havin' the scandal."

"The scandal? Can't be no bigger scandal than you lettin' Hettie and his three yella get live right under yo' nose. Right here on Thornton land!" Mama had taught Eula to always be polite, not that Mama had been. Eula hadn't really meant to hurt Fedora's feelings, but her sister-in-law was hard-headed sometimes.

Now Fedora turned red. Were those tears welling in her eyes? "Damn it to hell, Eula Mae!" She jumped up from the table, went to her dining room safe, and grabbed one of Mama Thornton's fancy fans—straight from New Orleans. She swished the beaded and lace creation about her face as she turned back to Eula Mae. "You actin' like I thought it was fairy-dust fine with me for Ben Roy to keep his other family on my own property." She planted her hands on the table, the cords in her neck stretched tight. "Well, let me tell you one damn thing. I hated Hettie, but I hated somebody else more." She straightened up. "You heard me right. There was days I hated your brother fo' what he done to me."

Sounds gurgled in Eula's throat. She stared at Fedora. "I...I'm sorry. Didn't mean..."

"Oh yes, you did." Fedora straightened, She stood while Eula remained seated. "You think I don't know your mama—" she jabbed a quick finger at Eula—, "didn't think I was good 'nough fo' Ben Roy?" She nodded her head. "That I was just a shade above po' white trash 'cause my pa didn't have no more'n twenty acres and five-hundred dollars to his name? I don't have your fine manners, Eula Mae. And, no, I can't talk proper like you. I say ain't and you say aren't. I say fo' and you say for." She pounded the table. "Don't you see, Eula Mae, that's just it. What kind of a way out is there for women like us?"

Us? Eula frowned.

"Not a word in you now, is there? Well, you give it a bit of thought 'cause while you was raised with more class than me, you, Eula Mae Thornton McNaughton, is still a female woman."

Eula shook her head like a dutiful child receiving a proper scolding.

"You think I don't feel the same pain you feelin'?" The muscles in Fedora's cheeks twitched. "Alex just brought his outside brat to stay in your house fo' a few days, and you think you 'bout to die 'cause of it. Eula Mae Thornton, the Good Lord has smiled on you. Think how I felt when Ben Roy brought not one, but all three of his colored bastards over here. And their mama, too! And it weren't for no three days neither." Tears splashed down Fedora's cheeks. "Twenty-one years, fo' months and thirteen days, I had to suffer me that wench sharin' my husband's body. Knowin' he wanted her more'n me."

Eula got up from the table and started toward Fedora. "I am so sorry. I guess I never thought..."

Fedora held up a hand. "Well, now is yo' thinkin' time. Eula Mae, I wanted to do just what you think you can do right now. Leave. Leave that cheatin' brother of yours 'cause he done broke my heart." Fedora used the sleeve of her Sunday-best to swipe away the wetness on her cheeks. "But, Eula Mae, I ain't had no place to go. Neither do you."

"Uhh," Eula's brain whirred. Everybody knew divorce was a sin. Reverend Hawkins said so. There were no two ways about it. But she, Eula, was a Thornton.

"Oh, I can read yo' mind all right. No, Ben Roy ain't gonna let you come here. If he did, he'd be confessin' to all of Lawnover that he was an even bigger sinner than Alex—him and every other white man in Lawnover! Yo' brother and no other man in all Montgomery County ain't 'bout to do that."

Eula stopped at the corner of the table, Fedora still some four feet from her. "But this is my home, too."

"No, it ain't. Law says it all belongs to Alexander." Fedora moved toward Eula. "Eula Mae, you is almost sixty years old. You can't get no job. I was a young woman when Ben Roy done that to me." She nodded. "Eula Mae, you know I was good lookin' back then." Fedora shifted her breasts upward. "And I knew how to make a man happy, but ain't none of that counted for nothin'."

Fedora stood so close, Eula smelled the Sweet William talcum her sister-in-law used only on Sundays.

Fedora tugged at the folds of her dress. "Yes, I wanted me a divorce, but what kind of a job is there for a woman like me other than sharecroppin' or whorin' up in Clarksville?"

Eula's mouth opened.

"Eula Mae, how you gonna feed yo'self, put clothes on yo' back? And how you gonna go to church 'cause won't nobody in Lawnover ever speak to you again if you divorce Alex—Thornton woman or no."

Eula felt her knees buckle. Fedora led her to the nearest chair and reached for the sweet tea.

"You tellin' me Alex won't have this girl in yo' house fo' long." Fedora shoved the tea glass into Eula's hand. "Ben Roy gonna give Alex three days to get that gal out of yo' house. You stay here 'til then. You're right, Eula, you ain't like me. Ben Roy won't allow you to live with yo' husband's colored get. Not the way he made me."

Eula lifted the tea glass. Fedora had added a hint of mint. Was she hoping the smell would be soothing? It hadn't. Eula's hand shook as she took a sip. "You want me to go home and do for Alex like everythin' peaches and cream?"

Fedora, who'd never before shown this much sense, had laid out the painful truth.

"No, Eula Mae. You don't have it in you to pretend that much. You ain't me. You go on back to Alex. That you gotta do, but you don't have to be no real wife to him no more."

"What?" Eula Mae looked at Fedora. "You mean you and

Ben Roy? You don't…"

"Not as much as he'd like."

"Oh my Lord. I thought…Reverend Hawkins… A wife's duty."

"Eula Mae, I know you better than that. You ain't paid that preacher man no mind for sixteen years. I know I haven't. Now get on up to yo' room. Give yo'self a good cry. Then get on back to yo' house in three days. Ben Roy gonna see to it."

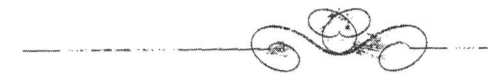

CHAPTER TWENTY

"Mama, did you get a letter from Dolly, yet? Sammy, put that down!" Lottie, still in her summer church dress, reached for the fork in her toddler's hand.

Annalaura kept her eyes on the bowl of turnip greens she'd just set on the kitchen table for Sunday dinner. If John paid his daughter any attention, he didn't show it as he poked his fork into the fried chicken platter Annalaura had laid on the table.

"Mama?" Lottie snatched away the offending fork and resettled Sammy.

John, sitting at the head of the table as usual, glanced up from his now full plate. "Yo' Rusty playin' trombone tonight?"

"Last night." Lottie, her church hat tossed on a chair in the front room, sounded less than happy. "He practices with his friends on Sunday." She cocked her head. "So he says."

John jabbed his own fork at Lottie. "Don't you go begrudgin' yo' husband a good payin' extra job. He'd takin' good care of all of y'awl."

Lottie nodded. Annalaura struggled to keep her mind on the back and forth between father and daughter. Her head had traveled to Tennessee and was having a dickens of a time getting back to Illinois.

"Annalaura?" John's voice called her out of her fog. "Everythin' all right? You look like yo' mind's done run off somewheres."

She looked first at John, then turned to Lottie. "No, I ain't had no letter from Dolly." She pushed closed the curtain on her kitchen window from letting in too much sun. "I just want my children back here in Brugestown." She let that accusing tone come into her voice.

John tackled his plate. Annalaura cut herself a slice of the still-warm-from-the-oven cornbread, and slathered it with her fresh-churned butter. John. Yes, she had done what no wife was allowed—possess the passing secret feelings for another man. But even if she was weak in putting aside what sometimes played in her heart, in that truth-telling moment deep in her mind, she had never really forgiven John. She'd done wrong, but so had he. All the new coal-burning stoves, fancy perfumes, linen table cloths, and fine cotton sheets he laid on her were not going to change her mind.

"I reckon we all want that." John held up a chicken-leg as he gave her a peculiar look.

She'd been right. It had been a test! Now did her husband think he was better than her for making their children the bait?

"Mama, does anybody down there have a telephone?" Lottie guided the spoon into Sammy's mouth.

John grunted as he chewed. "That's what I been tellin' you. Yo' husband thinkin' puttin' a telephone in yo' place."

"I just wish he'd hurry up and get to it." Lottie put greens into Sammy's spoon.

Annalaura's mind slipped away again. Had Leotha made good on her instructions? What did Alex want? Sunday afternoon. There were no stores open in Clarksville on a Sunday. The Lord had decreed the seventh day a day of rest. She'd have to wait at least until tomorrow. Did her children have until tomorrow? She lifted a hand to her head.

"Hey, Ma. Pa." Cleveland opened the back door and walked into her kitchen. He'd cut through the back yards of the two houses separating his from his folks. He reached for a clean plate in the safe.

"When's that wife of yours going to learn how to cook? The only time we see you is for Sunday dinner." Lottie could have more say against Lucille than either of Cleveland's parents.

"What my wife can and cannot cook ain't none of yo' business." Cleveland pulled out a kitchen chair. "Pass me the cornbread, please, Ma. You feelin' all right?"

Annalaura jerked her hand from her head. Lord have mercy. If only she could snatch back her Tennessee thoughts as fast. "I'm jest fine." She managed a weak smile.

"Don't look fine to me." Cleveland shot a passing glare at John. "Ma, you ain't workin' too hard, are you?"

"Fill up yo' plate and leave me be." Annalaura slid the cornbread and bowl of turnip greens in Cleveland's direction. She nodded toward the mashed potatoes and gravy while Lottie sidled over the platter of fried chicken.

She picked up her own fork and slid it under her mound of greens. Greens, string beans. Lord, she remembered that August day back in Tennessee—that year—when she'd cooked up the last of her summer vegetables, and had no seed money for fall planting. It was a pain she'd never forget. Her fork stirred under her greens. No, she'd never forget, and neither would Cleveland.

He'd been eleven that summer. Old enough to remember—probably Doug, too. Annalaura felt the water stinging her eyes as she stared at her plate, tears she always fought back. Cleveland, eleven years old, and she had to work him like a man. Her oldest child understood what it meant when his father took off down the road. When his daddy didn't come back after the usual two to three weeks away, Cleveland took it upon himself to be the man of the family, to look after Doug, Lottie, little Henry, and her. Cleveland would remember it all—Alexander McNaughton, his mama pregnant, especially the day John came back to Lawnover after his secret year gone to Nashville. The day John beat her.

The day Dolly was born. The...

"Mama?" What was Cleveland's man voice doing breaking into her memory? "You been starin' at those greens for five minutes. Ain't ate a one. You sure you're all right?"

"Yo' mama's just fine." John cut in. He slid a quick look toward Annalaura.

Her husband had never won back Cleveland, not all the way. Lottie, Henry, and even Dolly loved their papa without doubts. A parent's not supposed to have a favorite but, Cleveland, John's first born, had always been the one. John had tried his mightiest to win his boy back—helped him buy his house, although John couldn't stand his boy's floozy wife. Cleveland had said his polite thank yous, but his daddy had long since stopped being Cleveland's hero. To John, the loss of his son's love would always be Annalaura's misdoing.

"I is fine." She picked up her fork of greens. "I do fret 'bout yo' brothers and sister down there in Tennessee, but it's just 'cause I miss them."

"Uh-huh." Cleveland spoke between mouthfuls. "I know they ain't due back for another ten days or so, but if you that worried, I'll go down next weekend."

"Maybe, I'll go down with you." Lottie. "Take Sammy to see his Welles cousins."

"No!" Annalaura's shout brought four pair of eyes staring at her. "Ain't no need fo' none of that. Let Dolly enjoy her graduation present." She refused to lose all her children.

Where was Leotha? Lord, let Monday hurry on here.

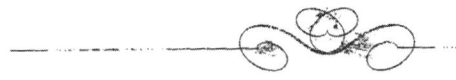

CHAPTER TWENTY-ONE

The Model-T whipped past the tree branch on the edge of the road, the leaves brushing the passenger side. "Little Ben!" Ben Roy shouted. "If you gonna tear up my car, I ain't 'bout to keep on teachin' you how to drive!"

"Oh, Daddy, give him a chance. He's not but seventeen." Tilly, still in her blue polka-dot, Sunday dress sat in the cloth-cushioned back seat, Wiley George beside her, drinking from the moonshine hooch he kept for right after Fedora's Sunday dinner.

"Well, let him learn on somebody's else's car." Ben Roy shaded his eyes against the on-coming sun. "Hey, ain't that the Welles' wagon comin' thisaway?"

The mule pulling the wagon neared. Ben Roy spotted Dickie Welles, Leotha beside him on the buckboard.

"Looks like they headin' back home." Wiley George took another nip from the bottle.

"What they doin' headin' out of Lawnover? " Ben Roy frowned. "Can't be comin' back from church. They headin' the wrong way." He peered past Little Ben. "Roll down the winda. I want to give 'em a holler." Ben Roy leaned across Little Ben. "What you folks up to?" Ben Roy called out.

Eula had made it clear the Welles gal as well as Alex's get had moved into her farm house. Lord, he'd heard enough moaning and groaning from his sister to last two life times.

"Uh...uh..." Dickie looked like he was about to fall off his own wagon. If Leotha had been a white woman, she would have passed out.

Ben Roy grunted. "I say, what y'awl up to this fine Sunday evenin'?" Ben Roy made the stop sign to Little Ben. The boy looked right, then straight ahead. He pressed on the clutch and the gas pedal at the same time. The car jerked and lurched to a halt. Dickie Welles tipped his hat and flicked the reins of his mule as he trotted passed.

"God damn it, Little Ben! They done got away!"

"Daddy!" Tilly harrumphed.

Like she hadn't heard her father cuss before.

"Sorry." Ben Roy muttered as he turned to Little Ben. "Boy, don't you know the gas pedal from the brake? I wanted to talk to those coloreds."

"You wanted to give niggers a 'how y'awl,' Grandpa?" Little Ben didn't have much more sense than his father.

"Boy, what did I tell you 'bout using that word?"

Now Little Ben pumped on the clutch and the brake at the same time. "What word, Grandpa?" The car growled under Little Ben's efforts.

"Lord, boy, will you watch it! I told you don't never use that word when there are ladies present."

"But you just cussed."

Ben Roy glared at his grandson. "There's the turnoff to your Aunt Eula Mae's house." The boy swung wide onto the road leading to the McNaughton farm.

"What ladies you talkin' 'bout, Grandpa?"

Ben Roy swiped Little Ben above the ear. "Knucklehead, don't you know your mama's sittin' in the back seat? Don't never say that word in front of polite company."

Little Ben rubbed his head right above his ear as the car aimed toward another tree. Ben Roy straightened the wheel as Eula's farm house came into view.

"Let me out of here before you kill us all! I'd let your pa drive if he wasn't drunk as a skunk."

The car ground to a stop, one wheel stuck in a rut in the path leading to the back of Alex's house. Ben Roy opened the door and jumped out. "Tilly, don't you let neither one of 'em get behind that wheel 'lessen I'm sittin' next to 'em." He headed toward the back porch. Lord, what was he going to find?

He walked through the always unlocked back-porch door. The smell of burned biscuits hit his nose first. He heard Kate Welles' scolding voice.

"You lucky, Mr. Alex ain't smacked you one."

Ben Roy stepped into the kitchen. "You the one burned the bread?" He looked at Dolly, her bobbed hair swinging under her chin as she washed the dinner dishes. Lord, that gal was way too good-looking for parts like these.

The girl shrugged. "I don't usually burn biscuits. I cook them at home all the time. I'm just not used to a stove that burns wood. We have coal at home." She stood there without a yes sir or a no sir coming out of her mouth. Worse. She didn't seem to know better.

This sure as hell wasn't going to work. This up-north girl had no proper training at all. Ben Roy turned to Kate. No use talking to that other. "Where's Mr. Alex?"

"He say he goin' to the barn to give the cows their evenin' milkin', suh." Kate Welles kept her eyes where they belonged—on his collar. He'd remind himself to tell Leotha she'd raised a fair-to-middlin' good girl after all.

"Kate, I see you got the windas wide open. Get a fan and get that stink outta here." Ben Roy walked out through the back porch and down to the barn.

Alex stood at the barn door, a pail of milk in one hand. He played with the door latch with the other.

"Alex, I come to talk."

Alexander turned around, his face showing no surprise. "Eula Mae settlin' in all right at your place?"

"All right? How in the hell can your wife be all right when you got...you got...all this mess goin' on?" Ben Roy pointed to the kitchen window.

"I told Eula it won't be but for a few days." Alex looked unconvinced.

"You ain't got no idea what you gonna do, now do you?"

Alex hunched his shoulders. "She ain't the kind of girl I can just put in some cabin I build in the back forty." He looked up at Ben Roy. "She graduated high school, you know." The man even smiled.

"Oh Lord, Alex, you can't have this. This gal ain't gonna work out down here. She's too set in her up-north ways."

"You kept three of yours with you for most of their lives 'til Het…"

Ben Roy put up a hand. "I know what Hettie done. I don't need you to tell me. Hettie had no count takin' my girls up north. I already sent two of 'em to high school. I was gonna fix 'em up real good."

"Like you gonna fix up my Dolly with the Davis cousins?"

Ben Roy squared himself in front of his brother-in-law. "I ain't sure that's gonna work either. That gal is way too northern for the likes of any fella here in Lawnover. Ain't but one thing to do."

Alex walked over the spring house, opened the door and set in the pail of milk, piling on what was left of Friday's ice-block delivery. "And I reckon, Ben Roy, you gonna tell me what that is."

Ben Roy licked his lips. The sun still had another three hours before setting, and the temperature had ratcheted up more than two degrees. He pulled out his handkerchief and swiped at his forehead. "You got to send her back befo' there's trouble."

Alexander jerked his head toward Ben Roy. "What kind of trouble?"

"Eula Mae, for one. She's up at the house cryin' her eyes out to Fedora."

"Eula Mae? What's she got to do with this? I ain't takin' nothin' away from Eula. In fact these girls can be of some help."

"Burnt biscuits?" Ben Roy shook his head. His brother-in-law was worse than a blind man with a Little Ben's mind sitting behind the wheel of a car. "She's gotta to go back up North."

"No."

Ben Roy figured Alexander for stubbornness. Always had been. Oh, Alex used to act like he was more God-fearin' than all the other white farmers in Lawnover. He didn't have him a regular colored woman like the rest of the planters in these parts for almost twenty years. Then he set his eyes on his sharecropper's wife. Ben Roy shook his head at the memory. Oh Lord, he'd had himself a time with Alex that morning, what with Alex screaming to the world about loving a colored woman—Eula Mae and Fedora just two rooms away. They'd had a scuffle, he and Alex. In truth, it was more like a knock-down-drag-out. Both of them suffered more than a few cuts and bruises. Ben Roy's black eye took more than a week to settle down. Alex never did understand the way things were supposed to go. Screaming out he loved her—Annalaura Welles—Ben Roy would never forget that moment. Ben Roy had just about preached himself blue in the face telling Alex that he couldn't ever say such a thing out loud, no matter how hard he felt the truth of the thing. And now here the man stood, telling Ben Roy "no" to the only sensible way out of this mess.

"No need for you to stand there lookin' at me, I ain't gonna change my mind." Alex folded his arms across his chest.

Both men had seen sixty birthdays. Ben Roy was in no mood to go the rounds again with Alex, but somebody had to knock some sense into his brother-in-law.

"Alex, you are my sister's husband. I'm duty-bound to help you help yourself. Now that gal of yours can't stay here in Lawnover, no matter what. No, you and I ain't gonna tussle again, but your worries are not 'bout me."

Alexander dropped his hands.

Ben Roy nodded. "Now you and I take a family interest in this gal." He sought Alexander's eyes. "But there's other men in this town who only see a very good-lookin'..."

Damn, if Alexander hadn't just laid a fist across his chin! Ben Roy backed up and held up his hands. "Alex, I ain't your enemy. You know what I'm sayin' is the God's truth. Now looky here. This here is Sunday. I want you to figure your way out of this mess before Tuesday. I'm bringin' Eula Mae back home to you Tuesday afternoon. I don't want her to find no 'hired-help' still 'round here when I do. If you need my help figurin' things out, just say so. I ain't got nothin' else to say." Ben Roy turned and headed back to the Ford. He'd be the one to drive Tilly home.

CHAPTER TWENTY-TWO

Alex squeezed the last drop of milk from the teat of his oldest cow, Sallie Sue. Been with him these ten years now. Eula usually got to the milking six days out of seven, but this morning all the chores fell on him. Maybe that's why Sallie Sue had been ready to give up her milk, but not to Alex's rough hands. To tell the truth, Eula's hands were not all that soft. Nothing like Laura's. Why, that woman's entire body— got to stop thinking about her. Alex tried just about everything to forget Laura. But whenever she crossed his mind, she still riled the man in him up.

He grunted as he hoisted the half-full milk bucket. Enough of those kinds of thoughts. Because today's chores all fell on him, he was late for Clarksville. The sun had come up a good forty-five minutes ago this Monday morning. Alex set the milk in the spring house and headed toward his kitchen door. Mmmm. Something smelled good. Bacon sizzling. Eggs frying, the brown crispness of their edges filling the air. The first hint of the tang of buttermilk floating from baking biscuits swarmed his nose as he stepped into his kitchen. Dolly, a tee-towel doubled in her hand, pulled open the oven door.

"Them biscuits smell 'bout ready to me." He called out to his daughter, remembering yesterday's baking disaster. "You 'bout ready to take 'em out?"

Dolly lifted the biscuit tin from the oven and set in on a free stove eye while Kate Welles flipped his eggs onto a plate. A pot of grits simmered on a third eye while the now empty bacon skillet sat on the fourth.

"Mr. McNaughton, I'd say breakfast is ready to be served." Dolly turned that smile on him. Laura's smile.

"Yes, suh," Kate interrupted, "take yo'self a seat." The girl laid down his filled plate.

Dolly frowned as she headed toward the kitchen table, a bowl of biscuits in her hand. "Kate, you only set the table for one." She put the bowl down as she headed for the kitchen safe.

Alex took his eyes off his daughter. There was something about that bowl—it was white, sprigged in blue with a thin sliver of silver near the top. Lord, was that Eula's wedding bowl? How long since he'd seen that thing? Dolly marched back to the table, set down one plate, pushed aside an old journal, and laid out a second plate. She pulled out a chair and sat. Alex heard the gurgle in Kate's throat.

"Uh, uh, Dol…I reckon…I think….I ain't hungry. I'll tend to the cleanin'" The girl ran from the kitchen and headed up the stairs.

Alex reached for a biscuit, his hand brushing against the book now laying at the edge of his kitchen table. He stared. Now where had that come from? Eula Mae's old account journal. Like the wedding bowl, he hadn't seen the journal now in…how many years had it been?

"How could Cousin Kate not be hungry?" Dolly stared at the bottom rung of the stairs where Kate had disappeared a moment earlier. She turned to face him.

Alex moved the journal closer to him. "Where'd you get ahold of this?"

"Oh, it was on the top shelf." Dolly pointed to the safe. "I saw the bowl. Thought it was pretty and would be fun to serve at breakfast, so I climbed on a chair and pulled the bowl down. That book kind of slid out with it. Looks old."

"Does your ma have a bowl like this one? Fancy, I mean." Now why had he asked that? Alex snatched up a piece of bacon as he inspected his plate.

"Mama? Oh, she's got lots of fancy things. Doesn't really use them, but Papa keeps buying them for her."

The bacon caught in Alex's throat. He gestured for a cup of coffee.

"Oops, guess we forgot to serve that." His daughter grabbed Alex's mug from the table, moved to the stove, and poured him a cup. She sat it down next to him before she took her seat. "I'm just not good at this maid stuff." She smiled again.

Alex downed half a cup without his usual cream and sugar. He cleared his throat as he resumed his breakfast. The questions and the pain pounded at him. No, his girl was terrible at being a maid. Hadn't Laura taught her? And what had his child said about John Welles? Dolly, the child of Alex's body, called another man—John Welles—Papa. Didn't the girl know the truth? Had Laura allowed their daughter to love another man like he was her father? Did Annalaura—he put down his biscuit and rubbed at the hurt in his chest—love John Welles, the man who had beaten her when she was in the last hours of her pregnancy with that very same Dolly?

"Mr. McNaughton. Mr. McNaughton?" Dolly's voice cut through the past. "I know I can't cook like my mama, not yet, but is everything all right?"

"Got to go, girl." He pushed back from the chair. "I've got me some business. You two set tight right here. I'll be back directly. And, don't let nobody in this house. You hear me?" He walked to the porch door, calling over his shoulder. "Breakfast was just fine. Especially them biscuits." He closed the door behind him.

* * *

Alex's truck swung a wide left onto Franklin street. He remembered he'd seen the Southern Bell telephone office somewhere around here. He'd come to Clarksville before, of course, but it wasn't like he knew every nook and cranny of the place. He could find his way to the feed stores, mercantile that sold and repaired his farm tools, and one or two dry-goods shops, but that was about it. He rarely took Eula Mae into Clarksville. What for? Oh, she'd go every month of Sundays with Fedora, Ben Roy at the wheel, but Eula Mae wasn't a frivolous sort of woman. What did she need with pretty dresses, sweet-smelling soaps, frilly drawers, and such? Those were things for Laura. He sucked in his lips as his hands tightened on the wheel. Lord let him forget about her for just a few hours.

Alex strained to spot something familiar up the street. He had little time to wrack his head over what ought to have been, and he had only a precious few hours to solve the problem of Dolly. His daughter had been right. She was not a girl who was going to sit home and clean house. And she certainly wasn't meant for the likes of the Davis cousins. What with Eula Mae coming home for certain tomorrow afternoon, what was he going to do about Dolly? Where was that damn telephone company? Alex steered right, and there, a few doors down from the Clarksville Feed & Grain, flapped the striped awning. Southern Bell of Northern Tennessee.

Alex parked the truck, stepped out and walked into the building. The counter man pointed him to the pay telephone, showed him how to use the contraption, and took his nickel for the privilege, telling him if he talked longer than three minutes that'd be another nickel. Alex handed over a dime. His mind was fuzzy. What Leotha blabbed to him about calling some woman with a funny-sounding name made no sense to him. What did this Illinois person have to do with Dolly? Alex fumbled in his pocket for the sheet of paper where he'd copied the name from that scrunched up scrap Leotha had showed him. She acted like she wanted to keep that paper for herself. While she stood there driving more wrinkles into that ragged scrap, Alex spotted Eula's old journal. He flipped open the back cover and yanked out a sheet of lined paper. There he'd written the name—Gina Maggiora. What kind of name was that? Sounded foreign to Alex. He lifted the ear piece just the way the counter man instructed.

"Number, please." A tinny female voice—sounded young. Alex raised the sound of his own words. "I'm calling up North." He looked at the ear piece. He hadn't much used a telephone, though Ben Roy had one up at the main house. Fedora had insisted.

"Up north?" The girl's voice came in a waver over the telephone line. "You mean up north here in Tennessee?" She sounded confused.

"No." Alex shouted at the voice that faded in and out of his ear. "I mean up North in Illinoise."

"Illinoise?" The voice paused. "You're gonna need the long-distance operator."

"What?" Alex heard clicking and clacking on the line. He dug into his pants pocket. Good. He had four nickels and six dimes. He'd need every last one of them at this pace.

"May I help you, sir?" A more northern voice.

"I'm callin' a G-i-n-a M-a-g-g-i-o-r-a."

"In what city and state, sir?"

"Oh," Alex unfolded the paper. He hadn't copied the name of the town but he remembered it. From Dolly. "Brugestown, Illinoise."

Alex hung on the line while the clickety clacking went on.

"That will be five cents more, sir, for another three minutes." The northern voice. "I have your party on the line."

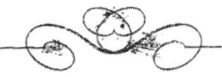

CHAPTER TWENTY-THREE

Gina pushed open Annalaura's screen door, her light-tan face now flushed. Her breathing came in stops and starts. A person might think Gina had just run around the block two times instead of stepping from next door. Her eyes opened wide like she'd seen a ghost or something else unexpected, when she spotted Lottie. Annalaura's oldest girl stood at the ironing board, folding the last of her Monday wash.

"Hey, Mrs. Maggiora. I'm just about finished. Had to use Mama's washing machine. One of my rollers is off the track. Of course, hers is not electric."

Annalaura gave her daughter that "I told you so' look."

"Give me that!" Lottie called out to Sammy as the boy rolled an ear of corn across the kitchen linoleum. "We've got to get home and start your daddy's dinner. 'Bye, Mrs. Maggiora."

Lottie, carrying the heavy-looking laundry basket, walked out of the kitchen, through the front room, and out onto the porch. Gina pushed both hands to her sides like she was trying to hold in her breathing until Lottie disappeared down the concrete porch steps, Sammy bounding ahead. Gina turned to Annalaura.

"Mrs. You hurry the feet!" She grabbed Annalaura's arm. "You gotta the telephone call!"

Annalaura's feet moved underneath her. She supposed that was because they could not resist the mighty tug Gina had on her. Annalaura saw her porch and driveway fly by. She imagined her shoes must be touching them, but her body refused to feel anything. Gina rushed Annalaura through the kitchen and into her living room. Her neighbor planted Annalaura directly in front of the wall telephone, its ear piece dangling from the cord. Annalaura tried three times before her voice finally decided to come out of her throat.

"Who…who…" Annalaura pointed to the hanging instrument.

"Edith tell me the call come from the Tennessee. I say who? She…Edith tell me a man, a Mr. Alex McNa…"

Annalaura watched Gina's lips move as she chattered on. But out of the corner of her eye, there it—he—was on the other end of that telephone line. Oh, Jesus, Lord Jesus, help her now. Gina picked up the receiver and tried to shove it into Annalaura's hand.

"No!" Annalaura drew back. The black receiver looked so much like a snake. Annalaura blinked. Was the thing writhing in Gina's hand just like some slithering creature filled with venom? She felt the water well in her eyes. Oh Lord, she couldn't do it. She could not hear his voice—that voice—not after all these years. Her feet moved her backwards from the phone. She had to get home. Weren't her snap beans on the stove? They'd burn without her tending to them. She held up a hand to Gina as she shook her head. Annalaura bumped against the kitchen door jam.

"Doug. Henry. Dolly." Gina, standing as straight as a prophetess of old, held out the phone, aiming it straight at Annalaura's heart. "You talk now."

Each step her feet made toward Gina felt like she was walking through a tobacco field pulling a fifty-pound bale with each leg. "I…I don't think…" That voice didn't sound like her own.

Gina snapped the phone into Annalaura's hand and lifted it to her ear. She poked Annalaura in the back.

"Oh," oozed out of Annalaura's mouth.

"Hello?"

Good God in Heaven! Sixteen years flitted away like a burning tobacco cigarette. Alex's voice.

"Anybody there? Are you this G-i-n-a woman?" He spelled out the name as though he were reading off a printed page.

The name, his name, came into her head long before she tried to get the sound out through her mouth. She tried three times before she managed, "Al…" She remembered her Tennessee manners. "Mr. McNaughton?"

The telephone line crinkled and crackled like always, but Annalaura could swear she heard Alex's breathing. Long and deep.

"Laura?"

Too late. The tears she held in check for all these years splashed down her cheeks before she could use the back of her hand to brush them away. "Uh-huh." Her voice strangled out of her throat. "Yes. This is Annalaura." She took in a breath. Sixteen years could not fall away this fast, could they? "Annalaura Welles, John's wife." She needed her own reminder.

Was that a groan she heard over that bothersome telephone line? Annalaura turned to Gina who stood within touching distance. Her friend's face nodded a "go ahead."

"Alex," What Gina said all those minutes ago finally sunk into Annalaura's head. Doug, Henry, and Dolly. Enough of this weak-in-the-knees foolishness. She had done right all those years ago. What was so in nineteen-fourteen Tennessee was still so in nineteen-thirty Illinois. "Alex, I needs to talk to you 'bout…'bout my children."

Annalaura looked at Gina. Her stomach and heart took turns rumbling and grumbling. Annalaura focused on Gina's face, remembering her friend's words. That smile she felt coming over her felt good. Annalaura was where she needed to be—doing what she ought to save her children. She frowned at the phone. How long had it been since she'd heard a sound from him?

"They're all right. Your children." Another pause—longer this time. "She's here. With me."

Annalaura took in a deep breath. "I knows. I knows she's safe with you, but I need her back here with me. To help out."

"Help out?" Sudden worry crowded into Alex's voice. "Ain't you feelin' all right, Laura?"

Oh, God. The man still called her Laura. Nobody else in this world had ever named her that. The muscles in her belly tightened, but the grumbling continued. She had to get this right. One thing had to be understood. Alex was still stuck in nineteen-fourteen, thinking things between them had never changed. "I'm feelin' fine 'cept I want my girl back home."

"She is home. At least, will be once I get a few things sorted out." His sigh cut through the noise on the telephone line.

There was something about this man that pulled Annalaura. The law, white folks, colored folks, her husband, time, the Bible—if you listened to the white pastors—all said such tuggings were not natural. Close to a sin. But Alex had a way about him of making her feel like she was something extra-special. In his mind, the Good Lord made the sun rise and the moon set only in her. The way he looked at her sometimes, the way he touched her. But she knew better. None of that could be for real. Alex had his own way of thinking, ignoring each and every fact around him. Just like the day he eased her birthing pains as best he could and, at the end, pulled Dolly out of her. She'd never seen a man so happy to look into the face of his first-born. Then his mind broke half-in-two. He'd insisted they'd all live as one big happy family—Alex, Annalaura, Dolly, and Eula Mae. And here he was, sixteen years later talking almost the same foolishness, taking no heed of what was. Annalaura felt herself stand straighter, her words flowing quicker. Like back then, she had to be the one to save them all.

"Alex, I wants my girl home. I told Leotha to ask you a

question. Hope you been thinkin' on an answer."

"Oh, I been thinkin' on one all right. I got an answer for you."

Annalaura felt her heart quicken. "Yes. I'll do whatever it is you wants if you gets all three of my children out of Tennessee and back up safe here in Illinois."

"Will you, Laura? Do whatever I want?"

Now, what had she said? "What is it you think you want, Alex?"

"An answer."

"An answer?" She looked over at Gina as though her neighbor knew both the question and the response. "To what?"

"I think you know to what. Laura, I…"

Had the line gone dead? Annalaura tapped the earpiece.

"I'll bring Dolly to you." Alex came back on the line, but each word took twice as long to reach her ears.

The tears threatened again and not from the bright summer sun flowing through Gina's curtains. "Oh, Alex, thank God, Almighty. Can my girl and the boys leave this afternoon?"

More emptiness on the other end of the line. Annalaura pressed the phone so hard against her head, her ear lobes hurt. She had to be patient.

"Dolly, she tells me she wants to go to college. Says there's some school up there in Illinoise. Don't rightly know where it is, but that's where I'll take her."

"Take her? You wants to send Dolly to Champaign? Whatever for? Just 'cause Dolly wants to see what she can't never have ain't no reason to allow it. It'll only break her heart all the more." Annalaura took in a deep breath. Truth be told, if she could, she would help her daughter become that teacher she always wanted to be. "We got no money fo' college."

"So she tells me." More crackling over the line. "She got schoolin' good 'nough for college?"

"Yes. She's a right smart girl. I jest wish…Alex, I don't

wants her travelin' by herself. Just put her in the car with Doug and Henry, and they can all be out of yo' hair by nightfall."

Annalaura stared at Gina's clock sitting on her round, doily-covered table next to the settee. How many clicks did the thing have to make before Alex spoke again?

"Laura, you want an answer from me? Here it is. No, I ain't sendin' Dolly nowheres. I'm bringin' her on up to this Champaign place on the train. We can leave tomorra. Tuesday."

"Train?" Annalaura heard her own shout into the telephone bounce back into her already sore ear.

"I don't want her on no train travelin' by herself. She just turned sixteen." Annalaura dug her nails into her palm. Why did she mention Dolly's birthdate? If anybody would know that day, it was Alexander McNaughton. "Just hand her over to Doug and Henry."

"Like I been sayin', we—me and Dolly—are leavin' tomorra mornin'. Doug and Henry can go on home any time they get good and ready. Ain't nobody gonna bother them down here."

"Dolly? You?" Annalaura finally filtered Alex's words. "You comin' to Champaign?" Annalaura shook her head so hard her neck hurt. "Ain't no need fo' that. Just..."

"Laura, you asked me a question. I just gave you my answer. I'll hand Dolly over to you day after next in this Champaign place. Wednesday. But, I'll only hand her over to you direct. And then only if you answer some things fo' me." Alex's voice sounded stronger and more certain with each word he uttered.

"Things? Me?" Annalaura fought to put Alex's words into some kind of sense. "You want me to go to Champ...go there to get Dolly? Wednesday? From you?"

"You talk to me first. I want a good long talk with you. I think I deserve that, don't you?"

Annalaura's heart thumped in her chest and played chase with her stomach. "You...Alex, you want to talk to me? But what we got to say to one another after all this time? Let me send Lottie. Easier fo' her to get over to Champaign. John...he might not..."

"No Lottie. Just you. I want my answers, Laura." More silence. "I can take care of Dolly just as well as you. Fact of the business, she can stay right here in Tennessee, not go back to Illinoise at all. I can make an arrangement for her."

Oh, Lord, Glory. Was the man bluffing? Anybody with a grain of sense knew a girl like Dolly couldn't stay in the South, not unless some white man... an arrangement? Annalaura felt Gina's arms around her as her knees buckled. The phone shook in her hand. Her fingers trembled as she put the piece back to her ear. She waved Gina away. "Alex..." her voice whispered. She tried again. "Alex, when you gets to Champaign with Dolly, I wants you to promise me two things befo' I can say yes to goin' myself."

"Promises? I know what store you set by promises." His heavy sigh came through the static on the line. "I recollect what you promised me, Laura. On the day our baby girl was born."

The grunt spewed out over the line before Annalaura could control it. Yes, she remembered her words to Alex that morning right after Dolly took her first squalling breath. She'd said the only thing she could to save both of the men in her life—Alex and John. If she hadn't, both would have been dead by nightfall—Alex by John's gun, and John by the nightriders. Couldn't he see that? "I...uh...Alex, I did what was best."

"Best for you. Best for John... Tell me what you want. Laura, I keep my promises."

Annalaura took in a big breath. This had to work. "First of all, I can't allow Dolly to travel alone with you on a train comin' out of Tennessee. You two can't sit together. Ole Jim Crow won't allow it. You knows that. Not 'til you hits the Illinois border."

"Oh." Alex sounded as though he'd forgotten his daughter was colored.

Alex in Illinois with Dolly. That would never do. Annalaura rummaged her mind. "Bring Leotha with you. Tell her I said she was to come chaperone Dolly. I'll pay the ticket."

"I can do all of that. What else you want?"

"I pray to the Good Lord you ain't said nothin' yet 'bout... who Dolly's papa is." Annalaura shut her eyes trying to lock out the furor in her girl's face if she ever learned the truth. "Tell me you ain't."

"We gonna talk 'bout that when I get up North. You and me. Til then, I won't tell her nary a word. That it? All the promises you want out of me?"

"Uhh. Jest one more."

"Yeah?"

"It ain't gonna be easy fo' me to get away from home for a whole day over to Champaign. Gotta figure me a way to tell John. But when you and I meets up, we just gonna talk 'bout Dolly, right? Nothin' else?"

"That promise you ain't gettin' from me. Now you want me to get the tickets or not?" Alex sounded gruff.

"I...uh...Alex, I'm still livin' with John. We married."

"Tell me, Laura. Will you talk to me in Champaign, yes or no."

Annalaura turned to Gina, who sent her a questioning look. Oh Lord, Gina doesn't have the answer either. Aunt Becky always said Annalaura had more sand in her than was good for a colored woman. Right now, Annalaura needed every grain the Lord had blessed her. Her shoulders shuddered. Yes, she could gather up enough courage to talk a few words to Alex—in public. Besides, she'd have Leotha standing right there by her side to stop Alex from wanting...

"Yes."

Did she hear the click of a phone being hung into its cradle among all that crinkle and crackle? "Alex?" No answer.

Gina gathered Annalaura into her arms before the phone reached its hook. Annalaura did not want Gina to stop the hugging.

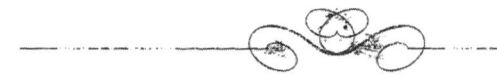

CHAPTER TWENTY-FOUR

Though he couldn't say it out loud, Alex had always given his praises to Eula for the way she had with money. His wife was a saver. Even with all this Depression talk, Alex's bank account was better than fair-to-middlin' good. After he hung up from Laura—he still couldn't believe he'd actually talked to her after all this time—he'd headed straight to the First National Bank two blocks down the street in Clarksville, and drew out the money for three train tickets—two in the Colored section and one in the whites-only chair car. Then he fretted himself over getting word to Ben Roy—don't bring Eula home 'til Friday noon. Alex figured that should be time enough—trains being faster these days. If he left Clarksville Tuesday morning, he'd be in the Champaign place by that very evening. Talk to Laura and set up Dolly on Wednesday. Then back on the Thursday morning train for Clarksville. He'd be home in plenty of time to receive Eula. But he still had one problem.

On the way back from Clarksville, he'd driven to the Welles place and delivered Laura's message to Leotha. Told Dickie to keep mum about where Alex was going when Dickie told Ben Roy to hold Eula at his house 'til Friday. Dickie and Leotha had looked at him owl-eyed, but when Alex hinted there could be trouble if they didn't answer to him right now, they both nodded their heads. One more thing—keep Doug and Henry in the dark until they heard direct from Alex.

This morning, standing on the Clarksville train platform, sweat already staining his fresh-ironed shirt even though the eight-thirteen train coming up from Mississippi was yet to be seen, he looked down at Dolly. She caught his glance.

"Mr. McNaughton"—that frown hadn't left his daughter's face since he told her last night about the quick return to Illinois—"why does my mother want me back home so soon? I just started my vacation. And what about my brothers?" She turned those blue eyes on him.

"Honey," Leotha's voice trembled, "don't go askin' too many questions. Jest do like yo' mama says."

Alex looked at Leotha. That woman's face of terror had long ago gotten on his nerves. The way she carried on, the world would think he was sending her straight to Hell. On the other hand, not a bad idea if the woman's fearful look didn't stop upsetting his daughter.

"Dolly, your mama wants you back in town. I told her I'd bring you." He turned to Leotha. "Your cousin here is the chaperone."

Dolly shook her head as she groaned. "You talked to Mama?

Alex held his breath. She gave him a curious look but nothing more. "I don't need a chaperone. I've got brothers." She tilted her head like she considered mounting a complaint, then thought better of it. "Is something wrong with Mama, Papa, Lottie, Samm...?"

"Ain't nothin' wrong with none of them." Alex heard the whistle before he turned to watch the locomotive puff around the bend. The droplets from the steam clouded the air and rained down on him. The train pulled to a stop, covering them all in one big burst of gray hot water.

"All aboard." The white conductor called out. "Coloreds to the back, white folks up front."

Alex carried Dolly's valise up the train steps, while Leotha struggled with her own cardboard case. He handed the luggage over to Dolly as the conductor pointed Leotha to the Colored train car. The man stared at Dolly, frowned, then motioned her to follow Leotha.

"You want me to go in there?" Dolly directed her question to the conductor. The man turned to Alex, confusion on his face.

"Yeah. Y'awl go on that side." Alex watched while Dolly peered through the window of the connecting train-car door. "I'll be back with some food directly."

He found his seat in the whites-only section and settled next to an empty space. Illinois. Up North. He'd never before left the South. Would he find the North as strange as Dolly plainly did the South?

*   *   *

Dolly looked at the dust covering the two empty seats three rows into the train car where Leotha decided they would sit. Dolly judged the car could hold almost sixty passengers, but she counted just ten beside herself and her cousin. On the last rows at the back of the car, she watched a group of five men sitting on the top of the seats backs. She leaned over for a better look. Yes, their shoes—those that wore shoes—rested on the seat cushions. As for the rest of their attire, their overalls had patches in them, and one of the men wore a checkered shirt with a torn pocket. The men stared back at her. She smoothed down her dress. When she first entered the car, she thought she heard the strains of a Louis Armstrong tune, but as she followed Leotha down the aisle, the music went quiet. Dolly met the eyes of the oldest-looking of the brown-skinned men, a nicked-up guitar strung around his neck. Another fellow—about Henry's age and wearing a straw hat with a sizeable chunk of straw missing from the back brim—held a beat-up saxophone just inches from his lips as though he'd stopped playing the instant Dolly entered the train car.

"Leotha, er, Cousin Leotha, we can't sit on seats that look like these. See all that dust?" Dolly crinkled her nose as she leaned in to her older cousin. "Besides, maybe somebody put their bare feet on the cushions just before we came in." Something smelled like day-old fried fish and the slime of yesterday's boiled okra. Dolly took one more look at the group in the back. At least two of them held chunks of catfish in their hands. Large grease-stained brown-paper bags sat on the seat cushions next to the men's feet. "Let's go up and tell the conductor we want to change our seats. Sit in the car with Mr. McNaughton."

Leotha grabbed her by the collar of her good dress—the one she was supposed to wear to church in Lawnover this past Sunday. "Lord, have mercy, girl, don't you know nothin'?" Leotha was still shaking.

Dolly did know something, but in all the excitement of these last two days, she'd pushed most of Mama's Tennessee lessons right out of her head. No wonder Leotha was so afraid. Things in the South were supposed to be separate and not equal for the Negro. Dolly took another look at the dust-covered seats, whipped out the hanky Mama always said a lady had to carry, and dusted off the aisle seat. If this was the way of the South, she supposed she could tolerate it for another few hours. And thank goodness, she didn't have Kate as a traveling mate. "Here, Cousin Leotha, you can sit. You look a little…a little…" What was that look? Dolly swiped some of the grit covering her seat, climbed over Leotha and ensconced herself next to the window.

"I'm sorry. I forgot about the South. This is my first time on a train, and I'm a little excited." Dolly settled herself into her chair, but she felt the probing stares of the men in the back rows on her neck. "Why are those men looking so hard at me? I washed my face and brushed my teeth this morning. Combed my hair, too."

Leotha turned a face that looked about to cry toward Dolly. "Don't pay them fellas no mind. They's probably goin' up to Chicago."

"To visit?"

"No, sugar, I specs those fellas is movin' up there. Come up from N'Awlins or maybe, Memphis." Leotha waved her train schedule. "This here train is the Illinoise Central. She goes clean down to Mississippi and N'Awlins and such." She peered around the edge of her aisle seat. "Looks like them fellas got themselves enough food to last quite a spell." She leaned in to Dolly. "I hear tell lots of our folks is movin' up to Chicago—especially them that can play some music."

"You mean jazz?" Dolly brightened. "Mama doesn't like jazz. Calls it devil music." She raised a shielding hand to her mouth. "But I like that kind of music a lot."

For the first time since she stepped out of Cousin Richard's wagon this morning at the Clarksville train station, Leotha looked as though she might live through the night. She laid her hand atop Dolly's. "Yo' mama's right. T'is devil's music, but some young folks sho' do seem to like to dance to it. Like my Kate."

"Hmm." Thank goodness bossy Kate was back home with Cousin Richard. Dolly settled back into her seat, a sprinkling of dust settling over her right shoulder. She flicked it off with her fingers. She tried to look out of the window, but the grime covering the pane limited what she could see of the rolling Tennessee countryside. "Cousin Leotha"—had her relative calmed down enough for Dolly to get to the real point—"why is Mr. McNaughton the one taking me home to Danville? Why couldn't I just come back with Doug and Henry or even you? And how did he talk to my mother? We don't have a telephone."

"Uh, uh," the wheels clanked against the rails as Leotha lips worked to come up with some sort of an answer. "That business with you and Kate. At that jazz juke joint."

Dolly grimaced. So that was it. Word had gotten to her mama in Brugestown. Who'd blabbed? Cousin Leotha or Cousin Richard? Neither. Probably that awful Dodie. Dolly groaned out loud. No wonder she was being sent back home. Oh, goodness, what punishment had her parents thought up for her? They'd already taken away her graduation trip, but if she understood Annalaura Welles at all, she knew her mama would come up with a doozy of a discipline. Papa might go easy on her—no picture shows for a month—but her overly-strict mama would lay down the law and maybe not even spare the rod. Dolly grumped. Like Annalaura Welles had never done a wrong thing in her whole life. Dolly stared out of the window, the muddied image of her mother jumping off the passing tobacco fields. She grunted. What a pain to have a mother who really had never done a bad thing. No, Dolly was being sent home because she'd broken a major commandment set up by St. Annalaura. And Dolly had to pay the price. But why with Mr. McNaughton?

Dolly rubbed a spot half-clean on the window to rid herself of Mama's image. A sign—Welcome to Kentucky—greeted her. She sat back in her seat. She'd give Leotha another thirty minutes to settle herself before she rephrased her question. Dolly closed her eyes. McNaughton had gotten her up awfully early this morning.

"Tickets. Y'awl hand over yo' tickets." The conductor's low, growly southern voice roused Dolly out of her sleep.

If she'd been dreaming, she couldn't remember a thing about it. She looked out of the window. The sun was almost directly overhead. Had she slept that long? Dolly watched while Leotha held out tickets to the conductor. Her cousin kept her eyes on the floor. Curious. Southerners—colored people—seemed to do that a lot in Tennessee. The white conductor snatched the tickets without touching Leotha's hand and nodded. He moved across the aisle and five rows down to the couple sitting mid-car.

"Cousin Leotha"—Dolly judged Leotha to be fairly calm after her own nap—"how long did Mama work for Mr. McNaughton?"

The way Leotha's mouth made those sucking air sounds worried Dolly. Her cousin had to be over sixty. Amazing she'd lived this long. Was she about to have a killing stroke?

"Uh, yo' folks, they...uh..."

Dolly leaned forward to get a better look at her relative who seemed to be tongue-tied. "They…" she encouraged, "they what, Cousin Leotha?"

Leotha must have spotted a mouse or a spider the way she stared at the dirty floor of their train car. "Sharecroppers." She finally raised her eyes to Dolly, a smile flitting across her lips. "Yeah. They was sharecroppers. Yo' mama and yo' p…" The smile disappeared as suddenly as it had come.

Dolly nodded encouragement. "Yes, I know they worked for him on his farm. Was Mama Mr. McNaughton's cook or something? She's awfully good in the kitchen, and he seems to remember her well."

"Uh, that's right. Oh, Dolly, I gots to get me to the rest room." She looked to the rear of the train just as the connecting door up front opened.

Alexander McNaughton strolled through. The Colored train car went silent again. Dolly felt the eyes of the car's occupants all trained on the white man.

"Brung you your lunch." He handed two wrapped sandwiches to Dolly. "We'll be in Illinoise before nightfall. Eat dinner there. Dolly, you doin' all—?" The train swayed as it rounded a bend, the blast of its horn drowning the last of his words.

"Mr. McNaughton, I was just asking Cousin Leotha about you and my mother." Dolly raised her voice. Did…" Why did that sudden flush color the man's face? "I was born in Tennessee, you know. But my parents brought me North when I was a baby. Did you know Mama when I was born?"

The train conductor quick-stepped down the aisle and stopped beside Mr. McNaughton. He, too, had a strange look on his face. "Suh, is there anythin' I can help you with?"

"These gal…my workers, they're travelin' with me. I just come to check on 'em. I'll be getting back now." He headed toward the connecting door leading to the "Whites only" train car without looking back at Dolly.

Dolly heard the sigh come out of Leotha like someone popped a balloon. The elderly cousin closed her eyes and lolled her head to the side as though she were going to sleep. But, how could that be? Leotha had just awakened from at least a two-hour nap. Dolly turned to the window. Outside she spotted rolling hills, trees, and lush grass with a bluish tinge. She folded her arms over her chest. Cousin Leotha, Mr. McNaughton. What didn't they want her to know?

Leotha roused herself to wolf down her Virginia country-ham sandwich. Then she did her best to pretend sleep. As the hours ticked by, Dolly switched between flipping through the movie magazine Mr. McNaughton bought for her at the Clarksville station and staring out of the window. They'd crossed into Illinois three hours ago. Another hour or less and they'd be back in Danville. She looked over at Leotha, whose eyelids twitched.

"Cousin, we're almost there." Dolly had nudged Leotha twice before, only to hear her relative groan and turn her back to her. "Shouldn't we be getting ready to meet...hmm..." She gave Leotha a hard poke in the side. "Who's coming to pick us up? My family's car is still in Lawnover with Doug and Henry."

Leotha rolled toward Dolly. "Not rightly sure." She let out a heavy sigh as she sat up and patted her hair.

"Well, Papa will be off work by now. I suppose he can come with Rusty. That's Lottie's husband. He's got his own car." Dolly reached into her purse for her comb.

"Urbana. Champaign." The conductor walked down the aisle from the back of the train. "Champaign-Urbana."

Dolly turned in her seat. Only the tops of the heads of those in the back row were now visible. They must have napped along with Leotha. The conductor strode up the aisle calling out the latest stop. None of the other passengers looked interested. He stopped next to Leotha.

"Okay, gal, this is it. Your stop."

When Leotha looked as though she saw a whole graveyard of ghosts, Dolly leaned over her cousin and looked up at the conductor. "No, we're getting off in Danville."

The trainman scanned her face. Dolly sat back in her seat.

She was getting tired of men looking at her like she had two heads.

"No, you're not. You two getting' off right here in Champaign." He reached into his pocket. "See, your tickets say so." He flashed the cardboard in front of Leotha, who looked turned to stone.

Dolly pulled the ticket from the conductor's hand. Sure enough, Champaign was printed in black ink across the slip.

"Hey, gal. Give them back. Now get yourselves off my train. Your boss-man's 'bout ready to pack up." The conductor reached overhead and pulled down Dolly's valise.

The clickety-clack of the wheels slowed just as Dolly spotted the buildings of a city on the near horizon. A Welcome to Champaign sign flashed by as the train dropped down another ten miles per hour. "Cousin Leotha?" Dolly pointed to the sign as the train moved past.

The conductor stepped back as Leotha struggled to her feet. The trembling in her cousin's body started again. While the conductor folded his arms, Leotha reached for her cardboard box. Dolly gave the train employee her most withering glare as she moved into the aisle. She was no longer in the South, and Mama's Tennessee rules held no water here. She pushed Leotha aside.

"No, Cousin, you'll hurt yourself." She turned her smile on the odious trainman. "It's this gentleman's job to take down your luggage." Dolly spotted the couple at mid-car, and the five fellows in the back. They all looked like the same stone statue that was now Cousin Leotha. Dolly shrugged her shoulders as she walked into the vestibule carrying her valise. Let the conductor and Leotha work it out. Dolly had to figure out why the destination mix-up. As soon as she opened the heavy connecting door, there stood Mr. McNaughton.

"I'm afraid there's been a mistake with our tickets. We're supposed to be getting off in Danville. Instead, here we are in Champaign."

"Where's Leotha?" The man took his eyes off her as the train slowed almost to nothing.

Steam rose. The train wheels ground to a stop. The conductor stepped into the little vestibule and dropped Leotha's cardboard box at Mr. McNaughton's feet.

"This is y'awls stop. Take 'em with you." The trainman jerked his thumb toward Leotha who stood just inside the connecting door. The conductor pulled out the folding steps leading to the platform. He moved down the train stairs, his hand out, palm open.

Mr. McNaughton grabbed his own valise in one hand and Dolly's in the other. He descended the steps.

"We really are getting off here?" Dolly stared after McNaughton. Champaign hadn't been a mistake, after all?

She scowled as she picked up Leotha's cardboard box and made her way down the train steps. Leotha followed, looking for all the world as though she'd just stepped into Hell. Dolly stared at Mr. McNaughton, who laid a quarter into the conductor's hand. No, Champaign was no mistake. For some reason he—the Tennessean—wanted her here. Dolly looked back at Leotha. And Cousin Leotha knew why.

*   *   *

Dolly kept quiet as Mr. McNaughton led the three of them to the Welcome Visitors desk at the Champaign station. They'd already tromped through the waiting room, and if her father and oldest brother had been there to greet her, she would have seen them by now. No, something else was going on, and it was plain to see that neither Leotha nor this Tennessee man were going to tell her outright. She'd have to trick it out of them.

"M'am," Mr. McNaughton addressed a woman just a little older than Dolly who sat behind the table with a welcome sign on it, "where's the colored hotels in this town?"

The girl, her brown hair cut in a bob just like Dolly's but with marceled waves, turned a surprised face to the Tennessean. "Colored hotels? Oh, you mean hotels that will accept"—she shot a quick look at Leotha before she lowered her voice—"the Madison or the Land-of-Lincoln, they both allow colo—Negroes." She smiled.

Mr. McNaughton gave her a strange look. "Is there a white hotel near these here two—the Madi..."

The receptionist cocked her head, a quizzical look pasted on her face. "Yes. Those two hotels have white guests as well as..." she nodded again at Leotha.

"Um. What about cars for hire and such. You got them for colored?"

The clerk looked at all three visitors standing before her. "Uhh, you can get a taxi right outside the station. By the curb. It'll take you—all of you—to the hotel." She held her hand in midair.

Dolly busied herself looking out the window of the taxi tooling down the street toward the Land-of-Lincoln Hotel. So this was Champaign—the place where Claire would be heading in about three months. A pang of regret swept over Dolly. Yes, she longed to see the college campus, the seat of the University of Illinois, but she hadn't wanted to trod its acres as a tourist. She wanted to be a student. She sighed as the taxi pulled to a halt in front of the brick building with the shoddy awning out front.

"How far to the campus?" Now why had she asked the driver such a silly question? It might hurt all the more if she actually laid eyes on the place she would never enter.

"Right over there, Miss." He pointed to a park like setting some two blocks down the street.

"I reckon we can walk over there." Mr. McNaughton talked to the taxi driver as he handed over the fare. "But not 'til tomorra." He turned to Dolly. "Not 'til I..." He grabbed the two valises and walked into the hotel.

Leotha, still resembling a statue like one of those Dolly had seen in her book on French sculpture, stood stock still. All right. Dolly had sorted it out. Just as Dolly hadn't known what to do in the South, cousin Leotha was absolutely lost in the North.

"It's okay, Cousin." Dolly picked up the cardboard box.

"Let's get to our room." A room where Dolly would try her mightiest to worm the truth out of her elderly relative.

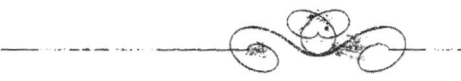

CHAPTER TWENTY-FIVE

Annalaura waited a good fifteen minutes after John, carrying his lunch bucket, piled into Cleveland's car and headed to the zinc plant. Usually, John rode with Doug and Henry, but they and the family car were still in Tennessee. When she was fairly sure John wouldn't return home to pick up something he'd forgotten, though he never had in all these sixteen years, she looked at the clock. A quarter to eight. Annalaura watched Lorenzo, his miner's cap on his head, start the two mile walk to the coal mine with most of the other foreign workers on her street.

Tuesday was going to be hotter even than Monday. More like August weather than mid-June. Annalaura took one more look at the clock in her front room. Can't hurt to wait five more minutes, her head told her—just in case—but her body twitched so bad her legs forced her to walk out her kitchen door, across the driveway, and tap on Gina's kitchen door. Her neighbor had to help her sort this one out.

"Come-a in, Mrs." Gina held the screen door open wide.

Annalaura stepped inside, spotted a kitchen chair and plopped herself into it. Son, Guido, had gone off to his summer job at the brick factory in Danville. The house was empty except for the two women. "You gotta help me figure this thing out." Annalaura put her hand on her chin as she leaned an elbow on the table. Her brain that usually served her so well had just about shut down.

Gina pulled out a chair with her foot, two cups of coffee in her hand. She set them down, spotted a fly, opened her screen door, and shooed the thing into the early morning heat. She returned to the table and sat across from Annalaura.

"Now tell me this thing again. You gotta go to Champaign to talk to this Tennessee man before you get you Dolly back." Gina recited what had pondered both their minds for all these hours.

Annalaura reached for her cup, the steam rising into her face. She pushed it aside. "I've got to get myself to Champaign sometime befo' noon tomorra." She shook her head. "Gina, how is I suppose to do that? What will I tell John?" The fog that held her in its grip ever since Alex hung up that phone two days ago still would not let her loose.

"You gotta the family, the friends in Champaign?"

"Nary a one." Annalaura played with the handle of her cup. "That's it!" Her hands flew up, brushing the cup. A few drops spilled on Gina's oilcloth-covered table. "Sorry." Annalaura got up and headed for Gina's sink. She retrieved the washrag and blotted up the spots.

"What is it?" Gina watched Annalaura clean up the spill.

"I ain't got nobody in Champaign, but you do." Annalaura sat down, the crumpled dishrag still in her hand.

Gina cocked her head. "No, Mrs." Gina's words poured out slow as molasses, "I no gotta nobody in Champaign. All my people are in Italia."

"I know that, but John don't know that. Leastways, he don't keep up. You could'a had a new cousin or such come this way from Italy a month or so ago."

"And I would no tell-a you this before the now? And you would no tell you husband?" Gina put her hands over Annalaura's. "It's no gonna work, Mrs. You no good at the lie. What about you Lottie? She can drive the car. My Lorenzo say woman drive the car is the scandal, but..."

"Lottie? Oh, glory to Heaven, no!" Annalaura shook her

head so hard her neck twitched.

Gina stared at her. "You Lottie the young woman. Young wives these days can do more of what they want. You, me, we have to get the husband's yes before we go anywhere. Not you Lottie. What do the young girls say? They say they can think for herself. Independent. I say it right?"

"Yes. No." Annalaura shook her head. "Yes, the young girls, they got mo' say over what they want to do than me and you ever had, but that ain't it."

Gina took one sip of her coffee and held the hot cup in her hands. "Then, Mrs., what is it?"

When had the clock on Gina's front room table ever ticked this loud? Annalaura counted the beats. Twenty, twenty-one, twenty-two.

"Mrs., we can sit here all the day if you want."

The clock faded away. Annalaura looked at her friend. Gina was a smart woman as well as one who knew when to keep her mouth shut. "Won't do fo' my Lottie to go to no Champaign. She was six years old back then."

Gina cocked her head. She had the question written all over her face, but like usual, Gina knew how much time to give Annalaura to let out the truth.

"When we left Tennessee….me, John, Dolly, the boys, and Lottie…." Annalaura brightened as she grabbed her coffee cup. "Gina, you reckon six is too young to remember much?"

Gina pursed her lips and arched her eyebrows. That clock again. Ten maybe twelve clicks this time. "Depends, Mrs."

Annalaura shook her head. She could return the favor. Give Gina time to get out her own story.

"I remember this and that when I was the six." Another sip. "My papa bring home the cameo. You know the cameo? It have the carving of the abalone—beautiful face of the woman. Papa bring it for my mama because he sold the pig for a lot of the lira. I was the six years and that cameo made my mama happy and my papa proud. That morning stay in the head of me all these years." Gina set the cup on the table.

"Nothing else from the six I remember because is not important. Is what you Lottie might remember important?"

Gina's words might just as well have been bolts of lightning shooting through Annalaura's chest for all the hurt they caused. "They asked me, you know. Both my girls."

"My boy ask me questions sometimes, too. About the days in Italia. What you tell you girls?"

"Both of 'em. Oh, not at the same time. Lottie, she asked me first, then Dolly. Both of 'em 'bout twelve, thirteen."

"Uh-huh."

Annalaura's mind flitted back to those days. She'd gotten away with it then. "Wanted to know why Dolly didn't look like the rest of our family. She the only one with blue-green eyes. The only one with straight yella-colored hair, the only one with nigh white skin."

"All Brugestown see that, Mrs."

"I told the girls," she remembered, "and Henry, too, Dolly was a throwback to my grandma, Charity. She was a full-blooded Cherokee."

"I new to America. Don't know that much about you Indians, but do they have the eyes of blue and hair of the yellow?"

Annalaura felt the chuckle coming on. Back then, she prided herself on her quick thinking. "Charity's husband," she giggled, "he was a mulatto." She looked at Gina. "That means his pa was a white man—with blue eyes and yellow hair." In truth, Annalaura had no idea the color of the man's eyes or his hair.

Gina smiled for the first time. "Mrs., you good. Now you worry about what the Lottie might remember about the Tennessee?"

Annalaura nodded again. "She wasn't but six years old. Would she recollect her mama's belly pokin' out? She wasn't there for Dolly's birthin'. I sent her out with my Aunt Becky. Still, there was a white-skinned baby in my arms the next day. She hadn't seen her papa in a year. Barely remembered the man. My Henry didn't recall him at all." Annalaura stared at

Gina. "Reckon Lottie could put two and two together?"

"At six? No. But you Lottie not six anymore."

Annalaura shook her head. "That's what I knows. Lottie goes to Champaign to fetch Dolly and sees her sister with Alex. Won't take her more'n a minute to put four and four..."

"And get the eight. Mrs., I see the problem."

"But, Gina, do you see the answer?"

Gina slipped her finger over her upper lip with its dusting of mustache hairs. Her forehead swept down into wrinkles. "No good for the Lottie to go, but she can do the talk to her papa. Tell him the why of you going to the Champaign place."

Annalaura sucked in her lips. She stared at Gina as she played out her friend's words. "No, Lottie can't be the one talkin' to John. To tell the truth, I've got to convince her 'bout Champaign as much as I does John."

Gina nodded.

Annalaura slapped down a hand as the smile crossed her lips. "Dolly. Her papa will do jest anything fo' her. I tells John I'm feelin' bad cause we can't send Dolly to that university she wants so much." She watched Gina's lips prepare their protest. Annalaura wasn't waiting to hear from her friend. She stood, walked around the table, bent down and grabbed Gina's shoulders. "That's it! I'm feelin' bad, and I wants to surprise Dolly when she comes back home. Surprise her with one of them college books on that French she loves so much."

Gina shook her head as she grabbed Annalaura's wrists and lifted them off her shoulders. "Oh, *Mama mia*, you believe your husband buy that story? What you tell him when you bring you Dolly back home ten days early?"

"Oh." Annalaura had always prided herself—though Aunt Becky declared pride a sin—on being a quick thinker, with Gina just a mite behind her in the thinking department. Not this morning. "You tellin' the truth. I ain't no good at this makin' up stories business." Annalaura stumbled back to her chair. Her head, right behind both eyeballs, started paining her. She slumped back into Gina's kitchen chair.

"Don't look like that Mrs. I never leave my Lorenzo in all the years I live here. I go to Danville only the two times. But if I ask my Lorenzo to go with you to the Champaign to bring back you Dolly, my husband, he say no." Gina grinned as she stood up and circled her hips. "At the first. But if I tell him you John say the yes to the Dolly emergency, but only if another woman keep you the company, then my Lorenzo…"

"You comin' with me then?" Annalaura clapped her hands. Gina had more smarts than a little bit. "You and me goes to Champaign to fetch Dolly. But John's not to fret 'cause Leotha is comin' with her." Annalaura started to stand. "But what does I tell John?"

Gina shook her head. "You Dolly, she have the homesick. She no want to spoil the vacation of the brothers so she come home on the train with the cousin of you." Gina looked satisfied with herself.

Annalaura wasn't the hugging kind, and Lord knew Gina's story wasn't all that hard to see through, but the woman had tried for Annalaura's sake. She wrapped her arms around Gina so tight her friend acted like she was gasping for air. Praise the Lord for Gina. Now all Annalaura had to do was polish up some of the truth for John—and find a way to get the two women to Champaign.

* * *

Annalaura was a good cook. Aunt Becky had seen to that. Declared her plain-lookin' niece would never get a husband unless she made her man's stomach jump for joy every day. This evening, Annalaura skinned and fried up the rabbit Cleveland brought over yesterday. She stirred up some corn succotash, flavored her green beans with smoked ham hocks, and made the flakiest of biscuits. She climbed down into her cellar off the back porch and picked out a jar of cherry jam. But she knew that wasn't enough. She'd gone out to the shed and pulled down the last of the stored coconuts. She taken a hammer to the thing to break into the shell. Seemed like it took her an hour to scoop out the coconut meat, but she'd done in all, and at the last minute stirred up a cake complete with frosting. It was all ready and sitting on the table when John walked in the door.

"What's all this?" He stood in the kitchen doorway, his work clothes soiled as usual. "I believes I smell me some coconut cake." He turned to his wife. "Annalaura, you feelin' all right? We don't have no coconut cake 'cept for Thanksgivin' and Christmas."

"Get yo'self washed up and set down fo' dinner. I got some news fo' you."

"Must be good news with all this business goin' on my kitchen table." He walked through the kitchen door to the outside pump, where he always cleaned up before supper. He walked back in and took his usual seat at the table head.

Annalaura took a plate and began ladling John's food onto it. She handed it to him before she took her own seat at the foot of the table.

"Go on, Annalaura. Tell it to me." He picked up his fork. "And I knows it ain't no good news. What done happened down in Tennessee?"

John wasn't a bad man. Annalaura always knew that even when he was throwing his fists at her. She'd just never been sure if he was the right husband for her. Lord knew, he'd tried awful hard ever since they settled in Brugestown. Bought her everything she asked for and then some. Didn't happen all that often, but John still had his gambling and bedding-other-women ways—whenever Richard Welles came into town. In the end, she reckoned John was like just about every other man. But he was a man who could figure things out way ahead of most others. Tonight, she'd tell him just enough to sound reasonable, knowing good and well he'd figure something else was up. But he would know anyway. He was the one who set up this test in the first place.

"It's Dolly. She didn't 'xactly hit it off in Tennessee." She watched his alarmed face. "No. No. I don't mean there's any trouble. Just that Tennessee wasn't like she wanted. Had Leotha bring her home."

"Leotha?" John poked his fork into fried rabbit. "What's Leotha got to do with it?"

"Cousin Richard didn't reckon it was right for a young girl to travel on a train all by herself, so..."

"Train?" John chewed between words. "What train? Where's Doug and Henry at?"

"Um." Annalaura caught herself. "I said to myself, ain't right to ruin everybody's trip 'cause Dolly got herself a mite homesick. Cousin Richard's thinkin', let the boys stay. Leotha can bring Dolly home."

John played with his succotash, "Leotha ain't never been up North in her life. Ain't never rid a train, neither. What's she doin' bringin' Dolly home?"

Annalaura shrugged. "Don't rightly know." She picked up a biscuit and stuck a knife into her jar of cherry jam. If she acted matter-of-fact, maybe John would let her be. Annalaura was no good at this stretching the truth business.

"So Cousin Richard gave the say-so for Leotha to bring Dolly back up here to Danville?" John laid his fork across his plate.

Annalaura stuck the jam-filled biscuit into her mouth. "Uh-huh." She hoped her muffled response could be taken for either a yes or a no. But Lord, had John said Danville? She took one more bite of biscuit. Her cheeks were about to puff out. "Champaign."

"Champaign? You say Champaign? What about that place?" John stared hard at her. "Annalaura, what ain't you tellin' me?"

She took her time chewing and swallowing her biscuit—time to come up with some sort of an answer. "Weren't no trouble in Lawnover." She held up her hand as she debated. John wasn't going to settle for nothing but the truth. But how much of that truth did he need to hear right now? "Cousin Richard and Leotha thought it best to get Dolly home quick like. I guess they got themselves confused over Danville and Champaign. Could be Dolly wanted to at least see that school she wanted to go to. Like make up for her disappointment with Lawnover." Annalaura forced herself to breathe as usual when all she wanted to do was hold her breath. She read her husband's face. Even if he thought she'd told a lie, would he call her on it?

"When's Dolly comin' home?"

Annalaura took in a tiny breath. At the least, he was giving her a minute or two more to get her story right. "Tomorra."

"Tomorra?" John shouted. "I can't pick 'em up tomorra. I got to work."

Annalaura scratched her cheek as though she were thinking. "I reckon I can take the Traction to Champagne. Pick the two of 'em up. All of us come back here tomorra night." She watched the frown climb over John's face. She counted to five. "I'll get Gina to go with me."

"Gina Maggiora." John broke apart a biscuit. "So she's in on this, too." He nodded his head. "And you two figurin' to take the Traction to Champagne?" He pulled the butter dish toward him. "Thought you was scared of the Traction. Said all them overhead 'lectric wires wasn't right. Fire makin' a train go couldn't be God's work."

Annalaura looked into her husband's eyes. Yes, he knew she wasn't telling the whole truth. So be it. He was the one who dreamed up this trap, and if John Welles thought Annalaura was supposed to feel bad about any of it, he sure was wrong. She kept her eyes locked onto his. John had planned this whole thing to get him an answer. Maybe Annalaura was the one who needed the answer. "Don't know when the Traction runs. Me and Gina will walk up to the highway to Bianchi's, take the bus into Danville, and catch the Traction from there." She picked up her fork. "Case we don't get back in time, I'll leave yo' supper in the warmin' oven."

Annalaura tackled her succotash, though John's eyes still bored into her forehead.

"If that's the way you say it's gonna be." John bit into his biscuit.

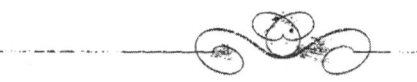

CHAPTER TWENTY-SIX

The knock on the door came in threes. At least Dolly thought she'd heard the tap-tap-tap series at least two other times before her eyes finally opened. She yawned. Sleeping hadn't been all that comfortable. Not only was the double bed lumpy and dosed with a whiff of unwashed bodies, the small, stifling hotel room with its one bureau, one nightstand lamp, raggedy carpet, drenched Dolly in perspiration, even with the window open. Tap-tap-tap. There it was again. On the outside door. Dolly stretched out an arm. Oops. She'd smashed her hand against Leotha's back. Her cousin lay curled up on her side of the bed, taking most of the sweat-stained sheet with her.

"Leotha!" Mr. McNaughton's insistent voice called through the closed door. "Open this door. I got to talk to you."

"Okay. She's coming." Dolly sat up. Must be morning, but how early? The room held no clock. The window shade, drawn last night, had at least a dozen pinprick holes in it. Beams of sunlight poured through. Definitely morning. Dolly shook Leotha's shoulders. Her cousin couldn't sleep through all this noise, could she? "Leotha, wake up."

"Uhh. You go to the do'." Leotha pulled the sheet over her head.

Dolly grunted as she stepped out of bed and covered her pajamas—now wringing wet with perspiration—with her night wrapper. She walked to the door, barefoot, and pulled it open.

"What you doin' up?" Mr. McNaughton moved Dolly back into the room as he stepped inside. He closed the door behind him.

"Uh..." Dolly looked to Leotha. No help there. Was a man supposed to be in her room when she was in her nightclothes? "Mr. McNaughton, how can I help you?"

He ignored her as he approached Leotha. He bent down. "Leotha, get yourself dressed." He turned to Dolly. "You, too. Leotha, you got to be at the station by half-past eight."

Dolly rubbed her eyes. "What time is it now?" She brushed away the sleep. "Eight-thirty? What station?" She stared at McNaughton, who stood fully dressed for the day.

"Where's her clothes?" He looked around the room, spotted Leotha's travel costume on the back of the only chair in the room. He walked over, gathered up a number of garments and tossed them at Cousin Leotha. "Get to steppin'. You gonna catch the eight-fifty-one back to Clarksville. Best if you call Dickie before you get on the train so he can pick you up in Clarksville tonight."

Leotha, still on her side, lowered the sheet to her chin. She stared at the man.

Mr. McNaughton threw up his hands. "Dolly, I'm steppin' just outside this door. You get your cousin dressed. I ain't 'bout to have her miss that train." He looked down at Leotha. "Gal, if you ain't out that door in ten minutes, I'm comin' back in and dress you myself!" He rushed across the room and slammed the door behind him.

Dolly stood flat-footed. She stared at Leotha, who still maintained her marble-statue look.

"Cousin Leotha?" Somebody had to answer her questions. "Why are we going back to Clarksville."

Leotha stared at her round-eyed. Dolly grunted. No time to bring her cousin back from the land of the living dead.

Dolly grabbed her own clothes, turned her back to Leotha, and dressed in under a minute. When she turned around, Leotha had managed to turn over onto her back though she still lay in bed.

"Oh, no, Cousin Leotha. I'm sorry about this, but I don't know what's going on and you're not telling me." Dolly pulled the sheet from Leotha, jerked her upright to the edge of the bed and pushed the dress over the woman's nightgown. Dolly grabbed Leotha's Sunday shoes and jammed them on her feet.

Ced up her own pocketbook, fished out the comb, and ran it through her hair. She pulled open the door. Mr. McNaughton paced the dingy hallway.

"Mr. McNaughton, what's going on here? Why are you sending us back to Clarksville when we just got to Champaign twelve hours ago?" Dolly didn't bother to hide her annoyance. This was Illinois, not Tennessee. "And what about my mother?"

McNaughton looked startled by Dolly's assault. No wonder. She wouldn't be surprised if she was the first female who'd ever spoken up to him.

He shook his head. "I told you, girl, I was takin' you to your mama. She's comin' here to Champaign. On the one o'clock Tra...whatever that thing is called."

Dolly stared at the man from Tennessee. She bit her tongue. She'd already been rude once, and whatever was going on, if her mama found out... She was already in enough trouble. "Traction. That's what it's called." She softened her tone. "My mother—Mama—is coming here—to Champaign—on a Traction?" Dolly tried to filter through the improbability of it all.

Leotha poked her head out of the door, her traveling hat sitting askew atop her head. "Uh, Mr....." Her words sounded dried up in her mouth.

McNaughton looked between the two females, his face furrowed in frowns. "Leotha, get a move on. You goin' back to Clarksville. Dolly, you and me, we're goin' to that school for a look-see."

"Look..." Now Dolly understood how Leotha felt when people around her were speaking gibberish.

Leotha began to shake her head. Slow at first, then so hard her hat wobbled. "No, suh." Leotha's voice rose.

Dolly pushed her own confusion aside. Who was that speaking out of Leotha's mouth?

"I can't do what you asks, suh. I gots to put Dolly in her mama's arms myself."

"No you ain't. I'll deliver Dolly to her mama in person."

Dolly was certain she saw Cousin Leotha sway. Only by grabbing the doorjamb did she keep herself from falling.

"I reckon I can't allow that, suh." Leotha held tight to the door frame.

Were colored women supposed to talk back to a Southern white man? Dolly was sure that was against Mama's Tennessee rules.

"If that's the way you want it, Leotha. But recollect, I can tell Dolly the why of it."

Dolly watched Leotha's knees buckle as the hat slid over one eye. Thank God her cousin didn't fall.

McNaughton glared at Leotha. "You think you 'bout ready to head off to that train station, now?"

Leotha nodded her yes while Dolly wondered about the "why" of it.

*   *   *

The chimes sounded out eleven times as Dolly sat on the bench next to an ivy-covered red brick wall. So this was the campus of the University of Illinois. Quiet now because this was summer—the heat of mid-June. She didn't need to close her eyes to imagine the place in September, when the leaves began to turn, students, hundreds of them, walking along the meandering pathways, carrying armloads of books, some strolling, others rushing to class. She took in a deep breath. To get this close—it felt wonderful. No, she would never be a student here, but now she had seen—lived—the student life. And he had brought her here. Mr. McNaughton.

"Hello there, Miss." A colored groundskeeper smiled in her direction as he mowed the vast expanse of lawn.

Dolly nodded back. For all the confusion going on around her, she was determined to enjoy each and every moment of this visit. After McNaughton had practically kicked poor Cousin Leotha onto the South-bound train, he walked Dolly over to the Illinois campus. All her efforts to sort out the mysteries of the why brought her naught. The man told her he had some business to conduct, and she was to sit on the bench until he returned. According to the Campanile clock, that was a good hour ago. He could stay as long as he liked as far as she was concerned. She would forever savor this—her pretend student time at the University of Illinois. She shut her eyes and imagined Claire and herself laughing, taking classes together, whispering about boys, speaking her already passable French with her best friend.

The clock bonged twelve. She opened her eyes. Mr. McNaughton was rapidly approaching from the direction of the Administration building.

"You 'bout ready?" He called out to her. "Your mama's Traction thing be here in just over thirty minutes."

Dolly slowly eased herself to her feet. She'd get her answers out of someone soon, but right now she wanted to enjoy every second. McNaughton had already turned up the path leading toward the train and outside the campus. She took one long last look around. She would remember this place forever.

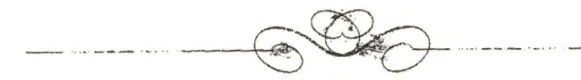

CHAPTER TWENTY-SEVEN

Alex looked at the oversized thermometer hanging on the outside of the two-story building where the Traction would stop. The thing read eighty-one degrees. Back home, this time of year—mid-June—it would have said ninety. He should have felt a mite cooler, but his body was boiling with sweat. Alex stared down the tracks, waiting for the first glimpse of this contraption that ran like a small train but had a big pole on top attached to overhead wires. The thing ran right through the middle of town.

"Mr. McNaughton…"

"Hush, girl. I think I hear the train a'comin." His daughter had peppered him with so many questions, he just about developed a headache, though it hadn't been all that hard to ignore her. She wanted to have him answer this, she had to hear him say that. He'd kept his promise to Laura. What he told their daughter depended upon Annalaura Welles.

"Does Mama know that Cousin Leotha won't be here?"

"Is that the Traction thing?" Alex spotted the round light on the front. Smaller than a regular train and painted in maroon and yellow, it glided toward him. But the only steam he felt, came off his body, not the Traction. Laura. What was he going to say to her? Everything he'd wanted to ask these sixteen years flew out of his head.

He looked around as outgoing passengers readied themselves to board. Most of them carried small parcels and valises. The Traction rattled closer. His heart thumped. As the first car passed, he looked into each and every window. Would he know her after all this time? The train ground to a stop. Dolly rushed toward the center car. Alex's feet refused to follow. He closed his eyes. If only he could offer up a real prayer—not the kind he said in church from memory. That kind didn't count for anything but show.

"Mama, Mama, here I am."

Alex opened his eyes to watch his daughter jump over and over. His gaze followed her waving arms to the Traction steps. A man stepped off, a big-boned woman with silver hair caught in a bun came next, and then... Good God, Almighty. Laura. She wore her traveling hat but he caught sight of the brown of her hair. This was, for sure, her. None other. Alex touched his own hair. Once blond, he'd gone almost all the way to gray. Eula was gray all over with a few white strands threatening here and there. Eula, who'd never had any kind of a figure in the first place, was now even thicker around the middle. But not Laura.

Why hadn't she changed? Was this more of the Lord's punishment? For what, he still didn't know. Laura. She looked the same as she did back in that Good-Glory-in-the-Morning summer when the feeling took over his heart and body back in 1913. No lines creased her face, and that body. Lord, old as he was now, that body of hers still made him just about go out of his head all over again. How could her tits still be sitting so high? Her as...

She spotted him. Laura. Dolly walked up to her mother, acting like she wanted to swarm Annalaura into her arms, gave it a second thought, and held back. That big-boned woman—a little dark complected but white, as far as Alex could tell—gathered Dolly into her arms. Could she be the Gina woman? Laura's eyes darted to the right, then stared at the ground. She looked straight ahead, then focused on her shoes. Finally, her head creaked to her left. Her eyes locked onto his own. Her mouth gaped open. Little tremors shook her though she struggled to break his hold on her. Her feet didn't move, and neither did his.

"Mr. McNaughton's over here, Mama." Dolly pulled herself out of the other woman's arms.

With one great jerk of her head, Laura broke the gaze and raised a finger to their daughter. "I know what you done." Her voice carried over to Alex. Did she raise it to make sure he would hear?

"I told you 'bout dancin' to that jazz music."

Lord, she even sounded the same. Alex had his mind set. All these years the why of Laura breaking her promise had driven him. He wanted his answers. That was all. Tell him the why of it, and he would head on back to Lawnover. He'd spend the rest of his life—if that's what a person could call that day-after-day dullness that greeted him every sunrise—with Eula Mae. But the sound of her—Laura—the look of her, Lord have mercy. He wanted her—all of her—just as much as he did when he first spotted her in that hiked-up dress back in his tobacco field. Nineteen-thirteen. Now it was too late.

Dolly turned toward him, her face looking more happy than scared. She grabbed Laura's wrist and headed toward him. Alex watched Laura pull back. Dolly tugged again. Annalaura moved not a foot.

"Mama! He's over here."

Laura stared at the pavement. The big-boned woman shook her head—she wore no hat. Alex's stomach washed up to his throat. Yes, he still wanted Laura, always had, if the truth be told. But just as plain—she didn't want him. He clamped his jaws together just as the Gina woman laid a hand on Laura's back. With Dolly pulling and the foreigner pushing, Laura finally made her way to him.

He knew better. Knew it was no use, but he couldn't help himself. He let his eyes roam over her frame from head to foot. Her traveling hat, summer dress, and squat-heeled shoes all looked serviceable enough, but nothing like the finery he would have laid all over her if she were his. He shook his head. This kind of thinking wasn't helping. If he could just get his answers. Annalaura finally lifted her eyes to the collar of his shirt—just like those first days in Tennessee. She didn't speak. He wanted to speak, but even if he could have found a voice to put to his words, his head refused to form a decent thought.

"Mama"—Dolly turned from him to her mother—"you two know each other? Remember?" The girl's face caught between curious and doubt.

"I Gina Maggiora." The big-boned woman stuck out a hand almost as work-worn as Eula's. "Pleased to meet-a you."

She sure sounded funny, but Alex took her hand. Unlike Eula, maybe a long time ago this woman might have been passable in the looks department. He nodded his greeting. His voice stayed in hiding.

"I take the Dolly for the dinner. You two do the talk." The Gina woman grabbed Dolly's hand.

"No," his daughter called out. "I want to know how these two met. I know Mama worked for him, but when?"

Ms. Maggiora shook her head as she clamped a hand hard on Dolly's shoulder. "You eat first, then you Mama tell you all the news."

"Uh-unh." Sound finally came out of his mouth. Alex cleared his throat. "No. We all goin' to eat at the same time." He looked at the foreigner. What had Laura told her? And what had the two of them cooked up? If he allowed them to separate, the foreign woman would take Dolly back to Danville on her own—sneak her away from him—leaving him with no hold on Laura. He pointed up the street. "There's a Five and Dime over there. The folks here in Champaign tell me we can all eat there together." He took Dolly's elbow and steered her toward the Woolworth's. Whatever those two women had planned for his daughter, he'd get his answers from Laura first.

*   *   *

It felt strange—not all that bad—but just not the way things ought to be as he led Dolly and the woman who said she was I-talian to the Five and Dime lunch counter. White and colored eating together in public. Couldn't be right. But one look told him this place would never do for the questions he had for Laura. He led her to the far end of the counter— Dolly and Miz. Maggiora were already busy reading their menus at the opposite corner. He pointed to an empty stool, four stools away from the nearest diners. Laura looked at him but did not take her seat.

"Laura, this ain't gonna do." He leaned in close to her. Lord, her skin smelled the same. Sandalwood and night-blooming jasmine together came out of her pores. "What we got to talk about, we can't do right here out in the open."

"We...I....Alex," she turned her eyes to his. "I wants my girl back. You done brought her this far, and I thanks you fo' it. But you must know it's best fo' us all if I gets right back on that Traction and go home with Dolly, right now."

"Home? In sixteen years you ain't never told me where 'home' is. You ain't never told me where my daugh..."

"Alex!" Laura stared down the counter line. "We can't talk like this. Somebody's bound to hear."

"Laura, I will have my answers. And don't bother makin' me no promises." He felt his head clearing. "You and me, we gonna talk. Here or somewheres else. But first, I gotta tell you what I done."

Annalaura grabbed the back of the counter stool. "Oh Lord, Alex, tell me you ain't told her 'bout ...'bout..."

"Set down." He guided her onto the stool and sat next to her. "Can you get Dolly's high school grades to the mailbox once you get back home?"

"Grades? What do you want those fo'? I told you she was 'dictorian of her class. Her and her best friend, they got the best grades of the whole graduation class." Laura looked at the menu in its holder. "'Course her friend's goin' to the college up here next month."

He wanted to lay his hand on her shoulder when he told her the news. This was the North, but not even in the North could a white man lay a tender touch on a colored woman right out in plain sight. Instead, he pulled the menu from its holder. The words blurred, but it wasn't the price of a hamburger, root beer soda, or a slice of apple pie that excited him, it was what Laura was going to say. "I done spoke to the Admissions Office."

Laura turned. "Admissions Office?" She looked at him as though his mind had slipped into old age. She leaned in closer. "Alex, what Admissions Office?"

He hadn't planned it. He wanted to be stern with her. After all, Laura had more than broken his heart. She'd given him his first and only happiness and then snatched it away. He wanted her to see that. But he couldn't help himself. He smiled. "I went to that college Dolly's so high on—the University of Illinois. I set it up so she can go. 'Course she's got to have good grades, but the lady, the Admissions lady, said they'd take her." He peered into Laura's face. "Don't seem to matter she's colored." He gave his head a slow shake. "Half-colored."

Alex couldn't determine which opened wider, Laura's mouth or her eyes. Both of them made little flutter-bird movements a half-dozen times before she got any words out.

"But...but that school—that college—it ain't free. It takes money fo' her to go there." Laura's hand made a move toward his, but jerked back like she'd just remembered it was poison ivy she was about to touch. "I...me and John...would have sent her if they was any way." She dropped her head and stared at the hand that had almost made contact with his.

Alex kept his arm on the countertop. He didn't dare reach out to her, but just maybe she might... "It ain't John's job to send Dolly to college." He watched while Annalaura stared at him. "It's mine. I'm her daddy."

Laura sucked in a breath. She grabbed at the top button of her dress—the one at her throat. She looked like she couldn't breathe.

"I put down money for her tuition. I covered two years' worth. I can cover a place for her to stay, too. You reckon that friend of hers would be her roommate? Admissions lady said I'd only have to pay half fare for that." He scanned Laura's face. "You all right?"

Lord, he wanted to hold her right now. Was that wetness he saw gathering in her eyes?

"You didn't...you shouldn't...you..." Laura fumbled in her pocket book and pulled out a handkerchief.

That square of cloth looked familiar. Hadn't he given her one just like that back in nineteen-fourteen? Yellow linen, with a dancing ballerina on it, lace around the edges? He'd bought that square of cloth in Clarksville the same time he bought that doll for Lottie and the horn for little Henry. Memories. No good for him. They hurt too much.

"I want you to know that I ain't takin' back college for Dolly, no matter what. But you and me, we got to talk. I don't need to tell her the how-come I'm payin' her school bills. Told the lady to tell Dolly she won a scholarship. Ain't that what you call it?"

Laura grabbed his arm, gasped, and let go. "You sendin' my dau..." she swallowed hard, "yo' daughter to college?" She blinked away the water puddling in her eyes. "And, you ain't told her 'bout me and you?" She swallowed. "I thanks you ever so..."

"Told her 'bout me and you?" He spoke to the counter. "The law might say we done wrong, but God knows we ain't done no such thing. That's all that counts with me." He glanced over at Dolly and the foreigner. "Dolly needs to go to that school and sign some papers. All of us, together, can drop her off there. Your friend can stay with her."

"No need fo' you to go back up there. Me and Gina can take care of that."

"No." He stared at Laura. She was trying her mightiest to make short shrift of him. "Once she's in that Admissions place with your friend, you and me are gonna talk."

"Talk? Where? Somewhere up at the school?"

"No school. We can't have nobody hearin' our words. We gonna talk at the hotel."

"Hotel?"

"In my room."

"Me and you? In yo' room? Oh Alex, I can't…wouldn't be right. John… he my husband."

He leaned in closer. "I reckon I know who your husband is." He sat up straight on the stool. "If you was my wife, I'd never left you for nothin'. Never mind a whole year."

"Uh…" Laura dropped her head.

"You know what I want. My answers. Laura, God's truth. I ain't never forced you into nothin'. All those years back, you coulda told me no and I'da listened. Wouldn't want to hear that word, no, from you, but I wouldn't force you into anything you didn't want to do. Ain't never forced no woman. I ain't 'bout to start now. You come to the room so's we can talk. I need that." He turned back to the menu. "Real bad."

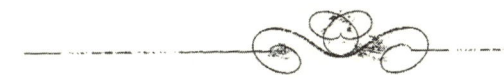

CHAPTER TWENTY-EIGHT

"Miss Welles, sign here, get us your high-school transcripts, and I just bet we can find a spot for you in the graduating class of fall nineteen-thirty-four." The Admissions Officer—the sign on her desk read Miss Morefield—smiled at Dolly as she handed over a fountain pen.

Dolly's hand shook as she took the writing implement. Would her signature even look like her own? "I don't understand." How many times had Dolly said those same words in the forty-five minutes since Mr. McNaughton and Mama dropped her off at the Campus Administration building and ordered Mrs. Maggiora to stay with her. As usual, the man would answer none of her questions, and mama, a woman who never cried, looked weepy.

"How did this happen? Any of it?" Dolly's voice hummed between ecstasy and skeptical. "I know you said something about a scholarship, but how?"

Miss Morefield busied herself with the papers on her desk. But hadn't she just done that?

Gina laid a hand on her shoulder. "Dolly, no look the horse with the present in the mouth."

"I didn't apply for a scholarship." Bless Mrs. M. She was trying. Dolly laid down the pen. "How did you—the university—know about me?"

Miss Morefield studied her ink blotter. "The donor wishes to be anonymous." She fidgeted with her inkwell. "Wanted to give a scholarship to a bright colored girl from a small Illinois coal-mining town." She finally looked up to Dolly, her eyes brightened. "After all, this is the Land of Lincoln." She stood and walked around her desk. "Welcome to the University of Illinois." She pointed to her office door.

"A bright colored girl? From a small town? But how did you—the U of I—know I went to Brugestown High?" Dolly sat still.

Mrs. M. clamped her hand on Dolly's arm and pulled her to her feet. Her mother's best friend practically shoved her through the door.

Dolly decided to try a different tact since the one she attempted with Cousin Leotha failed so miserably, "Mrs. Maggiora, mama said she and papa went to work for Mr. McNaughton years before I was born. But I forget if that was before or after my sister came on the scene. Do you know?" Honey poured from her mouth.

"Uh-huh." Gina Maggiora certainly was strong as she guided Dolly down one hall, up the next, down the staircase, out the Administration Building's front door, and across the campus.

"Mrs. Maggiora?" Dolly pleaded.

"You one lucky girl. My Lorenzo and me, we can only pay for our Guido to go to the college in the Carbondale. You win the scholarship, and all you do is ask the silly questions. Even if you don't know you good fortune, I pray the rosary tonight for you to do the understand."

"Tonight? What time does the Traction leave for Danville?" Dolly was grateful, she really was. A miracle had just happened, but sometimes didn't some people even question the saints?

"You mama tell me to take you back to the hotel. Wait in the room. She come for us when she through with the dinner and the talk."

The two stepped off the grassy path leading away from the

campus and onto the sidewalk of Champaign. This was enough. Dolly planted her feet on the pavement. "Talk? What do those two have to talk about that I can't hear?"

Mrs. Maggiora spun Dolly around. "You a smart girl, for sure, but you still not the grown-up. Until you be the grown-up, you keep the tongue in your mouth still." She clutched Dolly's arm, the left one this time. "Now come on and no more the questions!"

Dolly grimaced under Gina Maggiora's pull. She'd keep her mouth shut. For now.

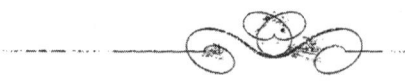

CHAPTER TWENTY-NINE

Oh, Lord, spare me this night. Annalaura stood in the hallway next to Alex's hotel room. He waited right behind her, the door wide open. Where was she supposed to sit? The room was small. She paid that no mind. Her rooms in Brugestown were just as little, even if she did have four of them. No, it wasn't the size of the room that bothered her. It was that bed with its dingy patchwork coverlet. Praise Jesus, she spotted a chair. She rushed into the room and pulled out the ladder-back chair before Alex could get to it. He closed the door, turned toward her and sat on the bed.

Her mind flew back seventeen years—to that August day. She'd lived in a barn just a mite bigger than this hotel room. Her platform bed was only four or five slatted boards nailed together, with a skinny corn husk mattress on top. Her bed. John's bed. Oh, Lord. Every word Alex said about not forcing her was true.

"What you want to ask?" She looked at Alex, who stared back at her. Back in nineteen thirteen, she'd said yes to him to feed her children but, Lord, what excuse could she give now?

Alex worked his mouth, shook his head, and looked down at his shoes. She'd never felt like she wronged John. Contrariwise, she put more than half the blame on her husband. All the excuses he gave her. Even before that first night with Alexander, she knew such a doing would hurt a husband, but if the truth be told, Annalaura figured John had left her forever. She was as good as a widow. But tonight, John wouldn't let go of her mind.

"I knows you don't want to hear it, Alex, but me movin' into yo' house back then wasn't goin' to work. Just like you tried to put Dolly up at yo' place this week. It wasn't clear thinkin'."

He lifted his eyes and shook his head. "You gotta do better'n that, Laura."

Would he ever stop calling her Laura? Every time she heard that name come off his lips she...oh, Lord, don't let her keep those kinds of thoughts.

"Alex, back then I didn't know I had a husband. Not a real honest-to-goodness one livin' in the house with me. Takin' care of me. Thinkin' 'bout me first over everybody else in this world." She took in a breath to give Alex time to sort out her words. He wasn't the only one who needed to do the sorting. "But, you, Alex, you had yo'self one then, and you got yo'self one now—a lawful wedded wife."

"Ahh," came through his parted lips. "You tellin' me you done what you done 'cause of Eula Mae?" He shook his head. "You know better'n that. What about your own Aunt Becky and Old Man Thornton?" His voice rose. "And don't tell me you didn't know nothin' 'bout Ben Roy and Hettie. Did you ever see Fedora cuttin' up and actin' all out of sorts over her husband's colored family livin' right there on her own back forty? Eula Mae woulda taken to the idea of you and Dolly livin' in the house after a spell."

Annalaura shook her head. "I thinks in yo' heart, Alexander McNaughton, you a good man. A lovin' man." She took in a deep breath as she stared into those eyes. "But you don't know squat 'bout women."

His lips parted again. "I know what I feels for..." he clamped his mouth shut.

"Miz McNaughton may be white, but at the center of it all, she a woman, first." Annalaura blinked her eyes closed for a second. How many women had John taken to his bed in these twenty-nine years? "I knows how I'd feel if my man took up with another woman. Fact is, that is how I feel." She'd said too much.

Alex stared the look of understanding at her. "Your John's a man. A fool of one for sure, but he's a man." His voice dropped as he cocked his head toward her. "Ain't many women like you, Laura. A man who had you for a wife don't need to stray. You're more'n enough for any man." He looked down at his hands as his fingers opened and closed. "But there ain't no women like you. So special." That redness came over his face. He looked up. "Wives like Eula, they expect their men to take their pleasures somewhere else ever' now and again. Know it's bound to happen. Wives don't take no harm by it."

"And you thinkin' Miz McNaughton would have taken no mind? I'd been livin' there right under her roof. Next to her kitchen where she takes her meals every day? Me and yo' baby."

Alex took fifteen clicks of the second hand on the bureau clock before he spoke again. "Eula Mae ain't why you broke your promise to me, Laura. Don't act like she's the reason. I've got to know." He kept his eyes on her. "Did you run up North with John Welles 'cause you…you had feelin's for him?" Alex looked like all the air had gone out of him. "Laura, today, right now, do you love him—John Welles?"

Love John? Why, in almost all these thirty years, hadn't that thought ever entered Annalaura's head? She'd married John because Aunt Becky called him the best colored catch in all of Montgomery County, especially for a plain-faced girl like Annalaura, way too smart for her britches. She hadn't thought about love back then. John asked Becky for Annalaura's hand. That was a miracle all by itself for a man carrying more than his share of God-given good looks. Her aunt said yes first. Annalaura just nodded her head when her turn came. "Love him?" She turned back to Alex. "He's my husband. I ain't got no choice. I got to do right by him."

Alex looked at her without nodding yea or nay. "I ain't asked you 'bout doin' right." He sat taller on the edge of the bed. "I ain't asked 'bout choice." Alex moved to his feet. "I asked if you loved John Welles. Was that why you left me and took off with him?"

Annalaura stared at this man who'd pulled her out of that deep hole of no hope back in nineteen-thirteen and sometimes made her heart glad for the doing. Oh, Lord, give her strength.

"Come here, Laura. I want to hold you when you give me your answer. If I can feel your body against mine, then I'll know if you answer me true."

Why was the Devil making her stand up from this chair? Who was it that pushed her feet toward Alexander McNaughton? Oh, Jesus, she was in his arms! He pressed her close—her breasts searching his chest. His hands moved her just enough so she could look into those eyes—so like Dolly's. Lord, help her remember her place. John's wife. Alex's lips curved into a little smile as his right hand went to the top button of her traveling dress. His fingers slipped the button through the opening without a fumble. Her knees trembled, but his other hand held her tight. Oh, Lord. She leaned her head into his shoulder as he flipped open button number two, then three, four, and finally five. She felt her chest fight to keep her heart inside when his hand reached under her dress. Thank the Lord she'd worn that new binder thing Lottie got her for Christmas last. Brassiere. That's what her girl called the contraption.

"Laurie." His breath brushed her neck as he ran his tongue around her ear. He slipped her dress to the floor. His eyes sparkled.

Annalaura hung on to Alex's waist as his hand traced the bottom of her brassiere around to the back. He pulled her close and unhooked the back of the binder, his manhood all the way ready. The white brassiere with its little rosebud center fell to the carpet.

"Uhh," She tried to get out words, but nothing came. Her

arms held on to Alex. Why didn't she cover herself?

Alex sucked in her nipples slow, one by one. He dropped to his knees and guided her feet out of the dress. He ran his hands up her cotton stockings and unrolled her best garters. Her stockings slipped to her ankles. Alex kissed the inside of her thighs as he lifted her feet, one by one, out of her stockings.

"Silk, I'm gonna put you in silk. Silk drawers. Silk stockings. Silk wrappin's around your tits. Nothin' but silk and lace for you." His voice muffled.

"Ale…" She almost got his name out of her mouth as he grabbed her around the hips and lowered her bloomers.

He pulled her naked body to his face. "Tell me now, Laurie…" his voice low and husky, "who do you love?"

Oh, Jesus. He spread her legs. His tongue explored…

"You."

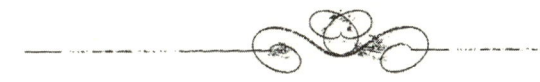

CHAPTER THIRTY

Eula Mae wasn't having it. No matter how many ways her brother told the story of why she couldn't go back to her house on Tuesday afternoon—had to wait 'til Friday—she didn't believe a word of it. Eula sat in Fedora's front room, the one where Mama Thornton had decreed only company could gather, and Fedora had dared not defy her mother-in-law though the woman had been dead these twenty-five years. Eula listened to the goings-on in the kitchen as Fedora gave what-for to her cook. Apparently the woman's custard pie had been too runny for Fedora's taste though the colored woman had worked for the Thorntons since right after Tilly was born. Fedora was no better at hiding the truth from Eula than was Ben Roy.

"Well, I got that fixed up." Fedora huffed her way onto Mama Thornton's chesterfield. "Had the nerve to say her niece stirred up that custard pie. Got the eggs from a hen that wasn't layin' all that much." Fedora fanned herself. "I hear tell this heat gonna break by Saturday mornin'. Jest two mo' days of this stuff."

"Fedora, when's Ben Roy comin' back to the house?"

"Ben Roy? He's out in the fields. Some of them sharecroppers is work-shy. You know how that is, Eula Mae. Why you askin' 'bout Ben Roy?"

"Cause either him or you are takin' me back to my farm."

Fedora looked as though Eula had just called upon Satan to pay her a visit. "You ain't supposed to go home 'til Friday noon. Tomorra."

"I want to go home, now." Eula tapped the arm of Mama's tapestried chair—her pride and joy and forbidden use by any of her children.

Fedora shook her head so hard, the top knot threatened to come undone. "It ain't time enough...I means you got to let this thing play itself out, Eula." She leaned closer. Was that a wink in her eye? "Now Ben Roy done fixed it so there's enough time to get the place cleaned up good befo' you come back home."

Eula looked at her hands. They'd never been pretty—knuckles stuck out everywhere, rough as a man's, and red as a rooster's comb—but they'd never been idle. "Wasn't it you, Fedora Thornton, who ordered me back to my house? Told me it was my bounded duty? Well, I'm goin' back to my house, all right. I'm gonna be the one stayin'. Law or no law. It's Alex who's gonna be keepin' you and Ben Roy company these next years."

Fedora frowned. "Eula, you talkin' out of your head again." She sighed like she dreaded telling Eula the same old story. "I told you Ben Roy was gonna get rid of that gal. That Dolly. Well, he done it."

"Where's Alex?" Nobody had come out and said direct that Alex was not at the farm, but with the looks her brother and sister-in-law tossed one another, even a person with one eye blind, and the other half out of the socket, could figure that Alex had taken off somewhere. That cramping in Eula's stomach that made Eula feel like she was about to lose her breakfast and lunch all in one big batch, swept over her again. Call it the Devil, or maybe it was the Good Lord, but she just knew in the marrow of her bones that Alex had gone up North with the girl. Maybe even to see her—that Annalaura—again. Why was Eula feeling pain now? She was dead. Had been since that day. She'd even written in her journal about her feelings and her promises. So why did it hurt so much now? She blinked at Fedora.

"Uh, you askin' 'bout Alex? I reckon, Eula, you don't need to bother yourself with the ways of the thing. All you need care 'bout is that gal is out of your house."

Eula stared at Fedora. Could her simple-minded sister-in-law be right? Why should Eula let anything Alex did or didn't do bother her now? He'd killed all the love she had for him when he took that woman not only to his bed but to his heart. In those first twenty years of their marriage, Eula loved Alexander McNaughton with everything in her. She couldn't tell him, of course. Didn't know how. That was then. Not now. No more tipping around her husband—making Alex happy no matter what he'd done to her. Cooking, sewing, running his farm, spreading her knees if and when he wanted. Never mind when and what she wanted. Do it all with a willing quickness and a smiling face because her world told her swallowing hurt was her wifely duty. Reverend Hawkins never did say a word about a man's husbandly duty.

"Fedora, I reckon I can walk to my farm. Not 'but three miles."

"Eula Mae, you can't do no such a thing. Not in this heat. You'll give yo'self a head stroke."

Eula stood, walked to the front hall and picked up her already packed valise.

"Hold on now, Eula Mae." Fedora sounded panicked. "I'll get out the old buckboard. I reckon I can take you home."

* * *

Most of the paint on the seat had peeled off the bare wood. The horse was a tad on the old side, but Ben Roy's buckboard still rolled along in working order. The conveyance didn't get much use these days. Ben Roy drove his Model T, and Fedora didn't go anywhere without Ben Roy's say so. This steamy Thursday noontide, Eula had given the say-so. Fedora flicked the reins, and the horse turned onto the path to Eula's farm house.

"Eula Mae, just go in and take a quick look around." If Fedora didn't lift that frown off her face, it would join the two dozen other wrinkles already covering her olive-complected skin.

Eula climbed off the buckboard while Fedora wrestled with stationing the horse. "No need for all that, Fedora. I thank you for the ride, but you can get on back home. I can tend to my own house myself."

"Lord, no, Eula Mae! Ben Roy won't…"

"I know. I know. My brother won't have it," Eula stepped up to her back porch. "There's gonna be plenty of things Ben Roy not gonna have. But there's one thing he is gonna have—Alexander." She walked through her porch and opened her kitchen door.

Fedora was still fiddling with the reins, trying to tie them to the old hitching post. Eula moved into her kitchen. She looked toward the top of the door. Yes, it was still there—the bolt lock that had hung up high way before she and Alexander ever moved into the place. Back then she wondered why in the world the previous owners had put a lock on their door. Not this morning. Eula stretched, grabbed the old bolt and wiggled it into its holding place on the door jamb. There. Let Fedora do her damndest to break her way into Eula's kitchen.

Damndest? Eula shook her head. She'd never been a swearing woman. Reverend Hawkins declared when a decent woman took to using such language, it was because she was too prideful. The pastor's cure for a woman thinking herself good for something more than groveling at her husband's feet? Work all the harder to be submissive, and never, ever, forget you're only a woman, designed by God to do your husband's bidding with nary a complaint. Damn Reverend Hawkins, too.

"Eula? Yo' do' is stuck." Fedora pounded. "Eula Mae, what you doin' in there I can't see."

"Fedora, why don't you go on back and get Ben Roy. Tell

him I want to see him." That should get rid of the woman.

"Ben Roy? Don't know when he'll be back. You be all right 'til he gets here?"

Eula put on her cheeriest voice. "I just need to see for myself. You run along. By the time Ben Roy gets here I might just have had my fill."

"You might be comin' back to my house, then?" Fedora sounded so hopeful. "Tonight?"

Quiet like, Eula let out a laugh. "I just need a spot of time." Eula listened as Fedora walked off the porch and climbed back onto the buckboard. As soon as her sister-in-law clicked her tongue at the horse, Eula turned to look at her kitchen. "Oh, my Lord!" She grabbed the back of a kitchen chair to keep herself on her feet.

When Alex announced the arrival of Kate Welles and that other one into Eula's own home last Saturday, Eula called on brother Ben Roy to rescue her. She'd run off like a scared rabbit. Left everything that was hers to them—to touch, to move, to do with what they pleased. Eula hadn't been there when one of them, probably Dolly, did this. There on her very own kitchen table sat the white bowl with its sprig of blue flowers and its thin ring of silver—her wedding bowl. She knew it wasn't much, but she'd put such store in it, used it only for Thanksgivings and Christmases. Then Alex ruined it all. Eula reached toward the bowl, but her fingers refused to touch. That night slammed into her head. Her husband had taken that very bowl down from its shelf, ordered Eula to fill it with a dozen of her best, batter-fried pork chops, and taken the whole thing to that woman—Alex's whore.

The tears came at about the same time her chest thumped in and out. Then the great howling sound ran out of someplace deep inside. Though for the life of her, she couldn't pinpoint the source of that wail of pain, Eula could good-and-well feel the trembling in her knees. She walked herself hand-over-hand around the chair to the seat, each step threating to throw her to the floor. She lowered herself onto the chair. Great anvils—two, maybe three, might have been four—pounded against one another in her head. Her breath got all caught up in her sobs. She had to lay her head down. Good Lord, have mercy! What was this? No, it couldn't be. Her journal? The one she used in the long-ago to keep account of all the workings of the farm. The one telling her that carefully accounted for supplies—jars of peach preserves, green beans, rashers of bacon—were missing. Gone because Alex had taken them to her—Annalaura Welles. Now here it lay on her kitchen table, splashed in sunshine. Eula's account journal. She smothered her face in her arms.

How long had she cried over that book? Her eyes were just about shut when she lifted her head off her kitchen table, but the sun still shone. Couldn't have been more than twenty minutes before she got her breathing halfway back. Her eyes pained her when she tried to open them wider. The first thing to greet her sore eyes was her wedding bowl. The silver looked like a mouth mocking her. She hadn't laid hands on that piece of crockery since the day she climbed on a chair and put it and the journal on the very tippy-top shelf of her safe. And Lord knows, Alex had never bothered to touch either one.

She arched her back straight. Could she do it? Could she touch the journal? Was it still there—the vow she'd written sixteen years ago? Eula pressed her hands against her eyes and swiped away the last of her tears, the way she wanted to wipe away all of Alexander McNaughton. She inched a hand toward the book. She saw fresh fingerprints on the dusty cover. Somebody had handled her book, laid their hands across its pages. Eula's fingers hovered over the cover. Her hand opened and closed. She squinted through the tiny slits that were her eyes. She wanted to see what she'd known all these years but buried within her soul— what a fool she'd been. She knew where the page was before she flipped open the back cover. A sheet of paper was missing, torn out, but it wasn't that sheet. Eula turned one page, then two, and finally four. Sure enough, there it was. The vow she'd made all those years back.

I, Eula Mae Thornton McNaughton, testify this day I have become, at last, the perfect Southern wife.

She shook her head as her finger traced the lines that other Eula Mae had written back then.

This day I resolve to do what I must. If, and when, my husband ever returns to my bed, I will hold him harmless for any pain he has ever put on me."

A whippoorwill called just outside her kitchen window. She looked up to see a hummingbird poking at her pink roses. The sun blazing through her window should have blinded her, but instead, she peered at the sunbeam landing across her scrubbed pine floor. Little specks and sparkles danced out of that beam. Eula felt the smile muscles in her face twitch and tingle. How long since they had worked? She looked down at the account book.

When he looks through me, I will always pretend that I don't know that it is the love of another he prays to possess. To my God, this day, I resolve to be the best white wife who ever lived in Tennessee.

They hurt, her smile muscles, when they first went into action, but the broader they spread the better Eula felt. She was old when she wrote those words, nigh close to forty-five. How could she have had so little sense? Eula turned toward the sunbeam. The truth put itself together out of those little sparkles. Mama Thornton had suffered through her husband's dalliances with Rebecca McKnight's mother and then Rebecca herself. Truth. Her father, Old Ben, really had taken his own colored daughter to bed and seeded her a baby. And Mama buried the horror of that pain deep and looked the other way.

Fedora still looked the other way though Hettie had been gone these two years. Eula stared at the last line on the page—her signature. *Eula McNaughton.* She'd not only been a fool all these years, she'd done a sin against God. Wasn't she commanded to love herself as much as her neighbor? When she allowed Alex to treat her worse than an acre of stunted tobacco plants destined to be plowed under, she'd defied the word of God.

Where was that writing pen? She spotted it on the floor. Must have rolled off the kitchen table when whoever tore out that last page in the journal and scribbled down some note or other. Eula bent down and picked up the pen. Now where was the ink bottle? There, on the bottom shelf of her safe. Eula got up, her smile muscles working good now. She grabbed the bottle and returned to the table. She shook her head as she turned the page on her vow.

Eula dipped her pen into the ink well. She scooted her chair closer to the table and bent over. On a fresh, clean sheet, and in big block letters Mama said only those with poor schooling used, Eula printed out the words:

PAGE TWO

I, EULA MAE THORNTON (won't be McNaughton much longer) AM A WOMAN WORTHY OF LOVE. I'VE GOT MORE THAN MY SHARE OF SMARTS AND GOD-GIVEN TALENTS. I KNOW IN MY SOUL THE LORD WILL NOT PUNISH ME FOR SPEAKING THE GOD'S TRUTH. I HAVE WASTED THITY-SEVEN YEARS OF MY LIFE LOVING A MAN WHO CAN NOT LOVE ME BACK.

I RESOLVE ON THIS JUNE DAY, IN THE YEAR OF OUR LORD, NINETEEN HUNDRED AND THIRTY, TO BE THE WOMAN GOD ALWAYS INTENDED ME TO BE. A WOMAN WHO RESPECTS HERSELF. A WOMAN WHO LOVES HERSELF EVEN WHEN THOSE SUPPOSED TO LOVE HER DO NOTHING BUT CAUSE HER PAIN.

NOO MORE. THIS DAY I TAKE MY HEART IN MY OWN HANDS. I WILL MAKE MY OWN HAPPY FORECER AFTER.
—Eula Mad Thornton

She left the book open on her kitchen table to let the ink dry. Eula had always been tone-deaf, just mouthed the singing words in church. This afternoon she heard her own voice singing out loud—"Praise the Lord and Pass the Ammunition." She walked up the stairs and into her bedroom. She marched over to Alex's chiffarobe, stretched and reached for Alex's valise. Gone. Uh-huh, Eula was right. Alex had taken off North. Never you mind. She pulled Alex's clothes from the chiffarobe and dumped them in the hall. She walked to the bureau and opened the drawer where he kept his things. She yanked the drawer from its moorings and dumped the contents over the hall bannister. Passing that ammunition sure felt good. Took her fifteen minutes to tote all of Alex's junk out through the porch back door. She had an armload, but she managed to dump every last bit—shoes, shirts, overalls, drawers, socks, his one good suit—all onto the bare ground. Good. Let the dust grind into each and every fiber.

"Praise the Lord, and pass me more ammunition!" She shouted to the cows in the barn and the chickens in the coop. She went back to her kitchen. Lord, it sure felt good to be free, and God, don't forget to damn Alexander McNaughton.

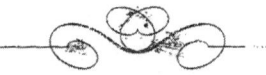

CHAPTER THIRTY-ONE

The electric street lamp with its harsh glow flickered through the window and across his shut eyelids, the shade not pulled down in Alex's haste. He'd been asleep, but it had been a light doze. The light roused him. Good. He couldn't afford to drift into a deep sleep, not this night. Was she really in his bed? Had they really made love a bit ago? Alex dreamed of this moment so many nights. Even on those few need visits with Eula, it was Annalaura Welles who drove him. As his fingers, hands, and body popped to life tonight, he was afraid to breathe. His right arm held shoulders and a back that felt made of the softest silk—just like Laura. But suppose he was still dreaming? He dare not move. His heart thumped. What to do? Lay still, not moving, not knowing, or trust that it had all been for real?

Alex moved his free arm across his own body, inching closer to the figure lying in his arms. Please, Lord, let it be for real. His fingers made contact with an arm—her arm? He lowered his hand. His fingertips explored the contours of a breast—firm on the inside, soft on the out—just like Laura's. And that nipple where he'd sucked last night—at least he thought he had in his dream. He had to find out the real from the workings of his longing mind. Alex lifted his knee and let his leg slide, gentle like, down the woman's hips. Curved and bouncy just like Laura's. He moved his hand to the belly and let his fingertips trace down to the woman's… She stirred. Laura.

"Laurie, you awake?" The street light washed out most of the moonlight. Alex couldn't figure the real time.

"Alex…I…we…me and you…" Her voice. Laura's. She laid her hand against his chest and wriggled away from him.

Thank God, Almighty, she was no dream. She, his Laura, laying there beside him in this hotel bed, was real. And so was last evening. "I heard you, Laura. I remember what you said." He tilted her chin toward him. The glare from the electric light washed her mouth in cinnamon. "I know you tryin' to find the words to tell me this is a dream 'cause the real can't be right." He withdrew his arm and turned to face her. "I'm married. You're married. That's what you want to say to me." He shook his head. "We both know them papers we signed so long ago don't have nothin' to do with what we feel for one another. We need this to be forever."

Laura searched his face from forehead to chin, but lingered longest on his eyes.

"I come up here to Illinoise to get me my answers." Alex laid a hand on her shoulder. "I didn't want to hear your words over no telephone line." Oh, Lord, the feel of her. "I didn't want to hear it with that friend of yours standin' right there. I had to see you, feel you, to know your words was tellin' me the truth." He kissed her forehead.

Laura's body shuddered. "Alex, I can't tell you no lie." She looked up at him. "Oh, I wants to all right, that's it's all right fo' the two of us to have feelin's for one another." She aimed her eyes just passed his head. "You and me, we both got peoples we made promises to." She worked her mouth as she turned to him. "But John—he broke his promise to me befo' I ever did to him. Alex," her words sounded strangled, "if you gotta hear me say it, then, in God's truth, I do have feelin's fo' you. Whether I wants them or not."

Her words, so quiet, barely reached his ears. Alex pushed her to her back. "I heard you right, then. You got feelin's for me." He felt the smile covering his face. "You ain't been out of my mind, not nary a night for sixteen years." His words came out faster than he intended. "Plantin' time, growin' season. Especially when the tobacco was no higher than your...than your thighs." That first time he saw her—his sharecropper's wife with her dressed hitched up in the heat of the field, those bronze legs—oh, Lord, his breathing came deep and slow. He pulled back the sheet and stared at those legs, as delicious looking as they were in the long-ago. "Ever' night, ever' day, I thought only of you. Even when I come into Eu..."

"Alex, I ain't never meant to put you in that kind of pain." Her face blinked out of his vision for a moment.

How had he lived with all that hurt? "I reckon I know how come you did it. Took off with...with John Welles. But I want to hear you tell it to me out of your own mouth." He fell onto his back.

"You wants to hear me say it? Why I settled on Illinois?"

"Why you settled on...him, John Welles."

"Oh, Alex, this ain't easy." She turned her head away. "Back then, I knew feelin's, no matter how deep, couldn't be paid no attention." She frowned as she turned back to him. "You understand?"

Understand? Alex had walked around these sixteen years with his heart wrung in two. "I told you 'bout Chicago. Me and you and Dolly could've gone up there to live. You ain't had no righteous cause to take off with John, leaving me with nary a word."

"I been livin' here—in Illinois." She turned to him while he stared at the electric light shadows on the opposite wall. "It's a good place fo' colored, but, Alex...even Illinois ain't no paradise for people like you and me."

"You and me?" Like the two of them—a white man and a colored woman. That was her reason? Could he bear to hear any of it? He turned his head to the far wall, the pain in his chest hitching up again.

Laura grabbed his hand. "Alex, you gonna hear me out. I

had me mo' babies than just Dolly to think about. Cleveland, Doug, Lottie and Henry. I couldn't leave 'em. I couldn't..."

"Laura, I ain't asked you to forget about your other children." He talked to the wall.

She squeezed his hand. His fingers couldn't answer back. Not yet.

He took in a deep breath. "I told you I had places to put each and ever' one or 'em. And I would have worked hard to send them all to school. Saw to it that they finished eighth grade." His neck creaked as he eased his head around to face her.

She leaned toward him and kissed his cheek. "I do recollects. Alexander, I tells you again, you a good man." She pulled the sheet to her chin. "I ain't never goin' to stop havin' feelin's fo' you, but I had to do what was right fo' all my children." She looked at him. "T'is the truth, Dolly's the only one finish high school, but all my others 'cept Cleveland went through the eighth grade." She rolled toward him, the sheet still in place. "They all fine men. And Lottie, she married a good, hard-workin' man. I know I ain't done right by you, Alex, but I done best fo' my children."

Alex laid a hand across her covered body. "I'm mighty pleased your young'uns have got on so well, Laura. I ain't never meant to take that from you. I just needed my answers." He looked up at the lightbulb hanging from the ceiling. "Maybe I shoulda done more thinkin' about your children. I reckon I did let that one slip by me, but, Laura, so did you." He turned to face her.

Her eyes met his. She frowned. "Slip by me? Children?"

He sat up in bed, his back resting against the wooden head rest. "Not your children. You ain't slipped there. I can just about understand the children part of it." He looked down at her. "But you did slip. Ever' night for sixteen years I wondered. Why did you leave me after you made me your promise? Why promise me anythin' at all if you wasn't goin' to your word?" His voice rose. "Why didn't you reach out to me sometimes? Sixteen years, Laura. Lord knows you musta wanted to write or telephone me the why of it at least one of them years."

Laura looked about to cry. "You right, Alexander. I knows you see that I done wrong by you." She worried her hands. "Why didn't I write you? Where to? Yo' missus would have found any letter I wrote to you." She shook her head. "What I done was wrong fo' you, but, Alex, you actin' like I had a choice." She searched out his eyes. "I ain't had no real choice. Wasn't gonna work with yo' missus, but that ain't all of it."

"No?"

She scooted up next to him, the sheet drifting to her waist. "John, he picked me and Dolly up right after you left Aunt Becky's cabin that morning. Laid us in the back of a wagon. Didn't know where I was goin'. Thought John had killed you and he was taking me to see yo' dead body."

He looked into her eyes. You thought…John… Laurie, I didn't know."

"I couldn't get my thinkin' clear. Oh, I thought I was doin' just fine that mornin', but I wasn't." She searched his face. "I just had yo' baby, one you pulled out of me yourself. It was a hard birthin'." She leaned into him and rested her head on his chest, her bare breast pressed against his side. "What thinkin' I could do told me you wasn't dead. Not yet. But I knowed in my heart it was up to me to save you." She looked at him. "John, he promised me he hadn't killed you. Yet. He ain't said, but I knowed to keep you safe I had to do what he wanted." She shut her eyes. "I just prayed you was alive. We was already in Illinois, I knew that 'cause I read the billboard sign, but John ain't told me nothin' 'bout where we was goin'."

He put his arm around her, squeezing her against him. "You tellin' me you went up North with John Welles 'cause of me? To spare me?"

"I did that, but it ain't like John didn't finally allow me to choose something." Laura blinked. "The train was already into Illinois when John come to me. He told me to pick."

"Pick? He 'llowed you to choose him or me? Fine time to

tell you that when you was almost to Chicago by then." He stroked her bare back.

"I reckon that's what he really meant—pick betwixt the two of you. But John just told me to choose the place to get off the train—Chicago or some little town. I knowed what he meant. Pick some place where you'd never think to look, or Chicago where you were bound to find me and Dolly."

Alex breathed in, his eyes moved back to the play of electric light on the far hotel room wall. "And when he gave you that choice"—his chest tightened and his hand stopped moving—"you chose him."

Laura played little circles across his bare chest. Oh, the touch of the woman.

"I picked Danville and a chance of livin' a decent life fo' my children." Her sigh caught in his ear. "I knows you don't want to believe, Alexander, but I chose what was right fo' you, too. That's why I ain't let you know where we was all these years. I knowed you'd come after us, me and Dolly. That would have been a hurting for all of us, including you."

He grabbed her wrist and pushed her hand away from him. "You done all this—kept me away from my daughter, kept yo'self away from me 'cause you thought it was best for everybody?"

She grimaced as she nodded her head.

"You thought you done right, keepin' me in misery fo' sixteen years?" All the years of pain pounded at him. "You tellin' me I got to accept that?" He searched her face. Lord, she was still beautiful. The pounding in his heart slowed. "Laura—Laurie—I can make myself believe you done what you did 'cause you thought it best fo' your children and...me. But I gotta to hear you say it again. What you said last night. Say it all this time." His heart played skippy-lou in his chest. "Me or John Welles. Say it."

She tugged at the sheet. "Alex, it ain't gonna do no good to hear me say it."

"Oh, I want to hear it offen your lips, all right. I've got to hear it more to really believe it."

She looked across the room where the outside electric light still made funny shapes across the wall. Her lips took nigh onto a minute to form the first words.

"You got to understand, Alex, John Welles ain't a bad man. He done everythin' in his power to make up fo' the way he treated me." She turned to him, her eyes damp, "I believes he might even have some likin' fo me." She swallowed. "It's just that I fear I ain't the only one in his life he treats like a wife." Her hands, both now clutching the sheet at her waist, opened and closed. "You, Alexander McNaughton, you always made me feel like I was the onliest woman in the world fo' you. The onliest one you ever loved. Ever could love." She laid a hand over his sheet-covered leg as she tilted her head toward the ceiling, her eyes closed. "God, Jesus, Aunt Becky and every colored woman ever been done wrong by a white man, all y'awl please forgive me, but I loves Alexander McNaughton over John Welles."

Alex watched those full lips as the sounds pushed off them like summer honey. His ears played the music sound of her words over and over. Had he heard right? Her eyes, those amber-colored eyes where he got lost every time he looked deep into them, they'd tell him if he'd heard right. "I believe you said the truth. It's me you love betwixt the two. Always have." Words stuck in his throat. His breathing felt hot, heavy, even in his own body, "I thank you for tellin' me. Now show me."

Laura closed her eyes. Her body swayed. She snuggled against his chest. Her hand moved to the top of the sheet at his waist. She inched the rough cotton half-way off his manhood. "This night, Alex, I'm yours. Teach me what pleasures you."

He led her hand to his manhood. What pleasured him? Annalaura Welles. All of her. Any of her. He laid back against the head rest while she stroked him top to tip. His hand found her tits. She stroked his manhood while he started his kisses at her forehead and traveled to her nose. He pulled her face toward his. He sucked those lips into his mouth. Laura gasped, and their tongues met. How long and how many times did they kiss? Time and place flitted in and out of his head. Laura lurched, and he laid her on her back. He continued his kisses down her throat to her breasts, still as pear-shaped as he remembered. He ran his tongue around her nipples. Something tickled his ear. Her tongue. Good God, Almighty. Her belly, soft and firm at the same time. He still got drunk in the smell of her—sandalwood and jasmine for sure, but more. Down there at her triangle of hair, she smelled like Laura—a scent that sent the shivers up and down his body over and over. Oh, Mighty Lord. She was planting kisses on the top of his head, her fingers stroking down his back. He spread her legs. Laura bent her knees. His chest felt ready to explode as he pushed himself up. Her hand, as delicate as the finest cotton lace, guided his manhood into her. Oh, Good God, Glory!

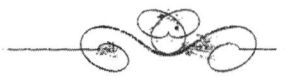

CHAPTER THIRTY-TWO

"Oh, my goodness, Mrs. Maggiora, what time is it?" Dolly shaded her eyes against the sun as she peeked around the edges of the drawn window shade in the hotel room. "Is it morning already?" Sunlight spilled across her bed. "Thursday morning?"

Gina Maggiora, sitting in the only chair in the room, fully dressed, looked worried. "And we been here in this room all the night."

"Didn't you sleep at all? When I laid down for my nap—Mr. McNaughton got me up awfully early yesterday—you were sitting in that chair. You're still there."

"Don't you-a worry about if I sleep or no. You get yourself up and the dress on."

Dolly, her head still fogged with sleep, looked around the room. Wasn't Mama supposed to pick up the two of them—she and Mrs. M.—right after her dinner outing with Mr. McNaughton? Weren't the three destined to catch last night's final Traction to Danville? Dolly frowned as she scanned the other side of the lone bed. A little rumpled like someone had laid on it briefly and then only fully-clothed—Mrs. M. No sign Annalaura even paid the room a visit last night. Dolly looked at the family's neighbor, "Where's my mother?"

Mrs. M. got up from the chair and retrieved her

pocketbook from atop the single bureau in the room. "You hurry it up. We call the sister of you." She nodded toward the pitcher sitting on the skinny, about-to-break-apart nightstand. "I bring you the wash-up water from the bathroom down the hall."

Dolly slid her feet to the worn carpet, her toe catching in the bare weft. She tapped her head to clear it. "Lottie? Didn't you call my sister last night to see who could pick us up in Danville? We'd get there about ten o'clock." She turned to Gina Maggiora as yesterday sorted itself out in her head. "The Traction, why didn't we catch it? I remember the train was scheduled to leave Champaign at nine-fourteen. That gave us plenty of time to get to the station." Dolly watched Mrs. M. pick up her pocketbook. Why did the woman keep her eyes from Dolly? "I guess I must have overslept when I laid down for a nap after dinner? Why didn't you or Mama wake me?" Dolly looked around the room for any sign, no matter how small, that her mother had been there. "She should have been back from her dinner with Mr. McNaughton way before nine o'clock."

Mrs. M. fished around in her purse as though Dolly had left the room for a leisurely stroll, leaving Gina Maggiora all by herself. Dolly reached into her valise and pulled out clean undergarments, her head trying to shake off the last of her fog-shrouded sleep. Let's see. Mama and Mr. McNaughton had gone to dinner leaving Dolly and Mrs. M. at the hotel. How long could one dinner take? Dolly turned her back to Mrs. M. and poured water from the pitcher into the little basin on the nightstand. Best to get dressed as quickly as possible. As she dabbed the threadbare washcloth over her body, thoughts shuffled themselves in her head like a deck of cards.

"You hurrying?" Mrs. M. sounded harried. "I wait in the hallway for you to put on the clothes." She opened the door.

"Has something happened to Mama?" Dolly raised her voice.

Mrs. M. stepped into the hallway as though deafness had

attacked her.

"Where's Mr. McNaughton?"

The door slammed closed. Dolly stared at the spot where the fleeing body of Gina Maggiora had just stood. Hurry. She tried to push the button through the opening in her midi-blouse but her fingers shook so. "This can't be right." Her own out-loud voice told her just the opposite. She'd heard of midnight suppers from the movies and the romance novels when she and Claire sneaked forbidden peeks. But her mother had never been the romantic type. Ridiculous. Why would Annalaura Welles want to have a romantic supper with Mr....? She laid a hand over her stomach. Dolly had been a star at Brugestown High in algebra, geometry and calculus. She could for sure add. And something here in Champaign didn't add up. Or, did it? Annalaura Welles and Mr. McNaughton? What could they have to do with one another? Yes, they both lived in Lawnover at one time. Yes, Mama had worked on Mr. McNaughton's tobacco farm, but that was all. Wasn't it?

Dolly felt her face grow hot. She plunged her hand deep into the water pitcher. She bent over and splashed her face. No, this couldn't be. But why had Mr. McNaughton really come to Champaign when her brothers could have easily driven her straight to Brugestown? Was his real interest not her, but...and if that was so...? Dolly straightened and searched the room for a mirror. She saw none. She grabbed her purse, yanked out the little looking glass Lottie had given her for graduation and held it to her face. Oh, God, who did she look like?

"You coming?" Mrs. M. popped her head through the just opened door.

Dolly rushed into the hallway. If anybody knew the truth, it sure would be Gina Maggiora. "Mrs.—my mother—she and he, Mr. McNaughton—they went off last night. Together."

"You mama?"

"And Mr. McNaughton. Dinner. They were going to

dinner to talk. Talk about what?"

"You mama tell me they want to do the talk...about the days of the old in the Tennessee." Mrs. M. didn't sound as though she believed her own words. She hurried down the hall, her back to Dolly.

"Talk about Tennessee? And talk all night?" Dolly caught up with the woman at the top of the stairway leading down to the lobby.

Mrs. M. scurried down the stairs, Dolly deliberately right behind the slower-moving woman. Gina Maggiora wasn't escaping Dolly, not when she held onto at least part of the truth. Mrs. M. grasped the bannister as she descended the stairs. Dolly stuck out her own arm. Oh, God! Dolly's skin was just a shade more tan than Gina Maggiora! She shook her head. Mama called Dolly a throwback to her Cherokee great-grandmother. Dolly felt her cheeks burning. Her stomach filled with cramps. Didn't Indians have red-tone skin? Then there was her brother, Doug. Sometimes, in certain lights, and mostly in profile, her brother looked like the Indians in the picture shows and her never seen but often described Cherokee ancestress, Charity—Indians.

"Ahh, we here." Mrs. Maggiora looked over at the empty hotel desk counter. "Where the clerk?" The panic was beginning to show in the woman's body as well as her face.

Dolly clutched her pocketbook. She stared again at her arm and hand. Not a red tinge anywhere. And her hair and eyes. Nobody else in her family had light-colored hair and blue eyes. Her eyes had always been a peculiar shade of blue, anyway—tinted with specks of green. Almost the same shade as... "Mrs. Maggiora." Dolly's voice squealed higher than she intended.

"Yeah?" The white desk clerk walked out of a nearby door leading to the lobby, carrying a coffee mug, the steam flowing off it. "What'd you want?"

"The telephone I want. For the long distance."

"Cost you fifteen cents for the first three minutes. A dime to the Illinois Bell and the rest to the hotel."

Mrs. M. dug in her purse for the coins. Dolly rushed up to her. Somebody had to tell her the truth. She tugged the neighbor's sleeve.

"Mrs. Maggiora, I know you know what happened—what happened between the two of them. My mama tells you everything. Even the stuff she doesn't tell my fath…" Oh, Good God, her papa! What had Annalaura Welles done?

Dolly stood transfixed in the hotel lobby, Gina Maggiora slipped away from her grasp, slapped down the coins, and reached out for the phone the stubble-faced clerk held in his hand. Dolly played it out in her mind as Mrs. M. shouted at the long distance operator. What had he said—Mr. McNaughton—he had known Annalaura since before Dolly was born? Dolly clutched at her stomach. She turned to Mrs. M., who held up a hand.

"Lottie, that you?" Mrs. M. clamped the mouthpiece tight against her mouth. "I talk-a too loud?" She moved the piece away. "Is better? Lottie, I no got the much time. I want you cook the dinner for you papa and my Lorenzo." She turned her back to Dolly and dropped her voice. "We come home as soon as we can. I can no leave you mama here. You please tell my Lorenzo that is the emergency right now."

Emergency? Was that what Mrs. M. said? Dolly rushed toward the counter and reached for the telephone receiver. If the neighbor refused to tell Dolly the truth, maybe Lottie would—if her sister knew. She'd been six when the family left Tennessee. Surely, she would remember if Alexander McNaughton paid frequent visits to their mother.

Mrs. M. spotted Dolly approaching. "Lottie, I got to do the hang-up now. Good-bye." She slammed the phone back into its cradle before Dolly could touch it. The hotel clerk swept the instrument to his side of the counter.

"Mrs. Maggiora. Gina!" Dolly shouted. "I've got to know."

Gina Maggiora checked to see if she'd snapped her purse shut. She smoothed her dress. Then she looked at Dolly. "Some things you don't need to know until you the woman."

She wagged her head. "I know you think you the woman because you very smart girl, but not yet." She turned to the counter clerk. "Tell-a my friend to wait here in the lobby. I take this girl to the breakfast"—Mrs. M. looked at Dolly—"but I no answer the lot of questions. I give her the time to think what good her questions do to her Mama and her Papa." Mrs. Maggiora patted her pocket book. "Her Papa, John Welles."

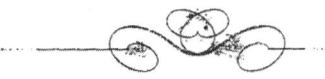

CHAPTER THIRTY-THREE

Annalaura slipped her head off Alex's arm and inched her way to the edge of the bed. His snoring told her he was still in a deep sleep. After three rounds of lovemaking last night, Alex finally fell into his slumber. She eased her feet to the floor and pushed herself off the mattress, taking care not to rustle the old ticking too much. She had to do this right. Annalaura tipped-toed to the chair where she'd carefully placed the newspapers she'd bought yesterday afternoon before she met Alex. She looked around for the clothes he had taken off her last night. There. She spotted her bloomers. She stepped into them and shimmed her dress over her head. She fastened the buttons to the top. No time for that brassiere contraption with its too-many hooks and eyes. She'd put that on later. Annalaura climbed back in bed, newspapers in hand. This time she plopped herself onto the mattress, upright, with as much noise as she could muster.

"Uhh." Alex grunted.

Should she kiss him? Annalaura wanted him awake for sure. The splashes the sun made on the wall told her it was ten o'clock, if not half-past. But if he awoke with her kiss, he'd want another round of lovemaking. The why of the bloomers and the dress. If he had to work to get her naked again... Not that she minded all that much—in fact, she'd never felt such a thing like Alex brought out in her last night. Three times. That feeling made her want to jump clean off the bed, soar to the heavens, and shout direct into the ears of the angels, but time was running out. She rustled the newspaper as she opened it to the Real Estate section.

His arms stretched, the fingers wide, Alex fumbled for her. One hand made contact with her dress-covered leg.

Alex jerked awake. "Laurie?" He sounded groggy and a little worried. "That you?" He opened his eyes. "You still here." Satisfaction poured out of his mouth.

She took his hand in hers. She did love this man. How could she make him understand that sometimes even love isn't enough? Alex squeezed her fingers as he struggled to sit up beside her.

"What you got your dress on for?" His grin was lopsided. "It's a brand-new day. We get to start all over." His hand went to the middle button of her dress.

"Hold on." She made herself laugh. "We got time fo' that later. I wants you to look here." She pointed to the newspaper.

Alex dropped his hand. "Look at what?"

"This here's the Places-Fo'-Rent section in the *Chicago Defender.*" She looked up at him. Alex had to believe the whole thing came from him—his choice. Lord, this hurt, but there was no other way.

"Places for rent?"

Please, Lord, let him see trust in her eyes.

"Up in Chicago. You and me." She gave him a gentle poke with her elbow. "Where we gonna live."

"Ohh?" Alex reached for the newspaper, curiosity on his face. "Chicago? Laura, you really mean it this time—thinkin' about us livin' together?"

She kept her eyes on the paper. "Can't be no marriage, though. Me and you together. Won't be no preacher sayin' words over us." She'd told him what she had to, but her words hurt her more than she ever thought. "My boys—ever' one of 'em—been up to Chicago. They say the colored people all live on the South Side. Near the water. Lake Michigan, I believe they call it."

"Colored people? South Side?" He shook his head. "We ain't gonna live there. I been up there"—he watched her face—"lookin' for you."

Looking for her? How many times? Oh, Lord, just what she feared. "But, Alex, there ain't no place else in Chicago for colored to live 'cept that South Side." She watched him work her words into his head.

"But, Laura, you'll be with me. Can't we live anywhere we want up North?" His forehead furrowed into a frown.

"Alex, I told you Illinois was a good place fo' colored—better'n Tennessee—but I ain't told you it was Paradise." She watched him stare back at her. Did he really think he could live right out in the open with her in a white neighborhood, even in Chicago? She clutched his hand. Lord, she didn't want to hurt this man all over again, but she had to do what was right for all of them, especially him. "Look here." She pointed to an ad. "Says we can rent two rooms, connected, with the bath down the hall. Thirty-five dollars a month."

He read the ad. "That's on the South Side. Don't want that."

Annalaura sucked in a breath. Time to bear down. "My boys tell me the North side of Chicago is the high-tone side. Probably only colored maids get to live there, and they only get a little room behind the kitchen in white folk's houses. But there's a lot of foreign folk—somethin' like my friend, Gina—livin' just outside of Chicago."

"No, you ain't gonna be no maid. Not when you with me. Tell me more 'bout these foreigners." The first hint of doubt crept out of Alex's voice.

"I hear tell they from a place called Poland. They likes to stick together. Gina, she from Italy. Said it wasn't no good place fo' her and Lorenzo to settle."

"Poland? Where's that?"

"Gina tells me it's way up north from Italy. She said that's in Europe."

"Hmm."

"Alex," she struggled to pace herself without him knowing, "This town up near Chicago—I think they calls it Cicero—the rents 'bout thirty-eight dollars a month." She looked at him. "I ain't got no money 'cept what John gives me. Can you pay thirty-eight dollars a month?"

He searched her face like she was speaking French out of one of Dolly's schoolbooks. "Thirty-eight dollars a month? I got me money in the bank—a nice chunk. I reckon I could..."

She forced a half-smile on her face. Lord, don't allow her courage to fail. "You can take care of the rent fo' me and you and Miz McNaughton, too?" Before he got out his answer, Annalaura hurried her own. "I reckon you don't need worry none 'bout Dolly's schoolin'."

He turned to her, his eyes flashing. "Dolly? Ain't nothin' gonna stop me from sendin' my girl to that school she sets such store on. As for Eula—why, I ain't...hmm."

"I knows you gots lot to think 'bout." She looked up at him under her lowered lashes—just like those first days in Tennessee. "Is we gonna rent up in Chicago forever? Together, I mean. You reckon we'll be able to buy a house someday? Got one now—in Brugestown. If somebody will sell us a house, you gonna have to sell the farm to pay fo' it?"

Alex jerked toward her. "Sell the farm?" His voice rose as he shook his head.

Annalaura clasped her hands in her lap. Lord don't let her plant these thoughts in his head too fast. "I'm tryin' to figure—tryin' to see how all this is gonna work. Alex, how you plannin' it?" She fixed her face to show patience and trust.

"Uhh...I reckon..." The little tics in his right eye told her he was struggling to think it all out. "Laura, I want you with me. I just ain't thought that far ahead 'cause I never ever believed this could happen anyplace outside my dreams. Me and you. Together."

She reached for his hand without planning the move.

Right now, she wanted to take away any worry he felt, but to do that, she had to hurt him a little to make things right for him in the forever after. "Alex, if this thing's gonna happen, best if you figures it out now." Annalaura glanced down. "I means, how we gonna do it? Run off to Chicago?" She looked up. For a second, she felt like such a thing could really happen. She shook sense into her own head. "What you reckon I should tell my children? Cleveland, he already don't say much to me. Reckon he remembers. Doug and Henry and Lottie, I think they was too young. When they do find out, I reckon my boys gonna have a time forgivin' me fo' what I done to their father. Lottie, too." She wanted to put a jog in his memory, but, Lord, she was the one surprised. Real tears watered her eyes. "You reckon, maybe Dolly, one day, might forgive me? She's thinkin' in her head that John Welles is her papa." Two tears trickled down her cheek. "Most likely, none of 'em ever want to see me again."

Alex gathered her in his arms. She knew she had to play-act to help him see the impossible, so why did she feel so sad? He brushed his lips against hers and stroked her back.

"Laurie, I ain't never gonna let that happen. You ain't gonna lose your children—not a one."

She reached her hands around him and hugged him close. She nestled her head into his shoulder. God help her. Why did this man always say the thing that made her want to sink into his arms forever? She bit down on her lip. She couldn't afford to get this comfortable. "I knows you only wants what's best fo' me. Same as I wants fo' you. I loves you so much fo' the way you is, but who gonna run yo' farm when we up in Chicago?"

"Uhh." He pushed enough away from her to look into her face. "Maybe Ben Roy could..."

"Mr. Ben Roy?" The name startled. She broke free of his embrace. "Miz McNaughton's brother?" She had to calm herself. "I reckon he would help out his sister, sure 'nough." She frowned. "He gonna be the one to run yo' farm and sell yo' tobacca?" She watched Alex's eye twitch. "You thinkin' he gonna share the money he gets from sellin' yo' tobacco with you? 'Specially since you'd be with me?" She waited while he figured out the rest. She squeezed encouragement into his hand, and this time, she meant it.

Alex worried his mouth. "Ben Roy, he ain't much of a forgivin' man. He's still riled up about Wiley George, and that's been close to eighteen years." His face lit up. "I reckon I could get me a man to run the farm. Pay him a bit and have him send the rest of the money up North to me."

Annalaura cocked her head like she was thinking serious about what he had just said. She had to give Alex time to figure for himself that this world just wasn't ready for the two of them. Not together.

He let go of her hand. "Hard to trust a hired hand to run the place. If I ain't there, no tellin' what Ben Roy will get up to."

Annalaura lowered her eyes. "Alex, what you know 'bout the law?" She talked to the floor. "Can Mr. Ben Roy take them acres from you and put 'em in Miz McNaughton's name if you come stay up North with me?" Aunt Becky always told her to make a man do right by his woman by asking him questions she could already answer for herself.

"Ben Roy don't own them acres." Anger barked out of Alex's mouth. "No, they ain't rich land like the Thornton place. But they can grow tobacco near 'bout as tall. And that land is all mine! I ain't Wiley George. I ain't never took nothin' from Ben Roy Thornton! Not even his sister."

She nodded. Alex was doing a fine job of working out the impossible all by himself. She'd just give him a little nudge.

"Miz McNaughton wouldn't want no divorce or nothin', would she?" Annalaura didn't wait for Alex to take the considerable time his face showed he needed to come up with the answer. "Tell me, Alex, how do the law work in Tennessee if the husband run off with another woman?" She held her breath. "A colored woman."

Alex tried to speak, cleared his throat, and looked at her. "Divorce? Colored woman? I ain't never thought...divorce?"

His words stumbled out. "Reckon divorce would be some kind of a scandal for Eula Mae." He parceled out his words like he was being asked to pay top dollar for a prized hog. "Eula don't want no divorce, I'm right sure. Truth be told, I ain't never thought much 'bout it." Alex worked his lips. "You don't reckon she'd..." He shook his head. "I can't believe she'd go that far."

Best to keep quiet.

The frown on Alex's forehead drew deep into his skin. "But Ben Roy don't want no scandal, that's for sure. He knows all about you and me. From sixteen years back. He won't say nothin' to nobody outside the family. Still, I reckon word would spread quick if Wiley George or Tilly got hold of the news that I'd run off to Chicago with you." He searched her face. "I could talk to Ben Roy. Bargain with him. Give him part of the farm to keep up for Eula if he can make sure Wiley George and Tilly don't find out nothin'."

She shook her head as slow as she could manage. Alex needed more of the for-real to sort this thing out. "I reckon I could work. 'Course you'd have to make what money Ben Roy did send up North stretch mighty far, what with Dolly's schoolin' and all." She lowered her eyes again.

"I could find me a job up there in Chicago." He reached for her hand. "Don't rightly know what kind of work. All's I know is farmin'. But, Laura, if it means bein' with you, I'll make a way."

Oh Lord, she'd have to dig deeper. "My boys say they got good jobs up in Chicago—in the stockyards. Pickin' up after the animals been killed. Stokin' the furnaces over at the steel mills. Hot work. Dirty work."

"Them's jobs for coloreds." He shook his head.

She kept her voice soft. "Alex, you'd be with me. We'd have to live in the colored part of Chicago and,"—s he sucked in her lips—"you'd mostly likely be doing colored jobs."

He grunted. "What kind of pay they give?"

Oh, Lord, was he really thinking about doing it? "Twenty-five cent an hour. Ten hours a day, six days a week if you can talk the boss man into lettin' you work."

He mumbled the figures in his head. "Fifteen dollars a week? 'Bout sixty a month." He looked worried. "Laurie, that ain't gonna be enough. Not with rent being 'bout thirty-eight. Lord knows, I can't depend on Ben Roy given' me my fair share from the tobacca sales."

She forced her face into its own frown. "I knows you don't want it, but I'll gets me a job. It ain't like you'll have yo' wife workin'. Can't nobody say you put yo' wife out to work, 'cause I won't never be that—yo' wife." The frown turned to real. She scanned the faded leaves in the carpet. "So's Dolly can get her schoolin'"

"I told you I'd take care of that." He sounded riled.

Good. Annalaura shook her head. She didn't want to, the Good Lord knew, but Alex was leaving her no choice. "I know you gonna take care of Dolly. She's yo' child." Annalaura let her words hang in the air. "'Course she can't know nothin' 'bout that...lessen you told her."

"Dolly? No, I ain't told her nothin'." He looked at Annalaura. "But I aims to."

Annalaura held on to her hands to steady herself. If, in all this mess, she could just keep Dolly from knowing. "She sets high store on John bein' her daddy." Her hands and her voice trembled. "I don't reckon my girl's gonna take to the truth too well—leastwise not when she find out 'bout me." She laid her hand on his cheek. "By and by, I knows she's gonna love you." No play-acting this time.

Alex slid her wrist from his cheek. "He's been good to her, then?"

"Real good." Annalaura's voice choked in her throat, and she hadn't planned it. "Give her time. She's gonna take to you real good, too." She looked up at him. Her eyes watered.

Alex wrapped his arms around her. He rocked her for one, two, three minutes as she lost the battle. Tears splashed down her face.

"What you tellin' me, Laura—high rent, low pay, Eula, yo'

children…" He kissed the top of her head. "This ain't gonna work, is it?"

The cries came up for her belly, rattled around in her throat, then beat at her heart. Her body shook in his arms. She wanted to spare him pain. Looked like all that agony fell on her instead. "No." The word gurgling out of her mouth carried on her sobs.

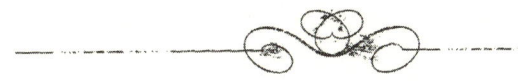

CHAPTER THIRTY-FOUR

"Little Ben, check that shotgun again," Ben Roy barked as he mashed down on the Ford's gas pedal. "Make sho' they ain't no shells in it." He looked into the rear view mirror. Wiley George sat splay-legged in the back seat, hungover as usual. Wouldn't do for his son-in-law to hold an actual loaded gun in his hands. The look of three white men toting weapons ought to be enough to scare the Welles boys back up North. With a message.

"Grandpa, I done checked this gun more times than I care to tell," Little Ben groused.

That boy was gettin' to be too much like his damned father. Ben Roy shot one warning look, then turned back to the road. Only one truck ahead of him, and that one was so far in the distance he couldn't even read the license plate. No other vehicle came at him from the opposite direction. Five more minutes, and he'd be at the turnoff to the Welles place.

"Hand me that gun." Wiley George wobbled himself upright and hung on to the back of Little Ben's seat. "Got to teach them nig...coloreds a thing or two."

"You get the damn gun when I says you can have it," Ben Roy shouted over the engine's clanking.

Wiley George wasn't worth cow dung on a stick, but he and Little Ben would have to do. Those Welles boys were

Northerners, and everybody knew Up-North colored didn't know anything about minding their manners.

"There it is, Grandpa! Comin up!" Little Ben pointed to the road leading off the highway.

"I got eyes, boy. I can see the turnoff." He steered off the highway and onto the road leading to Dickie Welles' acres and his house.

"Damn, if that don't look like that brand-new car I spotted a few days back." Wiley George plopped back into the seat when Ben Roy's right front tire hit a rut in the road. "Gimme that gun now, Ben Roy."

Ben Roy jerked the car to a stop and pulled out the ignition key. The engine rumbled itself down to nothingness. He looked over at the Model A. Sure enough, the Welles boys had come back from the Carruthers place. They'd know by now their sister was back up North. Leotha and her big mouth. What else did they know?"

"Little Ben, hand me that box of shells." Ben Roy, still in the driver's seat, slipped four bullets into the shotgun he'd be carrying, knowing good and well he'd only use the weapon if he absolutely had to.

Johnny, Rebecca's boy, never was all that far off his mind. One of those quick shivers ran over Ben Roy's body. He shot a fast look at Little Ben. Had the boy noticed? Thank the Lord, no. The kid was way too busy loading up his own shotgun. "You don't do no shootin' unless I give the word." Ben Roy glared at his grandson. "You got that in yo' head? And I don't want you havin' no more'n three shells in the gun no how."

Little Ben turned to his grandfather, "Three shells? But there be more than three colored in that house. Supposin' I miss?"

"This ain't no damn game, Little Ben!" Ben Roy shouted. "You gonna shoot Leotha, too? I knows she's colored, but she's a female."

The boy shrugged his shoulders. "Coloreds, colored. They misbehave—man, woman, or child—don't make no difference."

Ben Roy leaned over to the passenger seat and swiped a hand across Little Ben's left ear. "I told you this ain't no game. You ain't never been to no lynchin'. Ain't as much fun as you thinkin'. Now get yo' God-damned daddy out of my car!"

"Where's my shotgun?" Wiley George stumbled when his son opened the door and grabbed his arm. "Where's my shells?"

Ben Roy had on his best disgusted look when he heard the front door open.

"Mr. Ben Roy, suh?" Dickie Welles stood there in his work overalls like he'd just come in for dinner after working the fields this Thursday morning.

Ben Roy watched the man's eyes widen as he spotted the three shotguns.

"What is…?" Was that a tremble in Dickie's voice? "What can I do fo' you, suh?"

Wiley George pushed Little Ben aside and walked on unsteady legs to just behind Ben Roy. "You can get them up-North nig…" He shot a quick look at his father-in-law. "Them cousins of your'n. Get them out here!"

Ben Roy pushed his unruly son-in-law aside. "We just want to visit a spell with you and Leotha." He looked down at his shotgun, pointed at the ground. "We 'bout to go huntin' fo' possums. Them boys here? I sees their new car."

Leotha popped her head out next to her husband. "Y'awl like me to bring you some sweet tea?" Her eyes looked scared.

"Cousin Richard, who's that at the front door?" The shorter of the Welles boys pushed between Dickie and Leotha and took a step onto the front porch. "Possum hunting, huh? We've got good hunting in Illinois, too. I'm Doug, pleased to meet you."

Ben Roy wanted to shake his head at this boy's bad manners, but thought better of it. If he could get his message across without a fuss, so much the better. Get Alex back where he belonged, then teach these uppity colored a thing or two.

"Uh-huh. I'm Mr. Thornton to you." Ben Roy caught a glimpse of the second brother when he strolled up and pushed Leotha completely out of sight.

"And I'm Henry Welles."

Ben Roy watched Dickie clamp a hand on the younger boy's shoulder.

"I reckon I know who you are." Ben Roy stepped in front of Wiley George. "Your folks worked my sister's acres back befo' the Great War." He turned to Henry. "Reckon you don't remember me." He spat on the ground. "Been up North too long."

"That's fo' damn sure." Wiley George let out a noise that sounded more guffaw than laugh. "Needs some lessons in manners."

Ben Roy kept his eyes on the Welles boys, but he sure wanted to wallop Wiley George one. He'd get to him later. Both colored boys had their hands in plain view. Not a gun in sight, but where was Leotha? Was she getting the family shotguns ready just in case?

"I reckon Dickie told you your sister's back up North?"

Henry turned to Doug. Both boys nodded.

"Yeah, we just found that out. Came out here to take Dolly over to Clarksville for some shopping." Doug shook his head. 'She's a girl, and you know how women are."

Ben Roy almost nodded. Good God, Almighty! These up-North coloreds talked like they were almost as good as a white man. The sooner these two left Lawnover, the better.

"What you know 'bout women?" Little Ben was doing a good job of showing that he had almost as little sense as his father.

"Here's what we come to say." Ben Roy scowled in Little Ben's direction. "Leotha seen fit to take your sister home. I reckon it's time for you boys to head on out, too. Where's Leotha, anyway?"

Without looking behind him, Henry answered first. "Oh,

she's just making sure everything is right." He smiled. "With your sweet tea. Fact is, I was just getting used to being down South. Don't know if I'm ready to go home just yet. I'm enjoying myself."

"Well, I'll damn sho' tell you when you're ready to..." Wiley George grunted when Ben Roy's elbow connected with his midsection.

"Looky here," Ben Roy took another step forward as his hand stroked the barrel of the shotgun, "Fact of the business is, I got a message for you to take up North. Now this here's a serious message..." Ben Roy straightened the shotgun to elbow height.

Doug stepped back into the house, out of Ben Roy's view. Where was Leotha? Was she handing the Welles cousin her own loaded shotgun?

"What's this important message you want us to hear?" Henry.

"I know damn well what it is." Wiley George lifted his shotgun to his shoulder. "Yo' ma' and Al..."

"Yo' daddy's got sunstroke," Ben Roy called out to Little Ben. "Take him on back to the car. Then you come on up here."

"My mother?" Henry cocked his head. That smile he once showed turned into a frown. The boy's eyes narrowed.

Where was Leotha? Where was Doug? Hell, where was Dickie, for that matter? Ben Roy had to get this business cleared up mighty soon. Little Ben was likely to be as trigger happy as his dumb-as-a-post daddy. That's all the Thorntons needed. Even more cause for Lawnover talk that would never die down in fifty years! One of theirs owning up to having a colored child. And, Lord knew what else Alex was up to in Illinois. Might even have met up with that Annalaura. Eula Mae sure seemed to think it was a fact.

"What about my mother and who...?" Henry looked after Wiley George as Little Ben stationed him by the passenger side door of the Model T.

"The message ain't for yo' ma." Ben Roy spat on the

ground a second time. "I got reason to believe one of my kin might be up in Illinoise. It's him I want you to give the message to."

"What kind of message?" Doug's voice, but where was he? Ben Roy counted the heads he could see. One. Henry. "Name's Alexander McNaughton. You see him, tell him to get straight back here to Lawnover. Get back here and, uh..." Ben Roy didn't want to tell this colored everything.

"Get back here and what?" Henry.

"Tell him Eula—Miz. McNaughton—she's in a bad way. Needs him back here quick." What else could he think of not to tip off these up-North boys?

"Why us?" Henry took one step back into the house. "Just send the man a telegram. What's my sister got to do with any of this?"

Ben Roy grunted. "Leotha! Dickie! Get on out here befo' I tell these boys..."

"Here's yo' sweet tea, Mr. Thornton, suh." She stepped just inside the front door.

Ben Roy could barely make out her form through the shadowy inside of the house. Not a good idea to take another step closer, but what was that woman holding? He craned his neck. Thank the Good Lord, it looked like a tray holding three glasses.

"Tell us what?" Doug's voice again but no sign of him.

"Leotha?" Ben Roy waited.

She did a quick step through the door and laid the tray on the front porch, just at the top of the stairs. She straightened and walked backwards. She stopped as soon as she stepped into the interior. Ben Roy watched her disappear into the shadows again.

"Uh-uh..." Leotha's stuttering voice carried outside. "I reckon what Mr. Ben Roy wants to say is...is..."

"Hell, woman, say somethin' before I do."

"What is it you want to say, Mr. Thornton?" Henry called out from the shadows. "Does my cousin Leotha know something I'm supposed to understand?"

"She sure as hell..." the glint twinkling off the sun blinded his eyes. Ben Roy turned to the source—a window at the front of the house—ten or twelve feet from Dickie Welles' front door. What was that little flutter of Leotha's lace curtains? Ben Roy shook his head. Didn't know coloreds could afford lace curtains. In the back of his head, he needed to remember these Welles were uppity, but at the front of his head all he could see was that glint—the shine off a shotgun.

"Doug." Ben Roy swung his eyes back to the front door. Leotha was gone. Leastwise, he could no longer see her. Ben Roy strained to make out the figure of Henry. He still stood there. As slow as he could, Ben Roy sidled his eyes to the other side of the front door and its matching window at the left side of the house. The same lace curtains. No sun this time. Ben Roy shifted his weight to his left foot, careful not to let Henry Welles know he was on to something. Sure enough, the curtain was pulled back just a mite—enough for Ben Roy to get a quick look at the barrel of a second shot gun before somebody—Dickie—pulled it out of sight. He turned back to Henry, still standing more in than out of the doorway. "Where's your brother. I needs to speak to him."

"My brother? Mr. McNaughton, you can feel free to speak to me."

Ben Roy heard the rustle of Wiley George. This was no time to turn around to face his son-in-law.

"Them nig...coloreds is gettin' mighty uppity. Where's my shells?"

A wave of heat like the sun at high noon flashed across Ben Roy's forehead. Could even Wiley George be this dumb? "Put your pa in the back of the car." Ben Roy whispered out of the side of his mouth. "And take that goddamn gun away from him." He turned to Henry. Was that a grin on the man's face as he stepped into clearer view?

"You can talk to me, Mr. Thornton." Henry stood with his arms folded over his chest.

"It ain't you I want to talk to." Ben Roy raised his voice and watched the grin fade as Henry cocked his head. "Looky here." Ben Roy swept his eyes across the front of the house. Yep. Those curtains were still pulled back. Shotguns trained on him and his. "We was just drivin' by on our way to 'coon huntin' when I recollected I needed to get a message to my kin up north." Ben Roy's eyes swept the front of the house again. Still there, and no sign of Leotha. More'n likely she had a third gun at the ready.

"I thought you said you were hunting possum." Henry was grinning again. "Not raccoon."

Little Ben walked over to Ben Roy. The kid, holding the two shotguns, stood beside his grandpa. Maybe there was some hope for the boy after all.

"Have Doug come on out here so's I can talk to him. I reckon we don't need these whilst we drinkin' some of Leotha's sweet tea." He nodded toward Little Ben. "Lay them guns on the ground and fetch that tray over yonder."

Little Ben turned to Ben Roy. His face read like his grandpa had been caught between losing his mind and having a fit. The boy shook his head.

"Do what I tell you!" Ben Roy growled.

Even Henry could most likely see how bad Little Ben shook as he placed the two shotguns on the ground and walked his shaky legs to the front porch. Ben Roy hoped the child wouldn't pee his britches in front of these coloreds. By the time Little Ben got back to Ben Roy's side, half the tea had spilled out of two of the glasses, and the third was completely on its side, the contents dribbling off the tray and onto the ground.

Ben Roy pushed his grandson aside as he looked up at Henry, now standing sideways in the doorway. Waiting. Ben Roy grabbed the barrel of his shotgun with one hand and with the greatest of care laid the weapon on the ground. He straightened. "Would you get your brother, now?"

"What do you want to talk to me about?" Doug stepped through the front door. No shotgun in sight.

Ben Roy looked to the right. The curtains hung like they should. He went to the left. Oh-oh. Somebody still waited.

Dickie Welles.

"Me and you, we got to talk private." He turned to Little Ben. "Get on back in the car and keep your pa quiet."

Doug walked through the front door, across the porch, and down the three stairs. He crossed the yard separating him from Ben Roy. The men stood face to face. Eye to eye. Doug put his foot on Ben Roy's shotgun. Ben Roy looked down at the two other weapons. He laid his lace-up work boots across them.

Ben Roy nodded his head to Doug as he made his way to that right-side window. And no gun. Leastwise, not yet. He looked at Doug Welles.

"How old was you when y'awl left Tennessee?"

"Left Tennessee? I was ten. Why are you asking?" Doug narrowed his eyes.

He was a man now, but Ben Roy remembered the child. Not all that well. Doug's family had sharecropped Alex's acres, not his own, but when his brother-in-law took up with their mama, Ben Roy made it his business to see what was what. Back then the children had been respectful. Not now. Doug, little as he was in those days, had always seemed the brightest of the bunch. Now that Ben Roy put his mind to it, that whole family had been a little bit too smart for coloreds. Good thing they took off when they did. All the more reason to get the whole damn up-North Welles family gone from Tennessee for good. As much as it galled him to be that close to a colored man, he leaned in toward Doug.

"How much you recollect about...things before your folks lit out for Illinoise?"

Doug took a step back from Ben Roy, his nose crinkling. "What kind of things?"

"Looky here, boy—uh, Doug. I'm gonna ask you straight up. You recall Alexander McNaughton comin' to your house back then?"

Doug nodded. He folded his arms across his chest. "We didn't have a house. We lived in a barn." He hissed out the words.

"Yeah?" This boy wasn't telling Ben Roy anything he didn't already know. "Yeah. You worked for my brother-in-law. What you remember 'bout them times?"

"I remember I fell out of the rafters in that barn—drying tobacco." Doug folded his arms across his chest. "Broke my leg. I was nine years old." The strands in Doug's neck stood out.

Ben Roy scowled. What did any of that have to do with this colored's memories?

Doug's eyes roamed all over Ben Roy's face. Ben Roy clenched his fingers. Best not make a fist, though, Lord knows this colored had a good beating coming for daring such a thing. But now was not the time.

"Mr. McNaughton—Alexander—set it for me." He tapped his left leg before he nodded to Ben Roy. "I'll always be grateful to him for that." He dropped his arms from his chest.

"You recollect anythin' else?" Ben Roy held his gall inside him. A colored speaking a white man's first name out loud? Such disrespect called for a good old-fashioned tar and feathering.

"Like what?"

Ben Roy sucked in a breath. He had to separate what ought to be from what had to be. This colored wanted to play games with a white man. Ben Roy wasn't going to fall into that trap. Lord, let him get these smart-alecky Welles boys out of Lawnover before all hell broke loose. Ben Roy clamped his mouth shut until he could get his voice under control. "Like Mr. McNaughton"—he eased Alex's name slow—"did he come visit your family often? Your mama?"

Doug clenched his right hand and punched into his left palm. His eyes narrowed again. "What are you trying to say...Mr. Thornton?" He might as well as spit on the ground when he called out Ben Roy's name.

"I ain't got time for this. I was tryin' to spare your feelin's, but if you want to act all uppity, I'm just gonna get it out." Ben Roy clenched his own fists as he looked over at the

Model T. Both Wiley George and Little Ben were inside. "You and me, we got us a situation here that don't neither one of us want."

Doug blinked once, twice. "A situation?"

Could be he really didn't know?

"I don't know how much you knows. You was young, sure 'nough, when all that was goin' on, but you got eyes."

Doug shook his head. Ben Roy read more confusion in the boy's face.

"Your sister"—Ben Roy let the clock tick—"who you reckon she favors most? Her ma or her..."

"What the hell are you trying to say?" Both hands flew in front of Doug.

"Oh, we ain't playin' that game. Now I need your help and you need mine. I don't reckon your brother Henry knows the facts, and you seem a little hazy yourself, but your sister's pa ain't who you think he is."

Doug pushed his hands towards Ben Roy's shirt but must have thought better of grabbing hold. He dropped his arms to his sides and stared at the ground. Ben Roy shook his head. This boy had put two and two together.

"What kind of help are you talking about?" Doug kept his eyes down.

Ben Roy hadn't realized he'd held his breath all this time, not until he felt the air rushing into his lungs. "This is a thing best kept among the few of us what know." Ben Roy looked over Doug's shoulder. "I reckon your little brother is one of them that don't know. Up to you if you want to keep it that way."

Doug lifted his head to Ben Roy without nodding a yes or no. "Go on."

Ben Roy looked over Doug's shoulder, back toward the house. Only Henry was half visible, and only one arm at that. Could have been a shotgun in the other. "Leotha tell you Alexander McNaughton the one who took your sister up to Illinoise?"

Doug frowned. "Alexander McNaughton? No, Cousin

Leotha didn't…"

Ben Roy took a step closer to Doug and shaded his mouth. "What I don't want…" he jabbed a finger at Doug, "and you don't want, is for Mr. McNaughton to meet up with Annalaura Welles."

"Meet?" Doug had shouted the word. He took a quick look around, turned back to Ben Roy and lowered his voice. "Meet up with my mother? Why in hell would he do a thing like…?"

"I ain't sayin' it's your mama's idea." Ben Roy thought of Hettie, not that she was ever all that far from his mind. "But if my brother-in-law's in Illinoise, I reckon he's gonna move heaven and earth to see her…your ma."

Doug grunted and shook his head. If colored could look pale, Ben Roy swore Doug looked like he'd seen him a ghost.

"Here's the message you got to get to Mr. McNaughton. Alex…my brother-in-law's got to end this thing with Annalaura and get his ass on back down here to Lawnover. Won't be nothing but hell on earth if he does what I think he's a-plannin'." Ben Roy gave his head a slow shake. "Running off with your ma—most likely up to Chicago. That ain't gonna work no kinda way."

"Oh, hell no!" Doug's voice started up again before he got it under control. He whispered, "I'll tell you this Mr. Ben Roy Thornton, your Alexander McNaughton and my mother—that's never going to happen again!" Doug turned and stalked back toward the house. "Henry, pack up. We're heading home."

Ben Roy nodded as his chest loosened. Now to get Eula to see some sense.

CHAPTER THIRTY-FIVE

Mrs. M. did a good job at playing the stone face to stop herself from answering Dolly's questions.

"Scrambled eggs and bacon for you." The colored waitress set the first platter in front of Mrs. M. "Toast, eggs, and sausage for you." She smiled as she gave Dolly her plate. "Coffee coming up for you, ma'am, and cocoa for the young lady." She smoothed down the pink apron covering her white uniform, nodded, and walked away.

While Mrs. M. loaded up her coffee the way she liked it, Dolly took a look around the restaurant just three doors down from the hotel. It hadn't looked like much from the outside, not with its red-brick front appearing as though it never had a scrubbing since the days Abraham Lincoln rode the central Illinois circuit. But the inside had been a delightful surprise. Dolly liked the frilly lace curtains hanging at the window. While none of the ten or so tables had no white tablecloth, each and every one had been covered with a wiped-clean, flower-print oilcloth. The place wasn't crowded—not at this time of morning, caught between breakfast and lunch, but the five other diners enjoying their meals were all colored. Dolly picked up her fork. The smell of pancakes mingled with fried chicken floated from the kitchen on the far side of the dining room. Danville had such places, too. Spots with good food where only colored went to eat, but like Champaign, Danville had the Five & Dime where anybody could sit. She bit into her warm buttered, toast. Gina Maggiora couldn't hold her tongue forever.

"Mrs. Maggiora, what time did my mother tell you she'd meet us in the hotel lobby?"

Mrs. M. lifted her head, a half-dozen answers looked as though they paraded across her face. "We meet you mama when the time is right." She filled her mouth with a huge swallow of coffee.

"What time does the Traction leave for Danville?" Dolly was just getting started. She'd break this woman down.

Gina Maggiora shook her head as she stuffed an entire slice of bacon into her mouth.

"We should get back to Danville before dark, don't you think? Where's Mama? We can meet her wherever she is." Dolly put on her sweetest smile.

Now two forkfuls of egg joined the bacon. A wonder Mrs. M. didn't choke on the spot. She pointed to her mouth.

Dolly sat sideways to the front door, her mind planning its next attack on Mrs. M. She turned when she caught the blur of the restaurant door opening. A colored woman wearing a familiar traveling suit but no hat entered. Mama! And, goodness, who was that behind her? Dolly stared as the gray-haired, blue-eyed white man walked in right behind her mother. Mr. McNaughton!

"Mama?" Dolly knew her mouth was open, but she couldn't figure out how to close it shut.

Mrs. M. stood, almost knocking over her coffee cup. She planted herself between Dolly and Mama as though she didn't want Dolly to get too close a look at Mr. McNaughton. Dolly stared at the back of Mrs. M's own dark brown dress. No traveling suit for her.

"Annalaura, you-a ready for the Traction?" She waved an arm toward the door. Mrs. M.'s head bobbed as though she was mouthing some signal to the two in front of her.

"No, that ain't gonna work." Mr. McNaughton, standing a

head taller than either Mama or Mrs. M., brushed the neighbor away with the back of his hand. "Her mama wants to talk to her." He walked passed Mrs. M., pulled out a chair and stood behind it. "I'm gonna listen."

Dolly heard the gasps—oh, the other diners tried to cover their surprise as quickly as they could—but there it was. Mr. McNaughton waited beside that chair until Mama sat down. He turned to Mrs. M., who nodded and backed out of the restaurant door. He took a seat next to Dolly and across from Mama.

After all the planning, plotting, and questions she had pent up in her head, not one pushed itself to her mouth. The waitress, who had stood flat-footed just outside the kitchen door, now took slow steps toward their table, her order pad in hand. Was that a pot Dolly heard smash to the kitchen floor as the connecting door popped open? Who were all those kitchen staff people who craned their necks to get a good look at the white man who dared hold a chair for a colored woman?

"Can I take your order..." the waitress looked first at Mr. McNaughton, then at Mama, "...you first, ma'am."

"She'll have coffee, pork sausage, eggs, biscuits and gravy, and I'll have the same." He nodded toward her mother as he handed the menu to the waitress. "I hope your food is half as good as hers. She's a mighty fine cook."

Dolly's eyes felt like they were on a merry-go-round with all the swiveling they were doing. Mighty good cook? Why was he looking at Mama like that?

"Mam..." her voice stuck in her throat. She cleared it. "Mama...how does...did you cook for Mr. McNaughton when you lived in Clarksville?" Dolly grabbed at the collar of her midi-blouse. Today felt even hotter than back in Tennessee. She swiped at the perspiration coming off her forehead.

"I done some cookin'." Mama trained her eyes on Dolly like she was willing herself not to look at Mr. McNaughton.

Why didn't Dolly believe that was all there was to it? She

gulped in a big breath. "Mama, you and Mr. McNaughton...?" How was she going to finish that sentence? She couldn't bring up such a dreadful thing to her mother. Not Annalaura Welles and this white man. No. She grabbed her cup of cocoa. It felt cold.

"Dolly," Mama's voice sounded strained, "I'm mighty pleased you got that scholarship to go to the university over here in Champaign."

Scholarship? With all the turmoil she'd undergone these last twenty-four hours, she'd almost forgotten. She smiled as she slapped both hands on the table. She wanted to grab Mama's hands in her own, but Annalaura Welles had never been the affectionate kind. Come to think of it, Dolly had never even seen her mother kiss her father.

"It's the strangest thing. The scholarship, I mean. I don't know how the university even knew about me." Why didn't Mama smile back? And why was Mr. McNaughton, with those blue eyes speckled with green, staring at her so?

"Dolly"—why was Mama's face so strained? "You'll be livin' up here. In Champaign. All year. Holidays and things." Now Mama wrung her hands like she was twisting the soap out of the just washed laundry.

Dolly leaned on her elbows. "Mama, it's not like I'll be alone. Claire will be here. If her father can borrow a car to pick her up here in Champaign, I'll hitch a ride with them." She pushed back into her chair as the waitress laid down two fresh, food-ladened plates. "Besides, Doug, Henry, Cleveland, or even papa could come and pick..." Why did Mr. McNaughton go that funny color?

Mama looked at the food on her plate. She touched nothing, not even her fork. "Uh-huh. Maybe they can do that some of the time, but I wants somebody to keep an eye on you while you up here." She shot a quick glance at Mr. McNaughton.

The man's eyes shifted from Dolly to Mama and back again. "I get up here ever' now and again. On business. Be my pleasure to look in on you." He tilted his head like he was hoping for something. What? "If that would be all right with you?"

Dolly couldn't help it. Mama had taught her staring was rude. "Why?" Even though she couldn't force her eyes away from Mr. McNaughton, she certainly felt Mama's glare cut straight through her. "I mean...I mean you don't have to do that."

The man worked his mouth between a smile and a...? He laid a hand on the table. "It's somethin' I want to do."

Dolly folded her hands in her lap. Mr. McNaughton moved his arm a few more inches across the table—almost touching her mug of cocoa. He looked as though he wanted to take her hand in his. Like a fath...that was it! His expression—caught between a smile and pride. Pride in her? Dolly swung to Annalaura. "Mama?"

Instead of answering her girl—Annalaura Welles had never been shy about laying out the do's and don'ts of good manners to all of her children in no uncertain terms—Mama wore the most pleading face Dolly had ever seen on her mother. The woman's eyes climbed all over Mr. McNaughton.

He returned the look before a little smile broke free. "Oh, checkin' on you ain't no trouble atall." He turned to Dolly.

"I can see you're wonderin' why I want to check on you." Mr. McNaughton's smile faded.

Dolly managed to nod her head. She hoped that would be manners enough for Mama, who finally picked up her fork.

"Your mama worked for me. On my farm. Like I told you."

"My whole family worked for you." Dolly straightened in her chair. Hadn't that been what Kate had claimed?

Mr. McNaughton nodded. "That's right. Lau...your mama worked my tobacca acres..."—he turned to her mother— "did some cookin' for me, too."

"She cooked for you, and that's why you want to check on me at school?" Dolly strained to keep her eyes only on Alexander McNaughton. Even so, she felt Mama's hand take an imaginary swipe at the side of Dolly's head.

Mr. McNaughton looked at his plate, picked up a biscuit, and scooped up the gravy with it. He held the bread in his hand when he turned back to Dolly. "That's part of it." He waited, the uneaten biscuit in his hand. "Fact of the business is, I got used to lookin' after your mama…"—that little smile worked its way across his mouth again—"and your brothers. Little Lottie, too."

Little Lottie? Dolly's bossy, headstrong big sister? "How do you know…?"

"They was workin' my acres, you see." He laid the uneaten biscuit back on the plate, the gravy dripping over the sides. "Your family—back in 'thirteen—they was all my responsibility. They was just 'bout to go hungry if I hadn't stepped in after John Welles took off for a whole year."

Dolly jumped when Mama's fork clattered to the floor. The entire restaurant and kitchen staff must have heard Mama's groan.

"I… Sorry." Mama's hand shook when she reached down to retrieve the fallen implement.

Mr. McNaughton's hand slid across the table but stopped just before his fingers met Mama's. He turned back to Dolly. "John Welles, your mama's…husband…" why did that word catch in the man's throat? "He went off to Nashville to… work."

"What?" Dolly shook her head. "Did you say my father went to work in Nashville—for an entire year? And left Mama all alone with my brothers and sister?" She'd never heard such a story in all her life. She turned to Annalaura. "Is he right? Papa was gone for a whole year?"

Her mother grabbed a biscuit, slathered more butter onto the already buttered bread and slammed half the baked dough into her mouth. The woman nearly stared a hole in the plate. Dolly waited. Mr. McNaughton, his jaw clenched shut, looked as though he were communicating to Mama with his eyes. Dolly looked down at her hands, back to palm, palm to back. She hadn't meant it. Not really.

Yes, Dolly sometimes pondered wishful thinking. Didn't all the kids she knew believe they'd been given to the wrong set of parents at birth? Claire once told Dolly, when *Maman* was being especially Old World unreasonable, she was certain she was the descendant of Marie Antoinette, and she, Claire duBois, was the rightful heiress to the throne of France. Dolly joined in her friend's lament. Hidebound, rule-enforcing, Annalaura Welles couldn't possibly be her mother. A beautiful, never criticizing, always forgiving woman who was not Annalaura Welles had been deprived of her wonderful daughter, Dolly, by some evil-intending midwife. But Dolly had never even imagined such a thing about her father. Papa was Papa. Though she'd never tell Lottie, Dolly always felt she was her daddy's—John Welles—favorite child. Dolly laid her hands on the table, palms down. She examined the man who turned to slowly face her. She shook her head while Mama pushed her eggs around the plate with the clean fork the waitress had just deposited. It was more than his eyes, the arch of his eyebrows, the... Her birthdate—May nineteen-fourteen. Count back nine months—August nineteen-thirteen. Oh, God. She almost spoke the words out loud.

Claire sometimes took the Lord's name in vain, though it was in French, *Mon Dieu*, but Mama had forbidden such sounds to ever leave the lips of any of her children, even Cleveland, and he was twenty-eight years old, and married! Oh, my God!

"Did...did...you"—Dolly, co-valedictorian, and with perfect diction, stuttered—"you say my father was away working in Nashville for a year—nineteen-thirteen? Which month?" She leaned toward Mr. McNaughton, her heart thumping. "When did he leave in nineteen-thirteen?"

She watched Mr. McNaughton's eyes roam her face.

She swung to her mother. Dolly dipped her head low to search out Mama's eyes as her mother concentrated on her pork sausage like it was the most perfect diamond ring.

"But he came home for visits didn't he, Mama?" Each

word scratched her throat. "During the summer of nineteen-thirteen, I mean?"

"He put the crop in." Mama kept her eyes on that pork patty, acting as though she never smelled such fragrant sage in all her life.

Dolly strained to catch her mother's soft-spoken words. "The crop in?" Dolly looked at Mr. McNaughton, who watched her like he feared she might faint. "Is tobacco like corn?" She heard her own voice rise. "I mean, is it planted in the spring? April or May?" When Mr. McNaughton failed to answer, she turned back to her mother.

Annalaura looked as though she'd just heard every Negro in America was to be sent into slavery by midnight tonight.

Mr. McNaughton shot a quick glance at Mama that carried the look of reassurance. He turned back to Dolly. "John Welles," his words were slow, "wanted to surprise your mother with his good fortune. He come back from Nashville in May."

"But when did he leave?" Dolly's voice rose. She spotted the waitress, her mouth agape. A man wearing a tall white cook's hat peered over the server's shoulder, his mouth also open. "You said my father had been gone a year. He came home in May nineteen-fourteen. That means he left in May of..."

She focused on Mr. McNaughton. His cheeks moved in and out like he was fighting to keep words inside him. Dolly looked to her mother. Mama clamped her hands on the edge of the oilcloth. Neither adult answered her.

Mama had never said much about boys and men around Dolly. Oh, her mother told her to always sit with her knees clamped together and her dress long enough to cover. Dolly wasn't to be alone with a boy, and if one did creep up on her, she was to allow him no more than a hand-holding. Mama even frowned on kissing. But Dolly and Claire knew much more than that. Claire's *maman* told her daughter a thing or two about boys and men—the French way. If that wasn't enough, the girls had seen actual pictures—well, drawings, anyway—of men without clothes. Then that magazine Dolly found last year when she turned Henry's mattress during spring cleaning. Oh, my goodness. Those pictures! More women than men, to be sure, but both anatomically correct. And those how-to instructions! For certain, Dolly knew that for a baby to be born, a man had to be very close indeed to a woman nine months before the blessed event. And when Annalaura Welles gave birth to her last child, Dolly, that man had not been John Welles. Dolly's hand went to her throat. Her eyes stung. She coughed for breath. Alexander McNaughton pushed back his chair and knelt at her side before she got her first good gasp of air. He wrapped his arm around her shoulders.

"You understand then?" His face inches from her own, he laid soothing strokes down her back. "Why I want to check on you up here at that university? He looked as though he wanted to pull her into a hug but stopped himself. "I reckon you just got something stuck in your throat." His voice carried a huskiness. "You'll be all right. Always. I'll see to it."

A gurgle that sounded almost like a cry left Mama's lips. Dolly turned her head. Mama looked stricken with apoplexy as she turned to her daughter.

"Mama!" The shout came out when Dolly wanted a question. She looked at Mr. McNaughton, his face seemed to be pleading with her for understanding, not for himself but for that woman sitting across from him. Dolly had none to give right now. To either one of them. Dolly, tears splashing down her face, stood from her chair, Mr. McNaughton still on his knees. She covered her mouth with one hand.

"No." She shook her head at Alexander McNaughton. "You...you are not my fath... You can't be!"

He rose slowly to his feet. "Your mama means a whole lot to me. And so do you. I give you your name—Dolly."

Dolly swung around to face her mother. Her hand knocked over something. A cool wetness splashed over her hand. The half-full cup of cocoa? "Mama..." Her eyes watered as she shook her head so hard her bobbed hair whipped her face. Her lips felt tight. She could barely separate them. "Annalaura"—she spit out the name—"how could you do that to my papa?" Her eyes went to Mr. McNaughton as though they'd willed themselves. Dolly pushed over the chair and ran the gauntlet of tables to the front door, bumping into the waitress. "Mrs. Maggiora, where are you? Take me to that Traction, now!"

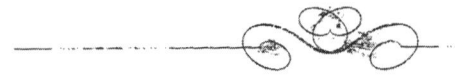

CHAPTER THIRTY-SIX

Eula sat at her kitchen table, her coffee cup at her fingertips, the journal opened to her last entry. She'd just finished her big breakfast—two fried pork chops, three eggs, six slices of bacon, and two biscuits covered in butter and topped with a jar of her strawberry preserves. She sighed as she leaned into her ladder-back kitchen chair. It sure felt good to eat a breakfast she'd cooked up herself without jumping up every two minutes anticipating what Alex might want. The smile on her face was broad. Alex. Eula turned to the closed pantry door where her almanac calendar hung from its nail. Friday. Let's see. The man had been gone since Tuesday morning, she reckoned. Probably got up to Chicago sometime late Tuesday evening. Tuesday night, Wednesday, Thursday, and for all she knew, Friday, Alex had laid up in bed with his colored whore. So be it.

She stood to get herself her third cup of coffee—she usually only had one because Alex gulped down almost the full pot—when she heard the truck rumbling up the road. She checked the calendar again. He'd come back after all. Probably to pick up his clothes before he moved North. She listened as the engine shut off, the truck door slammed, and Alex's feet crunched across the gravel. "Just you wait," she chuckled out loud, "more'n your clothes will be outta this house and my life."

"What the hell is this?" His shout came through the door.

Eula's smile grew wider as she made her way back to her chair, coffee cup in hand. The porch door and then the kitchen door swung wide. Alexander McNaughton stepped into the kitchen. He spotted her, frowned, and pointed to the back porch. His head bobbed like he was trying to come up with words that made sense. Eula waited. She was in no hurry.

"Eu…what…what's that out by the back porch?" He turned his head between her and the porch like he was trying to rattle all the pictures in his mind's eye into some kind or order. "Clothes. They look like my clothes and things. What they doin' out there in the dirt?"

"I thought you liked dirt." That good feeling welling up in her belly got better and better by the minute. "Seem to want to waller in it."

Alexander's face went from white to pink to red to plum. His eyes looked like they belonged in an owl. "Wha…?"

"Your clothes. I figured you'd want to take your things with you when you moved out."

He stared at her, one hand still pointing to the back porch, the other aiming a finger at her. Eula brought the coffee cup to her lips. Strange. In these last few days when she knew this moment was coming, she thought she'd be all atwitter. After all, she'd been married to Alexander McNaughton far closer to forty years than she cared to dwell on. But all she felt this morning was calm. She was ready for the scoundrel.

Alex shook his head as he turned to face her. "You right, Eula." He walked past his usual chair at the head of the table and took the seat next to her.

Right? Of all the things she'd planned for—imagined, coming out of his mouth—right wasn't one of them.

His eyes roamed her face like he was looking at his lawfully wedded wife for the first time. Eula felt a little tremor go through her body. "Right?" She managed to get the word out. Whatever game Alexander was playing, she was ahead of him. "I know, Alexander." She made sure she captured his eyes with her own. "I know where you been these past few days. And with who."

"You ain't never been stupid, Eula Mae." He brushed a lock of gray hair out of his eyes. "Come to think of it, I reckon I admire that 'bout you. But that ain't the most of it."

Eula tried to look away. Lord, how many years had she trained herself to be a respectable wife? Never give your husband the chance to believe you're challenging him. If you must look him in the eye, keep it as short as saying "jack rabbit" twice. Otherwise he'll think you forgot your place. Alex laid a hand next to her journal. He glanced down at the open page—each block print letter looking about two-inches tall. Eula felt her breath push out through her chest. She grabbed her coffee cup and hung on. She scowled at herself for that little twinge of nervousness that circled her belly. What did she care if her husband read her deepest thoughts? About time he knew.

Alex's forefinger drew down the written lines. Most of the time he kept his eyes on her. He flipped backwards through the pages. He stopped at one of her last nineteen-fourteen accountings of the supplies in the store room. Rashers of bacon, cans of pole beans, sides of ham. All missing. All gone to his colored woman.

His fingers traced her lettering. "I recollect I told you before how much I appreciates what you do for this farm." He turned to her. "Without you, Eula Mae, I wouldn't have much more'n a thousand or two dollars saved up."

Savings in the bank. Her breathing calmed. "That's one of the things I'm 'bout to tell you, Alexander."

He cocked his head, the look of surprise on his face. She'd never talked to him like this in all their married years. She'd never "told" him anything. Mama Thornton had trained her well: a husband is never to be told, only begged. Eula kept her smile to herself, but she liked the confusion that worked his face.

"You got somethin' to say to me, Eula?"

"Oh, I got plenty to say to you." Her fingers tapped the table. "I opened me up a bank account in Clarksville."

"Clarksville? How'd you get yourself to Clarksville?"

"I took the buckboard over to the Welles place. They were a mite surprised to see me, but Dickie and Leotha borrowed a neighbor's truck and took me straight to Clarksville." She pressed her lips together for a second. "Those two, they seemed to know a lot about where that up-North girl visitin' them might have gone off to. By the way, her brothers—those Welles boys—lit out back to Chicago a few days back." She ran her tongue over her upper lip. "You meet up with 'em?"

His wobbled his head like he hadn't heard her right. "You…got in the car…with coloreds? With no man around?" His forehead almost touched his eyebrows in their frown.

Hadn't he heard her? Eula picked up her coffee mug. "Wasn't nothin' to it. I just walked into the First Bank of Tennessee and told them to open me up an account."

"In times like these with the banks threatenin' to close, you opened a bank account?" he stared at her like she was talking gibberish. "'Sides, you can't open no account without my say-so."

"Don't need your say-so." She took a swallow.

Alex shook his head. "That ain't what I'm sayin', Eula. If you feelin' the need to have your own money, I reckon I could feel better 'bout that if I trusted the banks. But it ain't me that says you can't have no savings passbook on your own." He tapped a blank journal page. "You a married woman, Eula. Law won't 'low you to have money in a bank all on your own."

"A married woman, is that what I am?" She set down the cup. She knew the law good and well. She knew about all those New York banker fellows jumping out of windows. Folks just didn't trust banks. Not enough customers. That's why she reckoned she got that account in her maiden name—no questions asked, married woman or no.

The scowl on his face looked like it was settling down into

a permanent fixture.

"Alex"—she steadied herself—"I don't reckon you're hearing me."

His eyes bored into her. "Tell me what it is you want to say, Eula I suspects it's aplenty."

His voice was so low, Eula leaned forward to catch it. Her mind was set. Nothing Alex, Ben Roy, Fedora, or that hypocrite of a preacher, Reverend Hawkins, could say, was ever going to change her mind.

"Mr. Baxter—your banker at the First National—told me you took out every penny in the account 'cept ten dollars, earlier this week. Every dime I managed to wring out of these acres in almost forty years...it all went to you."

Alex looked down at the journal. He stared at another blank sheet.

"Nigh six thousand dollars. All in your hands." Eula spit out the words. "All I'm wantin' is two thousand. I reckon I've earned that and more." She sat back in her chair. "I'm using it to put seed in the ground this first year."

His head jerked up. "Put seed in the ground? I put seed in the ground, not you." He stared at her, his eyes climbing over her face like he was trying to read what terrible ailment consumed her.

"Alexander, I told Fedora and Ben Roy"—her fingernails, short as they were, dug into the palms of her hands—"I'm getting' me a divorce. You gotta leave the farm. Ben Roy and them, they'll take you in. I'm keepin' the farm."

His eyes opened wide then closed almost shut. He looked back to the journal and turned two, three more pages. "It's a divorce you're thinkin', is it? And leavin' me with that brother of yours? You with two thousand dollars." He raised his head, his eyes now steady.

The shaking started in her hands, but it took no time to reach her arms, her chest, and her head. "Alex, I can't stay with you no more!" She shouted out the words when, in all the planning she'd done, she practiced staying as cool as spring water. Her heart, that shriveled up thing in the center of her chest, twinged a teeny pang of pain.

Slow as making a way across an icy road, Alex turned his head toward her. His cheeks twitched. "I reckon it's more than a divorce you're wantin', Eula Mae. Sounds to me like you wantin' revenge. My farm."

"Revenge, you callin' it?" The pain of the last years cramped her heart. "I call it just and fair. Somethin' even a wife is entitled to." She felt her jaw harden. "I reckon I put in more than one woman's share into these acres." She held her gaze steady. "This here is my farm, too."

Alex dropped his eyes before she did. He turned two more blank pages of the journal. "I think I always knew you was a woman with a strong head." He flipped over another page. "You got cause to want to 'xact vengeance, Eula Mae. In all these years, I ain't never told you I love you."

The shock came like the one a person might get if she stood too close to a tree hit by a lightning strike. Eula jumped in the chair. "Don't say no more, Alexander McNaughton, 'specially 'bout love. These past seventeen years, I had me more than enough of your feelin's on which woman you love."

He thumbed through three more journal pages. The man sat steady in his chair, looking stronger by the second. "No, Eula, I ain't told you I loved you 'cause...," the blue eyes glowed, "I reckon I don't. Not like a man should love a woman. That I ain't never done with you." His fingers turned one more page without him glancing down.

Eula spotted it before she supposed Alex did—her Declaration in those big block letters.

Alex laid his hand across the page, his fingers splayed over the writing. He kept his eyes on her. "*I, Eula Mae Thornton...*" he recited the words without looking at the page, "*am a woman worthy of love.*" His eyes flitted across her face, her body, like he was undressing her soul. "No, Eula..." his voice went throaty, "I don't carry that can't-take-a-breath-without-thinkin'-of-you kind of love. Not fo' you. But don't none of that mean I ain't found you worthy of carin' for. I hold feelin's fo' you."

"Feelin's?" The sound croaked out of her throat. "You sayin' you got feelin's for me?" The words pounded in her ears like they were coming from a voice not her own. "The same kind of feelin's you got for one of your work mules that's done a good 'nough job for you?"

He worked his mouth and bent his head back to the journal. "*I've got more than my share of smarts and God-given talents.*" Alex slid his hand to the bottom of the journal page. He turned back to her. "A good work mule is somethin' a man can depend on. Reliable like. A creature that'll work his heart out just for you. Give you his soul if the Good Lord had blessed him with one." Alex glanced up. "Eula, you got all them things in you—all them high-falutin' words folks talk about—dependable, courage, devotion, intelligent. They all set well on you. To me, you ain't never been no work mule." He worked his lips over his teeth. "I ain't seen it in time. I reckon I was blind in one eye and couldn't see out t'other, but, you, Eula you got so many things I was looking for in a wife. Always had. You got yourself a mind to speak whenever you take a notion. You stand up for yourself when need be." His face fell into a frown. "Eula, truth be told, I ain't had much in the way of feelin's for you when we first got married. Took me a good long while to see the all of you, and ain't none of that put me in mind of no kind of mule." He shook his head. "No, I ain't got man-woman love for you, but I do have admirin' love for you." His jaw wobbled sideways as the kitchen clock ticked off close to half a minute. "Eula Mae, now you do the truth tellin'. I know I wasn't what your pa— Old Ben—had in mind for his bright-as-a-button daughter. I wasn't too many notches above po' white trash. Not worthy to have a Thornton for a wife. I knew that, and Eula, so did you." His sigh swept over the kitchen. "Was I just any ole man who could put a ring on your finger? Way before there was a Laura—Annalaura Welles—what kind of feelin' did you have for me?"

Eula couldn't keep her eyes off this man. What was he

saying to her? Trying to shame her into saving his acres? Why had she married him? To escape being an old maid. As gawky as she was, she was already the talk of Lawnover.

"My feelin's for you back then. You want me to say I loved you from the first minute I set eyes on you at the church social?" The blood rushed to her face. "You want to hear from me the time of night when my heart overflowed with love only for you?" She waited for his nod. It didn't come. "I'll give you your truth, Alexander McNaughton. I didn't love you when you asked Papa for my hand 'cause I knew damn well it was my pretty sister you really wanted. Her with her bosom sittin' all up high. Her behind round as a watermelon. Just like your Annalaura." She'd called out "damn", but it wasn't the word that made Eula work her tongue to get the bitter out of her mouth.

Alex jerked. No, he'd never, ever heard her utter a swear word in all these years. Let him jerk and jump all he wanted.

Eula folded her arms across her chest. "You thinkin' it was when I said, 'I promise to obey' in front of old Reverend Townsend." She shook her head, her lips forming a smile she didn't at all feel. "No, it wasn't that day either." Her mouth went dry.

Alex, his fingers stroking the Declaration, waited while Eula took two sips of her coffee.

"It was when she...my baby..."—the pain that should have been dead these thirty-seven years jumped out of her heart, cut through her chest, and rammed itself into a howl— "...died abornin'. That's when I loved you for sure." Water that she damn sure didn't want, flooded her eyes. "But you ain't cared a thing about that—not 'bout my daughter—these past sixteen years, 'cause you got yourself a replacement." She slumped in her chair, both hands over her face. Lord, have mercy. Not now.

Eula heard her own moaning. She jumped when his unseen arms went around her and pulled her to his chest. She heard the beating of her husband's heart. Eula worked her hands free, clamped down on his wrists and pushed him away with all her might. "No! Get...the...hell...outta here, Alexander McNaughton!"

His fingers relaxed as he slowly released her. He moved back to his chair. One hand closed her journal. His head tilted, he turned to her. "Eula, I told you. You are special to me. I know you may not take my words for true right now, but it's more than time I told you what you got business to know." He ran his tongue around the inside of his mouth. "This world won't allow me to have the woman I want. Ain't no secret from you and most folks in Lawnover that I love Laura Welles. But ain't no judge in the whole of the United States of America ever gonna 'llow the two of us to marry. Divorcing me on account of Laura don't make me no never mind."

Eula reached for the tea towel lying next to her cup. She dabbed at her eyes. Laura. That's what he'd called her—Laura—over and over. A secret name between the two of them.

"Some of that money you saved—and it was you who done the savin'—I'm sendin' up North to my girl. She wants to go to college." His eyes, trained on Eula, had never been so blue. "But, what I'm doin' for this daughter, I woulda done for my first born. Fact of the business, Eula Mae, I love Dolly all the more 'cause I lost her sister all them years ago."

Eula clutched the tea towel to her cheek. The baby cradle jumped into her head. The cradle Alex spent weeks crafting out of good poplar wood for their upcoming child—the same cradle where, twenty years later, he planned to lay his half-colored bastard Dolly Welles.

"No, Eula," Alex was just about whispering, "I can't have the woman I love, but the Good Lord sent me you to take away as much of the pain as He thought right." Alex tapped the shut journal. "You got business to know that I'll be goin' up North from time to time." He turned his full gaze on her. "To see my daughter. Not Laura. She won't have it. She won't have me. Not like this." He stood, and slid the book toward Eula. "You want me out of here? I can do that for a spell. You want your own bank account? You earned that money same as me. You want a divorce? I'm not leanin' that way. Hurt too many people—mostly your kin—and 'specially, you. But divorce or no, that one's up to you."

"I...want...you...out of my house. Ben Roy...Fedora... go there." Her heart felt seized in her throat.

Alex nodded. "I can do that for a week or two if Ben Roy don't put up too much of a fuss. You plannin' on takin' my acres? Say you worked hard for 'em? I grant you your hard work. Wouldn't no other wife done better, but that—my land—Eula Mae, that you can't have."

"Alex, don't make me have to tell the court 'bout you and that...colored woman."

"Eula, you got to do what you think is right. For me, I want you right here with me in this house. No, we won't be actin' like husband and wife. One day, I hope you understand what ever' man in Lawnover already knows—a wife ain't supposed to be a lover. But whenever you need me—you gets sick or broke down in your parts—I'll be here for you. You done me proud as a wife."

"You tellin' me we'll be friends—here in the house? But outside, we'll play-act bein' married?"

He nodded. "No different from Ben Roy and Fedora. No different from any of the other marrieds 'round here."

It was Eula's turn to stare. "No different?" Her words couldn't find a resting place in her head. "You want us to be friends while, for the rest of my life, I'm livin' a lie, knowin' you pinin' for your brown-skinned bitch?" Eula grabbed her journal to her chest. "Get your damn self out of my house, Alexander McNaughton."

He bent toward her. Eula stiffened. He drew closer. His lips grazed her cheek with a kiss. "In my fashion, I love so many things about you, Eula Mae Thornton McNaughton. I ain't never gonna be sorry I made you my wife."

He straightened, turned, and walked out the porch door. Eula, hands clasping her elbows, trembled as she heard the tossing of shoes, belts, metal-strapped overalls—all into the back of the truck. Her ears tuned in when the engine cranked up and the car's tires swirled against the gravel. She listened until the sound was no more.

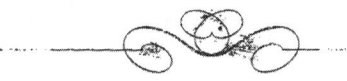

CHAPTER THIRTY-SEVEN

"Don't you do the worry, Mrs. You Dolly, she come around."

The Traction clattered passed cornfields on either side of the train, the stalks now just about shoulder height. The sound of steel wheels against metal rails almost drowned out Gina's words. Annalaura sat like a rock in her aisle seat when Gina pulled her into a quick hug. Annalaura broke free and leaned into the aisle. There was Dolly, a good five rows in front and on the right- hand side of the Traction car. The girl's shoulders shook like she was crying. Annalaura sucked in her lips as she turned back to Gina. The choking in her throat stopped her from getting out even one word.

Gina shook her head. "You hear my words, Mrs. You Dolly want that school the very much. The idea, it settle in her head. She do the figuring who pay the tuition. She see this man not so bad after all."

It took all Annalaura's fast-leaving strength to take one quick look at her neighbor before she trained her eyes on the back of the seat in front of her. She felt her lips tremble again. Annalaura opened her pocket book and reached for her handkerchief.

Lightning quick, Gina wrapped her arms around her a second time. "Annalaura, I know you think this minute you world, it will be no more." She squeezed her shoulders. "But it gonna work out."

Annalaura shook her head so hard her neck pained. "No, it ain't gonna work out." Her cry brought stares from the couple seated across the aisle. She turned back to Gina. "It ain't John I'm frettin' 'bout. He gonna put me out. I know that. I'm prayin' Lottie will take me in if Rusty don't put up too much of a fuss." Crying had never been a thing Annalaura allowed for herself. She'd cried more tears these last two days than in just about the whole of her life.

Gina patted Annalaura's back. "I know you do the worry for you Dolly. But I think, maybe, she not the only one." She put both hands on Annalaura and shifted her body around to look Gina Maggiora in the eye. "Don't fool me, Mrs. You cry the tears for him. That Alex man."

Annalaura's heart jumped. She scrunched up the top of her traveling costume as she let herself sink deep into Gina's arms. Her friend patted circles across her back. Oh, Lord, that felt good. Annalaura clamped her eyes shut. Jesus, let the blackness make Alex's face leave her head. The buzz of the Traction strummed a rhythm in her ears. First, the outline of his face blurred, then the ruddy color of his nose and cheeks faded, until all that was left were those blue eyes. How long had she kept her own eyes closed? When Annalaura finally left Gina's hug, she wiped at her swollen face. She looked out of the window passed Gina and spotted the sign. Danville. Ten miles. Ten miles, a short bus ride, a fifteen-minute walk from the Brugestown highway bus stop, and then—John. Annalaura sucked in her lips. Her hands grabbed the edges of her pocketbook to stop their shaking.

"Ten miles." Gina sat sideways in the Traction seat. Waiting. "You think you have the love for the Alex man."

Oh, Lord. Gina never did understand the need for easing up on a subject. Worse, that was no question Gina just asked. She'd stated what she saw in Annalaura's face.

"You ever love you John?" Now Gina leaned in close to Annalaura. Her voice was low.

Annalaura's fingers scratched at the leather edges on her

pocketbook. "He my husband."

"Don't you play with me, Mrs. We no have the much time. When I marry my Lorenzo, I nineteen years old. What girl that young knows what is the love?" She spread her hands wide as she sat back in her train seat. "Sometimes, we confuse the self."

"Gina, you a good woman. You tryin' yo' best to see the good in me." Annalaura looked down at the veins in her hands, popping out as she hung on to her purse like a snatcher was striding down the Traction aisle this very minute. "You ain't gonna find no good in me." She swallowed so hard she knew Gina must have heard. "I done the worst thing a wife can do to a husband."

Annalaura looked at Gina's face, but it was the voice of Alex that played out in her head. He told her she was a strong-hearted woman. If his words were true, she prayed to Jesus He might pour some of that strong into her right now. Annalaura's head felt like it weighed more than a dozen ears of corn strung together as she turned to look Gina Maggiora in the eye. Best to practice the strong-heart business on her friend before she had to face John Welles for the last time. "You don't know this country. That first time with Alex, I ain't had me much choice." She remembered that skinny mattress in the barn loft.

"You right. I don't know all the ways of the Americas." Gina lifted an eyebrow. "But I know the fair and the unfair. Like the *Cosa Nostra* in my Italia. The man with the power take everything from the one with the weakness. A *Cosa Nostra* man want him a woman, he take her. The husband— he say a word of the no—he die." Gina slid an open hand across her throat.

Mercy! Gina Maggiora understood far more about America's south than Annalaura guessed. She looked around the Traction car. The fellow passengers were either reading, dozing, or staring out of the window. Annalaura turned sideways to face Gina.

"When he first come to me in the smokehouse, I was so

scared I thought I might wet my drawers."

"You and the Alex?"

"He say he give food fo' me and my children. A roof over our heads, clothes, schoolin', money, everything."

"And you no want to tell this man yes." Gina nodded like Annalaura was telling her a story as old and as familiar as the Mississippi River.

"That first time when he come to my..." she swiveled around to check on Dolly. Her daughter still stared straight ahead at the seat in front of her. "When he come to my bed that first time, I just 'bout lost all my good intentions. I knew I had to tell him yes, but I was weakenin'. I was down to 'bout a cup of flour and even less meal. Henry, he wasn't but three years old back then, bawlin' every time his belly growled. Still, I didn't think I could let him—Alexander—do that to me." She stared at her fingernails. "It was my boy Doug who showed me the way. He done broke his leg—a fall from the barn rafters—and Alex set it fo' him." She looked up. "Real tender like. "I couldn't do it. I couldn't let my pride get in the way of savin' my children. No matter if I burned in hell fo 'ever fo' commitin' adultery, I could not allow my babies to suffer 'cause I held myself too good to say yes to a white man. Even if their pa done me wrong."

Gina's eyes widened for the flash of a second. "He no make you go to the bed—this Alex?"

Annalaura shook her head. "Wasn't no forcin'. I give Alex my yes all on my own. I got myself ready fo' the hurtin'." She looked Gina in the eye. "Colored women in that predicament don't like to talk 'bout what they go through. I reckoned it was gonna be mighty rough. Hurtin'." Annalaura waited for her words to put shock on the face of Gina Maggiora. Her best friend stared back at Annalaura, her hand making little "go on" signs. "I knowed it was gonna be bad." Annalaura tried to read Gina's face. "But it wasn't. From that first night in the barn, that man treated me like I was somethin' special. Almost like I would break if he mishandled me." Annalaura shut her eyes as that first night of surprise flooded her.

"You tell me the more."

Annalaura opened her pocketbook and pulled out the little looking-glass wrapped in its felt covering. She held it to her face for a second, then slipped it back in her purse. "Look at me. You don't see nothin' special, Gina. Even when I was young, I wasn't a pretty girl. You can see that. I got brown skin when everybody says light is right." She pulled at the hair she'd run a quick pressing comb through, "My hair's short and kinky when folks like yella-haired and straight. My eyes ain't blue." The muscles in her cheeks twitched. Lord, not another crying spell coming on. "Why would that man make me feel like the wings of the angels in heaven wasn't near as precious to him as me?"

"Whoo." Gina flapped a hand in front of her face. "And you John never make you feel like that? You husband, John, he do the thing wrong to you?"

Annalaura bit down on her lip. Not many folks in this world knew about John and that beating he delivered to her. Cleveland, for sure, maybe Doug, but that was it. Lottie and Henry, too young. She had never mentioned that awful day to anyone. Not even to John. "He beat me, Gina"—her sounds barely crawled out of her throat—"when Dolly was nine months in my belly."

"Mrs." Gina pursed her lips into the worst frown Annalaura had ever seen on the woman, "My Lorenzo, he hit me the one time. I no have the Guido coming yet. Me and my Lorenzo we marry just the six months. He come home one night with two big bushels of the dirty clothes of his drunk friend. The friend have no wife, and the friend's papa make him leave the family, so nobody to wash the clothes. Lorenzo say that will be me." Gina put both hands on her knees. "He tell me to go out in the night to get the well water and to-a scrub the clothes on the wash board all the night because the friend need his clothes clean for the morning. I tell Lorenzo I tired. I wash the clothes early in the morning when-a the sun can do the dry faster." Her face turned from its usual olive to plum. "Lorenzo hit me in the face with the fist. Here." Gina tapped her chest. "You know what I tell my Lorenzo after he do that to me?"

Annalaura shook her head.

"Husband. You stronger than me. You beat me this night. I can do the nothing." She leaned forward. "Not the tomorrow night, not the one after that, or the next one, but one-a night you eat the yum-yum dinner I cook with the special mushrooms, and the stomach pains, they start. Hour, maybe the two, you beg me to get the doctor. You dying, you say to me." Gina wagged her head. "Is the fault of me, if I no can hear what you begging me to do? I no hear the word 'doctor'. I no understand the words 'go get.' Even with his *prego*, the please—you do the die."

Now where had that laugh come from? Annalaura let go of her pocketbook. "Gina, I reckon you can handle just 'bout anything."

"You John, he beat you more than the one time?" The grin left Gina's face as she sat back in her seat. "I no hear you John do the beating. Not never in all these years we been the neighbors."

"He ain't a bad man, my John. He only beat me that one time, but he liked to kill me." She looked up at Gina. "I reckon fo' a long time I felt I deserved that beatin'." Gina was a woman who could judge the truth maybe even better than Annalaura. "John, he'd been gone fo' a year when he come home and found my belly poked out to here." Her hand drew a wide circle around her stomach. "He knowed he wasn't the papa. That's when he lit into me. Balled up his fist and smacked me in my face. In my chest." She fought down a cry. "In my belly."

Gina's groan was soft, but it was there. "That no good. But, he no hit you since?"

"Not nary a time." She felt the tears coming back. "Since we come up here to Illinois, John, he done everything he could to make up fo' that time." Sixteen years flitted by in her head. "He give me one of them Victrola things. My stove got two ovens. Sweet smellin' colognes." She patted the skirt of her outfit. "He even bought me this travelin' suit though I don't go nowhere but to Danville and Springfield a time or two." She leaned closer to Gina. "That man done all in his power to say his sorrys to me. And he's good to Dolly. Treat her like his own."

"You John, he know the feelings you have for the Alex man?"

Annalaura shook her head. "We ain't never said Alex's name in all this time we been up here. We just go 'bout the business of livin' day by day."

"But you no happy."

She folded her arms. "John, he give me everything. Ain't no thing I wants fo'." Annalaura frowned as she looked up at Gina. "Things. I get them all from my husband." She sucked in her lip. "Alex, he give me things, too. But they's different. What he give me, they like perfume fo' my heart. Gideon's balm fo' my soul." Her lip trembled.

"A man who put the song in the woman's heart, he hard to replace," Gina soothed. She reached for Annalaura's shoulders "The world, Mrs.—sometime it not the fair. This Alex, you love him, and he sure the hell love you." She pushed Annalaura's head into her shoulder and rubbed long strokes from neck to waist. "You take that kind of love to the final place where you gonna lay your head. You cry you tears. The weeping always make us women feel the better. You heart will make itself well someday, but…" Gina pulled Annalaura up and looked into her eyes. "…you-a, Mrs., got to give you John the chance to put the new song in you heart."

The Traction slowed to a stop on Main street, right across from the Court House. Danville.

CHAPTER THIRTY-EIGHT

The fumes off the Danville-to-Charlestown bus blew a black cloud in their faces. At least, in hers and Gina's. Dolly had already toted her valise across the Brugestown highway, dodging a gray Model T Ford. Annalaura wrinkled her nose as she breathed in the smell of gasoline.

"That girl is right mad at me." Annalaura peered through the lingering dirty gray cloud. She spotted an opening in the traffic traveling down the only highway leading from Danville, past Brugestown, and on to southern Illinois. "Let's make a run fo' it while we can," she shouted to Gina, who stood in front of Bianchi's market that tripled as a bus stop and a speakeasy. Her friend hugged her valise to her bosom and huffed across the road.

"That'a highway always give me the scare." Gina breathed as she put a safe foot on the gravel sidewalk. "You Dolly sure walk the fast." She bent over and caught her breath. "In this heat."

"That's so's she can get to the house befo' me. Tell her papa what a awful, sinful woman her mama is." Annalaura looked up at the sun. Mines and factories closed for the day. Men at home already. She turned to Gina. "What you gonna do 'bout yo' Lorenzo?"

Gina straightened, swung her pocketbook over one arm,

and caught up with Annalaura on the unpaved walkway. "Lorenzo? He be the mad, all right. But he no go hungry." She grinned at Annalaura. "I tell Lottie to fix the food for Lorenzo and you John."

Annalaura stepped beyond the little road leading to the neighborhood colored church, Nazareth Baptist, her shoes brown with dust. "My John? That's what you callin' him?" She shook her head. "Not fo' much longer."

"I tell you, Mrs., you Dolly come around the one day."

"Dolly?" She shot a sideways glance at Gina. "Oh, I ain't frettin' over Dolly. You was right. My girl's not but sixteen. Just turned, at that. Everythin' still pretend with her. I wants to keep her that way long as I can. She'll be a grown-up woman far too soon fo' my likin'." Annalaura sighed. "Learn fo' herself that what she wishes could be most likely ain't what's gonna happen."

Gina puffed her extra pounds to keep up. "In my Italia we call it the *cio che wil essere sara cio che wil essere sara*. In you English, 'what-will-be-will-be.'"

"Yo' Lorenzo, he ain't used to you goin' off by yo'self." Annalaura stopped in front of the red-brick school where all her children except Cleveland finished eighth grade. The paved sidewalk announcing the entry into Brugestown proper began here. "He ain't gonna hit you or nothin', is he?"

Gina tilted her head as the two moved toward the little grocery store right before the turnoff onto Lattier. "I keep-a mushrooms in my cellar." She winked.

Annalaura looked down at the sidewalk she'd stepped on so many times. First laid in nineteen-twenty-two, the stamped concrete read. How many more times was she going to walk these steps? She slowed a few yards before the corner. "Gina, I wants you to know if you ever need help with them mushrooms...or anythin' else, I'll get to you lightning quick." She moved toward her neighbor. Never in her memory could Annalaura ever recall being the one starting the hug. She pulled Gina into her arms and let her go almost as fast. "I ain't never had me a friend befo', not a real one. But I reckon

I gots me one now."
Gina, a woman Annalaura reckoned could have fought the Great War all by herself—and won—looked like she was about to cry.
"Who got water in they eyes, now?" Annalaura joshed. Felt good. "My cryin' times 'bout over, thanks to you. Got no mo' tears in me. But they done me good. Oh, I ain't sayin' it's laughin' time. Not just yet. I got to sit still and stay still while John lights into me. It's his right." She turned the corner and passed Lottie's house, two doors down. She heard Sammy shouting his two-year-old no's through the open front window.
A few more houses and she'd be there—the place she'd call home not much longer.
"Mrs., I always say to myself, that Annalaura, she one smart woman. Maybe you do the wrong when you sleep in the bed with you Alex. Maybe John do the wrong when he sleep in the bed with the other women in the Danville." She stopped one house away from Annalaura's and her own. "But he no have the right to 'light' into you."
This time Annalaura's hug was longer and deeper. "You have that Edith operator get in touch with me on that telephone contraption of yours. I'm hopin' to be at Lottie's, but I could be workin' somewhere up in Danville. Lots of maid jobs up there."
"Mrs., don't pack you suitcase just yet." Gina waved a hand in front of Annalaura's gray house. "I know some of the America way. The two wrong no make the one right." She walked down the driveway toward her own back door. And Lorenzo.
Annalaura sucked in a breath as she made her way up the concrete steps. The front door was closed. Dolly wanted to make this as hard as she could for her mama. Lord, let life be far more gentle to all her children, especially her girls, than it had ever been for her. She stepped across her porch and turned the knob.
"Papa, you know I can cook almost as good as Lottie."

Dolly's voice drifted out of the kitchen. "I'll cook all your meals." She paused. "But just for you, not her!"

Annalaura stepped through the front door. John, standing by his daybed looking for all the world like he was ready for her, turned to the whiskey cabinet for which he, alone, held the key.

"Don't look like Dolly had much of a time in Lawnover." He glanced over at Annalaura his eyes steady, his cheeks sucked in. John fumbled with something in his hand.

She looked at her husband, the man she'd been married to for nigh thirty years. Time enough to learn to read his face. That he had already pronounced her guilty flashed out of his eyes. He opened his fist. There, dull and gray, lay the key to John's locked cabinet. Annalaura matched her husband's face—no frowning, no pretend glad-to-see-you grin.

"I don't reckon you went up there to have a good time fo' yourself, now did you?" His voice was as quiet as his face. He slipped the key into the lock.

Now his eyes narrowed on Annalaura. Strange, her breathing came as slow and regular as the rest of her. Her husband stood there—waiting for her to come up with an answer. Annalaura walked around the square-built furnace and over to her own bed and dropped her valise. She turned to John. She held her gaze on him, but she reckoned it was the Lord she should thank for keeping her mind and body settled. Dolly bounded out of the kitchen. The child stopped when she spotted Annalaura.

"Oh," Dolly crinkled her nose like she'd just stepped into an outhouse. She turned her back on her mother. "Papa, I've got the best news to tell you."

"Ain't been much good news 'round here these last two or three days." He kept his eyes on Annalaura while Dolly rushed him into a hug.

"Hey, girl!" He jumped back.

Annalaura watched her daughter. John wasn't the hugging kind, and Dolly knew it. His arms went slow to Dolly's shoulders as she grabbed him around the waist and laid her head into his chest. Not since Dolly started first grade had her Papa hugged her. Oh, John bounced her on his knee until she turned four or five, but he'd never been the kissing type for any of his children. John looked over his daughter's head and planted his eyes on Annalaura.

Dolly let go, stepped back and clapped her hands. "I won a scholarship to the university, Papa. The University of Illinois. Over in Champaign. I start in September."

That did it. John took his eyes off his wife and turned to his daughter, his forehead buried in a scowl.

"What you mean, you won a scholarship? What kind of scholarship?"

"I…ah…" Dolly's fair skin flashed cherry-dark. She swung toward her mother, then switched back to John. "It was…Mrs. Maggiora…she took me to the…"

Gina had been right, again. Sounded to Annalaura like Dolly figured out who really stood behind her schooling. And now she was trying to stumble out a lie to her papa. Annalaura turned to her daughter. The girl had never been much of a liar. When she was little, she told her share of fibs, but they were plain to see. Annalaura wasn't about to have her girl start lying now. She wasn't good at it.

"I hear tell Gina took Dolly up to see that school in Champaign. Somethin' 'bout an anonymous donor."

"And you was where when Miz. Maggiora, and not you, took my daughter up to that school?" If John was the hanging judge, his hand just slipped the noose around Annalaura's neck.

"Papa," Dolly jumped in, "I know you would have found a way to send me to college. You knew how much I wanted to go." She wrapped her arms around him again. "You're the best father in the world."

John patted her back. "I is, is I? The best papa in the world?" His hooded brown eyes refused to release Annalaura. His mouth looked set in cement until he turned back to the girl. "You my favorite youngest daughter in all this world." John switched back to Annalaura, a question in his look.

"Now you take them plates back on up to Lottie's." He laid his hands on Dolly's shoulders and aimed her toward the kitchen. "I gotta talk to yo' mama." His voice landed in Annalaura's ears like the feel of a pick hacking away at a block of ice.

Dolly shook her head, that nigh straight hair of hers flying around her face. "Talk to…her?" The girl took no pains to hide that little shudder of disgust. "Remember, Papa, I'll always be here to take care of you." She looked over her shoulder at Annalaura. "Just you." Dolly ran into the kitchen and rushed back to the front room, carrying two washed plates.

"Go on now, girl. Git." John pointed to her suitcase. "Take yo' valise with you. Spend the night with Lottie. Doug and Henry, they back, but they bunking with Cleveland."

"My brothers are back? I didn't want their trip spoiled, too…" She clamped a hand over her mouth, looking like she remembered who had made her angry. She held the plates in one hand and snatched up her valise with the other.

"Papa?" Dolly turned from her father to Annalaura and back again. "Uh, Mama…she didn't…" Dolly shrugged and walked out the front door.

John watched Dolly until she walked across the porch, down the steps, and onto the sidewalk. He moved to the front window and looked at his girl until she was out of sight. John turned his back to Annalaura as he headed to his cabinet. She heard him slip the key into the lock and turn. Without a word, he pulled out a bottle of whiskey. She couldn't tell if the container was full or empty. John brought out a shot glass.

He turned around. "Drink fo' you?" His head tilted toward his right shoulder.

"I don't do no drinkin'."

"You don't do no drinkin'. You don't do no swearin'. Don't wear yo' dresses too short." His words came out like rocks stoning a woman to death in the Old Testament. "Annalaura," he drew out her name, "you got me and ever'body else in Brugestown believin' you is a right Christian woman." He pulled the stopper from the bottle. "But tell me this, Annalaura. You don't do no drinkin', no swearin', no wearin' floozy clothes, but do you do some...fornicating'?" He poured the liquor into the glass and held it out to her. "You gonna need this."

First, she looked at her husband's forehead, then her gaze drifted to his eyes, looking hard as black marble, then she went to his nose. She couldn't rightly see his nostrils flare, but she heard the sounds of thick breathing. She settled on his mouth, clamped so tight it looked like his cheeks might explode inward. Fornicating. By all rights, she should be shaking and quaking in her boots. But right now, she'd been delivered a calm that draped itself over her like one of those tight dresses Lucille wore. Annalaura looked at the glass in John's hand and gave her head a slow shake. "No, thank you."

He nodded. "So be it." He set the glass and bottle down on the table by his daybed. "I reckon I knows who that miracle anonymous scholarship donor is." He reached into the cabinet, moved a cigar box, two books, and a snuff can. "Bet you couldn't wait to tell Dolly who her real pa was." His back blocked Annalaura's view. When he turned around, he held out his right hand, his fingers clutching something. She saw it, all right. Right through his spread fingers. Black and metal. It had never been shiny. Always a dull color like a mangy cat caked in Mississippi mud. She'd never held the thing in her own hand, but it looked heavy—and mean.

"I ain't told her. Neither did Alexander. 'Sides, you is her 'real' papa."

"Alexander, is it?" That half grin-half smirk on his face looked like it best suited an executioner. "Not Mr. McNaughton? Not even Mr. Alex like ever' colored person in the whole of Tennessee is hide-bound to say, lessen they wants to die?" John opened the fingers of his right hand, one by one. There in his palm lay a pistol. "Sho' you won't have that drink?"

Annalaura lowered her hands to her sides. "I reckon when the time comes fo' me to do my talkin' to St. Peter, I wants to do it sober." She raised her face to John. "I don't need no liquor." She lifted her hand and drew a circle around the left side of her chest. "Here. John Welles, if you gonna do yo' shootin', do it here. My heart—it's already broke."

John worked his mouth and his cheeks as his right hand slipped to the pistol grip. With his eyes never leaving her face, John cocked open the gun. He took two steps backwards, fumbled his left hand inside the cabinet. Annalaura watched as he pushed away a sheaf of papers. There, at the back of the cabinet, she spotted the flat box marked "shells." With his eyes still on her, John pulled the box forward. He flipped open the cardboard top and took out two, three, five, six bullets.

"One, two, three, fo'..." John slipped the bullets into the chamber, one by one.

"This day been a long time comin', John Welles." Annalaura took three steps toward her husband and squared her body. "You gonna do what you gonna, do, but don't you give me that 'my-woman-done-wronged-me-and-can't-nobody-blame-me' hangdog look. This here thing goes two ways, and you damn sho' know it."

Whether he meant to or not, Annalaura couldn't tell, but John's mouth—that thing that looked like it'd been baked into hard clay by the sun—opened up. He stared at her, his hand, holding the last bullet, poised in midair.

"Don't look at me like you shocked." She pointed to the gun. "Befo' you get yo'self so big and bad 'nough to shoot yo' cheatin' wife, I wants you to answer yo'self and me one question." Annalaura leaned forward as she poked at her own chest. "Why me? Why of all the colored women in Lawnover, did you ever pick somebody as plain-lookin' as me to put in all this misery?"

"Misery?" John's shout sent Annalaura back a step. "Woman, that's what you callin' what I tried to do fo' you?" He pushed in the last bullet and snapped the weapon shut.

"Misery, that's what I say you done to me." He took a step closer. "Did you or did you not lay up with that white son-of-a-bitch in Champaign?" "Did you or did you not lay up with two, three, fo' dozen womens—I don't even know they color, and I don't care!" If the Good Lord was about to call time on her, Annalaura determined to speak her full mind.

"It ain't the same." John punched the air with the gun.

"You tellin' me it ain't the same?" Annalaura didn't bother to hold back that little laugh. "Talk 'bout fornication. You wanted them women. You took yo' good-lookin, slicked-up self and chased after each and ever' one of them happy-to-give wenches."

"And you ain't just come back from givin' yo'self to that white man?"

Annalaura took a deep breath. How many more minutes did she have on this earth? "I ain't gonna lie to you, John. Though I know that's what you hopin'. Me makin' up some excuse." She nodded toward the gun. "No matter what I say, you ain't gonna take it fo' truth. But St. Peter gonna know my words is honest. Wasn't none of my idea to go to Champaign. I ain't had no plans to sneak off and be with Alexander. Ain't had no contact with him since that mornin' we—me, you, all of us—left Lawnover." She shook her head. "He done all that—gettin' Dolly away from Richard, takin' her to Champaign with Leotha—knowin' good and well I'd come over there to fetch her home. Do 'bout anything to keep him from claimin' her." She felt her spine stiffen. "He had her, and if I wanted her back...fo' you, I'd have to come to Champaign and talk to him in the bargain." She stopped for breath.

"You done mo' than talk to him. Get on with it, woman. Tell me what I already knows."

"What you knows, or what you think you wants to hear? You wants me to say different words. To confess. Did I go to bed with Alexander McNaughton in Champaign?" She ran out of air.

John steadied his arm, straightened his elbow and aimed the gun straight at Annalaura's chest. "This ain't no time to stop talkin'." His voice came out colder than a February icicle. "Get the hell on with the rest of it, woman!"

"Get the hell on with it? Here t'is, John Welles. Yes, I slept with the man, but that ain't 'nough fo' you. You wants to hear more. All right, let's start by you askin' me the words you been stewin' over all these sixteen years." She put her hands on her hips. "If you wants to hear more, then go on, John Welles. Fix yo' lips to ask that question."

He squinted one eye as his finger twitched on the trigger. "I ain't got no questions fo' you. Plain to see what's standin' in front of me…a fifty-cent ho'. Did yo' white man even pay that much?"

The shudder started in her shoulders, but Annalaura drew the tremble inside herself before it reached her belly. "Think all the evil 'bout me you wants to. Call me all the low-down names come into yo' head. Ain't no name yet for a man ho', now is they? When they is, you'll be first in line to claim it." Her lips felt dry. "John, this ain't 'bout name callin'. You ask me what you been dyin' to know since you come home back in nineteen-fo' 'teen, all puffed up with yo' earnings from Nashville. Money you got from workin' in a ho' house!" Annalaura hoped her shout hadn't carried over to Gina. That woman would most likely come running.

John looked down at the gun as he shook his head. "We ain't talkin' 'bout no ho' house in Nashville. I told you. I done all that fo'…"

Annalaura walked over to her husband and stopped, the gun two inches from her left breast. "Uh-uh, John Welles. I told you this was a two-way street. You do the fornicatin', and it's all right in God's eyes 'cause it was to save yo' family. I do the fornicatin' to feed yo' children and keep the winter snows off they heads, and I'm supposed to burn in Hell." She shook her head. "This ain't 'bout no 'fornicatin'' 'cause me and you ain't had no choice. This is 'bout that question burnin' in yo' chest these last sixteen years."

Was that a little tremble in John's gun hand?

"Keep yo' words to yo'self, Annalaura. I don't need them. I got eyes."

"Too late fo' all that. You gonna hear what you think you been knowin' all this time." Her throat longed for water. "Did I love Alexander McNaughton when he first took me in that barn?"

The gun jerked to the right and away from her body.

Annalaura stepped to her left, back in front of the gun. "God's truth, no." She held up her right hand. "Did I love Alexander when he pulled Dolly out of me after you—John Welles—beat me most to death? Him, wantin' me to run off to Chicago—just the three of us—him, me, and Dolly. You, crazy mad with a gun, doin' yo' best to kill Alexander McNaughton. Well, listen up good, John Welles, fo' here is words true 'nough fo' Jesus Himself to hear. That day, I ain't had no full love fo' Alexander, but I had me plenty of good feelin's." Her chest hurt. "Feelin's fo' him and... fo' you. I didn't want neither one of you dead."

"Annala..." John's finger spasmed on the trigger.

"Oh, no, John Welles. You been waitin' fo' this day every minute of these sixteen years. Waitin' and hopin' I'd give you some sign. You even done set up this little test to trap me. Send Dolly to Tennessee to see if you could flush out Alexander and see what come of it. Would I make some excuse and hie me off to Tennessee just so's I could drop my drawers, lickity-split, in front of Alexander McNaughton?"

John waved the gun in front of him as his head shook. "Use Dolly? You knows I would never ever hurt that girl. Ain't none of this on her. I loves her ever' bit as much as I love Lottie. I wasn't never gonna put Dolly in no kind of danger, even if I did have me good cause to speculate 'bout you and..."

"I knows you love her, John." Annalaura's voice dropped down in her throat. "But I reckon you hates me far mo' than you loves her." She kept her eyes on him. "That's what our old life—Tennessee—brings out in folks. Stick coloreds in a place where we bound to hurt one another. Well, here be yo' last question you hear from me, and yo' last chance to hurt me."

"I don't needs to hear me no mo' questions!" John's shout banged in her ears. "You already told me what you done. You already put the pain in me." His hand tightened on the pistol grip. He picked at the bodice of her dress with the gun, searching for her nipple. "You laid up with him, and this wasn't no Tennessee. He ain't made you do it. You coulda said no."

"No mo' questions? I coulda said no? Here's the one question you really wants me to answer. The words you really wants me to say. I laid up with Alexander all right, and no, he didn't make me do it. But you wants to know the why of it. That's yo' question. Why?" Her breath came faster than she could get out her words. "Do I, at this moment, love Alexander McNaughton? John Welles, here is yo' damn answer. The one you been holdin' tight against yo' chest all these years—both waitin' to hear, and scared to hear." She took in a quiet breath. "I failed yo' test." She watched John poke out his lips like he was trying to rid himself of poison. "I done it because, today—at this minute—I do love the man."

John swayed more toward the furnace than to her daybed.

"Here's yo' why." The sounds scratched her throat. "Cause he makes me feel like a full woman. Ain't no color with him. I'm just the one who fills his world. The only one."

Something in her head told her to close her eyes. The gun's metal opening, as round as a nickel, pressed hard into her breast. At least she wouldn't see the bullet when it came. But she couldn't listen to her inside-head voice. She kept her eyes open. "Get ready to do yo' shootin', John Welles, but if you man 'nough, you'll do me the same favor I just done you. Answer me my one question befo' you pull the trigger. Why did you pick me to marry up with?"

The barrel of the gun scraped across her chest when John shoved her backwards and slammed her down on the daybed.

Annalaura landed on her side, a spring in the lumpy mattress poked through the ticking, tore through her dress and pricked her. Her right shoulder folded under her head. She struggled to free her arm. John shoved the gun to the side of her head, his body pinned her left arm under him. He held her sideways, pressed into the mattress.

"You got one last question, do you?" He hovered just over her face. "One last answer from me, and you thinkin' that's gonna do it? That give you the right to quit me and run off with yo' white lover man? Run off to California someplace and live happy-ever-after?" He twisted the gun into her temple. "Well, Annalaura, I ain't havin' it. You ain't never gonna see yo' white man again. But I'll tell you what I am gonna do. I'm gonna give you yo' last wish. I'll answer the damn question."

Annalaura winced. Her eyes closed at the pain. She willed herself to open her eyes. "If you is the last sight I sees, you answer me, John Welles, so's I can tell St. Peter."

His hand, holding the gun, wobbled, raking her head from temple to ear. "Why did I marry you?" He drilled the barrel into her ear. "'Cause you was the best thing around." His voice threatened to crack. "I ain't talkin' just Lawnover. You was the best thing in all of Montgomery County. In all of Tennessee. Goddamnit—in all this world." He twisted the barrel into her ear canal.

If the Good Lord would just allow her to keep her eyes open against the pain long enough to see his mouth tell her more, she'd go to Heaven or Hell, whichever, with a smile on her face.

"You knows the best part?" His breath, smelling like Lottie's cooking, dampened her face. "You ain't knowed nothin' 'bout how special you was." His voice dove into his throat as he pulled back, easing the gun out of her ear. "Made you all the mo' precious. You talk 'bout yo' white man thinkin' you so special. Hell, woman, any man with only half a good eye could see wasn't no other woman, black or white, come even close to matchin' you. Annalaura, you one of a kind."

She lay still on her side, her right arm throbbing pain, the other still trapped by John's body. "Nice words, John Welles, but if…I…" she grunted to clear her throat, "was so 'special,' why'd you run off with anythin' looking like it might wear a skirt some day? First…you run off fo' a night or two, then a week…finally, you ain't come back fo' a ye…"

The gun dug back into her ear. "And, that's why you took up with that white bastard? "'Cause I was tryin' to do better by my family?"

She winced. "You know damn well it ain't." Air enough to float one of those new-fangled balloon airplanes suddenly filled her lungs. "If I was so special to you, why…"—now the pain came from her heart, not her ear—"did you have so many womens? I ain't never thought I was 'nough of a woman fo' you. Couldn't give you what you wanted."

He jerked the gun away while his eyes roamed her face. "Not 'nough of a woman? What kind of foolishness you talkin'? Annalaura, you don't know, do you? You give me 'bout everythin' the Good Lord ever intended a man to have." He shook his head. "Them other women—they ain't meant a damn thing to me. I just needed them fo' what they could do fo' my family. Fo' you."

"'Fo' me? Needed them?" She scrambled her right arm free. Pins and needles shot through from shoulder to wrist. "I know you needed them to give you a better time in bed than I could."

He scooted backwards, freeing her trapped left hand. She raised herself on her right elbow, her side trickling blood where the bed spring had gouged into her.

John tapped the pistol on the bed covers. "I wanted you, my children, to have it better than bein' a sharecropper's family." He looked at her, his forehead still in a frown, but his jaw moved into softness. "Like I told you, them other women, they wasn't nothin' but business. I ain't had no feelin's fo' em." He slid the pistol back and forth across her summer coverlet. "Is that it, then? You had to hear me to say words to you? My doin' 'fo you wasn't good 'nough?" He shook his head, his eyes looked like they were on some other place. "You had to hear me tell you I ain't never seen no woman as beautiful as you? Ain't never been cared fo' like you was takin' care of me. In the bed and out. That's what you wanted to hear?" His eyes blinked at her like he'd just given her a puzzle that only she could put together. "Then it would have been all right?"

Annalaura eased herself up on the daybed. She slipped both feet to the floor. She searched his face. The man she'd known all these years looked like he was about to melt into somebody else. "I reckon that is what I was wantin'. To hear you tell me, ever' now and again, that I did mean somethin' mo' to you than a good cook and a free housemaid." She looked down, her eyes found the gun still in John's hand, but both now rested on her daybed. "I just ain't knowed it 'til now." She raised her head. "I ain't knowed how you felt 'bout me. That in yo' eyes I was somethin' special."

"A man can't tell a good woman no such thing—how they ain't no other woman can even touch the bottom of her shoe. He can't tell her she the reason why he lay his life on the line if any man say a bad word 'bout her." John pulled the gun closer to him. "Back in Tennessee, ever' time I had to go with my hat in hand bowin' and scrapin' to ever' white man come my way, I done it 'cause I knowed when it was all over, I'd come home to the best woman in this world."

Annalaura reached for John's left shoulder. "Why ain't you told me none of this, befo'? Why'd you have me thinkin' you ain't cared fo' me the way a man's supposed to care 'bout a woman? Had me thinkin' you used me at night 'cause you had nothin' better to do. Left me and yo' fo' children all alone with nothin'. No food. No money. You made me make a way the best way I could fo' all of us."

"I ain't never meant to leave you with nothin'. Ain't never meant fo' you to have to make a way all by yo'self." John's eyes looked like they were trying to jump into her soul. "But, Annalaura, I knowed how strong you was. Ain't never met a woman with even half yo' smarts. I knowed whatever trouble come yo' way, you could work yo'self out of it." His head shook again. "But a man ain't supposed to tell none of that to his woman. Wrong to lay sweet words in her ear. If a man tell his woman he'd rather die than see her leave him, she see him as weak. Tell her she mean everythin' to him, it'll just turn her head. The old folks say, lay pretty words on a good-lookin' woman and it'll ruin her. She'll get to thinkin' she too good fo' you. Jump up and leave you for somebody better. I was too weak a man to take that chance. I love you too much." He worked his lips. "And the old folks was right. If you coulda, you'd left me fo' Alexander McNaughton."

Annalaura blinked. Have mercy, more tears watered her eyes. "Did I hear you say, you...love...me?" Her voice rose.

"Loved you 'befo I married you. Loved you even after Dolly was born. Love you now, Annalaura Welles. Ain't never stopped lovin' you. Why you think it hurt me so much to hear you say you got feelin's fo'...him?"

She looked down at the floor. "I can't take them back, John. My feelin's for Alex." She lifted her head. "But I got my feelin's fo' you, too. I reckon it's gonna take me a spell to sort out what I'm feelin'." She searched her husband's face. "Does I have that much time?"

John looked into her eyes without a blink. He held them there for thirty ticks of the second hand on the clock. He worked his mouth. His right arm, on the bed, moved. He lifted the pistol and pointed the barrel. Annalaura watched the blackness of the opening come closer.

ENDING NUMBER ONE

Bang!

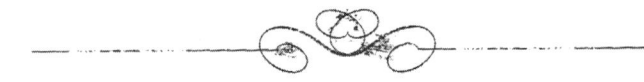

ENDING NUMBER TWO

"It ain't gonna be no easy thing, Annalaura." John tilted the barrel of the gun toward the ceiling, stood, and walked to his cabinet. He opened the weapon and took out the bullets. He slid the pistol behind two books, shut and locked the cabinet door. "Me and you. I reckon I wanna try."

Annalaura got to her feet, walked to John. "I ain't never gonna see Alexander again. I told him the two of us never gonna work fo' a whole lot of reasons. He got to stop pinin' fo' me and thinkin' things is ever gonna change." Her head moved in slow little circles. "If you can go on breathin' knowin' that, I reckon it's time me and you fo 'gave one another."

She watched John Welles nod his slow yes.

ACKNOWLEDGMENTS

Writers put words to page because we're driven to get out the story, but without a legion of supporters behind us, that drive would never come to fruition. Without ongoing support of the critique groups at the California Writer's Club—Berkeley Branch—A Waltz in Tennessee would still be disjointed pieces of my mother's story running around my head. Their unerring feedback has kept me always at the core of the story I'm driven to tell. Thanks to all of you. A special thanks to my family and friends who continue to support me. Doug and Hank you always come through for me, and I welcome Lidia who's joined their ranks. As for you, Gilles, you have always believed in me. Thanks to the people at Amazon Publishing who continue to remember me.

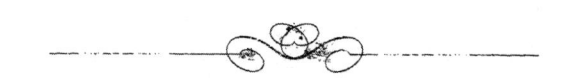

ABOUT THE AUTHOR

Francine Thomas Howard is a product of the San Francisco public school system where she learned the art of writing. A graduate of San Jose State University and the University of San Francisco, Ms. Howard left a rewarding career in pediatric occupational therapy to pursue her other love—writing down her family stories. Her efforts were quickly rewarded with the success of *Page from a Tennessee Journal, Paris Noire, and The Sisterhood Hyphen*. She is the mother of two handsome sons, a marvelous daughter-in-law, and two grandchildren. She continues to reside in the San Francisco Bay Area.

Copyright Barb Pic #2

Made in the USA
Middletown, DE
27 July 2015